KATHERINE QUINN

THE
AZANTIAN
TRILOGY

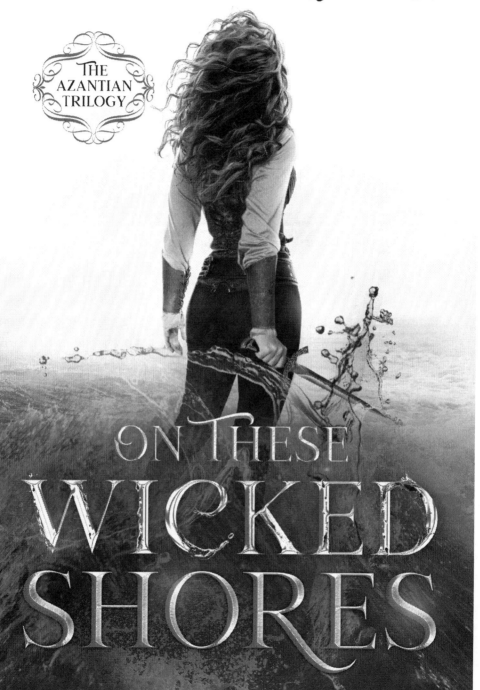

ON THESE
WICKED
SHORES

ON THESE WICKED SHORES

KATHERINE QUINN

CITY OWL
PRESS

ON THESE WICKED SHORES
The Azantian Trilogy, Book 2

CITY OWL PRESS
www.cityowlpress.com

Cover Design by MiblArt. All stock photos licensed appropriately.

Edited by Charissa Weaks.

For information on subsidiary rights, please contact the publisher at info@cityowlpress.com.

Hardback Edition ISBN: 978-1-64898-213-2
Paperback Edition ISBN: 978-1-64898-151-7
Digital Edition ISBN: 978-1-64898-152-4

Printed in the United States of America

To my mother Nancy, who is my biggest fan.

PRAISE FOR KATHERINE QUINN

"Forbidden romance, whispers of hidden gods, and the mysteries of the roughest seas animate this adventure while leaving plenty of potential for future installments. Fans of the enemies-to-lovers trope will be pleased."
— *Publisher's Weekly*

"Quinn's writing style is lush and lyrical, her premise unique and spellbinding, the love story magical and full of heat. Readers will cheer for Margrete and Bash and gasp at the twists and turns."
— *Ashley R. King, Author of Painting the Lines and Forever After*

"A sweeping and extravagant fantasy weaving in romance and adventure that takes the reader in a voyage into a world they'll never want to leave."
— *E. E. Hornburg, Author of The Night's Chosen*

"My stomach is a riot of butterflies. This book is phenomenal and a new favorite with romance that is both HOT and sweet and just makes me yearn. And the end is so, so good. My heart is racing."
— *Desirée M. Niccoli, Author of Called to the Deep*

"The world building is phenomenal. The descriptions of the buildings, the castle, the ship on the ocean, everything is so vividly detailed you feel like you are there... You will be enthralled with this tale."
— *Beyond the Stars Book Blog*

"Filled with heart-wrenching twists and an addictive, sexy romance, *On These Wicked Shores* delivers a tantalizing escape into a dark and dangerous fantasy adventure where the lines between good and evil and love and hate blur. Readers will beg for more of Quinn's lush world."
— *Charissa Weaks, Author of The Witch Collector*

PROLOGUE
DARIUS

Darius had worn many faces over the centuries of his long, *long* existence, and he'd gone by twice as many names. Yet as he hovered over a sleeping Margrete and her Azantian king, he found himself wishing his *true* name would slip past her lips, for once free of derision or scorn.

He'd forgotten what it was like to feel.

It was both a blessing and a curse that Margrete Wood helped remind him.

For months, he'd infiltrated her dreams, sneaking through the cracks of a fragile reality. Like seeds, he planted thoughts, watering them until they grew. Oftentimes, they served his purposes—to make Margrete yearn for the power she refused to express. He'd witnessed her struggle over the long weeks. She couldn't tame his brother's magic and had no idea *she* was to blame for her own failure—because she didn't remember.

Remember what she once had been to him.

But that had been another life, Darius supposed, and he couldn't fault her for her ignorance. He only recently allowed himself to get close enough to glimpse the familiar soul shining beneath. At first, he'd foolishly believed her to be some unassuming human, lucky enough to have been in the right place at the right time, gifted with the powers of a god. How very wrong he'd been. Darius saw the truth now, and it blinded him.

If only she would remember me.

But she didn't, and she wouldn't—unless he forced his hand.

So every night he opened his soul—his own magic seeping into her veins, giving her just a taste. Eventually, she wouldn't be able to hinder herself and hide from who she was, and then she'd take her place beside him. All would be right again.

When dawn chased away the night, Darius would melt into the shadows he commanded. But he never truly left her.

Not when this woman was the key to his salvation.

Margrete Wood carried Malum's heart, his brother's divine essence. The final boost of power he needed to reign as the sole ruler of the boundless waters. That, and she'd inadvertently stolen something else, something far more precious than his brother's magic. But that would all come to light later. He'd make sure he revealed his cards at just the right time.

Of course, Malum's final act—done just before Darius ended him once and for all—had been to place a symbol of protection upon Margrete's skin, a roiling wave grazing her collarbone. That damned mark made it impossible for Darius to steal her newfound power, but more importantly, it denied him complete access to her mind. Sure, he could slip inside for moments at a time, but he couldn't stay long, and Darius was never fond of being a bystander in a game of his own making.

He decided he'd create a new game.

One with rules *he* could control.

Darius was resourceful and notorious for bending the rules, and something told him Margrete would be a challenge he wouldn't soon forget. If she was who he knew her to be, then he would expect nothing less.

A smile blossomed as he watched Margrete's eyes flutter in her sleep. Soon their fates would be irrevocably tied together, and he would finally,

finally, no longer be alone. The thought made a foreign warmth settle in his chest. The sensation was a nice one.

Below his towering shadow, Margrete hooked an arm around the Azantian king's bare waist, her pert nose nuzzling his hair. So at ease, so sickeningly happy. The unconscious act of tenderness made him clench his fists.

The love Margrete possessed for her king vexed him to no end, and when Darius thought too long of it, his vision became painted in red.

That should be me.

During these long months, he longed to reach out and feel the softness of her skin. He'd held back during his nightly visits, afraid of reliving the overwhelming emotion that had assaulted him the last time he touched her. But he grew tired of his role as a silent observer.

Against his will, Darius remained at her bedside until dawn beckoned. She appeared so frail in her mortal body. Weak and easily broken. Still, he felt her spirit, her *soul,* and it sang to him until the early morning hours.

With a frustrated growl, Darius turned to leave, knowing there was much work to be done to fix a mistake committed a thousand years past. But his feet abruptly stilled as though an invisible cord snapped and grew taut. That cord pulled him back to the bed, and this time, when he reached out, he didn't stop himself. He couldn't.

Darius trailed a lone finger down her cheek, the skin just as soft as he recalled. Better, even. She felt like summer itself—warm and light and full of hope. His heart pulsed erratically, and in that captured moment in time, memories he hadn't allowed himself to hold on to rushed back to him.

He smiled. Maybe he could right the past and change his future.

Maybe he could have it all.

CHAPTER ONE

MARGRETE

MARGRETE WOOD BOLTED UPRIGHT IN BED.

Someone had been here.

Watching her.

Touching her.

For months she'd felt eyes upon her, even in her sleep. But this time, when she woke with a gasp, her cheek prickled as if the graze of phantom hands lingered. She brought her finger to touch the tingling skin as she glanced at her king.

Thank the gods, he still slept. He'd been restless as of late, and she'd sensed a great change fall upon him like a poisonous shroud. Then again, they'd all changed since that fateful day her father attacked.

Margrete shifted to brush the strands of hair from Bash's brow when something crinkled in her lap. She went still. A brittle black leaf, outlined in crimson, lay on her thigh. Frowning, she picked it up and spun it around, admiring the intricate black swirls that were reminiscent of waves. She'd never seen anything like it on Azantian, or the mainland for that matter, and she was well versed on the subject of botany. Just as she brought it closer, wanting to inspect its elaborate details, a powerful gust of wind from the balcony stole it from her fingers. The leaf fluttered in midair, as if not wishing to leave, right before the breeze swept it up and away.

Instinctively, she reached out, driven by an inexplicable need to catch it—

A wave of ice shattered against her mind.

Margrete gasped, and the smell of salt clogged her senses. Where she'd touched the leaf, her skin prickled, but she didn't have the strength to focus on that—she mostly felt a sweeping surge of crushing power flooding her veins.

Her back bowed violently, and she fell against the pillows.

The coldness in her hands stretched to her neck, where it wrapped around her throat like a noose. Her lips parted, a pathetic puff of air escaping.

It was happening again.

Another vision.

Another nightmare come calling.

She fisted the sheets as her loose grip on reality was wrenched away. Slowly, painfully so, she sank further into the velvet darkness of her mind, dragged to an endless void that housed only horrors.

Delicate wisps of black shadows swirled behind her eyes, and flashes of silver sparked like enraged lightning. It was unnatural—the light, the tendrils of ashen fog rolling through the obscurity like long, spindly fingers.

A breeze reeking of decay and rot swept through the abyss, the scent pungent and bitter. It blew across the expanse of nothingness until it revealed a grand ship she knew all too well.

The *Phaedra*.

Steel clouds curled about the vessel, and ghoulish silhouettes rose like withering blooms from the waves. Higher and higher these wraiths ascended until they arced and plummeted to the wooden decks, descending across the ship in a single falling wave.

Margrete blinked, willing away the creatures, the demons. Their shrill screams pierced the foul air and rattled her bones, leaving her ears ringing. *Evil.* Whatever they were, they reeked of malicious intent.

Abruptly, the scene shifted, and the night sky quivered forcefully. In place of the mighty *Phaedra*, only wasted sails and splintered wood remained. A sliver of a wary moon cast the world in an unearthly white glow, and the charcoal waters cradled the ruins of a devastating shipwreck.

The *Phaedra* was gone.

In this distorted hallucination, Margrete heard Bash's name. Nothing but a whisper at first, it became a song sung by a chorus of sinister voices that twisted it into something devious and wicked.

His name was a haunting chant as the haze cleared and an obscure island took shape in the distance, well beyond the wreckage of the ship. She squinted, but the image never settled, and all she managed to see was a single figure standing on its shores.

She choked back a scream as the figure blurred and erupted into a fine misting of gray dust. He might've vanished, but Margrete knew who it was, who had stood on those shores. But rather than fear, she felt...warmth.

It was a harsh, metallic scent in the air that shook her from her daze. The edges of reality slowly sharpened at the corners, and the sea-glass walls of their chambers wavered back into focus.

She lowered her eyes to the source of the smell, her heart racing. Blood blossomed on her palm from where her nails dug into the flesh, four curved lines of crimson a reminder of the horror she'd witnessed.

This had been the fifth hallucination—or whatever one could call them—since her father attacked Azantian months ago. Since Darius slayed his brother and vanished into sea-foam.

And she'd been left to pick up the shattered pieces.

Although brief, what Margrete saw during these episodes, these cryptic glimpses, left her reeling. Sometimes she saw the outline of a shadowy couple, their limbs entwined in a fervent embrace, black trees rising up all around them. Their faces were obscured, but something about them held a trace of familiarity.

Other times, like tonight, death greeted her with open arms.

Just as she had every other time these visions plagued her, Margrete sought the safety of the man nestled at her side.

Bash, the King of Azantian, looked rather angelic when he slept, though she would never admit that to his face. Bash was many things, but self-conscious, he was not. Now that he was unconscious, she freely admired him without his cocky grin making an appearance.

A grin she very much loved.

Bash's tattooed chest rose and fell rhythmically, his well-defined body sculpted by the gods themselves. He wore a linen shirt, though the buttons were undone, and her eyes trailed lower still, following the fine dusting of dark hair that crept below the blankets. Heat warmed her cheeks. Even though she'd explored and tasted every inch of him, he still managed to wring such a heated reaction from her.

She let out a sigh. At least she hadn't woken him.

Over the last three months, she'd done her best to ignore her fleeting visions and pretend she didn't feel the impending sense of doom hovering on the horizon. A week after the attack, Bash had caught her in the throes of a vision, but she claimed exhaustion—a cowardly excuse. Margrete recognized the doubt that stretched across his face at her poor explanation. The quiet alarm that rolled off him in waves as her lips spun sweet lies.

She hid things from Bash because she didn't want to worry him. Not until she understood the extent of her new powers. Besides, she wasn't ready to ruin the happiness they'd found. She deserved to be a little selfish, right?

At her side the king twitched, his eyes fluttering in his sleep as if outrunning his own monsters. This was one of the rare nights he slept, and when he did, he was difficult to wake. Tenderly, Margrete smoothed the strands of deep-russet hair curling around his temple, her thumb working to alleviate the tense worry lines marring his forehead.

Only when his brows unfurled did Margrete slip out of bed, the mattress dipping beneath her weight. Bash grumbled but didn't wake, although he reached out as if to pull her back to where she belonged.

While she longed for nothing more than to stay enfolded in his arms, hidden away in their own secret place in the world, the sea—as it so often did—called to her from beyond, demanding an audience.

Margrete padded to the open balcony doors, dancing her fingers over the fine wooden furniture covered in mystical designs—of sea monsters and nymeras and stunning beasts she once believed were myths.

Oh, how wrong she had been.

Outside, wearing nothing but a thin slip of pearly lace, Margrete fixated upon the rising sun waking the untamed sea below.

Since the day Malum's essence awakened, Margrete wasn't alone. Like a humming beneath her bones, she sensed the abundant life of the sea, each wave a song only she could hear.

If only she could hear the damned beasts that escaped.

For weeks, they'd heard nothing—no attacks, no sightings. The crushing silence was unnerving.

"Hello, old friend," she murmured to the waves. A playful wind gathered the long strands of her dark hair and brushed it out of her face. The breeze wound around her torso and picked at the hem of her nightdress, cooling her sweat-soaked skin.

"Thank you," she answered back, and her lips curled into a soft smile. The magic inside of her thrummed, a heat coiling about her heart and gently squeezing. It was a reverent touch, a caress of power. Almost as if Malum's essence desired to show its affection. If magic *could* show affection.

Her fingers drifted to her collarbone, absentmindedly tracing her little wave. The tattoo appeared the morning after the attack without any explanation. Though sometimes, she'd catch herself stroking the wave as if it were a pet to be soothed. Margrete suspected Malum had his hand in its creation, even if the god no longer roamed the waters.

Still, his *heart* did, lost somewhere in the depths after the *Iron Mast* went down. Margrete hadn't sensed its presence, though she certainly tried. Day after day, she reached out and sought the empty vessel of the god. Nothing.

Shutting her eyes, she took in a deep inhale. A storm would arrive at these shores in two days' time, the smell of salt and raging passion reminding her of the scent of a potent jasmine bloom. Margrete couldn't explain her new sense of...intuition, but there was so much she had yet to learn.

"There you are."

Two muscled and tanned arms wound around her waist, tugging her against a solid chest. Immediately, her body relaxed, and she melted into the embrace.

"That's the longest you've slept in," she said with a grin, her attention on the waters.

Bash rubbed his scruffy chin against the back of her neck, tickling the sensitive flesh. She shuddered, inhaling his salt and sandalwood scent.

"Maybe because someone was tossing and turning all night. I've never been kicked so many times." She opened her mouth to protest, but he cut her off. "Although," he began, a lilt in his voice, "your form is improving. You managed to kick me off the bed entirely at one point."

Margrete rolled her eyes.

"So very funny, *Sebastian*," she mocked, twisting to face him. She craned her neck to meet his gaze. Bash stood well over six and a half feet, and compared to her five-foot stature, he was a giant.

He let out a strained groan. "You know I *hate* that name."

Margrete smiled from ear to ear, wickedly delighted. Adrian let Bash's full name slip one night after dinner when they'd had too much wine. Apparently, his mother had named him, and after her death, Bash's father refused to call him by anything other than his nickname. Bash often said Sebastian was too grand of a name for him, claiming it sounded pompous and arrogant.

So of course, Margrete used it to tease him whenever the opportunity presented itself.

"Listen here, princess," Bash began, placing both hands on either side of her on the railing, thoroughly caging her in. His warm breath fanned across her mouth. "Must I remind you what happened the last time you called me that?" He quirked a brow.

Oh, she remembered all too well. Instantly, a blush rose to her cheeks. They'd broken his desk, and when guards rushed inside their chambers at the sound of the crash, they certainly got more than an eyeful of their king's backside.

"Well, Sebastian seems too proper for you anyway," she said smoothly, wiping off invisible lint from his shoulder. The blush remained on her cheeks. "It would make you sound like some stuck-up lord who can't dress himself without assistance."

The spark in his eyes returned.

"Well, we both know I sometimes require assistance *removing* clothing." Bash shot her a playful wink, and she lightly smacked his chest. He feigned a groan of hurt.

"Damn, woman. You really *are* getting stronger." His tone held a measure of genuine awe, and she smiled.

In fairness, she'd been training with Adrian, Bash's commander and Bay's boyfriend, every day for months. She had a long way to go, but sheer determination ruled her. Even Birdie, her little sister, joined their combat sessions. The eight-year-old was a natural, according to Adrian, and quite adept with the bow.

Aside from combat lessons, Adrian, and sometimes Bay, taught her how to swim should she not have her newly blossoming powers to aid her. Seeing as she intended to stay on Azantian, the skill seemed abundantly necessary.

"Are you intimidated by me, pirate?" Margrete asked, trailing a finger up and down Bash's right arm. His starfish tattoo shot out from beneath his sleeve, curling around the tip of her finger. Out of the many moving and living creatures that inked his golden skin, the starfish was by far her favorite.

Bash groaned, the rich sound of it causing her stomach to flutter.

"Quite the opposite." He leaned down to run his tongue across the seam of her lips, tasting her as he took his time exploring. Her mouth parted as a soft pant escaped her. "Watching you become a fearsome warrior has me feeling anything but *intimidated.*"

"So how *does* it make you feel?" she asked in a breathless whisper.

Bash placed a tender kiss on the tip of her nose before pressing himself even closer. His growing hardness pushed into her belly, and her lids shuttered.

Bash's chest rumbled as he let out a low chuckle. "I do love a woman who can knock me on my ass." He grasped her hip, his fingers digging into her silky gown.

"Don't tempt me," she warned, struggling to speak. "I'm more than happy to make that dream of yours come true."

"Promises, promises." He tsked against her lips. "Whatever will I do with you?" His midnight eyes sparkled with mischief and longing. Eyes that had once been the color of emeralds before Margrete brought him back to life. The day when the sea tried to lay claim to his soul.

"I have a few ideas," she said, shrugging. "But I'm not sure you're up to the task." Last night he'd passed out from exhaustion before she could get her hands on him. Her need for him had grown insatiable.

"You wound me," Bash said, pulling back enough to bring his hand to his heart in mock affront.

She grabbed his hips and yanked him back. "Good. I wouldn't want your ego to swell any more than it already has. You wouldn't be able to get through the door."

Bash arched a brow. "Are you sure we aren't talking about *you*?"

"Egotistical *and* delusional." She shook her head. "And people think you're threatening." She snickered, fisting his unbuttoned shirt. His gaze fell to where she held him, and his eyes gleamed with molten desire.

"I *am* threatening, princess. It's not my fault you don't see it for yourself."

"Like I said. Delusional. Absolutely delusional."

Margrete beamed up at the man who'd stolen her heart. A king whose unwavering faith in her lifted the weight of the unknown.

Raising her hand, she brushed her fingers along the sharp edges of his chiseled jaw, delighting in the subtle prickle of his stubble. With his hair thoroughly disheveled and sleep framing his depthless onyx pools, his rumpled appearance made the poised ruler seem almost boyish. Though Margrete had learned that Azantians aged at a much slower pace compared to their human counterparts.

Yet another problem they'd yet to address.

Margrete wasn't sure if she would age the same as a mortal or as an Azantian. Or if she would age at all, with what lay inside of her.

She moved to play with the silken strands at Bash's nape, giving them a gentle tug. His lids fluttered closed as he sighed contentedly.

"I suppose I'm lucky then that you keep me humble," he finally replied, moving back to idly stroke her through the thin material of her chemise. She cursed the damned silk. Judging by the look on his face, she suspected he felt the same way.

Rising to the tips of her toes, Margrete kissed his full lips. They were delectably plush and tasted of pure sin. Bash snaked his arms around her waist before sliding a hand into her hair. He fisted the long strands and exposed her neck, his eyes burning as he leaned down to plant a reverent trail of kisses up and down the column of her throat. Margrete's heart skipped several beats as he returned to her mouth, taking his time exploring, worshipping, losing himself in her.

Gently sucking her lower lip into his mouth, Bash's tongue teased as he tasted her, and another low groan reverberated deep in his throat. The noise was borne from desire and adoration, and Margrete lost herself to the intoxicating sound.

Minutes passed before Bash gradually pulled back, onyx eyes hungry. Their inky hue was a shade darker this morning, but perhaps the early light of day cast shadows upon them.

Bash heaved a frustrated sigh. "I hate to leave so early, especially now that you're blushing for me." He cupped her cheeks, and she leaned into his caress. "But I better get ready. The council is meeting this morning. Something about the mortal world."

Her world.

Prias and her human home felt like a lifetime ago. A time when she'd been a perfect *lady* about to marry the traitor, Count Casbian.

"What is the meeting about?" Margrete's skin buzzed in warning, that familiar trepidation settling in her chest.

Without a doubt, it had to do with the unleashed beasts. Maybe they'd *finally* made an appearance. Her spine tingled with swelling adrenaline.

Bash clutched her arms.

"You know I'll tell you everything. Gods know I've learned I can't hide anything from you anyway." His eyes grew wide. "Not that I ever would, mind you," he added in a rush.

One corner of her mouth pulled up. Bash was smart enough to understand she would pester him until she got her answers. Although, their arguments often led to a much more enjoyable form of...battle.

"You better tell me everything, pirate, or your bed will be rather chilly this evening," she threatened, settling against his chest and hiding her heated face from view. Margrete took a greedy inhale, shutting her eyes and relishing in the beauty of this single moment.

She understood all too well that nothing beautiful lasted forever.

As they watched the steady rise of the sun, consumed with the nearness of the other, a foul breeze—much like the one from her vision— swept in from the east.

And Margrete knew without a doubt, that this would be their last peaceful sunrise together for some time.

CHAPTER TWO

MARGRETE

Since Adrian was busy with the council meeting and there'd be no training today, Margrete wound up at the shore beyond the palace. Slipping off her boots, she dipped her feet into the cool waters and shivered as the now-familiar rush of energy raced down her spine. The moment she connected with the sea, her body buzzed, and a pleasant tingling vibrated across her skin.

Sea spray dampened her rolled-up pants, but she welcomed it, sighing contentedly when water coiled around her calves. The clear, blue water spun up to her thigh before playfully weaving back down.

She'd been...practicing. Manipulating the waters, that is. While she might've commanded the colossal wave that sank her father's vessel, she hadn't been able to do much more than raise the surf a few feet in the air since then. It was altogether frustrating.

Margrete could *feel* the ocean, but she certainly didn't own it as she once had. Perhaps that was the reason she crept out here after training, hoping to hone the powers no mortal possessed before.

Her heart thrummed wildly, and she briefly shut her eyes as the wind tickled her cheeks. The sea was in a joyous mood today. She sensed its elation as it snuck into her soul and explored.

Raising her hand, she twirled her finger in idle circles, murmuring the same ancient words she'd used months ago. "Arias moriad."

The approaching swell jerked but didn't cease its advance. She repeated the words, louder this time. The waters grew ever so slightly, but the wave didn't stop until it collided with her shins. Margrete growled.

She turned to her next target, determined to replicate the impossible magic she'd commanded. Again the wave struck the shore, but at least Margrete managed to lift it three measly feet. A sheen of sweat coated her brow. She pressed on.

Another wave came, and this time, when she uttered the old words of the mystics, the crest rose high in the air, well above five feet. While unsteady, it didn't falter, not even when it crashed against the sands of Azantian's shoreline, thoroughly drenching Margrete from head to toe.

She gasped, closing her eyes as she swiped her sopping hair from her face, smiling like a fool. Progress, however insignificant, lifted some of the weight of her incompetence.

When she opened her eyes, the meager pride she felt vanished. Instantly, her body shook and her pulse thundered, blood rushing to her ears and drowning out the whooshing waves.

Him.

Across the swells, face obscured by a deep-cobalt hood, stood the man —no, the *god*—she'd dreamt about for months.

Darius.

Even when he fought his brother, he'd never shown his true face, a silver mask concealing every feature. Yet Margrete could *feel* him, his darkness, just as she could that night.

She dragged in a sharp inhale. What brought him here after all these many weeks? She told herself she'd be prepared for the day he'd come, but now that he stood before her in the flesh, crushing fear stilled her limbs.

Miss me? A voice entered her mind, one she remembered well. It sounded seductive and deep. Silken. Her knees trembled.

She might possess most of his brother's essence, but Darius was still a *god*. She had every right to be fearful.

What do you want? she asked, eyes narrowing and back going ramrod straight. She wouldn't cower, not even as her pulse quickened and sweat dripped down the curve of her spine.

This talk was well overdue.

A chuckle wafted to her ears. *You have something I want but cannot have.* There was a pause, and she could practically feel the frustration rippling across the waves between them. *But I've learned to be patient, thanks to my dear mother,* he spat. Surria, the Goddess of the Wind and Sky. *And I find I no longer...desire to kill you.*

Margrete frowned, uncertain as to what he meant. She'd expected him to come and steal Malum's essence right from her chest the second he was able—even if he had to carve it from her body.

Should I be thankful? Margrete snapped. *You did your best to kill the king, but you failed. I won't let you hurt me or anyone I care for ever again.* A rush of icy air snaked around her throat, twisting in her hair and pulling at the strands. She could taste the bitterness of his ire.

Tell me, Darius. What. Do. You. Want?

Margrete wasn't the same naive woman she'd been when she arrived in Azantian. Facing her father and almost losing Bash to the sea had hardened her heart. Made her resilient.

Life was cruel, but she was stronger.

She had to be.

Come with me, the god demanded, his voice nearly a growl. *Not only will it be easier, but I won't hurt your* loved *ones.* He hissed the word, which dripped with venom. *It is well past time you learned the truth so we can begin our work. I have bided my time long enough.*

Steeling her spine, she forced a mask of bravado. His threat hadn't gone unnoticed.

There is no we, Darius. If you are the almighty God of the Sea, then clean up the mess you and your brother made. The sea monsters are products of your squabble, after all.

The breeze picked up at her words, the fabric of his cloak lifting just enough for her newly sharpened sight to glimpse the corners of his lips curling into a grin. Her heightened vision was another gift from Malum, it seemed.

While I am strong, years of being trapped in a mortal body have weakened me. Malum's protective mark certainly hasn't helped aid me. His eyes flickered to the tattoo on her collarbone. *And months spent in the ancient advisor's body only made matters worse.*

Margrete gritted her teeth, seething.

Ortum.

I knew the brand they found on Ortum's body was yours, she said, her vision streaked with red. *Since the moment I met him, it was really you. But why? Why go through the trouble of using his form?*

Darius didn't speak, not even as she continued, her anger rising.

Are you that fearful of showing your true *face that you used another? Are you that hideous?*

Margrete couldn't help but provoke him. In fact, she took immense joy in doing so. It was a rush she felt now, the same kind of rush she'd felt during the attack when he'd met her eye across the waves.

My face is hardly hideous, darling, he said, voice dangerously light. He almost sounded amused. *I had my reasons for using the advisor, and I might tell you about them...one day. But first, I implore you to come with me before I'm forced to resort to more drastic measures. Or I might find myself finishing what I started that night on the waves.*

Bash.

Darius made it clear he wanted the king out of the picture.

Why him? She cocked her head and took a bold step in his direction. At her back, she felt the waters rise to her thighs, the sea's fury matching her own. *You will leave him out of this.*

Whatever *this* was.

Darius chuckled. *So attached to your king. I wonder what you'd think if you knew his* true *face.*

Margrete's brow furrowed.

Bash's *true* face? Darius was speaking in riddles. She knew Bash. Knew of his passion, his bravery, his kindness—even of his temper and impatience. His flaws were still a part of the man she'd grown to love.

Margrete closed her eyes and swallowed down her rising bile. She wouldn't let Darius threaten her. It was time he revealed his true intentions.

She opened her eyes. Nothing but that familiar expanse of blue sea lay before her, the cloaked figure but a distant memory.

Darius was gone.

As was that rush of electric adrenaline that had stormed into her veins. Her knees wobbled, and she took in her first full inhale since Darius's unexpected arrival.

Unable to fight the surge of dizziness any longer, Margrete let herself sink into the knee-deep waters. She dug her fingers into the soft ivory sands as the power of a god sputtered and died out.

She closed her eyes, and in that split-second, an image flashed across her mind. Maybe it was her weakened state or the shock of facing Darius, but what Margrete glimpsed sent a violent shiver down her spine.

Behind closed lids, she saw herself and Darius...

She was in his arms, holding him tightly against her body, her fingers woven into his hair. And she was smiling, gazing up at the god with a brilliant grin borne of *love*.

She felt sick. The image looked too real, *felt* too real, almost as if she'd lived it before.

Margrete opened her eyes with a start, though the picture of her in Darius's embrace lingered. And as if he somehow knew what she'd envisioned, Darius whispered across her mind one final time.

I'm coming for you.

CHAPTER THREE

BASH

Bash knew the peace of the morning spent with Margrete wouldn't last.

She'd seemed distracted when he found her on the balcony, those calculating blue eyes scanning the waters for answers that eluded her. She thought he didn't know of her visions, but Bash was more perceptive than she could possibly imagine.

Especially where she was involved.

He strode down the corridors of the palace to the council chambers with two stoic guards on his heels. Smartly, they averted their attention whenever Bash glanced their way. But he surmised their apprehension to meet his gaze had more to do with his newly changed eyes than him being their king.

Apparently, many found the black pools unsettling.

Right now, he couldn't blame them. It didn't help that the dark circles below his eyes were a nasty shade of purple, a sign of his restless nights and haunting dreams. Nightmares that had him waking in a cold sweat.

Glimmering eyes.

Dark waters.

An island full of ash and bones.

There was a reason he clutched Margrete extra tightly in the middle of the night, why his body shivered even in the warmth of their bed. It didn't matter what ghastly demons inhabited his dreams. Bash could handle it. There was no way he'd add more weight to Margrete's shoulders.

His father once told him that a king should show no emotion, and certainly not an ounce of weakness. Whenever young Bash would come to his father with tears in his eyes, the old king would scowl and demand he "fix himself." It wasn't until nightfall that the king would visit Bash and take a seat on his bed, relaying a tale of one of his many adventures.

Bash understood those visits were his father's way of showing his affection, however subtle. Each second of those rare nights was more precious to him than any crown.

Margrete taught him differently. She showed him that while he could be a formidable ruler before his people, he could also just be a man. Even a vulnerable one.

Bash.

He flinched at the sound of his name, nearly losing his step. The guards said nothing as he righted himself. It had been a hiss of a noise whispered into the shell of his ear—one he'd heard before.

Come to me.

Goosebumps danced across his neck, and his muscles tensed. This was the third time the voice dared come to him during the light of day. It had grown bold. Gods, he wished Ortum were alive to offer some insight.

They'd yet to discern what happened to the advisor, but Margrete suspected the brand that marred his decayed flesh belonged to none other than Darius, the same deranged god who'd tried to kill Bash. He could still envision Darius's narrowed eyes as his power barreled into him during the captain's attack. He'd glimpsed such hatred in that fleeting moment before he'd been dragged under. Hatred and some other unnamable emotion he couldn't place. Or perhaps, one he wished to ignore entirely.

Either way, the god wanted Bash dead, and clashing with the divine wasn't a fight he was certain he could win.

Rolling back his shoulders, Bash schooled his features into that of a formidable king. Just as his father had taught him all those many years ago.

The council members, robed men and women of varying ages and positions, trickled into the expansive chambers, murmuring among themselves. He knew them all personally, as he'd practically grown up in these rooms. Bash would sit in the corner as his father delivered a new decree or settled a dispute. His first visit had been at the tender age of four. Needless to say, he hadn't had much of a childhood. Another lesson from his father—there isn't time for play. Only preparation.

When everyone took their seats in chairs of gold and azure velvet, a dozen eyes turned his way, their gazes full of expectation.

Focus, Bash chided himself. He could wallow later when more pressing issues weren't at hand. Namely, the silence of the sea's children. For creatures bred to wreak chaos and crave blood, this quiet unnerved Bash greatly. What the hell were they waiting for?

"Everyone assembled?" he asked, addressing the room. His advisors nodded, anxiously awaiting the news Nerissa had promised the day before.

"Let's not waste time then." Nodding to Nerissa, the court's seer, Bash urged her to begin. The sooner they learned the basis for this impromptu meeting, the better. He itched for action. Sitting around and *waiting* was driving him closer to the edge, and not having any semblance of a plan had his need for control spiraling. Control meant order, and with all the bedlam soon to unfold, he clutched at whatever scraps of it he could.

Nerissa cleared her throat, her dainty features contorted in concern. *That's not a favorable sign*, Bash thought, clenching his fists in anticipation beneath the cover of the table. Seated to his left, Adrian, his oldest and most trusted friend, reached out to quickly pat his hand. His warmth enveloped him, his hand an anchor, keeping him from being swept away by his own panic. Adrian always knew when Bash needed his support. He gave him a quick smile in thanks.

"The cities of Castion and Malor have been demolished." Nerissa's melodic voice sounded so at odds with the news she delivered. The room fell into a tangible hush. "The beasts of Azantian, of the sea, aim to wipe away everything in their path. It won't be long before the land of men will be destroyed. I've seen it, and the destruction reaped will be great," Nerissa warned, her eyes creasing at the sides. "We must act fast...hunt the sea's children before it is too late, and the balance is further damaged."

Adrian let out a deep breath, the rush of air sounding loudly in the hushed room. Bash also heard the rustling of fabric as the council members shifted uncomfortably in their seats, most peering through their lashes at their king. The gates opened under *his* reign, and Bash would fix his mistakes, with or without Malum's heart to imprison the beasts.

If Malum's physical heart was indeed gone, then the majority of the god's power would stay with Margrete. Adrian had told Bash of her practice sessions down by the shore, and as much as he hated her placing herself in more danger, he knew that harnessing the magic would be the only thing to save them. Fate had entrusted the woman he loved to wield such power, and Bash put his trust in her completely...even with his father's cynical voice telling him otherwise.

The whispering council members hushed as Bash lifted his chin and placed both hands on the table. It shook beneath his palms.

"How many dead?" he grated out.

Nerissa grimaced before glancing at the stone tiles. "The waves have taken out thousands so far. The docks and ships that carried thousands more went down as well."

"How many?" Bash repeated, shoving down the guilt that rose like bile. He may not trust the humans, but they didn't deserve to die.

"At least ten thousand."

He bit back a foul curse.

"Adrian?" He twisted to his friend and commander. "Thoughts?"

Bash needed a moment to process. Much would go into building an army great enough to defeat such monsters of legend.

Rising to action, Adrian addressed Nerissa, his golden-brown skin rippling as the muscles in his neck tensed.

"They're taking out ships?" he said. "Coastal cities and islands?"

She nodded.

"Any idea which creatures are responsible?"

Many beasts escaped that night, most notably the Drathion. While similar to the sea serpent that was killed the night of the attack, this beast was double the size and twice as deadly.

"The Drathion," Nerissa began cautiously, "and the Collossious. Though it tends to roam the deeper waters, it has taken down dozens of ships thus far and doesn't appear to be slowing."

The Collossious, one of the fiercest predators the deep had ever known, was well over thirty feet in length, its hide supposedly impenetrable, and its thousands of serrated scales sharper than the finest Azantian daggers. While possessing similar features to a shark, it was said it could sink a ship with a single snap of its maw.

"Sir..." Nerissa started, lifting her gaze. "There's something else."

"Yes?" Bash pushed, impatient for the bad news to be over and done with. He needed to go to his office and begin executing a plan. There was so much to do already. "What is it?"

A sharp stinging radiated from his chest, and Bash brought his hand to where his most secretive of tattoos had been hidden by his shirt. The nymera, unlike the others, had been immobile for his entire life. But yesterday, he could've sworn he saw her smile.

As if to answer his dark thoughts, Nerissa replied.

"We still have to contend with the nymeras. According to the few ancient texts our historians located, they might possess the ability to venture beyond the shoreline using the most twisted of the dark magic from which they were born."

The nymeras—half-human, half-monstrous creatures of the deep. They sucked the souls straight from the mouths of mortals, feeding on them. They'd been weakened from their time beneath Azantian, and Bash suspected they'd hunt for souls until they were satiated, killing thousands if not more.

The tattoo on Bash's chest thrummed, and a sickly sweet taste coated his tongue. If they attacked...

It would be beyond chaos, beyond Bash's control. *Anyone's* control. They were far more deadly than the sea's other children, as they were clever and calculating, and an ancient dark magic flowed through their viscous, black blood.

"I also sense..." Nerissa paused, sighing through her nose. Bash could tell she was hesitant to relay this next part.

"Yes, Nerissa, what is it?"

"I sense that one of the gods is working with them."

The room gave a collective gasp.

"I'm assuming Malum's brother?" Bash asked. Nerissa gave a quick nod.

"I'm not sure what they're up to, but my visions have been filled with gray sands and a hooded man radiating divine power. He's surrounded by a horde of nymeras, the sea rising at his command."

Bash wondered if things could possibly get worse.

"Something tells me that you shouldn't step foot off these shores," Nerissa said. "But I know you have to leave in order to contain the beasts."

"You're right," he said firmly. "I cannot sit back while my people hunt the creatures that were my responsibility." The council members mumbled in agreement. He gritted his teeth, ignoring their tangible disappointment. He needed out of this suffocating room.

Nerissa opened her mouth but quickly shut it. She knew him well enough to know when he'd made up his mind. She took her seat without another word, but her inquisitive eyes shifted his way. He could feel her studying him.

Adrian lifted to his feet, dispelling the hushed whispers. "If you're planning to set sail for the beasts, then I'll have the men prepare the *Phaedra.* If any ship can withstand—"

Adrian droned on, but Bash only heard the depraved whispers that plagued him—the corrupt hisses he'd become all too familiar with.

Bash's world was changing—his *mind* changing—and with this new world came the promise of spilled blood.

CHAPTER FOUR

BASH

Bash's outspoken subjects argued well into the heated afternoon, the council chambers burning like an oven. Sweat trickled down his back, gluing the white button-down shirt to his skin.

When Bash finally called an end to the absurdity and relayed his final orders, he turned to Adrian. "Ready the men and prepare them for what is expected. I want the *Phaedra* equipped with a hundred soldiers."

He'd send word to Adrian once they identified the nymeras' movements, and his commander would launch a full fleet to aid in the battle. It wouldn't make sense to send all of their soldiers out in one go.

Adrian gave a slight tilt of his head, his bright green eyes brimming with unspoken questions he'd surely unleash later. He knew better than to speak to his king so candidly before gossiping subjects.

Nodding to the grim-faced council members one final time, Bash exited the chamber, his legs yearning to pick up the pace. To run and get the hell away from that stifling room.

It was all the *noise* that drove him to escape—the voices of his discontented people that mingled with the demented hisses of his swelling insanity. Everything blurred dangerously together.

As if on cue, the whispers returned.

Let them die.

You don't belong with them.

Mortals are worthless.

Spineless.

Unworthy.

Every slippery word dripped of loathing and animosity, the chorus of voices rising to a shrill ringing in his ears.

Beyond the council chambers, Bash thrust his back against the wall of a shadowy alcove and pressed his hands onto the cool glass. He greedily sucked in air.

Stop, he silently commanded, his breaths coming out in strained pants. *Fucking stop.*

He didn't want this, didn't want to hear any more voices. Voices speaking of killing and cruelty.

Voices he knew shouldn't exist.

Let them die, die, die...

The word repeated on a loop until Bash shivered in fury. The sheer malevolence of the voice brought out something within him he didn't very much like. The darkest part he'd suffocated for years. The *wrongness* of it wasn't him, not the man he'd worked so hard to become. It couldn't be.

Bash hissed in frustration, and the need to lash out, to feel *anything* other than this wickedness, had his body itching, tingling, *burning*. It was too much all at once, and try as he might, he couldn't turn off the damned voices. No. They grew louder, more forceful.

Die, die, di—

"Aghhhh!" Bash spun around, slamming a white-knuckled fist into the sea glass wall. It cracked, tiny rivulets of fractured glass spiderwebbing from beneath his bloodied knuckles.

Instantly, the pain silenced the song of death. *That's it,* he coaxed, trying to take in a deep breath even as his chest shook. *It's not real.*

"Are you all right, my king?"

A sugary sweet voice broke through the roaring in his ears, severing his concentration. Bash turned, finding Shade staring at him with a cool expression etched across her delicate face. The hairs on the back of his neck rose.

He didn't want anyone to see him in such a state.

"I'm fine," he ground out, twisting away from her penetrating gaze. He couldn't explain himself to his court treasurer, even if they were friends. Or, *used* to be friends. Lately, Shade had made herself scarce, only showing her face to honor Ortum at his memorial months ago.

"It doesn't look like you're fine," she replied, her voice free of emotion.

Bash clenched his knuckles, the skin cracking. *Yes. Focus on the pain.*

"This doesn't concern you, Shade," he managed, seething. He sounded cold and cruel and so unlike himself.

"Perhaps you need to let off some steam. Maybe I could summon Adrian to the terrace—"

His temper flared again before he could rein it in.

"Do not presume to know what I need." Bash took her in, from the crown of her fiery red curls to the depthless green of her eyes.

If his bite wounded, she didn't let on.

No. Shade *smiled.*

"As you wish, my king. As always, I only aim to please." Her last words dripped with acid, and she lingered for just a moment, a spark in her green eyes flashing. They looked exceptionally vivid today, nearly *too* bright. But before Bash could think too long on it, Shade bowed her head and glided back to the hall, vanishing as quickly—and as silently—as she'd appeared.

He'd deal with her later. Whatever she truly wished to ask of him could wait. It would have to.

Without another thought, Bash abandoned the alcove and shoved past a startled Adrian.

"Bash!" his friend called out, his voice drenched with concern. "We need to talk!"

"Later!" Bash snapped over his shoulder, continuing his relentless pace. Adrian spoke his name one more time, but Bash had already turned the corner and left him in the hall. He felt like an ass, but his mind was a mess of emotions, and there was only one person on this island—in this entire realm—who could soothe him now.

Before long, he stood outside the royal chambers, curling his hand around the handle before pushing inside.

The second the door slammed shut, Margrete bolted up from her favorite chair, a thick leather-bound book tumbling to the tiles. Since she'd moved into his room, she'd added color and light to the previously barren and impersonal space.

Woven tapestries hung from the walls, and brightly colored pillows decorated the bed. Even his desk, which once contained no more than pen and paper, held small trinkets found in the marketplace. Now, his rooms were a home. A place of comfort. Hell, he didn't even mind the clutter.

Much.

Bash shoved his bloodied hand into his trouser pocket before Margrete had the chance to spot it, although she'd find out soon enough. The skin was already working to knit itself back together thanks to an Azantian's ability to heal quickly.

Margrete stood frozen across the room, her tiny hands clutching the silk robe tied tightly around her waist. Her brown hair was damp and curling around her face, and she smelled of lavender and soap. She must've just returned from the shore.

"Bash?" His name held all her questions. Her love, doubts, and fears.

She knew him better than most, and it didn't help that the façade of calm indifference had shattered the moment he'd exited the council chambers.

Bash let the remnants of his mask slip.

"The beasts that escaped have attacked the ships and islands of the mortal world," he began without pretense, sauntering farther into the room. "There have been many casualties."

The tips of her ears turned red, a spark of fire flashing in her blue eyes. "How many?"

"Ten thousand."

Bash's skin prickled as a gust of wind rushed into the room, the air turning icy.

"I need a vessel," Margrete demanded without hesitation. "Darius... this has to be him. He has to be the one commanding them. If we take out the beasts, then they can't be weapons for him to command."

Darius. The name was a curse on his tongue.

"Nerissa thinks he's working with the nymeras for some reason. I'm sure he's planning something."

Margrete sighed, running her hands through her damp hair. "I saw him today."

Bash stilled at her revelation, every muscle tensing.

"He wanted me to go with him. He made threats."

Threats.

Bash's blood boiled. "He appeared to you? Did he...harm you?" He clenched his hands into fists. If Darius so much as touched her, he'd make it his life's mission to hunt the bastard down. Why couldn't he just leave her the hell alone?

Margrete shook her head. "No. He didn't hurt me, Bash. But I don't think it's the last I've seen of him. He mentioned a protective mark Malum placed on me." She touched her wave tattoo. "But I have a feeling he wants more than his brother's power. He...he said something about me learning the truth? Whatever that means."

"I won't let him harm you. God or not." He seethed, his eyes narrowing into slits. White-hot rage slithered into his veins, making it nearly impossible to breathe, impossible to think about anything other than driving his blade through the god's heart. Bash swallowed down his fire, his blazing fury, and forced the next words out.

"Where were you when he approached you?" He'd have to double security and—

"By the water. He kept his distance, but he wanted me to come with him. He threatened you, *again.* Among other things."

Bash opened his mouth to argue, but she cut him off.

"And he admitted Ortum's death was his fault. That he was the one commanding his body. For weeks, he used him, convincing you all he was the man you'd known and admired."

Bash didn't know whether to be more angry with himself or with Darius. He *should* have known Ortum wasn't the same. Should've known that the warm and gentle man who'd always been a steadying presence in his life had changed. Ortum had practically been a second father to him.

"The council wants to send the *Phaedra* out with one hundred men in the morning. We will hunt them, don't worry. But in the meantime, I'm doubling your security. I'll make sure Darius doesn't have another chance to...come to you again." He averted his gaze, his anger a tangible beast. He feared he wouldn't be able to control it much longer.

A rush of air blustered and Margrete stood before him. She gently grasped his jaw.

"I'm going with you. Even if Darius isn't involved, the sea's children need to be killed before they take more lives. I'm as much a part of this as you."

Bash's throat constricted painfully, a crushing weight settling in his chest. If she came and something happened...

"Margrete, it's too dangerous. I'm not letting you—"

"*Letting* me?" she questioned, incredulous. She dropped her hand from his jaw, one brow raising. "Letting me?" she repeated. "I believe *I* was the one who saved this island. I destroyed the captain and—"

"Margrete!" Bash raised his bloodied hands to grasp both of her arms, giving her a gentle shake. "I was there. I know what you did, and I also know you nearly died because of it!"

An image of her flashed across his mind, right after he'd pulled her from the waves. The day he'd lost her to the sea, and she'd been reborn.

He couldn't go through that again. It would break him.

"I was fine, and you know damn well I can handle my own. Probably more so now that I have *this*." She gestured to her own heart. "Once I learn how to use it, who knows what I'll be able to do. I've been practicing every day."

And yet she hadn't managed to achieve the same force as when she destroyed her father's ship. Selfishly, Bash felt relief.

If she couldn't expose herself to whatever untested power she possessed, then she'd be safe, tucked away on the island where he could protect her. But Bash also knew she needed no protecting. While her ignorance would put *him* at ease, he'd vowed to her he wouldn't keep her caged. A promise he'd honor. Even if he would die an early death from worrying.

Just then Margrete's eyes drifted, catching sight of his knuckles. He began to drop his hands, but she snatched them, her lips thinning.

Shit.

"Bash? What happened?" She flipped over his hand, inspecting the dried blood with a furrowed brow. Instantly, her anger transformed into concern.

"It's nothing," he assured weakly. "I lost my temper. Nothing more."

"Lost your temper on *whom?*" When Bash's lips remained shut, she pressed, "Who did—"

"A wall, all right?" he said, heaving a forlorn sigh. "I lost my temper on a wall. It was an impossibly long meeting, and I'd just learned that thousands of people died."

"So you punched a *wall?* What else aren't you telling me? You may be quick to anger at times, but never like...this. I know there's more you're hiding."

"It was nothing more than that," he lied, the weight of the false words burning his tongue. "I was just disturbed by the news. Frustrated that I let it happen."

He could tell she didn't believe him, that she wanted to push him further until she gleaned every ounce of truth. But instead, she sighed and said, "I'll get a rag. You should wipe that off before others see."

Bash stopped her. "I still don't want you going."

"If you think for one second I'm not—"

"*Please*," he gritted out. He wasn't accustomed to answering to someone else. But she had to see reason. She needed to be safe.

Bash wasn't sure of the exact moment he found himself loving her, *needing* to protect her more than he required air. But the feeling rooted itself deep inside his core, and there was no getting rid of it now. She'd become as much a part of him as his racing heart.

Margrete's ears flushed crimson as her chest rose and fell rapidly, her full lips opening to protest. Before she could, Bash silenced her with a desperate kiss.

She went still for a heartbeat, but when his hands tangled in her hair and his tongue traced the seam of her lips, she gave in. Sighing in defeat, she wound her arms around his torso, snuggling in closer.

When he invaded her mouth and tasted her sweetness, Bash nearly forgot they'd been fighting at all. That was until Margrete drew away, her eyes sharper than daggers.

"You can't kiss me every time you wish to win an argument." Although determined, her tone softened, turning woeful. "I *have* to do this, and I can't stay here holed up any longer. I can't just sit back and wait. Darius wants me *and* Malum's heart, and I won't be waiting for him to take it."

Bash growled his dissent, but he knew he'd lost.

Cursing, he squeezed his eyes, letting loose a weighted exhale. One that said more than any words.

"Then it's settled," she said. "I'm coming. And with me onboard, you and your crew might actually have a chance if something unnatural occurs."

Sensing his resolve weakening, she reached to cup his face, her small hands cool against his heated flesh. The touch was like a balm, and his tense muscles slowly relaxed.

"I'm not the same woman you first met, Bash," she whispered, leaning forward, her lips inches from his own, teasing him. "You'd do well to remember that."

Damn this woman.

"I know you're not," he relented. She'd always been fierce, but what lived in her soul spoke of magic beyond his reach. "You may be my reckless little warrior, but I'd prefer it if you didn't leave my sight."

Margrete gave him a cheerless smile, rising onto her tiptoes to plant a gentle kiss on his lips. "I'm so glad you see reason."

Bash let out a weary groan.

"Just...just listen to me for *once*," he added, watching her melancholy smile surrender some of its weight. "I can't lose my focus if you're in trouble. And you're quite distracting."

Margrete rolled her eyes—her trademark sign of annoyance. It used to drive him mad, but now it was...endearing. It was *her*.

"As long as you listen to *me* as well, pirate." Her old nickname for him loosened the tension in his shoulders.

"I do so love following your commands, princess."

CHAPTER FIVE

MARGRETE

Margrete hadn't stopped thinking about Darius's last words.

I'm coming for you.

Even after Bash stormed into her chambers and shared the news of the sea's children, the god's threat never left her thoughts. It dug into her mind like talons, its grip refusing to loosen.

Now, at dinner, her churning stomach could barely manage a bite of food.

"What's wrong?" A tiny hand poked into her side.

Margrete turned from her full plate of seared fish and fresh vegetables and took in her sister's beaming face. Birdie had taken well to the mystical island—her skin tanned and smile dazzling in its radiance. Margrete had never seen her smile so pure, and the sight warmed her heart.

Seated at the head of the table, Bash paused his meal, eyes wandering in their direction. He'd been watching her nonstop as he shoved his food around his plate. She hadn't seen him take a bite.

Ignoring him for now, Margrete cradled her sister's cheeks. "I'll be leaving tomorrow with Bash and his men, little bird, but I'll be back before you know it."

Birdie scrunched her mouth. "Do you have to go?"

The sadness in Birdie's small voice wrenched something deep within her, and she knew the darkness clouding her sister's blue eyes stemmed from Margrete vanishing months ago. Even if it was hardly her *choice* to be kidnapped by Azantians. Still, she carried the guilt of leaving her sister to fend for herself against their despicable father.

"I'll be here!" a cheery voice answered before Margrete could form the words. Shade grinned from the other side of the table, her crimson-painted lips stretched wide. "You can be my apprentice."

Birdie mumbled a reply, but Margrete focused entirely on Shade.

Margrete's grip on her sister's hand tightened.

Ever since she'd spotted the peculiar burn mark on Shade's neck the night of the Full Moon Feast, Margrete had been apprehensive around the beautiful treasurer. She told herself it was paranoia, but after the brand they'd discovered on Ortum's body, she couldn't settle her tumultuous doubts. It didn't help that Shade seemed to go out of her way to cover her neck, that luscious red hair always combed meticulously in place.

Stop. Margrete shouldn't make assumptions. Her mind went to the story Bay had once told her, about how Shade had lost both of her parents to a fire when she was young. She had been sent to the orphanage, where she'd met Bay. Margrete knew better than anyone how a painful childhood could force you to hide yourself from the world.

Besides, if anyone should make her feel uncomfortable, it would be Nerissa. The woman hardly paid attention to Margrete, though tonight she caught the court seer's eyes stuck on her more than once.

A fork clattered loudly, jolting Margrete from thoughts of Shade and gods and monsters. At her side, Bash let out a soft curse, barely audible to the full table of hushed guests. Not glancing from his plate, the king continued to stare at his dinner, oblivious, or simply unaware that he'd captured every eye in the room. The flames of the sconces glinted off the metal fork in his grip, and the refracted light caught the traces of silver in the blacks of his eyes.

"You all right?" Margrete asked under her breath, clasping his thigh beneath the table.

He flinched, though he finally lifted his gaze from his meal.

"Yes. I'm fine. Fine." He shrugged, bringing a mouthful of food to his lips. He grimaced as he swallowed.

As if she believed that.

"You're doing an exceptionally awful job at hiding yourself tonight," she chastised, forcing a smile to her lips, attempting to get a rise out of him. "You haven't even once commented on the chef's generous use of salt, and that is so very unlike the prickly pirate I've come to know."

Food was one area in which Bash was fastidious. She found it rather amusing.

The others seated around the dining table dutifully ignored their hushed conversation, though they appeared lost in their own brooding thoughts this evening. Bay and Adrian were wrapped in a tense exchange, the former uncharacteristically sullen.

Margrete did the only thing she could to break the silence. Tonight was their last night together for some time, and she hated that it would be spent in such awkward quiet.

"Bay told me about your first date," she blurted, glancing at Adrian.

Immediately, two pairs of eyes flickered in her direction. The shadows clouding Bay's blue irises cleared, and Adrian lost some of the rigidity in his shoulders.

"Oh, he told you, did he?" Adrian scoffed. "That man's idea of a romantic date is swordplay."

"And wine!" Bay added, his tone was light.

"Yeah, and wine," Adrian conceded. "But being stabbed on a date was not how I imagined it would play out."

"Excuse me?" Margrete dropped her silverware. She hadn't heard the part about Adrian being *stabbed*.

"Yes, you heard me correctly. Bay got too cocky with the dagger throwing and literally stabbed me."

Bay sat up, a finger jabbing the air. "It was just a flesh wound! I *barely* nicked your arm. Always so dramatic."

Adrian broke out into the kind of laugh that should've been conta-
gious had the night not held such weight.

"You're lucky I thought you were so attractive," Adrian said. He
snorted when Bay shot him a vulgar gesture. "Had it been anyone else..."
His voice drifted off, and he shook his head. Margrete adored the smile
playing on his lips.

"There was never anyone else." Bay reached out and seized his
boyfriend's hand. Lifting it to his mouth, he placed a gentle kiss on his
knuckles. Adrian blushed a deep crimson.

After all these years together—and a stabbing—they still blushed in
each other's presence. Margrete grinned. They were sickeningly
adorable.

Thankfully, conversation picked up after that little tale, and an hour
passed before excuses were made to retire for the night.

Bash offered Margrete his elbow before bowing low to slip his hand
into Birdie's. Her sister chatted merrily as they walked from the dining
room, speaking of all the new maneuvers Adrian taught her yesterday.
Bash commented and smiled, but his mind was elsewhere.

Just before they reached the spiraling stairs, an airy voice called her
name.

"Margrete. Can I have a quick word?"

Nerissa.

She stood in the center of the main hall, her hands clasped behind
her back. To anyone else, it might've appeared a relaxed pose, but the
slight flicker in her delicate jaw told Margrete the woman held more
tension than she let on.

"Of course," she replied, giving Bash a quick nod. He bent down on a
knee and asked Birdie to show him some of her new combat moves. The
ensuing squeal that left her rosy lips almost made Margrete smile in
return.

"Everything all right?" she asked Nerissa. She seemed to be asking
that question a lot lately.

The seer swallowed hard enough for Margrete to track the bob of her
throat. That couldn't be a good sign. Her hands instantly grew clammy.

"I wanted to say a few things," Nerissa began, bringing her hands to rest before her. Margrete saw how she wrung them, almost as though she were apprehensive to speak.

Margrete dipped her chin in acquiescence, not sure where she planned to go with this speech.

"I haven't been fair to you." Nerissa sighed. "I judged you from the moment you set foot on these shores, and I haven't been...welcoming."

An understatement. Margrete hoped her features didn't betray her.

"You're good for him, you know. Sebastian—Bash, I mean." She paused to give her a wry, knowing smile. "And I haven't seen him so happy in years. Well, maybe ever, actually." She fidgeted on her feet before bringing her gaze to Margrete's. "I care about Bash like a brother—a very annoying one—and maybe there's room for a new sister as well. A sister who has shown she is far more worthy than I'd imagined."

Nerissa didn't seem prone to sentimental talks, so the words sent a jolt of warmth shooting into Margrete's chest. There was no hesitation as she responded.

Grasping Nerissa's hand, ignoring how she flinched, Margrete pulled her into a hug. The woman stiffened, but seconds later, she relaxed into the embrace.

"I like you all the more for protecting him," Nerissa whispered into her ear. "It shows your heart, and in this often brutal world, such love is rare."

Margrete drew back and held Nerissa at arm's length. "You're a strong and loyal person, Nerissa, and I'd be honored to become your friend."

Nerissa clenched her jaw, but Margrete could just make out a fleeting spark of gratitude in her eyes. The seer took an abrupt step back.

"Be careful tomorrow," Nerissa whispered in warning. "And be on your guard. I sense very rough seas ahead."

As did Margrete, but they'd be on the *Phaedra*, a ship that could weather any gale.

"I will," she said. "Don't worry about us."

Nerissa's lips thinned, and it looked like she wanted to say more, but she just gave a curt nod instead. It left Margrete feeling uneasy.

"Well, goodnight," the seer said, loud enough for Bash and Birdie to hear. Bash's returning smile was borne of pride more than anything. Apparently gaining Nerissa's acceptance had been quite the feat.

"She likes you," Bash said on the walk up. "And gods know she doesn't give her friendship to just anyone."

Margrete couldn't help but feel like she'd been given a gift more precious than gold. There was something ethereal about the woman, something Margrete couldn't put her finger on.

When they reached Birdie's room—two doors down from the chambers she shared with the king—Margrete embraced her sister before tucking her in for the night. Bash waited patiently in the hall. Usually, he'd come in and tell Birdie some outlandish story of sea monsters, gods, or other such myths, but not tonight.

Only after they'd ventured to the royal chambers, the door shutting behind them, did Margrete turn to Bash.

"What aren't you telling me?" she asked, getting right to the point. She wove her fingers between his icy ones. Ever since his rebirth, his skin hadn't retained the same heat, but she was too thankful that he was alive to question the change too deeply. Maybe she should.

"Nothing is wrong, princess. I promise."

"You're a terrible liar. You've been acting odd since the meeting. Tell me. Now."

Enough was enough.

Bash's eyes turned cold, hardening at the edges. Shadows seemed to curl around his frame, flashes of steel sparking in his irises. Margrete inadvertently shivered beneath the unfamiliar gaze, warning bells sounding in her mind.

Bash's demeanor shifted as the shadows swelled, and for a moment she could've sworn she glimpsed a gaunt face amid the black clouds. She blinked, and the fog vanished.

"Why can't you just leave well enough alone?" Bash asked, his lips twisting. While the shadows had dispersed, the foreign glint in his eyes had not.

Margrete took a step back, not sure who stood before her. Surely not the man who owned her heart.

A muscle in Bash's jaw ticked, and a heavy cold settled in the pit of her stomach. In all the time they'd been together, Margrete had never been the subject of his wrath, this cutting *bitterness*. It was so pungent she could taste it on the tip of her tongue.

Bash flinched, seeming to realize what he'd said. The cruel way he'd fashioned his words. His lips parted as if in shock, and he brought a hand to his hair, running it through his curls.

"Bash..." She took a hesitant step forward. Something was off. *Wrong.*

"I—I'm so sorry," he murmured before scrubbing at his face. "I don't know why I just said that. I would never..." His eyes glazed over, and fear clouded his irises. "I need to go."

Gods, he couldn't even look at her, his gaze drifting to his boots. Shame and confusion radiated off him like a scorching noon sun.

"There's so much to do before we set off, and I need to make sure we're ready." Taking an unsteady step in her direction, Bash gently grasped her hand and placed a chaste kiss on her knuckles. "I promise I won't be too late."

Her brows furrowed as he plastered on a smile she knew to be fake. When he turned for the door, her instincts screamed at her to reach out and hold him, to convince him that whatever plagued him could be solved.

He suffered from more than merely the fear of the sea's monsters.

"Bash!" she called out just as the door to their chambers shut. But the king didn't turn back, and his steps echoed loudly in the corridor beyond. She cursed.

Darkness.

Margrete had felt and *tasted* the darkness that rippled off him. It was rotten and foul and reminded her of someone she wished she could forget —her father.

He's not him, she repeated in her mind. *He's not him.*

Bash had a lot thrust upon his shoulders.

That was all. Right?

Or was she choosing to ignore the traces of magic she tasted in the air whenever he entered a room? How his eyes shifted and changed and became something belonging to a stranger?

A salty wind wound through the hallways of the palace as if perceiving her anxiety. It coiled around her frame and tickled her goose-pimpled arms.

"What's he hiding?" she murmured to herself, nervously wiping her clammy hands on her trousers. The chilly breeze gusted around her loose linen shirt in response, the fresh sea winds answering her body's unspoken request. Instantly, her skin cooled. "I'll find out soon enough."

Margrete squeezed her eyes briefly before urging the lingering breeze back to the waters it hailed from.

FOUR HOURS LATER, WELL INTO THE DEEP CALM OF THE NIGHT, Bash returned to their chambers. Margrete must've fallen asleep because when she opened her eyes, the remnants of a dream clung to her vision.

A soft grunt sounded as a boot dropped to the polished stones. The potent taste of fear she'd sensed from him earlier saturated the air. Bash must've stumbled again, for the second boot dropped with another loud thud, followed by the clatter of his belt.

Margrete feigned sleep. She'd get her answers tomorrow, and tonight wasn't the time to push. They were both mentally exhausted.

Seconds later, icy hands wound their way about her middle, hugging her close as his breath warmed her hair. His nose nuzzled her curls, and she heard her name fall from his lips in a murmur.

It didn't take long for the King of Azantian to tumble into sleep, snoring softly in her ears. Margrete sighed, and although irritated at his lack of transparency, she leaned back into the comfort of his chest.

Perhaps a decent night of sleep would clear both their minds, and

Bash would realize she was his partner. Someone he didn't need to hide from.

Margrete lay awake in bed for an hour. Her mind might've been weak with exhaustion, but the heavy presence of foreboding kept her alert.

She'd been thinking of Darius and whatever sinister plans he'd envisioned for her, when the arm slung about her waist gave an abrupt jerk. Bash's fingers dug harshly into her middle, and she flinched.

"Bash?" she called out behind her.

No answer.

She prepared to flip over when the weight of his arm vanished entirely. The mattress dipped, and Margrete twisted to see Bash stumbling into his abandoned clothes.

Both her brows arched, and she clutched the sheets tightly between her fists as she watched him clumsily dress.

"Bash? What are you doing?"

He didn't respond, just continued shoving his feet into his leather boots. Margrete opened her mouth to call out again, but shut it, swinging her legs to the floor and ambling for her silken robe.

The king was halfway out the door when she caught up, one slipper secured as she fumbled to cover the other foot.

"What the hell are you doing?" she hissed again, racing ahead of him. When she peered into his eyes, she found them to be glazed over—glassy and unseeing.

Was he sleepwalking?

Birdie would sleepwalk from time to time, but she'd always end up in Margrete's bed, hogging the covers and hoarding a stash of treats.

Something told Margrete this wasn't the case.

Retreating, Margrete decided to see where his unconscious walk would lead them. Maybe he'd reveal more to her in his sleep.

Bash took the steps to the main floor of the palace, thankfully bypassing the dreaded throne room she'd avoided since the night of Darius's vision.

Margrete scurried after her pirate as he picked up his relentless pace, his feet carrying him down a corridor she recognized all too well. When they passed a vibrant emerald door framed in antique gold, Margrete's heart plummeted.

It was the place where they'd shared a kiss beneath lavender and plum fireworks. A cavern below the palace that glistened with saltwater and glimmering magic.

Bash was headed for the depths of the Adiria Cavern.

The door that once held captive the vicious nymeras.

A door that was now wide open.

CHAPTER SIX

MARGRETE

MONTHS AGO, IN THIS PLACE OF BOTH HAUNTING DARKNESS AND luminous light, Bash and Margrete had created a magic all their own. A night she would never forget, the memory of it would reside in her soul always.

Now, Bash led her back to the Adiria Cavern—though this time, his eyes were glossed over and his usual spark had dimmed. They weren't two lovers running away to the shadows, swept up in a moment of need. No. Bash had been driven here by some unexplainable force, and Margrete intended to uncover the reason.

Her steps were light as she followed, intuition her only guide. Should she wake him? She hesitated, recalling how dangerous it could be to rouse someone in such a state. But the cold, hard truth of the matter was that she selfishly wanted him to expose the secrets he hid.

She should feel shame over the admission, but her need for answers outweighed anything her conscience could throw at her.

Bash never fumbled or lost his way across the jagged rocks and dipping crags. He only stopped once to light a torch at the entrance, his fingers clutching the crude wood tightly. All that stood between Margrete and an unholy darkness was Bash's flickering torch, the scarlet and rust flames casting eerie shadows across the king's glazed features.

Margrete's hand trailed over the uneven planes of the cavern, her breaths coming out in short pants as they neared the final bend. Hastening to keep up, she turned the corner, her lips parting when she glimpsed Bash standing motionless beneath the apex of the cave.

Droplets glistened like tiny stars on a clear night, the sharp edges and spiked rock a complex design of coarse splendor. Though it was beautiful, Margrete sensed a gravity here, and the many untold mysteries pressed down on her shoulders and weighed each hesitant step forward.

This place was much more than the center of Azantian. It felt...divine.

Sacred.

And Margrete was trespassing.

Beneath the zenith, the hazy night sky filtered through a narrow opening in the center, the shy moon lending little to no light. Only Bash's torch fought against the gloom, and even that was no match.

The absence of his mind gave the man before her an inhuman quality —an empty shell decorated by impassive features of beauty. Margrete arched a brow, waiting for him to make a move, for him to make *any* move at all. Yet he stood as unyielding as a statue.

Maybe she should end this now and wake him.

Just as she dared a step closer, Bash's face came to life, as did the rest of the cavern. Where lavender whorls and sweet plums had once flickered and pirouetted across the span of rock, a dark silver and obsidian smoke curled about Bash's torso. The quivering beams bounced off his frame, rendering his weak torch useless.

Margrete held in her gasp, digging her fingernails into the flesh of her palms as the world shifted on its axis. The smell of dark magic wafted to her nostrils, the scent overpowering and rotten. It landed on the tip of her tongue, and her throat constricted in response.

Every nerve became electrified, and she itched to move to Bash, to yank him free from the spell he'd fallen under. But she halted, frozen in place by the sight of the ghostly wraiths slithering up from the rocks underneath his feet. These spectral apparitions wove and bent as they caressed him, swaying leisurely as they ascended. Apparitions that looked eerily similar to those from her vision. The ones that had stormed the sides of the *Phaedra* and consumed it whole.

Her lungs ached for air, and a searing heat scorched her insides. Something nefarious was at play, and even with the heart of a god within her, Margrete paused.

Her pulse quickened, and she fumbled back a step, closer to where the narrow passageway led to the palace. An engulfing heat flowed through her veins, and she knew it had to be Malum's essence awakening, responding to whatever blasphemous deed took place here.

Instinctively, her hand drifted to the necklace Bash had gifted her, the purple-blue stone he'd carved from the cavern itself. It usually brought her steadying comfort, but now it was ice against her fingers. She dropped her hand with a hiss.

In horror, she watched the wraiths spin, and more and more silver shadows slipped through the jagged cracks of the cavern floor. They climbed the walls, and a few tendrils of smoke escaped through the zenith's fissure.

"Soon," called out a voice that wasn't a voice. It was a whisper of a thing, a hiss. Guttural and savage. Not altogether human.

It didn't belong to Darius. No, she knew his voice as well as her own.

Whatever spoke held the type of darkness that devoured and ate away at one's soul.

"We'll be together soon." The sound echoed, raising the hair on the back of Margrete's neck. The scent of rot grew heady, and she stifled a cough against her palm.

Evil.

Whatever this was, it was evil.

"I will," Bash promised the unseen entity, his voice a rasp. "I'll find you."

Who exactly was he speaking to?

Margrete inched closer, about to race to his side and damn the consequences, when Bash dropped the torch and condemned the world to a devastating darkness.

CHAPTER SEVEN

BASH

"Bash!"

Someone called to him. A voice that held a slight lilt, one he recognized even under the fog that drenched him. A voice he'd know anywhere.

Margrete?

His vision swam, the shadows he glimpsed curling around the edges of his sight. Faintly, he could make out a steady dripping, and the smell of salt grew overpowering.

Where the hell am I?

Bash tilted his head, finding a sliver of light filtering down from above, the moon highlighting jagged rock.

The Adiria Cavern.

His name sounded once more, and this time Bash cried out in reply, Margrete's name a plea on his lips. Maybe this was all a nightmare, and he'd wake in bed with her tucked against his chest.

"Bash!" the voice grew closer. Before he could open his mouth to respond, the scent of lavender engulfed him like a crashing wave.

Slim arms wove around his torso, gripping him harshly enough to bruise. But it was her, his Margrete, not some apparition or spectral copy haunting his dreams.

Bash wrapped a trembling arm around her waist, using her as a lifeline, a hold to this world. Against him, Margrete's breathing grew chaotic and uneven, and he brought his hand to cup her cheek. A drop of wetness fell onto the pad of his index finger, and he frowned, his heart aching. Why was she crying?

"What...what happened?" He scanned their surroundings. "Why are we here?"

After the hellish day he'd had, after he fled Margrete, he'd indulged in a glass of his finest liquor, drinking alone in his study as he contemplated a grim future. He didn't even finish a full glass, but the rest of his night remained frighteningly blank.

Gentle hands grazed his cheeks, warming his ice-cold skin.

The moon's light peeked through the cavern's zenith, illuminating the fear contorting her lovely features. Its glow taunted him, showing him a truth he didn't wish to see.

"You were sleepwalking. And these shadows"—she shook her head—"or *whatever* they were, spoke to you. I didn't know what to do, if I should wake you or not. But then you spoke to a voice, and I froze. I did nothing."

Bash's brow furrowed. None of what she said made sense. Another tear slipped over his thumb as it slid down her cheek. Margrete rarely cried. It could only mean whatever she'd seen frightened her so thoroughly that her steely resolve had melted.

He'd take her anger over this tangible sadness. It broke him in a way he hadn't known before because *he* caused her tears. His hands lowered to her hips, and he gave her what he hoped was a reassuring squeeze. He wanted to ease her fear but didn't know how.

"I don't remember anything," he reluctantly admitted when the silence became too much to bear. "You said I was sleepwalking?"

He'd never done such a thing in all his life.

"Yes. You bolted out of bed and practically ran here. I followed when you didn't wake. I was worried you might do something reckless." She let out a throaty chuckle devoid of all humor. "Looks like I had a right to worry."

Bash often came to the Adiria Cavern when he wished to be alone. It was one of the few places in the kingdom where he felt at peace. But why did he come here tonight? And why did his skin crawl and his heart race as if he'd just engaged in a battle?

"We should leave," he said quickly, taking hold of her hand. Maybe once free of this sacred place, his head would clear.

He noted the slight bob of her head, but her lips remained in a tight line.

"Hold on to me," he instructed, beginning the short walk back to the palace. Bash didn't need a torch to find his way. He'd been sneaking down here since he learned how to escape his governess.

Margrete was unusually quiet as they trekked through the cavern, the only sign of her trepidation, the clamminess of her palms. Still, she never released his hand. Her trust was enough to steady his thoughts, though her silence worried him.

If he'd learned anything at all about Margrete, it was that she freely spoke, even during times of distress. Bash didn't break the uneasy quiet until the light of the corridor gleamed against Margrete's caramel skin, which was a full shade paler.

"Let's go back to our chambers," Bash offered solemnly, schooling his features. Margrete kept her hand in his, but he knew her well enough to know her mind was consumed with his midnight excursion and every-thing it could mean.

Only when the door to their rooms snicked shut behind them did Bash speak again.

"Tell me. What was it I did down there?"

Secretly, he didn't want to know. Knowing would make it real.

Margrete perched on the bed and placed her hands delicately upon her lap. The sight of her uncharacteristically full of nerves had his chest tightening with guilt.

He took a seat beside her on the bed, and the mattress dipped beneath his weight. She tensed, but he closed the distance, resting a hand on her thigh, anxious to fix what plagued her.

Bash should tell her about the whispers. The ones that had followed him for the past few weeks. He could open his mouth right now and plant worry in her already troubled head. Tell her what he should have from the start. It wasn't as if he didn't trust her...

No. He was a coward.

Bash swallowed his frustration, the shame, and needling exasperation churning chaotically in his chest and leaned his head against the sloping plane of her shoulder. The intoxicating scent of her hit him like a punch to the gut, and Bash inhaled the sweet perfume that coated the strands of her silken hair. She was home, safety. He took in another deep breath.

"I'm sorry I woke you," he eventually whispered against the shell of her ear. It wasn't what she wished to hear, but he couldn't find the words. Or at least, the *right* ones. Perhaps he didn't know them himself.

Margrete shivered, goosebumps rising like fallen raindrops on her arms. Seconds ticked by before she relaxed at his side. Snaking her arm around his torso, she gripped his shirt, her hold firm.

Bash smiled grimly. Even after tonight, he could always count on this. On them. He wasn't sure what he'd ever done to earn her unwavering trust, but he greedily accepted it.

"I don't understand what occurred down there, Margrete. At all." That was the truth. He had a blurred image of curling darkness, a figure dancing amid silver, but other than that, nothing. "But I should tell you something..."

The words were out now, and his heart thudded so loudly he was sure she could hear its erratic beating. Sweat banded across his forehead as tingles of alarm slid down his spine.

"I-I should tell you about—" His voice cracked, the confession trapped in his throat. It was physically painful expelling the truth, and his hands shook.

"About what?" she pressed.

Bash opened and shut his mouth. He felt as if a steel band had wrapped around his neck, preventing the words from escaping. Why couldn't he just tell her? She deserved the truth, and he should've had the courage to tell her weeks ago.

"Hey. It's all right," Margrete soothed, trailing her fingers along the underside of his jaw. He immediately closed his eyes at the contact and leaned into her palm. "I'm not going anywhere," she promised.

"I've been having..." His breaths turned uneven, and he felt his entire body give a forceful shudder. He couldn't do this. Not now.

Margrete tilted his head up so she could stare directly into his eyes. Worry clouded her gaze. "It's late," she finally said, her eyes flicking to his shaking hands. He went to hide them, but she seized his wrists and squeezed. "We can talk about everything tomorrow, but for right now, I'm just happy you're safe. Though I hope you know nothing you tell me could ever scare me away. And no amount of darkness could ruin this." She nuzzled her nose against his sweetly.

Bash nodded, and that band around his throat loosened. He focused on the steadying feeling of her fingers, how her very presence calmed his pounding mess of a heart. It was easy to lose himself in Margrete, and for him, falling into her depths was inevitable.

Slowly, so very slowly, he brought his lips to hers, thanking her for her understanding in the only way he was physically able.

Under the spell of her soft touch, sparks flashed behind his closed lids, and soon the nightmare of his lost time beneath the palace gave way to a reality more beautiful than any dream.

Yes. He could face his demons with the rise of the sun.

Margrete returned his kiss, which had started out soft and cautious, though when she gently nipped at his lower lip, heat swelled in his chest. Without warning, he scooped her into his arms and positioned her higher up on the bed.

This was real. *She* was real. And she was possibly the only thing keeping him tethered to this plane. With her, the voices were silenced.

"Stay with me," she begged, as if she knew where his thoughts had gone. "Focus only on me. Nothing else."

Her eyes were hooded, and her chest rose and fell rapidly as he hovered above, his muscles straining to hold himself aloft. He could see the pulse point on her throat flutter, and he wanted nothing more than to kiss the spot, to sink his teeth into her skin and taste her.

Bash caught her stare and held it. He recognized the need in her eyes —it matched his own.

"How did I ever get so lucky?" he mused, taking his time to slip off her robe. He slid the material down one shoulder at a time, the glimpse of her bare skin teasing him. His calloused fingertips were rough against her smoothness, but she arched into his touch. Her lips parted as he undid the belt and allowed the rest of the silk to fall open, her body on full display. "I grow more bewitched by you every day."

He trailed both hands down her arms, reveling in the sight of the goosebumps he left in his wake. Up and down he moved until he brought his hands to caress the sides of her full breasts, her waist, her hips. Her curves would be the end of him.

"I doubt I'll ever get enough of this," he said, palming one breast. Her eyes fluttered when he rolled her peaked bud between his thumb and forefinger. "You're so godsdamned beautiful it hurts."

"Going sappy on me, pirate?" she asked, though he noted how wetness lined her lower lids.

He smiled. "Only for you, princess."

Crawling up her body, Bash trailed leisurely kisses along her inner thighs, gently nipping. She shivered beneath him, her hands moving to grab at his biceps, coaxing him higher. He resisted.

"You're teasing me," she whispered as he kissed each hip bone. He'd discovered it to be one of her most sensitive spots.

"I would never," he murmured against her warmth. Lifting his head, he found her eyes the deepest shade of blue. Desire burned bright, and Bash lost the little control he possessed. He brought his hands to the neckline of her dainty slip and tore the fragile fabric down the middle with a satisfying rip.

A small gasp escaped her lips, and the beast inside of him stirred at the sensuous noise.

"That was my favorite," she rasped. Her sultry smile utterly wrecked him.

Bash flung the scraps to the side of the bed.

"I'll buy you a new one. I'll buy you dozens of them." He'd give her anything if she asked.

"As long as you keep ripping them off of me, you'll have to." She beamed up at him, her bare chest heaving. "Now please, finish what you started, king."

"Gods, I love it when you're demanding."

He dipped his head and took one nipple between his lips, sucking on the peaked bud before sinking his teeth into the tender flesh. The small hurt elicited another throaty moan, the noise music to his ears.

She was a queen laid out before him, a goddess. And he planned to worship her until he forgot about everything else but her and the sweet sounds she made just for him.

"I want you, Margrete," he murmured into the shell of her ear. He needed to hear her words before he continued. Tonight had been alarming for them both, and he wouldn't take what she didn't wish to give. He prayed she needed him just as much.

"You have me," she responded, arching her hips against his growing hardness. "No matter what happens tomorrow."

He held her gaze, reading the words she didn't speak. The vow she made. Bash hoped she wouldn't come to regret staying at his side.

"I don't deserve you," he said, drinking in the adoration, the complete and utter trust glimmering in her irises.

"No," she argued, her features turning hard. "Never say that. You're everything I never thought I'd have, and not a second goes by where I don't want you. *All* of you. No one has ever *seen* me the way you do. You encourage me to be stronger than I ever thought possible."

Only because he wanted her to see herself the way he did. She was magnificent.

With a relieved curse, he rose, yanking off his boots and clothing before returning to the siren who sang to his heart. Lifting to his elbows, careful not to crush her beneath his weight, Bash kissed her full lips. She tasted like summer and open waters and something divine and unnamable—something that was entirely *her*.

Margrete grasped the nape of his neck and wove her fingers through his hair, lightly pulling the strands. She didn't need to be soft or unsure with him, and she eagerly took what she wanted.

Bash groaned into her mouth, his kisses turning greedy. He slid his hand to the apex of her thighs and rumbled his approval at what he found.

She was wet, ready for him, and Bash let go of his shadows, his doubts, his fears.

And then, he allowed the beast control.

"First, you're going to come on my fingers," he commanded against her lips, relishing in the way her body shuddered at his demand. "Then, you're going to come when I'm deep inside of you. I want to feel you when you shatter for me so sweetly."

"Yes," she murmured, grasping his wrist, silently urging him to quicken his movements. "Don't stop."

Playing with her, he took his time, bringing her close to bliss before slowing, knowing full well how the unhurried ministrations tortured her.

"Bash," she protested, lifting her hips to meet his fingers. He withdrew them slightly. "Don't tease me. Please."

He adored when she begged. When she pleaded for him to fill her.

Like the gentleman he was, he picked up the pace, rubbing her most sensitive spot until her lips parted, her soft whimpers filling the room. Just before she found her pleasure, he plunged two fingers into her core, causing her to gasp, her eyes nearly rolling to the back of her head. She was so close, and he worked her with ease, his attention never once leaving her face. He leaned down to wrap his lips around a peaked nipple, biting down at the same time he added a third finger.

That had been the push she needed.

Her legs shook violently, her entire body tensing up and her breath hitching. He lifted his head at the exact moment she cried out his name.

Watching her fall apart was his favorite thing in the world.

Her chest rose and fell frantically, and then she clenched around his fingers with a choked cry. He continued to move in and out of her, wringing every ounce of pleasure from her satiated body, not relenting until she went lax, fully spent from her release.

"I could watch you come all night," he confessed, placing a kiss on the corner of her mouth. Bash brought his fingers to his lips and sucked them into his mouth. Her breathing picked up as he licked himself clean.

"You taste like heaven. Like sin itself. You taste like you're mine," he whispered, her savory sweetness on his tongue. He could drown in it and die a happy man.

Maybe he would.

Before she fully recovered, Bash shoved her thighs apart and leaned down, sweeping his tongue across her wet core. Her taste exploded on his tongue, and when he rumbled his approval, another breathless sound left her lips.

He swirled his tongue around her throbbing center before sucking her into his mouth. He smiled when her hands flew to his hair, and she pulled hard on the strands. She rode his face, panting, desperate, taking control. Bash welcomed it.

"Bash, I need you inside of me," she whispered, yanking on his hair. "Now."

The sheer command in her tone had him slowing. He ran his tongue across her once more before lifting and caging her between his arms.

"I wasn't done, princess," he said, tsking. "You interrupted my fun."

She swore, swallowing hard. Bash tracked the movement, his lips flying to the hollow of her throat before kissing his way up to her jaw.

"You know exactly what I want," she said, her nails digging into his skin.

A soft curse left him as the world tilted and moved. Margrete had flipped onto his back in the span of a blink. Hmm, he liked this turn of events.

She beamed above him as she straddled his hips, a victorious smile gracing her swollen lips.

For someone so petite, she was a force. It made him want her all the more.

"I know how much you love it when a woman knocks you on your ass," she teased, bringing her mouth tauntingly close to his. Before he could taste her, she retreated, a coy grin twisting her lips.

"You wicked thing," he murmured.

Margrete squealed when Bash rose and grabbed the back of her neck. His lips collided against her with near brutal force, and she kissed him like it was a match to be won. A fight she easily won the second she reached behind her and brought her fingers to his length, tracing up and down his hardness. He would come undone from her touch alone, but Bash had other plans for their night.

"So very cruel, princess. Especially since I've dreamed of being inside of you all day. Imagined your addictive warmth wrapped around me." Margrete's fingers curled at his words. "The sweet sounds you make for me when you come on my cock."

He watched as she swallowed hard, her lower lip trembling.

No more playing.

In one fluid motion, he grabbed her hips and threw her on her back. She let out a rush of air, a mix between a moan and a sigh as she bounced on the bed.

"Much better," he whispered, the husky tone of his voice belonging to the savage she turned him into. Bash positioned himself at her entrance, rubbing up and down her slick heat.

"Tell me, Margrete..." His lips trailed along the curve of her jaw, torturing her further. "*How* do you want me?" He pressed against the bundle of nerves between her thighs, enjoying the way her lashes fluttered at the contact. "Would you prefer my tongue? My cock? I could make you come on the balcony again? Or maybe—"

"I swear, I *will* kill you if you don't move," she threatened, her cheeks deliciously flushed and red. She wanted him now, and Bash hated to disappoint his princess.

"Hold on," he warned, just before thrusting inside of her in one go. They both groaned, Margrete's nails already digging painfully into his back. A pain he craved more than any tender caress.

Gods, they fit together so damn perfectly.

Bash moved in earnest now, every thrust sending Margrete sliding farther up the bed. He wanted to fuck her until she forgot all else existed outside of this room. Until she knew only his name.

His mouth found her breast, and he swirled his tongue around her rosy bud, giving it a gentle nip. When he pulled away, she let out a groan of protest, the sound turning into a shocked gasp as he flipped her onto her stomach and wrapped his arm around her waist like a steel band. Lifting her to her knees, he kissed up and down her spine, his hand gently wrapping around her throat.

He gave her no warning as he entered her. A sinful cry filled the room, and she fisted the sheets as she chanted his name over and over like an unholy prayer.

"You feel amazing." He pressed himself flush against her back, the arm supporting her tightening when her knees trembled. "But you taste even better."

He'd grown addicted, and he longed to feel her come on his tongue.

Margrete whimpered at his words, pushing her hips back to meet his thrusts. "If you're good, I'll allow you another taste later."

"I think I'm being good right now," he panted, driving into her as she chased her release. He could feel her clenching around his cock, her walls gripping him mercilessly. "Now show me how good I'm being, princess. Come for me."

Bash cursed as Margrete's entire body tensed, and then she pulsed around him. She screamed his name as she came, and Bash held her shaking frame aloft, driving into her ruthlessly as he found his own pleasure.

Gods above, if he could stay inside her for the rest of his life, he'd happily do so.

Minutes passed as he recovered from the aftermath of his release, his lips constantly seeking her skin, planting kisses along her back, her throat. When he finally caught his breath, he eased out of her warmth and pulled her satiated body against his chest, resting a hand on the small of her back.

Bash lifted a stray curl out of her face and tucked it behind her ear.

"You've stolen my black heart, princess."

She might've stolen his soul as well.

"It was always meant to be mine, pirate," she said, a hand wrapping around his biceps, holding him to this plane. Keeping him from floating away.

"My little thief." He kissed the tip of her nose, savoring the way she melted at his touch. If only she knew how deeply she affected him. He wondered if the realization would frighten her. He prayed to all the gods she felt just as desperate.

"Bash?" Her voice came out soft, hesitant.

"Yes, princess?"

"Promise me you'll never lie to me?"

After what they'd just shared, the question caught him off guard.

Bash hadn't told her the truth for weeks. How could he explain the events of tonight when he didn't even know the answers himself? When he tried to tell her, nothing had come out. Yet he knew he would have to try. For her, he'd get over his fears and accept whatever judgment she delivered. He had faith in them, in *her*.

He placed the barest kiss upon her lips. "Tomorrow. We'll talk about everything tomorrow," he vowed, tracing his thumb along her jaw, relishing in the feel of her against him.

Yes. The demons of today could be faced tomorrow. Tonight, he held an angel in his arms.

CHAPTER EIGHT

MARGRETE

MARGRETE PACKED WELL BEFORE DAWN, BASH STILL SOUND ASLEEP in bed. She was eager to leave for the human world, ready to hunt down the beasts and kill them before they slaughtered more innocents.

She hoped to distract herself. From Darius, yes. But also from Bash and all the secrets she knew he held close to his chest.

Snapping the locks on her trunk, Margrete turned to the King of Azantian. Her pirate looked so very innocent in his sleep. Last night she'd planned on interrogating him for answers, but the plea in his haunted eyes stayed her tongue. She'd never seen him look so lost, so fearful, and he'd needed her just as she needed him. Being intimate was a quick remedy to their plight, but not a cure.

As if he felt her gaze upon him, Bash shifted in bed, his heavy eyes opening to pinpricks.

"Morning, *princess*," she greeted, forcing a note of playfulness into her tone, hoping to lighten the mood.

Bash groaned, flinging the covers from his body and revealing his muscled abdomen that rippled with every movement.

"Morning," he responded, throat scratchy from sleep.

Margrete's eyes flickered across his tanned skin, a rosy blush creeping up her cheeks as she lowered her attention further. And further still.

She cursed him.

"For once, I'm not looking forward to setting sail," he said, oblivious to her lingering scrutiny. "I can't shake this sense of disaster and all things doom." He chuckled, though the brittle laughter was far from genuine. He grabbed fresh clothing from the dresser and pulled on his trousers. Margrete cocked her head as she took in his rigid movements.

Before he could begin buttoning his forest-green shirt, she rose from the bed. "Let me," she said, waving away his hands. Silently, she fastened his pearl buttons as he quietly watched her fingers work, his stare glazed.

Margrete finished the last button, and then she gripped his stubbled chin.

She was losing him.

"I thought I told you to stay with me," she reminded him. "If you *must* get lost, get lost with me."

A muscle in Bash's jaw flickered. "About last night..." he began, taking a step back and scrubbing his face with his hand. "I don't remember much. There are a lot of blank spots. But the last thing I *do* remember is having a drink and passing out at my desk."

Margrete shook her head. The lump in her throat grew.

"You were in the Adiria Cavern, surrounded by shadows. Wraiths. You stood at its center and spoke to a voice without a face. It promised you'd be together soon."

Bash gave her his back, and she bristled. He couldn't run from her.

"You weren't yourself, Bash. You haven't been for weeks," she continued, undeterred.

Why did he insist on shutting her out?

"I-I've been busy dealing with the council, and maybe I've been overworking." The muscles in his neck strained. "Gods know I haven't gotten much sleep lately. That has to be it. Maybe the palace healer can fix me a tonic. I don't know what else it could be."

It sounded as though he were trying to convince himself.

"We both know that's not the answer."

Bash's gaze fell to the waves beyond the open balcony, and the silence that followed grew painful. Still, she refused to let this go.

Margrete smelled smoke in the air. She inhaled, nearly choking on a breeze of what she likened to burning flowers. Whether a warning or an omen, she pressed on.

"Bash," she said, softening her tone. "Tell me."

The scent of smoke grew pungent.

Definitely a warning.

"I'm not made of glass, and I can handle whatever you throw my way," she said, just as Bash whirled around. "You promised we'd talk about everything today, that you wouldn't hide any longer."

His dark irises expanded, growing in size until the whites of his eyes were but a sliver. She shivered. They didn't look...human.

Bash edged closer.

"Sometimes I think you're only here because you have Malum's power inside of you. That you feel some obligation to my people to protect them." His eyes were entirely black now. "Would you stay if you had the choice? Would *I* be your choice? Or have you had your fill of playing queen?"

His words robbed her of air. She couldn't focus on the chilling sight of his eyes, only his cutting accusation.

"Don't you dare revert back," she said, barely above a whisper. "Don't push me away just because you're used to doing things alone. Sorry to tell you, but I see right through your act."

A sweeping shadow fell across the room, the early morning sun blotted out of existence as storm clouds formed in the sky. All her frustration was directed at Bash, who turned his attention to the balcony, his otherworldly stare widening as he took in the approaching clouds.

Was it fear she glimpsed? Or something else?

With every step Margrete took, thunder rumbled the palace, and three jagged bolts of lightning struck the now roiling waters.

Bash turned his head back to Margrete, who stood only feet away. A searing bolt of fizzling electricity crashed nearby, illuminating the sharp planes of his face.

She might've heard the barest whisper of a hiss before his irises shifted back to normal, losing the eerie dullness that had shrouded them seconds before. Bash blinked rapidly, his face contorting in confusion.

There could be only one explanation for what just happened. She'd smelled dark magic last night, and she'd recognize its aroma anywhere.

"I—" He scanned the room as if searching for something, the crease between his brows deepening. Shock muddled his handsome features when he turned back to her. "I shouldn't have said that. Gods, I-I didn't mean it."

"Maybe you secretly did."

Bash swiped a hand through his hair and grabbed at the back of his neck. "I was trying to push you away. The one thing I promised myself I wouldn't do." His chest was rising and falling rapidly, and he scrubbed a trembling hand across his face. "The truth is, I've been hearing voices for weeks. Hearing things that aren't there. A voice urging me to do unspeakable things. Murderous things. I feel like something horrid is growing inside of me, and it's taking everything I am to keep it at bay."

"You've been hearing voices?" she asked, her irritation waning.

He thought he would sound unhinged, but she'd been *seeing* things. Visions.

Gods.

Death.

"Yes. I've been hearing voices. Specifically, one. I didn't want to tell you because I know you've had a lot to deal with on your own." He shot her a pointed look. "Don't think I haven't noticed you waking up every night covered in sweat. Or seen how your eyes sometimes glaze over in the middle of a conversation. I never wanted to push you, but I know you've had visions. I've watched Nerissa for years, and I know what they look like. And you haven't once confided in me. Not once trusted *me*."

The heat in her belly lessened to a simmer.

Oh gods, she was a hypocrite.

She hadn't told him of her visions. Bash wasn't her father, not cruel and heartless. He wouldn't have seen them as a weakness, some ailment that tainted her. The realization struck her so swiftly and suddenly she was knocked back a step.

She should've already known that, but her past had returned to haunt her.

The waves ceased their frenzy, and the storm clouds slowly parted to reveal patches of blue sky. Instead of the smoky breeze clogging her senses, fresh air wafted into their chambers, caressing her heated cheeks.

Whatever spell had befallen her king was gone.

This was *Bash*. Her friend, her lover, her *home*, and he struggled as much as she did. They each fought to understand the consequences of the attack on Azantian. Both were trying to cope the best way they could, and they both were used to dealing with problems by themselves.

It was time to change that.

"We shouldn't have hidden so much from one another," she finally said. Margrete grasped his hand forcefully and banded her fingers around his, her grip firm. "I didn't realize you knew of my visions. Not that it's an excuse. I *should* have told you, but I didn't want you to worry."

Bash briefly squeezed his eyes and shook his head. "And I didn't want *you* to worry about what I've been hearing. The shadows that follow me, waking *and* in my dreams. It's difficult to talk to someone about it, even you. *Especially* you. Even Adrian doesn't know me completely, and he's the closest thing I have to a brother. I can't promise to change overnight, but I *am* trying. This is all new to me. It was instinct, trying to push you away, but I only want to keep you safe. Safe from *me*."

Bash heaved a sigh, and the defeat she saw had her wondering if she'd imagined the telltale signs of dark magic all along.

She knew she hadn't.

"Well, *enough*. I know we both had...unusual upbringings, and trusting another person isn't easy for us. But we end that right here and now. And once we slay the sea's children, we'll figure out what's happening to you." He wouldn't be alone in his fight. "But no more secrets. We can't hide anymore. Not if we want to succeed."

Bash used his free hand to grasp her chin, forcing her to meet his eyes. She shivered under their intensity, afraid that if she looked too closely, they'd morph into those of a stranger. Again.

"I'm sorry. Truly. Not just for keeping the voices a secret, but for the harsh words I just spoke. That darkness I told you about? It comes and steals me away, and it scares the living hell out of me." His head dipped in shame. "And in all honesty, a part of me thought you'd want to get the hell away from me once you learned the truth. I don't ever want to hurt you. It's the *last* thing I want, but I'm frightened, Margrete. I'm genuinely frightened that I'm losing my grip on reality."

Margrete shook her head fiercely, tempted to shake some sense into him.

"I won't allow the man I love to be taken from me." His entire body went rigid at that. "I love you, not because you're a powerful king or because you think I'm trapped here. It's because of how you make my blood boil at the same time I want to kiss you. I know that no matter what happens, you'll be a constant figure at my side. My lover. My closest friend and ally. The home I never thought I'd find." She brushed off the hand on her chin. "You insufferable man. You are truly a fool—"

Bash's lips silenced her, and his hands wove through her hair and gripped the strands. He kissed her with a deadly combination of relief and desperation.

When he finally pulled away, leaving her breathless, she noticed the tiny bursts of silver sparkling in his eyes once more.

"You love me?" he asked, as if he needed to. His voice was raw, hesitant, and more fearful than when he'd spoken of his voices. They'd never said the words, but she'd assumed he knew.

When her cheeks flushed, the corners of his lips lifted.

"I'm not saying it again."

The heaviness of the moment before vanished, swept away by the same unnatural breeze that had commanded the skies.

"I love you too, princess. And I'll say it as many damned times as I please."

He kissed her again, a shy smile on his lips as he stole her breath, her very soul. Their fight no longer seemed significant. Not when their declaration brought new air into her lungs.

"Tell me you forgive me," he asked, pulling away to stare into her eyes. Gone was the smirk, the elated joy, replaced with the same fear she'd seen earlier—the same vulnerability he'd never show anyone else.

Only her.

"I forgive your words. But you're no longer the lonely king who isolates himself and pushes everyone away, and I'm certainly not the same woman who first came to these shores." She cupped his cheek, and he immediately leaned into her palm, closing his eyes. "From now on, we move forward as one."

"You strike a hard bargain, but I accept."

"Together," she affirmed, hope blossoming.

"Together," he echoed.

Her chest tightened as the divine warmth of a god spread across her insides. This power throbbed and pulsed, every inch of her body buzzing. Margrete couldn't help but sense the warning as she clutched Bash, Malum's essence seeming to recoil from his touch.

But she shoved her instincts aside and held him, content to ignore the threat she smelled in the air.

The threat that was the King of Azantian and the dark magic that had embraced him.

CHAPTER NINE

BASH

A DARKNESS LIVED DEEP WITHIN BASH'S SOUL. DARKNESS HE'D spent his entire life shoving down. It hadn't been nearly as difficult to smother before, but he could feel it now, rising to the surface, begging release.

And he knew one day, soon, he wouldn't be able to contain it.

A shroud of black had swarmed his vision this morning. When he spoke those callous words to Margrete, he almost felt as though he were someone else, watching a stranger from above, unable to do anything but internally scream.

He wasn't that man, and he refused to give in to whatever supernatural forces haunted him. Bash had to be stronger.

His heart tugged as Margrete waved him over to where she stood before the *Phaedra*. Long brown locks whipped at her cheeks, rosy from the harsh wind, her eyes gleaming with anticipation. Yet it was that crooked smile of hers that both broke and thrilled him.

She was the most stunning creature he'd ever seen.

Bay trailed at her side, as he so often did, a coy smirk playing on his lips. One wouldn't guess by looking at him that he could have a man flat on his back in the time it took to blink. Many would assume he was simply having a conversation with a friend, but Bash noted how his eyes scanned the docks, the bustling crew, the horizon, silently searching for any sign of danger. Always the protector.

"Aren't you supposed to be bossing your crew about?" Margrete asked when Bash drew close. She jerked her chin toward the hundred or so sailors ambling up and down the plank. "I wouldn't want you to miss out on the fun. I know how much you love hearing the sound of your own voice."

Bay snorted as he elbowed her playfully in the ribs. She returned the gesture.

Bash's lips quirked. Gods, he wanted to kiss the sass right out of her. No. Maybe not out of her—he enjoyed it far too much. Besides, he appreciated her teasing. It was a welcome distraction.

"And deprive you of my company?" He took her hand in his. "I wouldn't dream of it."

"I see you're back to your old self. Cocky as always." Her lips twitched as she fought not to release her smile.

Bash leaned close so only she could hear him. "You wouldn't love me if I weren't."

When he pulled away, her cheeks were pink. She *loved* him. Few people had ever spoken those words to him—his own father only said them a handful of times.

Margrete's love felt different though. Precious. Fragile. *Dangerous.*

"Sister!"

Birdie's little voice was strong and sure as she called out from aboard the ship. From the looks of it, Atlas had been putting the young girl to work carrying supplies up and down the ramp. Then again, she didn't seem to mind. Margrete's sister took any chance to impress Atlas. Bash suspected she did so because Atlas felt impossible to impress.

She was just like her older sister in many ways—clever, impossibly kind, *stubborn*—and Bash smiled as she came down the ramp and flung her arms around Margrete.

"Remember what I told you, little bird—"

"Yeah, yeah. Don't irritate Adrian." Birdie rolled her eyes. "At least not *too* much."

"I didn't exactly use that word, but yes. I suppose that's right." Margrete laughed, rubbing the top of Birdie's curls and thoroughly messing them up. Her sister made a face.

"Gods, I'm gonna miss you," Margrete said as she yanked her in for a hug. Birdie rolled her eyes again, but she hugged her sister just as tightly.

"Me too," she mumbled against Margrete's shirt. "Bring me back something interesting from the journey?" Birdie drew away, wetness lining her eyes.

"Always asking for things." Margrete grinned and flicked her nose. "Behave, and I'll think about it."

Bash watched the sisters hug once more before Nerissa appeared at his side. He often compared the seer to a ghost, always moving on silent feet and able to sneak up on him when he least expected it. While it might unnerve some people, Bash found it remarkably impressive. Besides, he liked Nerissa's quiet yet centering demeanor—it had a calming effect on him as well.

"Watch her," he instructed under his breath, his voice low. Bash trusted his people with Birdie's care, but he knew how dangerous the seas had become, and she had become a light in his life. She'd become family.

"Always," Nerissa replied coolly. "I'll protect her with my life."

Bash turned toward her, looking at his seer for the first time. She appeared haggard—her straight black hair uncombed and her dress wrinkled. It was unlike her. He opened his mouth to ask if she was all right, but Atlas called out, shouting across the deck that push-off was in ten minutes.

So instead of words, Bash shot Nerissa a look of thanks and gently gave her arm a squeeze. Her eyes lit up with a glowing warmth.

"Ready?" Bash released Nerissa and turned toward Margrete. The seer held out her hand, and Birdie hesitated for a second before taking it.

Margrete wrinkled her nose playfully at her sister, then slipped her arm through his. Silently, he led them up the long wooden slat leading to the vessel. His crew flowed around them, and Margrete gracefully dodged and swerved out of their way. She'd grown rather agile since the night of the attack. Sometimes he didn't hear her approach until she was right behind him.

Once they were situated on the starboard side, as alone as they could be, Margrete spoke.

"You seem better," she remarked, eyes cast to the crew. "But you'll let me know if you hear the voices again?"

"I will," he promised, meaning it. He wasn't alone in his fight anymore, and he'd never hide from her again.

Margrete nodded, glancing away from the *Phaedra* and to the waves. She did that often lately. Bash wondered if she could see the answers out among the blue.

Bash sighed, grabbing her hand once more. "I should speak to the crew," he said, rubbing his thumb in tender circles on her skin before forcing himself to let go. Leaving her side was the last thing he wanted to do. "We'll talk more after we set sail and form a plan," he assured, savoring the soft kiss she bestowed upon his lips in reply.

Willing himself to leave her at the railing, Bash turned toward the frenzy.

From the corner of his eye, he spotted Adrian on the docks. His oldest friend would remain on Azantian while Bash oversaw the hunt. Adrian would rule in Bash's stead, and there was no one else he trusted more.

He'd spoken with him briefly this morning, and thankfully, his friend hadn't brought up Bash's state after the council meeting. Instead, he'd tugged him in for a fierce hug. Words weren't always needed, and Adrian understood this well.

Now, Adrian glided to Bay's side and slid an arm around his waist. Gently, he lowered his head to his boyfriend's, their noses nuzzling. Bash watched as his second-in-command planted a sweet kiss upon Bay's grinning lips, his hands moving to cup his face.

He warmed at the sight of his family before leaving them to say their goodbyes in peace. Guilt already weighed him, and he hated that Adrian would be separated from Bay for so long.

The time had come to address the sailors, the Azantians he'd personally selected to hunt the beasts. They were the ones risking their lives, and they deserved a proper speech worthy of their sacrifice.

He was about to open his mouth and command their attention when he heard *it*—a whisper of a threat that sent shivers down his spine, a voice only he could hear.

Our reunion approaches, young king.

Every muscle locked in place, his shoulders tensing with alarm. Why, *why* couldn't it leave him alone?

Go away, he silently gritted, nostrils flaring.

No one paid attention to the inner battle he fought. They couldn't see how he struggled to maintain his grip on reality. He clenched his fists and dug his nails into his palms.

Get. Out. Of. My. Head.

The voice didn't reply. It didn't need to. The threat had been delivered.

Somewhere in the recesses of his mind, Bash heard a chuckle like nails dragging across glass. A sound of triumph. Of someone who'd already won.

You'll give in soon, king.

CHAPTER TEN

MARGRETE

MARGRETE'S HEART ACHED AT THE SIGHT OF AZANTIAN GROWING smaller with every swell. While she'd called Prias home for twenty-three years, it had lacked the sense of belonging, that indescribable feeling that a *true* home yielded.

They would return soon.

They had to.

Margrete made her silent vow on the stern, losing herself to the lulling sway of the *Phaedra* as it glided across the crests. She turned to the skies, catching sight of something floating down from the clouds. The seconds ticked by until the object reached her, and when it landed precariously on the railing beside her hand, her heart stilled.

A single black leaf. Just like the one she'd woken up to days ago.

She didn't believe in coincidences anymore.

Something was coming for them. Whether it appeared in a minute or an hour, she was convinced the beginning of their voyage would be tainted with death.

Hours later, Margrete couldn't find Bash. He wasn't above deck nor delegating in the captain's quarters. It was unlike him to hide. He wasn't a king when aboard this ship, and he liked showing his face among the crew.

It might've been intuition or sheer paranoia, but Margrete raced down to their cabin, heart thrumming savagely in her chest. After what he'd confessed, she wasn't going to take any chances. She knew all too well that some voices wouldn't cease until they destroyed you.

The door squeaked open, the linen shade closed over the single port-hole. Margrete made out a pacing figure, his hands covering his eyes.

It was Bash.

"Stop," he pleaded to no one at all. "Just *stop*."

"Bash!" Margrete rushed to his side, grabbing both wrists and revealing his face. His black eyes were wide and fearful, and wholly unrecognizable.

"What is it? What's wrong?"

Bash hissed. "That voice," he gritted out, the admission paining him. "It's getting louder, *closer*, and I can't fucking stop it!" His voice rose to a loud shout, startling her. Still, she didn't pull away. No, she pulled him closer.

"Shhh." She wound her arms around his waist, nuzzling her cheek against his chest. His heartbeat pounded erratically. "It's okay. Just hold on to me. I'm right here." And she wouldn't leave.

You couldn't pick and choose times to love someone. Love meant both sunshine-filled days and cold, hard nights. Trying to avoid the night would be akin to never leaving shore for fear of a storm. But storms eventually passed, and rain ceased, and the sun never failed to return.

She was no stranger to darkness, and if she could be Bash's light, she would.

Bash grasped her tightly, his stubbled cheek rubbing against her skin, his breath hot on her face. "Shit. I'm sorry I'm such a mess, but this time feels...different, like there's more than one voice. And they're all screaming in my head," he hissed, trying to push away. Margrete didn't allow it.

Bash tried again, but she held firm, and when he lifted his head, his eyes were full of surprise. She'd grown stronger over these last few months. And not just from training with Adrian.

"I'm not leaving," she said firmly, grasping his chin. "We don't leave each other when times are rough. That's not how this works." Bash tried to run, yes, but he also meant to *protect* her.

Gripping the back of his neck, she yanked him close, his lips colliding against hers. He tasted of panic and desperation, but beneath the bitter fear, she tasted *him*. The sea and salt, and the open skies.

He just needed a reminder of all that he was.

Margrete kissed him hard, hoping he felt her love in his very marrow. She kissed him to show she stood right before him, *choosing* him. Broken parts and all.

Bash startled, but only for a moment, his lips frozen against hers. With a sharp intake of breath, he stole her air, and then he kissed her back as if he'd die without her lips on his. Margrete grabbed hold of his shirt, her hands fisting the linen.

When he pulled away, gasping for air, his eyes sought the shadows lurking in the corners. Margrete turned his chin back to her. "Stay with me," she demanded.

As if her voice vanquished his doubts, his swelling panic, Bash's arms snaked around her waist, his palms pressing into the small of her back, holding her like she'd float away if he let go.

She felt his chest rise and fall against hers, his warm breath fanning across her exposed skin.

"The only time they leave me is when I'm with you," he murmured. "Everything—the voices, the nightmares, the darkness—it all goes away when I kiss your lips and feel you against me. It's like your very presence chases it all away." He shuddered, his grip on her body turning fierce. "As long as you're beside me, I'm never truly lost."

He moved his hand to her hair and gripped the strands, angling her face so she had no choice but to get lost in his eyes.

"But you have to promise me something, Margrete."

She stilled at the sound of her name, how he spoke it with such weight.

"If the day ever comes when I'm not...myself, I need you to run. Run as far away from me as possible. And if you can't run"—he paused, his eyes narrowing into determined slits—"then you do not hesitate to defend yourself. *Whatever* it takes."

Margrete frowned, understanding his meaning. "That'll never happen—"

Bash placed a finger against her lips. "I don't know what's happening to me, but please, *please* promise me you won't allow me to ruin you."

She went completely rigid. A part of her sensed the lurking darkness hiding just below his skin, but the other part—the part that was stubborn and refused to ever let Bash go—argued she could vanquish it.

Instead of speaking her truth, she simply nodded. Bash needed her to agree, if only for his sanity, but he didn't need to know it was a lie.

"Good," he breathed, his hold loosening a fraction. He placed a kiss on her brow. "You may be the key to protecting my people, but you've become something far more precious to me. Until I am...cured of what plagues me, I want you to be on your guard. Do not lower it, even if you think I'm fine."

She hesitated, and Bash lifted a brow.

"I'll be wary," she conceded, the vow bitter on her tongue. "But know I won't allow anything bad to happen to you. My powers may be new, and I may not know how to use them yet, but I *feel* the magic in me, and it is powerful. When I finally understand it, do not doubt I won't eliminate any threats to you."

"So stubborn," Bash whispered, sighing. Sadness creased his eyes before he rested his forehead against hers.

"You like my stubbornness."

A chuckle caused his chest to rumble. "I admit nothing."

They remained in place, neither daring to move, unwilling to shatter the illusion of peace. All she focused on was how his breath fanned across her cheeks and caused warmth to spread in her belly.

Soon they would face monsters, and then, if they survived, they'd have another battle to contend with—dispelling whatever demons haunted Bash. Until that time came, Margrete would cherish every damned second.

It wasn't until a knock shook the walls of the cabin that Margrete begrudgingly lifted her head and met Bash's wide eyes.

Moments later, the sound of alarm bells and frantic shouts rent the air.

Margrete took in a deep inhale.

And just like that, their fragile calm was shattered by the rotten stench of death.

CHAPTER ELEVEN

MARGRETE

THE WATERS SLICED AGAINST THE SIDES OF THE *PHAEDRA* LIKE sharpened knives, hell-bent on consuming the vessel and its crew. From above Margrete's cabin, shrill cries of men and women wafted to her ears, the falling rain muffling the frantic orders of the quartermaster.

"I'm coming with you," Margrete said to Bash. "I can help."

He hesitated for only a moment, then gave a reluctant nod. "Please stay far from the port and starboard sides," he begged, moving to grasp her shoulders. His eyes were a swirling vortex of darkness and uncertainty, and it looked like he wanted to say more. Instead, he leaned down to place a tender kiss on her lips.

She felt everything he couldn't manage to say in that one single kiss.

When he drew back, Bash entwined their fingers and shot her one last look before leading them out the door and into the chaos. A wave sent them crashing against a wall, the ship veering precariously to the left. Margrete nearly lost her footing, but Bash tightened his hold, fighting to bring them to the stairwell.

The last time they'd endured a storm on this ship, she'd nearly drowned. That was *before*. Now, she wouldn't waste a moment twiddling her thumbs while the brave crew grappled for control. She wasn't some fragile damsel. Margrete held the heart of a god inside her, and she intended to at least try and use it.

Powerful winds whipped at her hair as she and Bash struggled above, the *Phaedra* careening back and forth in violent waves. Margrete tucked her hair behind her ears and forced her eyes open against the biting breeze, embracing the sting of saltwater as her entire body shuddered.

She licked her lips. The rain that made its way into her mouth tasted foul. *Unholy.* Instinctively, she knew this wasn't a storm, not in the way these sailors were used to.

No. Something ancient was at work here.

Dark water sloshed onboard, murky and clouded as it soaked the wood, every inch of the *Phaedra* glistening with the assault of the sea. Margrete swerved and dodged a flying rope only for a rocking wave to send her crashing into the thick column of a mast. She lost her grip on Bash, who went soaring in the opposite direction.

She reached for something solid to hold on to, trying to gather her bearings while internally screaming for her power to show itself.

Her magic flickered, but the spark didn't catch. Malum's essence was a gentle thrum when she desperately needed a vicious roar.

"Stay there!" Bash screamed from across the deck, his eyes wide and pleading. His men called his name, and his head swerved in their direction only to turn back to her a second later. She knew he wouldn't leave to help unless she agreed. Even if she didn't intend to stay put.

Margrete gave him a quick nod, praying he didn't see past the lie in her gaze. Bash lingered for a moment longer, regret and fear twisting his features. When his name sounded again, he took off with a grimace.

Now, she had work to do.

Squeezing her eyes, she delved into herself, searching for the pool of power she'd harnessed the day she sunk her father's ship—that ethereal blue and yellow light of the gods.

Deeper and deeper she dove, her body swaying, her mind focused and determined. Margrete felt herself scream into the storm—both the one in her soul and the one transpiring around her physical body. Gritting her teeth, she thrust ahead.

Only to meet a wall.

She jerked backward, her eyes flashing open as rain pelted her face.

Help me, she pleaded, splinters biting into her palms. Frustration rose in her throat like bile. *Tell me how to use this damned power.*

What was the point of carrying this burden if no good could come from it?

Fucking tell me!

Lightning struck dangerously close to where she braced herself. She flinched in horror as violet sparks fizzled in the aftermath, metallic silver cascading down from the skies. No ensuing thunder rattled her bones, but the taste of decomposing flesh continued to permeate the breeze.

"Gods," she breathed, sucking in air. What the hell was this?

Releasing her grip on the mast, Margrete scrambled to the upper deck, a massive wave nearly sending her overboard. She flung her hands out to seize the railing, and her fingers dug into the damp wood. It bit into her sensitive flesh, but the sweet pain heightened her senses.

Help me! she beseeched again, her head tilted toward the pouring skies. *Please.*

She didn't know how to control Malum's essence, and she'd been a fool to think she could master such power by herself. Sheer, unbridled panic flooded her veins, turning them icy.

I knew you'd need my help.

The voice slithered around her mind and constricted like a snake, and Margrete instantly recoiled.

Darius.

Of course.

Tell me how to aid them, she demanded of her enemy. More violet lightning struck the main mast, crew scattering in all directions as it cracked and splintered. She knew she sounded desperate, but she didn't care. She *was* desperate.

Ah, now you're begging. I think I rather like this.

Margrete clenched her hands into tight fists, every instinct screaming at her to spurn Darius, to shut him out. But she wasn't thinking properly. Not when she caught sight of Bash racing across the planks, helping his men battle the winds and fasten the sails. His deep-red hair was plastered to his face, his lips contorted in a thin, determined line.

She couldn't let her pride be the end of them. Not when magic was involved.

Everything will be as it should, Darius said coolly, no trace of derision in his voice. *The waters will take you where you were always meant to go.*

What the fuck does that mean? she asked, her frustration overwhelming the little control she held over her power. *You claim you don't want me dead, but this storm will be the end of me!*

Darius only answered with a soft chuckle. The noise rattled around in her head until it vanished altogether, as did the god himself.

She was alone. The waters continued to rail against the belly of the *Phaedra,* much like a small child who'd been told no. Silver sparks fell from above her head, the scent of magic heady in the air.

Dark magic.

Just as she'd experienced before.

Fine. She should've known better than to engage with Darius, but it didn't mean she'd stop trying.

Focusing on the impending crest heading their way, building with each breath, Margrete bit her lip as she thrust her hands into the air, curling her fingers as her mind tried to grasp the wave's force.

For a ticking of a heartbeat, Margrete was no longer fastened to her mortal frame—she was drifting, higher and higher above, a phantom without bones to imprison her will.

Margrete focused on an approaching swell that towered well over thirty feet above the ship. Seizing the strength she'd been gifted, she commanded the advancing wall of water to fall.

Margrete's skin prickled with the bite of a thousand needles, a frigid cold sweeping down her frame. Her vision swam and her body swayed, but she homed in on the wave that struggled to disobey. She didn't let it.

If anything, its defiance made it easier to seek the source of her magic, and just before the wave battered the hull, she felt a surge of energy burst free from her body.

The wave collapsed in on itself, and when it hit the side of the ship, there was minimal damage. Cheers soared above the cries of turmoil.

Margrete's knees shook, as did her palms. She glanced down at herself, noticing a few sparks of light sizzling out in the center of her hands. Her power had barely shown itself, and she knew she was capable of so much more.

If only she weren't on the verge of fainting.

Even as the crew celebrated the seconds of reprieve, the gale appeared nowhere near its end. It had taken *everything* from her to capture but a few moments of peace, and she knew she couldn't keep this up forever.

The *Phaedra* jerked abruptly, sending Margrete flying onto her backside, her concentration severed. Scrambling for a hold, she gripped the wooden edges of the ship, screaming into the unnatural lightning and rain.

The slick planks gave no purchase for her fingers, and as much as Margrete tried to avoid sliding across the deck, the ship shifted dangerously to the left. As one side of the mighty vessel skimmed the indigo waters, Margrete took in a bone-chilling sight...

Shadows.

Hundreds of slithering shadows crawled from the deep waters. Margrete's eyes widened as the rain pelted her, and she strained to make out the details of the sinister shapes slowly coming into focus.

Men. Or creatures with the bodies of men. They appeared almost human, but behind their darkened silhouettes, swirls of onyx, silver, and lavender plumes trailed in their wake. The dancing lights rose and fell every time one of the creatures drifted back into the waters, illuminating the sky upon their return to the air.

Before Margrete could study them further, the *Phaedra* rocked swiftly upright, the force sending her roughly into the railing. Fiery hot pain shot across her ribs as she sputtered. Bruises and broken bones could heal, but there would be no returning from death. And death certainly wished to claim them today.

Where is Bash?

Using what energy she could muster, Margrete lurched up, white-knuckling the ship's wooden sides and staggering to scan the crew. Bash would be up here with his men, struggling to maneuver them out of this gale. He was a leader, and a leader always stood beside those who fought for him.

Margrete found a familiar face, and although it wasn't the one she searched for, relief flooded her chest.

Bay.

He was attempting to tighten a sail, his blond hair plastered to his temples. Margrete half-stumbled, half-lurched her way to him, his eyes catching hers as she gripped his biceps. The roar of the storm made speaking impossible, but Bay understood what her eyes pleaded.

Where is he?

Bay shook his head, frantic and glassy-eyed. There were only screams of turmoil and the blur of bedlam, all the faces morphing into one giant haze of sinking hope.

Margrete shoved away from her friend. "Bash!"

Another sail ripped, the surge of the downpour masking the cracking of wood. There was no longer a question of whether they would over-power the storm. Without any doubt, Margrete knew one thing with all of her being: The *Phaedra*, the prized vessel in the Azantian fleet, would succumb to the waters.

Just like her vision.

Margrete pushed past the fallen foresail to the forecastle deck, her boots gripping the slick wood as she heaved herself up the steps. A rush of bodies and fog swirled, but her eyes landed on a lone figure by the jutting bowsprit.

Bash.

He'd rooted himself to the deck, unmoving and gazing out at the waves before them. Margrete screamed his name but was met only by more lightning and thunder in reply.

By the time she reached him, her chest was heaving. She was spent, broken from her silly attempts to control something she had no idea how to command.

"Bash!" she roared as she approached, reaching out to grasp hold of his arm. He didn't move, didn't turn at her words or her touch. The man before her was transfixed by what lay ahead, lost in his own world.

Under the same spell as last night.

Margrete grasped his stubbled chin, tugging it to the side to gaze upon his glazed-over face. Rain and sweat clung to his skin, his shirt glued to his muscled frame.

Margrete's heart sank somewhere deep, lower than the ominous shadows that swam alongside the doomed vessel. Nothing lived in those murky eyes of his, not a single hint of recognition. It was as if he were a shell of a man, and the sight of him chilled her to the bone.

Margrete wrapped her arms around his torso and yanked him back, but Bash was too strong, and he remained rooted in place.

"You need to come with me!" she pleaded. "Please, Bash!" she added like a prayer. But who was she truly praying to? Her anxious pleas went unanswered, her exhausted arms screaming in pain with every tug.

He didn't move an inch.

Tracing the side of his stubbled jaw, Margrete searched for *anything* in his eyes, any hint of recognition. He stared blankly ahead.

Where did you go, pirate?

The *Phaedra* pitched forward, and Margrete collided into the solid muscle of Bash's chest. All the while, Bash held onto nothing, his feet cemented by some unseen force.

The skies opened, crackling with purple streaks, gracing the decks with sharp pelts of hail. The ice stung as it cut into her skin, the tiny pinpricks of blood quickly washed away by the rain.

"Bash, please!" she implored, frantic and dying on the inside. He'd die if he remained here—they both would.

Before she could even try to move him once more, shrill screeches pierced the air. The inhuman shrieks mingled with the howling of the wind and hail, a spine-chilling melody of garbled voices and cutting screams. The blaring noise swelled and shattered her eardrums, but Margrete couldn't block them and seek relief. She had to maintain her hold on Bash. She had to save him, and letting go wasn't an option.

The shadows she'd glimpsed earlier, trailing the rocking ship like vultures, were back. They rose into the chilled air, their spindly feet dangling above the thrashing waves. Moving as one, they formed a barrier around the *Phaedra*.

Gods.

Margrete stared open-mouthed as monsters swarmed them on all sides. Their upper bodies appeared human in nature, but their lower halves were covered in sharp scales working down into two serrated fins.

Nymeras.

She might've screamed, but her voice was too hoarse to carry. She held Bash flush against her chest as the unnatural creatures drew closer still. They trailed their fingers down Bash's cheeks, his jaw, his chin. They touched him gently, *reverently,* even.

Margrete's hands shot out, hoping for a spark of Malum's power, for just a sliver of magic.

Nothing happened.

"Please, come back to me, pirate." Margrete grasped Bash with both hands, holding him as the haze of beasts flickered over his tanned skin.

The *Phaedra* dipped dangerously close to one side, but Margrete held on, searching Bash's eyes one final time.

There.

Deep within his pools of night, she saw a flicker of recognition.

Bash tilted his head so slightly it might have gone unnoticed. But Margrete caught it, saw how his eyes creased and sharpened.

"Bash?" she whispered.

"Princess. Is th—"

A hissing, frozen wind carrying the stench of death sliced the air between them. In an instant, the gale wrenched Bash from her arms and shoved her back against the rails, knocking the breath from her lungs.

The nymeras wrapped her king within their arms and consumed him until not a trace of Bash remained. She reached out, frantic to grab hold of him, but the wraiths were too quick. He plummeted overboard and into the waves.

Gone.

Margrete couldn't breathe, couldn't think. There was only the piercing sting of her loss, a shattering agony that tore her insides apart piece by piece. She stumbled to the rails and peered into the waves. Nothing. Not even the moving shadows grazed the vicious crests.

She might've screamed, might've reached out, but a massive wave sent her careening backward, her body slamming onto the deck with gruesome force.

Water surged into her mouth, suffocating her as her fingers fruitlessly sought purchase. A wave struck the hull and she went sliding, screaming as the world tilted.

A dreadful snap rent the air, and the wood beneath her fractured and cracked. The cries of the crew joined hers as masts collapsed and sails tore. The mighty *Phaedra* broke apart piece by sacred piece, and the relentless swells kept coming.

The final wave of pure devastation struck.

Margrete shrieked, the planks groaning as they splintered and broke. She fell down, down, down until water rushed up and swallowed her. Malum's essence flared, but she was too frantic to concentrate, too rattled to focus on the powers she couldn't control.

She'd failed Bash.

Failed herself.

Margrete sank deeper into the waters. Unconsciousness claimed her seconds later.

CHAPTER TWELVE

MARGRETE

Margrete woke to darkness.

Water crashed all around her, and she sputtered and gasped for air. She lay on her stomach, her hands outstretched above her head, wet, packed sand beneath her.

Gods. The *Phaedra* had wrecked. It had actually gone down, a feat she hadn't believed possible.

Crawling on her hands and knees, Margrete scrambled up the beach, her limbs sore and aching. She felt as if she'd been tossed repeatedly against a stone wall, though she thankfully didn't smell blood in the air. She'd made it whole, it seemed.

Her next thought was of *him*.

"Bash!" she called out, her voice hoarse.

Those monsters stole him. *Nymeras*. She might not have set eyes upon one in real life before, but she knew what they were deep down in her soul. Or maybe the divine essence she contained had recognized them.

As if she'd called it forth, heat flared in her chest, and slowly, warmth stretched down her torso and legs to her toes. It numbed the pain and chased away the desire to just lie down and let unconsciousness take her again.

Margrete scanned the moonlit beach.

There, no more than fifteen feet away, was a body. Someone lay motionless on the sand, their back to her. She scrambled to her feet, lurching toward the other survivor. When she staggered over and flipped the body upward, glimpsing his face, her heart gave a bittersweet tug.

Jonah. A sailor from the *Phaedra*. Not Bash.

Margrete shook him, coaxing him to open his eyes. He was young and untried. This had been his first official outing with Bay's crew. He couldn't have been older than eighteen.

Jonah's black hair fell across his face, a tangled mess of midnight strands.

"Wake up," she begged, pushing against his chest. The sailor gave a powerful shiver, and then his pale green eyes shot open, and he lunged to his side, spewing saltwater from his lungs.

Margrete rested on her heels, breathless, as she watched Jonah come back to life. Silently, she thanked the gods that he lived, but her gaze still swept across the beach, hoping to see her king. Hoping against all odds he'd evaded the nymeras and wind up here. Wherever *here* was.

Instead of Bash, a familiar head of blond hair glimmered in the moonlight. Margrete jumped to her feet and bolted to the warrior's side, a bolt of fiery hope coursing through her veins.

"Bay!" She frantically pushed against him as she'd done Jonah. It took longer to rouse him, but eventually, Bay, too, woke with a gasp.

"Margrete? W-where are we?" he asked when he regained his breath. She shook her head in response. It appeared a simple island, though the sands were a shade of slate gray. Brittle trees with deadened leaves lined the edge of the beach, the reedy branches swaying in a cautious breeze. Something about them had her pausing, and she focused on the darkened leaves that reminded her of Bash's eyes. Realization struck in a sickening rush.

She *had* seen them before...

The night of her vision and upon the *Phaedra*.

Margrete felt dizzy at the memory, and she knew deep down that the unusual leaves appearing here, on this island, wasn't a coincidence. It couldn't be. There was something about this place that had her head buzzing, as if there was a trapped memory she couldn't quite access. She shoved that thought to the back of her mind to examine later.

"Have you seen Bash?" She turned her head and scanned the endless grains. The island curved slightly. Perhaps he'd wound up farther down the coast. Yes. He was strong, and even if he'd been pulled overboard by those creatures, he would've fought them off and made his way to these shores.

"I saw him go overboard," Bay said, sitting up. He rested his head between his knees. "Those things took him. Nymeras. Had to be." He rocked back and forth, a hand going to his mouth as if battling a surge of nausea.

"Bash is alive," she said, no trace of doubt in her voice. "I would've felt it if he died." If he lost his life in the sea. The part of her she'd only just begun to explore argued as much, and the warmth she knew to be Malum's power seemed to pulsate at the mention of his name.

"I'm going to search for others." Margrete stood, unsteady on her own two feet. She didn't care. It would take much more than weak knees to stop her from searching for Bash.

Bay swallowed down whatever rose in his throat. With a grimace, he lifted himself up and gave her a curt nod. "We spread out," he said, tilting his head behind him. "If you find survivors, send them back here."

Margrete grasped his arm before he could turn away. She gave him a reassuring squeeze. "Bay? Be safe. Please."

They had no idea where the hell they were. For all they knew, enemies lurked around the corner. Or worse—the nymeras were near.

Bay shivered, but he brought Margrete in for a hug. She gripped him just as tightly before releasing him. "We'll find them," Bay said, backing away. "We're Azantians, remember? Hard to kill." His mouth twisted into a grim smile, but the usual spark in his eyes was absent.

Margrete watched as Bay turned and raced off down the beach in search of the *Phaedra*'s crew. They couldn't be the only ones to have washed up here. Right?

Something sharp prodded against her chest, right beside Malum's power. This place felt wrong. Off. Even the air smelled stale, like the island had been sealed within a trunk for decades. The sheer wrongness of it all sent her into a panic.

Margrete took off running.

She didn't stop until a towering figure with blonde hair approached from the distance.

Atlas.

"You see anyone else?" Margrete asked when she halted at Atlas's side. "Bay is looking farther down for more survivors." The words were hard to form and stuck to her throat. Every thought she possessed returned to Bash. The longer she went without finding him, the more her nerves frayed. Her pulse doubled when Atlas nodded.

"Grant is helping Mila. She must've broken her leg, though she should heal shortly."

And just like that, her hope fell. Not Bash.

Sure enough, two more figures came hobbling closer, a smaller one leaning against a brawny sailor with stark white hair she'd recognized from the first time she ventured to Azantian. That had to be Grant.

"She's better, but I suggest she get off her leg so the bone doesn't set wrong," Grant muttered, his voice deep and gravelly, like he'd spent his life on the water shouting above roaring winds. Margrete suspected he had to be in his late forties, though guessing an Azantian's true age was nearly impossible.

Mila nodded in agreement, her short red hair plastered to her sweat-soaked forehead. Margrete knew little about Mila, but she could plainly sense her courage as she ground her teeth and lugged her broken leg across the beach. She directed them in Bay's direction.

To Atlas, she said, "Head back with them. I'm going to search for more."

"Margrete, wait." Atlas caught and pulled on Margrete's hand. "I washed up a mile down, and no survivors were in sight." She shook her head sadly. "I think it's best we regroup with Bay and figure out the next plan of action." Atlas scanned the tree line and shivered. "This place gives me the damn creeps."

"Understatement," Margrete said. "But if it's all the same, I'm going. Tell Bay to stay in position until I return. Please."

She gently slipped her hand from Atlas's and dashed off before the warrior could argue with her further. There wouldn't be a point.

Margrete ran until her legs turned to jelly. When she couldn't feel them at all, she *still* pushed ahead and didn't stop until she sensed the shifting of time. Hours must've passed, and she'd only come across one other member of their ship. She hadn't slowed her pace other than to instruct him to continue on to Bay.

She found no others.

Eventually, her legs gave out entirely, and she stumbled forward, collapsing onto the sands in an ungraceful heap. She tasted it in her mouth, the grains making their way down her parched throat. It burned as she swallowed. She'd have to get fresh water. And soon.

With a groan, she shoved up. She could hardly stand. Margrete knew that finding Bash like this was a fool's hope, and the unexplored coast was endless.

He may not be dead, but the King of Azantian wasn't anywhere nearby. If she continued in this direction, she might not have the energy to get back to Bay, and then she'd be well and truly screwed.

Margrete cursed, the foul word piercing the too-quiet air. Tears threatened to escape, but she held them back, swallowing hard. There wasn't a need to cry, not until she saw proof of Bash's demise. How many years had Margrete stayed strong for others? She could pull herself together and do so now for the remaining crew. For Bay. For Atlas.

Whether she wished it or not, the Azantian people had begun to look at her like their hope. Their savior. She couldn't fall to pieces when so many depended on her to be strong. Herself included.

Margrete spun on her heels, about to begin the trek back, when her boot struck something hard. Furrowing her brows, she bent down and brushed away a layer of sand.

She cursed again.

At the tip of her shoe rested a coin. And not one she'd ever seen before. Not a coin used in any port or bay across the realm.

This coin *glowed*.

With trembling hands, Margrete scooped up the shining silver piece and brought it closer for inspection. A person with any self-preservation might've dropped the *glowing* coin, but Margrete was too far gone to care.

On one side, an eye was inscribed. The motif was simple, crude even, but Margrete squinted, making out a number etched inside the pupil.

"One?" she murmured out loud. Flipping it over, she examined its other face. Elegant script at odds with the rudimentary design of the coin was engraved on the metal.

Beware the Eternal Night.

A shiver wracked her body, and her hands began to tremble. She nearly dropped the coin when Malum's power sparked before extinguishing completely. The coldness left in its absence was somehow worse.

She felt like she'd seen this coin before, but just like the island itself, she had no clear memory of it.

She pocketed her finding and forced herself to move. Maybe Bay would have some insight, and any clue he could provide had to be better than nothing. Something eerie was at play here, though she didn't understand what.

Her life had shifted from one mystery to another.

First Azantian. Then her powers. Battling a faceless god.

Recalling her nightmares had her remembering her vision. The one she'd had but nights before.

She'd seen the *Phaedra* go down. Saw the wreckage, the splintered wood, tattered sails, and broken masts. Margrete came to a halt, the night spinning and blurring into one line.

She could've prevented this. Prevented *all* of this.

And she'd done nothing.

She dropped to her knees, fisting her hands in the sands.

She opened her mouth and screamed, releasing all the guilt and grief and rage she'd bottled up so the crew didn't see. And from inside her pocket, she felt the coin shudder, vibrating against her leg.

This was no ordinary island.

CHAPTER THIRTEEN

MARGRETE

Margrete managed to pick herself up, dry her tears, and find Bay and the others some hours later. Her friend had raced over, his eyes scanning her from head to foot in search of injury. He'd find none he could see. Her wounds lay below the surface.

The reality that they hadn't found Bash came barreling into her, and it took every ounce of willpower to fix her face into an emotionless mask. There were nine survivors in total, including herself.

Nine.

Out of the hundred men and women they'd departed with. It made Margrete's rage spark, and the tips of her fingers buzzed. The powers she'd tried to harness back home, on Azantian, were fluctuating here—calm one moment and untamed the next.

"I found this on the beach," she said, reaching into her pocket and retrieving the coin. The light it radiated hadn't dimmed, and Bay's eyes widened at the sight.

"Let me see that," he demanded, his voice growing cold. He seized it between his thumb and forefinger, turning it this way and that. "This symbol"—he pointed to the eye—"belongs to Surria."

"Then why is it here? And please tell me there's a reason it's glowing." *Tell me it's just a damned coin and not some ominous clue after we narrowly eluded death.*

"I've only ever seen one of these before, and it was held in Azantian's vault." When Margrete raised a brow, Bay explained, "Where we keep other relics and crown jewels. It's not anything Bash would've thought to tell you about, seeing as the man doesn't care for such 'obscene luxuries' as he calls them. A waste, if you ask me," Bay grumbled.

"Focus, Bay," Margrete prodded.

He sighed. "Well, from what I was told, there were supposed to be only three of these in existence." Bay turned it over to the side where *Beware the Eternal Night* was written. Margrete leaned closer. Nothing. Not a clue as to what it could mean. No symbol other than the eye on its other face.

"Apparently, Surria crafted these after the birth of her children. Millenia passed before she brought them to an island of her making and forced the brothers to undergo a great trial when they found a coin. The goddess wanted to ensure they were worthy to rule over the seas, and so her sons had to prove themselves. Once all three trials were complete, they were gifted with a surge of divinity. After that, none of the other gods could ever deny their birthright. Apart, they could be defeated. But together? Together, they were more powerful than any of the gods combined."

Margrete shivered at the thought. If Darius and Malum hadn't despised one another, they might have combined powers and done great things. Or ruined the entire realm.

"What kind of trials did they undergo on the island?" she asked, the hair on the back of her neck rising. None of this seemed like a coincidence.

"Of that, I don't know," Bay whispered, his brow creased in thought. "Though I imagine they weren't pleasant." He continued flipping the mysterious coin over and over until she reached out and grasped his hand, stilling his movements.

"Bay. First, we find Bash. I doubt this is the actual coin from legend." Even as she spoke the words, she knew they were a lie. The cursed thing lit up like a beacon. It certainly didn't belong in this world. Not the human world, that is.

Besides, she couldn't ignore how the coin had made her feel. And she felt too much already.

"I'm hoping Bash fought his way out of the nymeras' hold. My friend isn't one to give in so easily." Bay wiped a hand through his short blond hair. The ends stuck up at all angles. "I say we build a fire and settle down for the night. Once morning arrives, we can continue our search. Adrian always says no good thought comes after dark."

Adrian.

Margrete found herself thankful he had remained on Azantian. She lifted her gaze to Bay, finding his eyes watery, filled with tears he refused to shed.

Instead of asking a foolish question, she merely hugged him to her chest. Bay may not have lost his boyfriend to the waves, but he'd lost his crew. The men and women he'd trained for years.

She couldn't fathom how he felt. The pain he must feel.

"We'll find him, Margrete," he whispered into her hair. "And then we'll destroy the monsters that took him."

Morning came slowly. The skies remained overcast, gray, and solemn. The sun barely penetrated the dense clouds surrounding it, and the light that filtered past the haze cast the island in an unnatural glow.

The fire they constructed last night smoldered, dying out. It hadn't provided much warmth anyway. Margrete and Bay had settled down beside one another, finding body heat that way. She suspected he craved the nearness as much as she did.

The rest of the crew remained where they'd eventually passed out the night before, most tucking their knees to their chests as they gazed at the waters. The lapping waves did little to calm anyone's nerves, not when the blackened trees rose behind their makeshift camp—an ominous reminder of where they would soon head.

"Anything new?" Margrete asked Bay as he inspected the coin for the hundredth time, his lithe body hunched over by the fire.

"No," Bay groaned and handed it to her with a frustrated scowl. The moment it fell into her palm, a spark raced down her arm.

She flinched.

"What was that?" he asked, catching the subtle reaction.

"Nothing," she lied. Bay raised a skeptical brow but didn't press. She was thankful.

Instead, he said, "We need to search for water." Bay stood and wiped away the sand from his trousers. His eyes landed on the trees. She suspected the mighty warrior and sailor before her wasn't keen on venturing deeper into those woods.

She rose as well, thankful they were doing *something* useful rather than sitting around and waiting for nothing to happen. Besides, every time she blinked, she saw Bash and relived those last horrid moments when her grip slipped. When she let go.

"Better hold on to that," Bay said, eyeing the coin she held. Malum's essence seemed to recoil from the sight of it. Margrete clutched it tighter in her palm.

Around them, the weary crew turned their gazes away from the weak fire and to their leader. They, too, sensed the impending journey.

"I'm hoping we can find some fresh water inland," Bay spoke loudly enough for them all to hear. "Water is our first priority. But keep your eyes open. Report *anything* that seems amiss."

His sailors nodded, Grant grunting in reply. The older man kept his sights on Mila, the red-headed sailor who'd broken her leg. She grimaced when she shifted on it, but one wouldn't know of her injury by looking at her gait. Another few hours and it would be like it never happened.

"We head out in five."

Bay gave his crew his back as they went about their preparations—which weren't many, seeing as they had only the clothes on their backs and no food to consume. Thankfully, a few had canteens, which they'd fill once they found water. They'd have to share. Hopefully, they wouldn't be here long enough for their limited resources to become a problem.

A shrill cry sounded from the trees. Margrete and Bay both spun on their heels, glancing wide-eyed in the direction of the forest. It sounded like a bird, though not one she'd ever heard before.

Almost as one, Bay and Margrete sucked in a deep inhale. Her hand drifted to Bash's necklace, the icy facets piercing the pads of her fingertips. The sting grounded her.

"Are you ready?" Bay asked, his jaw clenched. He peeled his attention away from the woods and the unknown beasts it contained. "You still have Adrian's dagger?"

"Always," she said, reaching down to her thigh sheath. The simple blade had belonged to Adrian's father. When her friend and trainer had given it to her a month ago, Margrete had nearly cried. The gift meant more to her than he could ever have imagined.

"Good. Keep it at your side." Bay patted her shoulder. "If you get injured, Bash will definitely kill me when we find him."

His attempt at lightheartedness failed, though Margrete forced her lips to lift.

"Then I suggest we find him before I meet my untimely death."

Bay grinned at that, shaking his head. "Always so optimistic, Margrete."

Ten minutes later, the crew found themselves deep within the spindly forest. The branches licked at Margrete's skin, nicking at her exposed forearms. Already they were covered in small cuts and scrapes, yet she hardly felt the sting.

This place had the hair on her arms rising and her stomach in a constant knot of anxiety. She couldn't explain it, but while her body reacted fiercely to their new surroundings, there was a pacifying buzzing just beneath her bones, and she had the overwhelming sensation of déjà vu.

Margrete shook off the peculiar thought. She'd never been here before. Gods knew she'd remember such a horrid place.

That same cry from earlier sounded three more times. It grew louder, more piercing, making Margrete's heart skip each time. They were nearing it, whatever *it* was.

Margrete gripped her dagger, her palms clammy and cold. The weather here wasn't normal. It shifted every couple of minutes, from warm to frigid and back again. The only sound—aside from the shrieking —was the wind. It shook the frail leaves and battered the crew. Margrete sniffed, detecting some foreign spice.

Abruptly, Bay raised a fist in the air, and they all came to a halt. He shifted his head right, and Margrete's gaze fell to where the trees parted, a barely visible path coming into view. Without a word, their leader began down the narrow pathway, his steps light. He moved like a ghost.

Mila stayed close to Grant, and Margrete wondered if they were related. The young sailor continuously stole glances at him as she followed Bay. Behind them, a pair of siblings walked side by side, their matching blue eyes wide and alert. And finally, a blond-haired man walked alone, his hand never leaving the blade strapped to his hip.

Margrete picked up the rear, waiting until the last member of their modest group trailed after Bay. As she followed, her eyes drifted to the skies. Hardly any light made its way through the branches and the onyx leaves, and it was difficult to discern how much time had passed.

The tips of her fingers buzzed once more, and Margrete moved them in front of her, twisting them at the wrists. Nerves. It had to be nerves.

Yet even as she assured herself nothing out of the ordinary was at play, the coin in her pocket seemed to thrum with life, to beat in tune to her every heartbeat. If the coin was real, if it truly belonged to the goddess, then—

Margrete slammed into the back of Grant's broad back.

All the air rushed from her lungs when she drew back, an apology dying on her tongue. There had been a reason the crew had all come to an abrupt halt—and the scene before Margrete froze her in place.

Bones.

Human bones.

They lay scattered in a clearing, some broken and splintered, others whole. A few held traces of decayed muscle that refused to part.

"Holy gods," she said on a breath. "What the hell—"

Her words stuck in her throat as she collapsed to the ground with a yelp of pain. Her leg *burned*, prickled like a thousand tiny needles were being jabbed into her skin. In the muddling agony, she must've reached into her pocket, because she felt the coin hidden within throbbing angrily in her hand. Copper wafted to her nose, and warmth pooled in her palm.

As Bay staggered to her side, Margrete held out the coin, gritting her teeth as she stared in awe. In fear. The coin no longer glowed an eerie white.

Blood.

It dripped from the token like falling tears.

Margrete turned to Bay just as the first droplet fell and the island gave a brutal rumble. The rest of the crew toppled to the ground, knocked straight off their feet.

Bay held onto her as he fought to keep them steady. She clutched at his torn shirt with both hands, turning her face to his chest, shuddering as violently as the earth.

A breath later, it all ceased. Everything stilled. The gray world righted itself.

Margrete peered from beneath the safety of Bay's arm. Fog the color of midnight charged toward them, weaving through the trees and thicket. Its pace left them no time to run, to race back to the beach. It moved as if sentient, as if it sensed their presence and wished to suffocate them below its thick blanket of poison.

Her eyes shuttered closed as the fog enveloped her, stealing her air and sight. She made out the faint pulsing in her hand, the coin's thunderous beating slowing. It stopped throbbing altogether when Margrete took her final breath.

CHAPTER FOURTEEN

BASH

SOMETHING HEAVY LAY ON TOP OF BASH.

He woke seconds before, the smell of rotting flesh clogging his nostrils. When he attempted to get up, to do anything to escape the pungent odor of death, he couldn't move an inch. Couldn't *see* anything but gray and white.

Panic immediately surged in his blood, and adrenaline sent his arms jerking, thrashing against the layer of white that shrouded him. The objects piled on top of him felt icy to the touch, hard yet brittle, and smelled altogether vile.

A crack sounded overhead, the noise urging him to continue his fight. Eventually, he could lift his arm a few inches, and he used this space to curl his hand into a fist and bang against the remaining barrier.

There wasn't time to consider where he was or what trapped him. Bash only knew if he didn't get out soon, he'd slowly suffocate. Already he was growing dizzy from the lack of oxygen, and the poignant aroma had bile rising, searing the inside of his throat.

Bash swallowed his fear down, as he so often did, and focused on the task at hand. He concentrated on small movements, the trivial shifts that allowed more air to filter through and to his nose. Little by little, he displaced the objects holding him down, and with his sight all but useless, he pictured the one thing that always calmed him. The one *person*.

Her image bestowed him strength, and with a roar, Bash thrust up both arms at the same time and shattered the final layer of white keeping him captive.

He broke free, desperately filling his lungs, panting as he calmed his pulse. Even as he blinked, he couldn't seem to clear his vision, and a fine dusting of powder floated in the air, casting everything in a chilling mist.

Where the hell was he?

Bash groaned as he pushed himself up and off his elbows. Something hard snapped underneath the weight of his hand, and his gaze instantly shifted down. He almost wished he hadn't looked.

Fuck.

The adrenaline that had saved him moments before came back in full force, though this time, the anxiety that accompanied it sent the world spinning.

He'd been buried beneath bones.

Bones.

He scrambled up with another yelp. Human remains didn't frighten him, but waking up entombed by them? Buried as if he were another soulless body left to rot? Yeah, that certainly was enough to set off his panic.

Bash scrambled up and off the pile of human remains, purposefully not looking where he stepped. Memories of the *Phaedra* going down nearly had him doubling over in horror, but he pushed forward, gritting his teeth. He had to get to wherever Margrete and his crew had washed up. He made for a copse of trees to his right, took a careless step forward—

And fell.

The moment of freefall was quick to end. One second his heart plummeted and his stomach twisted into fine knots as his boots dangled in the open air, the next he made impact.

Frozen water rushed around him and swallowed him up. He fought against the current carrying him down a narrow stream, patches of white fog lining the banks.

He lost precious seconds when he'd opened his mouth to scream, and he knew that he didn't have much time before his air ran out. Azantian or not, he couldn't *breathe* underwater. Not like Margrete could.

At the thought of her, Bash kicked harder, treading with more vigor. What if she'd been buried, same as him, beneath a pile of human remains? What if she was calling out to him for help, and he drowned because he'd been too panicked to see straight?

Bash bared his teeth, fighting the current. He couldn't die. Not like this, and not with Margrete's safety in question.

As he'd often done in the past, Bash gave himself over to the water, using the current to aid his plight. He relaxed his body as best he could and closed his eyes, seeking the pulse of the water, its life force.

Azantians were made for this, and Bash's instincts took over.

A great jolt went through him the moment he connected, and the resistance holding him back dissipated. With the woman he loved in his thoughts, Bash split the surface.

The stream carried him still, cradled him as they both moved, but he filled his lungs with fresh air and life. Well, fresh wasn't exactly what he'd call it. The breeze held some exotic spice that mingled with the general decayed aroma of his surroundings.

Bobbing up and down, Bash barely took in the deep charcoal trees and their slender branches, could hardly see the blackened soil that rushed by on either side. Yet when his legs started to tingle, the sensation was all he focused on. It began slowly, the trembling, the prickling numbness. It worked up his toes and crept beyond his boots and calves.

Bash thrust to the side, kicking with his unsteady limbs, hoping to reach the bank and haul himself to dry land. It took three tries, but eventually, he grasped one of the gnarled roots dipping into the water. With the root in his ironclad hold, he lifted himself from the stream, grimacing as he struggled to toss his upper body onto the black soil.

He collapsed with a groan.

Bash lay there, motionless and thoroughly stunned. That odd prickling in his legs ceased, and he moved his toes around in his soggy boots. Crawling up the bank, he flipped onto his back, his eyes cast overhead to where the barest hint of sky shone through the trees.

The *Phaedra* had wrecked.

The obvious question, of course, remained how he managed to wind up covered in bones far from the shore. He should've washed up on a beach with the others—if there *were* other survivors. It didn't make any damned sense.

Bash brought his hand to rest on his wildly beating heart. Now that he didn't face imminent death, he had to discern his location and formulate a plan. Sitting here wouldn't give him answers, and it certainly wouldn't tell him what happened to Margrete or his friends.

He rose into a seated position—about to push up from the ground—when he paused. He caught sight of his right hand.

That fear he'd been battling to shove down broke free.

Black ink touched the bottom of his fingernails near the nailbed, his skin stained a matching shade just below. Bash brought his hand closer, using his free one to wipe away the black. It didn't rub off. If anything, he could've sworn he saw the ink spread, just the slightest.

He cursed, more loudly than he'd meant to. It could be anything, some sort of dye that would rinse away, but it was how the ink appeared to swirl and move that destroyed his composure. Absolutely shattered it.

Deep down, he knew it wasn't ink at all.

Bash shot to his feet and turned his head left and right, surveying the ghostly woods rising all around him like charred skeletons. There were no calls of animals nor the chirping of birds, none of the typical sounds one would hear in a forest. Only the noise of the stream and the whooshing winds reached his ears, the breeze carrying that damned smell of rot.

Calm. Bash had to focus on finding his calm. Because right now, stranded and alone gods knew where, he was awfully close to losing his mind. He ignored his instinct to call out as loud as he could, to scream for his missing crew. For Margrete. Instead, years of tactical training with Ortum had him slowing down, assessing the situation.

Moving to the nearest tree, Bash trailed his inked hand across the roughened bark. He'd never seen or heard of a tree with black leaves before, which told him this island hadn't been reported in the Azantian library—which was rather odd. The keepers of the sea would know of any island or coast where waters grazed the shore.

Lowering his hand, Bash continued through the thicket, muttering a hundred new curses under his breath. Fallen branches viciously snagged at his torn trousers, and Bash detected the faint smell of his blood in the air.

A few minutes of aimless walking brought him to a clearing of sorts. A lone tree had been situated in the very center, and while it appeared similar to the others, its trunk was wide and thick, and its black leaves glimmered with specks of gleaming silver.

Bash shouldn't have closed the distance. How many stories had he read where the hero knowingly touched the cursed or divine object during one of their quests? Those tales never ended well, and he'd always assumed he would've made a better decision had he been in the protagonist's shoes.

Maybe he wasn't as clever as he imagined.

Feet away now, Bash took in a mess of swirls and flaking wood. Some sort of writing had been carved into the trunk.

Beware the Eternal Night.

Unable to help himself, Bash touched the inscription, rubbing at the peeling bark where it had been engraved. A speck of red shimmered just beside the letter B. He leaned in, watching in horror as the speck of red bloomed, as it turned into a trickle of crimson. Bash darted backward.

He smelled blood—and not his own.

Blood poured freely from the carved letters now, and Bash stumbled on his feet, desperate to get as far from the *bleeding* tree as possible. In his haste, he spun around and tripped over a fallen branch, flying face forward onto the ground. He grunted at the impact.

Adrian would be laughing his ass off had he seen his king showcasing such ungainliness. Bash had trained for years to be a silent killer, a formidable opponent, but now, he'd been bested by bones, a stream, and finally, a mere branch.

Bash hoisted himself up for what seemed like the hundredth time and brushed his dirtied hands on his trousers.

He put together what he knew—Margrete below deck, the storm, the *Phaedra* on the verge of sinking. But a particular memory, a memory with blurred edges, snagged his attention. He'd seen some sort of shadow, one that moved toward him, hands outstretched as if to grab him. The gale had raged all around Bash, and he wondered what he'd been doing by the bow instead of with his men. He never would've abandoned them during a storm, he—

A shriek sounded.

The wind ceased to blow.

The air turned chill, weighed down by ice.

Bash stilled, his body going ramrod straight. Years of training finally kicked in, and he swiftly pressed his back against the nearest tree, ears perked as he listened for the shrill noise to sound again. That couldn't have been a damned animal.

He waited for many long minutes, holding his breath in fear that whatever had made that noise would come upon him and strike. Yet no twigs snapped or leaves crinkled, no sign that someone or something approached. Bash cautiously shifted from behind his hiding spot, eyeing the forest through narrowed slits.

Keep it together, he chided. Adrian would've told him to—

Bash saw movement just ahead, just the barest glimmer of gray. He reached for his dagger as a black and slate fog crept around the trees like steam. It rushed in his direction, too fast to outrun and too dense to see beyond.

Couldn't he just have a moment to catch his breath?

The fog seemed to speed up in reply.

Guess not.

Twisting on a heel, he bolted, swerving around fallen trees and logs, jumping over shrubbery and the thick underbrush. His heart raced and sweat dampened his brow, but he refused to stop.

While determined, Bash knew his sheer will alone wouldn't be enough to carry him away from the fog. It was at his back now, chasing him, eager to swallow him whole. He pushed his legs forward, wishing his body didn't feel so sluggish, so weak.

When the mystical haze slithered from behind him and wrapped around his body, Bash gritted his teeth, still struggling to run. To fight.

Once the fog filled his lungs, Bash fell, toppling to the ground. He struck his head on impact, and black spots dotted his vision. Within seconds, the blackness took over everything else.

Bash ceased breathing.

He closed his eyes, a nightmare of claws and teeth and scales sweeping over his mind. He screamed into the void, all the while knowing there was no escape.

CHAPTER FIFTEEN

MARGRETE

MARGRETE OPENED HER EYES. SHE STOOD ON A ROCKY CLIFF bordering the sea. Alone. The sky, which had been gray and cloudy, was swept away by a vibrant blue, the sun shining down on her in full force. She spun around.

Prias.

Somehow Margrete had found herself back in Prias, atop the cliffs overlooking the bay, the ones right beside her father's keep. Her brow furrowed. While the breeze cooling her face was welcome, it didn't smell of home. Mingling with the familiar scents of the docks below the keep was a spice she didn't recognize.

Wait.

She *did* recognize it. Though she first scented it back on the beach—the same one they'd washed up on after nearly losing their lives.

Everything came back to her in a sickening rush, and the last thing she remembered was a fog...then nothing at all.

Without a clue as to why or *how* that peculiar fog had brought her here, of all places, Margrete made her way across the rocks toward the keep. She'd barely managed a few feet when something clinked inside her pocket, and she reached within, only to pull out the coin she'd found while searching for Bash.

Beware the Eternal Night.

The warning stared back, taunting her. What the hell does that even mean? And how had the coin ended up back inside her pocket? Her list of questions grew.

Margrete quickened her pace, uncertain of everything, every move she made, every breath she took. She just moved. Farther from the cliffs, away from the sea that called to her, Margrete didn't stop until she opened the main gates to her father's fortress and stepped inside.

Silence greeted her. Not even the usual sounds of the staff met her ears, and she peered around the corners as she passed through the halls, searching for any other soul. Again she found herself utterly alone. As if instinct guided her, Margrete grasped the railing on the staircase and tiptoed up to the second landing.

The keep she'd called home for twenty-three years felt too vivid to be real, like she was staring at an artist's rendition of it and they'd used far too much color.

She was about to climb to the third floor, where she'd find her and Birdie's room, when the hair on her arms rose. A soft lullaby played somewhere nearby, a soothing melody that she'd not heard before. It reminded her of summer and innocence and everything she hadn't had as a child. She couldn't stop herself as she moved toward the source.

Her limbs became fatigued with every step, her mind growing heavy as well, and whenever she focused on anything other than the lullaby, darkness crept around the edges of her sight.

Margrete didn't realize where she stood until it was far too late.

She was in the center of her father's study. The place where her trauma began.

That intoxicating song continued to play, taunting her. She had to find it, became desperate to hold the music in her very hands and keep it all for herself. It was a promise of a future, the melody one of joy and endless possibilities.

Margrete shuffled to her father's mahogany desk, and while the noise demanded she continue to search, her feet stumbled. She didn't want to be here, back in this room. Her panic flourished, and sweat dampened her brow. The room began to spin, and she feared her savagely beating heart would escape from her chest.

She was having some sort of attack.

And she couldn't breathe. Could hardly move.

Margrete shut her eyes. The room spun and blurred, and she just wanted it all to stop, wanted to be anywhere else in the world. Suddenly, she was a child, crying for her father to open the door to her box, begging for him to love her. That's all she ever wanted, such a simple thing, and yet it might've been the only thing he couldn't give her.

When Margrete opened her eyes next, she stood in total darkness. She screamed and the sound echoed, growing louder, more shrill as the seconds passed. Instinctively, her arms shot out, only to be met by the solid wood paneling of a prison she knew all too well.

The box.

The weapon her father had used to control her. An attempt to bring the stolen divinity out of her soul and back into the sacred stone in his possession. He'd failed to retrieve her magic, but he certainly had succeeded in making her scared, in turning her into a lost child, frantically begging for air, for light. For love.

Margrete pounded on the wood, kicking at it and screaming until her throat turned raw. She didn't stop until warmth spread across her knuckles, until her blood dripped to the floor. Gods, she couldn't be here. Not again.

When she unleashed her next scream, the ground beneath her boots trembled and shook. She lurched to the side of the box, bumping her shoulder and howling in pain. She must've cut more than her fists, because the smell of blood grew more potent.

This could be a dream, a figment of her imagination, and it wouldn't have mattered to her. As long as those walls surrounded her, Margrete couldn't think straight.

The box shuddered violently, and then she was rolling, tumbling around and around as if her prison had been thrown off the keep itself.

Margrete folded in on herself, sputtering for air as she spun in an endless cycle of torment.

She couldn't think of Bash or Birdie or the island they'd landed on. All that consumed her was the overwhelming sensation of being confined. Being here brought all her pain back, the crushing weight of never being enough, as if she were waste to be discarded whenever the captain saw fit.

Margrete's fear devoured her.

Twisted and turned her inside out.

She gasped when the box made impact with something that felt harder than rock. The air rushed from her lungs, and she held both arms out, touching the walls of her cage. She'd stopped rolling but...

She heard waves.

Smelled the sea.

Felt herself *sinking*.

The scream of pure, unadulterated terror that slipped past her lips shattered her eardrums. Her nails were bleeding from clawing at the wood, trying to escape like some crazed animal. She could feel the box dropping, could feel herself descending into the waves.

Water shot through the gap in the door. It streamed onto her face, into her mouth. This was her greatest nightmare—to be trapped and dying in this box of horrors. To take her final breath in the contraption built to destroy her.

Margrete always believed herself capable, that she might think quickly enough to save herself when thrust into a life or death predicament. But she knew better now.

Fear, the *purest* form of it, rendered you immobile.

She heard herself speak Bash's name, but it sounded far away, unlike her own voice. Her words were distorted and shrill. Unhinged.

Stop.

The voice that carried into her mind didn't belong to Darius. To Bash. To Birdie.

Somewhere in the distance, she made out the steadying commands, all telling her to calm, to remember none of this could be real. And...that voice?

It belonged to her.

Somehow, *somehow*, a small part of her rose above the alarm and panic and demanded she fight. Margrete held onto this voice tightly and welcomed it closer. Squeezing her eyes, she listened to every dominant syllable, ignoring how she trembled.

He failed. He could never break you.

The captain had tried, and he hadn't succeeded. He'd tortured her for *years*, and whenever he opened that door, she would lift her chin and force a smile. In that small way, she showed him he couldn't crack her armor, and that he would never be able to fully steal her soul.

A soul that wouldn't let him win.

That's it, came her own voice, guiding her. *Deep breaths. He's gone. Dead. Unable to take anything more from you.*

Margrete kept her eyes shut, pretending the water hadn't climbed up to her hips.

You're stronger than this. Than him.

She'd endured hell and come out on the other side, and she had been lucky enough to find happiness and her soul's missing half. Margrete had suffered, like so many others, and she'd risen.

The sound of the rushing waters grew stifled, and slowly, she tuned it out altogether.

Margrete envisioned Azantian, the island where she'd changed her fate. She pictured herself lifting on top of the wave that had destroyed her father, and she relived the moment where she allowed that lethal wave to fall, killing her tormentor.

Instead of the shame she'd felt for months following his death, Margrete felt...justice. The sense of righteousness that came with facing evil incarnate and triumphing.

All the noise stopped, and the air came alive, vibrating so hard that even the planks beneath her boots quivered.

When everything stilled and a blanket of peace fell across her weary soul, Margrete opened her eyes.

CHAPTER SIXTEEN

BAY

ADRIAN'S CHARRED BODY DIDN'T MOVE. HIS CHEST DIDN'T RISE AND fall in the steadying breaths that often lulled Bay to sleep. His eyes didn't open and spark with his own subtle mischief. The man Bay couldn't go through life without lay dead upon the stones outside Azantian's palace.

Bay didn't care that the palace itself had burned down. How could he? He shook his lover, his tears falling on Adrian's scarred cheeks, dripping onto a face that was nearly unrecognizable from the burns. A face that would never light up his heart again.

"Come on, Adrian. Open your eyes. *Look* at me," Bay sobbed, throwing himself against Adrian's broad chest. Bile rose in his throat when the scent of burnt skin and hair reached his nostrils, choking him. He swallowed it down and squeezed Adrian tighter, hoping his love could save them both, because if he died…

Bay didn't know if he'd recover.

He'd been alone for so damn long that when Adrian came into his life, he realized how broken he'd been. How lonely.

As an orphan, Bay never thought he'd find that connection with another. Believing and hoping led to disappointment and pain, and he had enough of that as it was. Instead, he had focused on training, weapons, and becoming someone who garnered as much fear as respect. He ignored the soldiers who told him he was too small or too weak to become one of the revered Azantian soldiers. Bay ignored them all.

He never cared.

Adrian *made* him care. And then he couldn't seem to stop.

Bay lifted himself up from Adrian's chest. The palace roared with flames, the blaze causing the top floors to crumble and fall. It would reach him soon, and if Bay stayed here any longer, he'd be swept away with the rest of the rubble.

Bay didn't move. The fire could take him too, because anywhere Adrian went, he'd follow without thought.

How the blaze started, he didn't know. All he remembered was a flash of orange sparks, the scent of dark magic, then utter disaster. He'd lugged Adrian's body outside the gates, and he hadn't moved since.

Maybe he deserved this end. Was always meant to die alone and undeserving. Pathetically unwanted.

His right arm began to shake uncontrollably. He could almost feel phantom fingers squeeze into his muscle, digging beneath his shirt and bruising his skin. Whatever had taken ahold of him turned relentless, and Bay's vision swam as he was tossed to the side of Adrian's corpse.

Far away, someone called out his name.

His eyes drifted to the sky as he fell to his back. The shaking never ceased. It grew until the sun itself seemed to flicker in and out, the clouds turning gray instead of white.

The palace wavered in and out of focus, even as Bay looked to the highest window, catching just the barest trace of red hair.

Bay!

The fingers he felt on his arms squeezed, and then another pair grasped his other arm.

Wake up!

It sounded familiar. Like it belonged to someone he loved. Someone who loved him back.

Bay stared blankly at Adrian's closed eyes, knowing he'd never see the spark in them again.

It's not real.

The ground he lay upon trembled. The sky turned dark, and he could make out flashes of charred leaves and black branches.

Don't leave me.

Bay jolted upright. The air didn't smell right, not like his home. It smelled wrong. Just as it had on...

The island.

Bay had been on an island with gray sands, and Margrete...that was *her* voice begging him to wake up, to come back to her.

As the rush of awareness assaulted his senses, the air he knew to be wrong grew heavy and thick. He shut his eyes and focused on the voice that was able to reach him when he couldn't reach himself.

Come back to me.

CHAPTER SEVENTEEN

BASH

Time ebbed and flowed, and Bash couldn't distinguish one breath from the next. A cruel void of shadows had his skin itching, stinging—the feeling akin to a thousand spiders dancing across his body, biting at his flesh.

Bash whipped around, finding nothing but endless darkness. He stood upon stone, smooth, onyx stone with white veins that reached out like the branches on the island.

He must be dead. Or dying. There wasn't another option.

Footsteps approached from the distance, a soft pattering of bare feet. Bash held his breath and waited, every muscle in his body tensed and prepared for a battle. While he might have left the mortal plane, Bash wasn't especially keen on rolling over and accepting his fate. If something came for him, he'd fight it tooth and nail.

His breathing caught altogether when a woman emerged from the smoky gray and black nothingness, her gown crafted from pure white silk. Long, raven hair hung limply down her back, the ends appearing almost singed. Glimmering black scales caressed her chest and wound around her neck like a gruesome noose, and the tips of her toes were blackened as though they'd been seared.

This hadn't been the opponent he expected, and Bash stilled, immobile beneath the weight of her cunning stare. This woman wasn't a woman at all, even with legs in place of a spiked tail. No. Bash realized with startling clarity what she was.

A *nymera*...and one who appeared more human than he'd imagined possible.

Bash formed his hands into fists as she neared, as she moved idly, unhurried, smiling as if she took pleasure from his swelling unease.

The creature appraised him with keen interest, her beady eyes sliding up his form with what he could mistake for curiosity. His pulse quickened in response, a choked scream trapped within his chest. He knew from the few books on nymeras that they were quick, though they were typically found near the sea where they drew some of their energy. In this supernatural abyss, the sea was absent. And yet this woman, this thing, thrived, drifting closer.

When she stood—no, *hovered*—no more than five feet away, she stilled, cocking her head to the side and curling her fists. In horror, Bash glimpsed her serrated talons, which clicked rhythmically against one another. He lowered his gaze, taking in those perfectly honed weapons at the tips of her fingers. He had no doubt they could inflict unimaginable pain.

Maybe that was why he merely lifted his eyes to greet the demon dressed in such a deceivingly pure white gown.

Hello, dear boy.

Her raspy welcome shot straight into his mind, her cracked lips unmoving. The sound echoed in Bash's skull, each syllable pronounced and cutting. It was a voice he'd heard before—in his dreams, during the council meeting, under the palace, in the Adiria Cavern. This was *her*. The beast that called for him.

"Who are you?" Bash demanded, raising his chin. Fear wasn't an option. Bash knew these monsters fed off turmoil, inhaling fear to bolster their strength.

He only wished he could see his opponent properly, and that the air didn't weigh his bones, making everything feel painfully sluggish.

The nymera raised a hand, black ink spiderwebbing like gnarled veins across porcelain skin. Bash couldn't help but flinch. If he made a grab for his dagger, the creature would strike.

Bash couldn't move. Gods, he could barely stand.

A phantom pressure landed on his shoulders, willing him to his knees. He struggled, not bending easily.

A wicked smile curved the nymera's lips, and she leaned forward, placing a lone finger beneath his jaw. Her touch was tender, if not reverent, and she trailed her razor-sharp claw down to his chest, pausing above his wildly thudding heart. It was there that she lingered.

Throughout her leisurely perusal, Bash held her stare. He was a king. And this *thing* didn't deserve his fear. Still, something gnawed at him the longer he looked at her. He sucked in a steadying breath, though the troublesome feeling remained.

You grew up well.

The nymera lowered her hand, beaming wide enough to display a set of jagged teeth, sharper than any predator in the sea.

"I grew up well?" he echoed, hackles raised. He wanted to lash out and strike the grinning abomination, but his body refused to follow his command. The woman—nymera—smiled, a knowing kind of smile that set off all of Bash's alarm bells.

You'll find out what I mean soon enough.

Frozen, stunned, *helpless*, Bash watched as a rolling fog—the same one that had assaulted him in the woods—came rushing across the empty space. Shrill howls sounded, growing painfully loud as the clouds neared, and Bash made out hands moving amid the chaos. Tails. Faces.

Yes. Bash could make out several faces in the fog, all sickly pale and hollow, their dark irises matching his own. A rotten wind carried the horde of monsters, and as one, they stretched out their elongated fingers, reaching for Bash.

He couldn't control his fear any longer.

Bash screamed, trying to move, to run. His fight was futile.

Trapped. Bash was trapped and nothing could save him from the wave of creatures with fangs made to puncture skin. Fangs attached to monsters that could suck the soul straight from their victims' bodies.

You are your nightmare, came the female nymera's voice from somewhere far away. Bash couldn't twist his head to search for her, but he sensed her presence.

Bash wanted to shake his head, deny her words. They might not have made sense to anyone else, but he understood them all too well.

He'd felt that darkness inside of him for far too long, and ever since the attack on Azantian, his hold on his inner beast had been slipping. Bash's fingertips tingled again, and as his eyes were the only thing he could move, he peered down to his sides.

The ink on his fingernails.

Gods.

His blackened nails grew before his eyes, long and sharp and grotesque. He might've cried out as blood pooled around the beds, as the skin stretched and accepted the claws protruding from both his hands, yet he heard nothing but his pulse.

Nothing about this place felt real, even if Bash felt a severe and biting *pain*. It was like being trapped inside a lucid dream, fully aware and fully susceptible to whatever horrors invaded his mind. And he couldn't do a damned thing about it.

Bash lifted his eyes and met his reflection. The supernatural fog that had stolen him from reality swirled chaotically, dancing around a silver mirror lined with broken pieces of dark sea glass.

Look. Look at your true face. The voice echoed, its haunting melody a cursed taunt.

Bash glimpsed his face, his black eyes, and...his now black hair. The curled strands had turned from russet to the murkiest of black, and his jaw dropped, disbelieving that the creature he stared at was himself. Scales wound around his neck, snaking down to dip below his tattered shirt, their edges unfiled and sharp.

He blinked, and the woman in white stood before him, the mirror and his reflection gone.

She dipped her chin in welcome.

There you are, my son.

CHAPTER EIGHTEEN

MARGRETE

Margrete hovered over Bay's sleeping body. She shook him roughly, trying desperately to break him free from whatever spell they both had succumbed to. That damned fog...it must've been what delivered the poisonous hallucinations.

"Wake up!" She gripped his arms hard enough to bruise, not accepting that she wouldn't see his mischievous smile again or feel the too-tight hugs. He was her friend, and she needed him so much more than he knew. "Please come back to me!"

Bay opened his eyes with a wheezing gasp.

He lurched to his side and dry-heaved, nothing but choked air coming up from his empty stomach.

Thank the gods.

"Shhh," Margrete soothed, rubbing his back. Her heart thrashed against her ribs. She thought she'd lost Bay to the underworld. Gone forever.

From the corner of her eye, Margrete glimpsed a few of the crew beginning to shift and jerk in place, coming back to life, awakening from their own visions. Atlas brought herself onto her elbows, panting, and Mila let out a whimper as she rolled to her side.

"What was that?" Bay asked, seizing her arm, using her for support. His entire body trembled as he sat upright.

"The fog..." She glanced over her shoulder, scanning the woods. "It had to have been what caused this."

"Did you dream of—"

"I dreamt of my worst fear," she finished for him. Bay swallowed thickly.

"It felt so real," he murmured, sounding slightly out of breath. He scanned the rest of the crew with creased eyes. "I felt myself drowning in my pain, and then I heard you. Begging me to wake."

They'd all surrendered to unconsciousness at the same time, and if their visions were as horrid as Margrete's, then she knew they'd suffered an encounter worse than any nightmare. She only worried why some had yet to open their eyes.

"This place..." Bay swallowed thickly. "It's not right."

They'd already agreed as much, yet they still had no answers as to why.

"The coin." Margrete hadn't released it from her fist. Slowly, she lifted her arm and twisted her wrist. Bay held his breath as her fingers unfurled, his forehead creased with leftover fear.

Margrete opened her hand.

The eye carved into the metal stared back at her, and she could've sworn she saw it blink.

"The number is gone," Bay observed, bringing her attention to the spot where the *1* had been marked inside the pupil. Her friend met her stare and held it.

Numbers don't vanish...unless the damned coin had belonged to Surria, and in that case—

"Margrete!" Atlas shouted from across the clearing. "Come here!"

She broke contact with Bay and shoved the mysterious coin back into her trousers. Racing toward Atlas, Margrete found her hovering over a sailor with bright blond hair.

"He's the only one who isn't waking up."

Mila elbowed past her and Atlas. She dropped to her knees and placed her finger on the younger man's pulse point, her breathing uneven as the long seconds passed.

"His heart's barely beating." Mila rested her head on his chest. The sailor's skin held a sickly hue to it, and dark bruises formed beneath his eyes as if he hadn't slept. The redhead turned to Margrete, fire in her eyes.

"Fix him."

Margrete inched away from the woman's pleading stare, the biting demand in her tone. Mila looked at her as if she held the power to snap her fingers and wake the comatose man below them.

Gods. Maybe she *did*, but that didn't mean she knew how to access such potent magic.

"Mila..." Grant warned, sidling up and placing a hand on her shoulder. "I'm not sure if she...if she can do that."

"I don't care!" Mila snapped. "She saved our king once before, and now she can save *him*." Her eyes finally fell to the blond. He was handsome, possessing a strong jaw, high cheekbones, and an aquiline nose. From her memory, she knew he had bright blue eyes and a kind smile. She felt guilty that those traits were all she could recall.

"I—" Margrete stood frozen in place, the eyes of every crew member on her, waiting, *hoping*. It was too much. "T-that happened out there"— she tilted her head toward the direction of the shore, to the sea—"and I don't even know how I did it in the first place."

"Useless," Mila spat, standing. Her venomous stare turned watery. "They all act as if you're some kind of savior. A goddess among us. You're just full of shit."

Margrete choked on a gasp.

The words stung, mainly because she'd thought the same thing herself. But what if Mila was right? All that practice after training had been a waste. What good was lifting the waters five feet in the air? Sure, she'd saved Azantian once before, but Margrete hadn't called on it. It had come from her rage, birthed from her tangible hatred for her father.

"See, she can't even deny it," Mila sneered, backing away. She shook her head before bumping Grant's shoulder and vanishing through the trees. Her companion immediately followed, her name on his lips.

"She didn't mean that," Bay whispered, squeezing her shoulder. Margrete brushed him off.

"No. She most definitely did."

Margrete shut her eyes. She attempted to remember what had gone through her head when she saved Bash, *how* she'd summoned so much power. She'd been so desperate when Bash had laid unmoving and pale, and something inside of her had snapped. It had just...happened.

The blond sailor she hovered over had a pulse, albeit a slow one. Margrete gritted her teeth. If she had done it before, she could do it again, and it had to be easier than raising a man from the dead.

Nevertheless, she'd used the words of the ancients that day in Azantian, and now she didn't know if she needed to speak for her magic to work. But there was no whispering of commands belonging to a mystical language. There was nothing at all.

Still, she wasn't giving up just yet.

Placing both hands on his barely moving chest, Margrete pictured the wisps of glowing magic that had skirted across her vision that fateful day. Like fireflies in the night, she chased after it, hoping to home in on a spark and trap it.

The murmuring noises of the crew fell to the background. She heard the waves and listened to their song. She followed the sea's call and begged it to help her.

All the while, she reached for that fleeting power that evaded her grasp, and every time she failed to capture it, her heart plummeted into her stomach. She began to silently plead with it, that light, praying beneath her breath, praying to the gods she didn't particularly like. She resorted to bargaining anything and everything, and still, the magic didn't listen. If anything, it recoiled further. Margrete didn't understand.

Did she have to touch the waters? Perhaps that was the issue. She heard the unconscious sailor's weakly beating heart thud in her ears, and her skin turned to ice when it skipped several beats, slowing. She wouldn't have the time, but if they made it to the coast—

It stopped.

The pounding *stopped.*

Margrete's eyes shot open, her hands still on his chest, centered over his heart. She pushed, thrusting against him, her movements rough and uneven. In her panic she was barely aware of the change in his body, how it went completely limp. She continued to push on his chest until his lips parted and...

A forked tongue poked out to lick at his lips, his chin. It looked like something was *inside* of his mouth, moving, causing his cheeks to bulge.

She froze, horrified as two serpentine eyes stared back at her, the head of a black snake opening his jaw impossibly wide.

No. She couldn't be seeing this. This wasn't real. It had to be another hallucination.

But it wasn't a hallucination. In absolute terror, Margrete watched as a black snake escaped, slithering out of his mouth, its long body still trapped in his throat. She could see how it moved beneath the thin skin, causing the man's neck to swell and ripple.

Someone screamed, maybe her, maybe one of the others.

Faintly, she heard Bay say her name, felt his touch on her shoulder, but she continued to push on the man's chest in vain, even as another snake worked its way up. It hissed at her, flicking its tongue at her in warning, its eyes a sinister red.

Her magic dissipated at the sight, and she felt nothing but suffocating fear.

And the worst part was that the snakes kept coming.

"Margrete, stop!"

Hands reached around her torso, and she went flying back, pulled off the motionless sailor she couldn't save.

The snakes, their lithe bodies ringed in blood red and yellow, crawled over the body, their elongated fangs sinking into his slowly cooling flesh. They punctured every inch of him, hissing as they wrapped themselves around his arms, his legs, his neck.

Margrete's feet kicked out as she fought to return to the nameless sailor, to try and find his life force and banish whatever dark magic cursed him. She couldn't let Mila be right, couldn't let *herself* be right. There had to be a way to tame her power and use it to help those in need. Margrete didn't want to spend her life being a mere vessel. She was destined for more than that.

"He's gone," Bay whispered into her ears once they were past earshot of the remaining crew. Margrete peered around her friend's shoulder. The Azantians all stood at a safe distance from the boy, most clenching their fists in apparent frustration that nothing could be done.

How they must hate her.

"Mila was right!" Margrete said, nearly growling. "I can hardly raise a damn wave, and yet they look at me like I could've saved him. Like I *should* have saved him. Hell, I didn't even know his *name*."

Margrete hadn't realized she'd begun to cry until salty tears slipped between her lips. The tears made her all the angrier.

"No one expects you to know how to use the powers of a god, Margrete," Bay said, clutching her face to his chest. "We all saw the snakes, all felt the dark magic. I doubt you could've done much of anything. And I suspect the only one who could've saved him was himself. Those dreams, hallucinations, whatever...they were a test. A test I would have failed had you not reached me in time." His arms wound around her back, and he held her firmly in place. She let him.

It didn't matter if she somehow saved Bay and freed him from his nightmare. She still felt responsible for not saving the life of that sailor.

"I brought Bash back, and yet I couldn't do the same today." Mila's disappointed face flashed across her mind. Her eyes had been filled with such animosity, such vehement hatred.

"His name was Jace," Bay said softly. "Mila had been seeing him in secret for a few weeks now. She thought Grant didn't know, but he liked Jace well enough. He approved."

Margrete peeled back to look into Bay's eyes. "Is Grant her father?"

Bay shook his head. "Not biologically, but he's her father in all the important ways. He took her in when his brother and her mother died."

Bay pushed back her hair and tucked a loose strand behind her ear.

"You can't help everyone, Margrete. We all know your journey will take time, and Mila said those things out of grief. She didn't mean them."

Margrete didn't say anything in return. There was nothing she could say that would change a damn thing. Instead, she reached for the coin and brought it between her and Bay. Her friend eyed it with rightful fear.

"I lived out my greatest fear back there. I felt like I was dying, *actually* dying. I saved myself at the last minute, but gods, it had been so close. Too close."

Margrete flipped the coin over and ran her thumb across the inscription.

Beware the Eternal Night.

Bay dropped his hands and stepped back, his eyes fixated on what rested in her palm.

"If the legend of Surria's coins and their trials are true…then that was only the beginning, and Jace didn't pass," she murmured softly. "He succumbed to his nightmares. Snakes, so it seems." Margrete curled her fingers into a fist, the metal digging into her flesh. She gritted her teeth. "And I have a feeling it won't be long until we discover the second coin."

And then more would die.

CHAPTER NINETEEN

BASH

Bash woke up in the same place the fog had taken him.

Jumping to his feet, he began walking, holding no grasp of direction, only the need to get as far away from that clearing as possible. If his brain couldn't explain what he'd just seen, then he'd move until it all made sense. It *had* to make sense eventually.

He wandered for most of the day, not wanting to admit that his encounter with the nymera hadn't felt like a dream at all. If anything, it had been a ghastly hallucination nestled in reality. Both real and not of this world.

Just like the island itself.

But the man he'd seen in the mirror...he'd been Bash's worst nightmare. That creature who wore his face was the embodiment of how he felt when the dark thoughts overpowered all else.

Sometimes he felt eyes upon him as he walked through the forest. Yet when he'd turn, fists raised and ready for a fight, nothing stood behind him. All that greeted him were hisses, the noise more feral than human, though he could've sworn they all breathed the same word.

Follow.

He ignored it. Ignored it all.

There wouldn't be a point in listening, and all he'd accomplish would be an unhealthy dose of panic.

By the time twilight approached, he barely had enough time to find shelter. An overturned tree lay across a dip in the earth, providing room for him to settle below, the reedy branches overhead blocking most of the biting wind. He leaned back against the packed earth and brought his hands to rest beneath his head.

A lock tumbled over his brow, a curl obscuring his left eye. Black. His russet hair was gone, changed forever after he'd glimpsed into that wretched mirror.

The words he'd tried to ignore all day came back to him.

Beware the Eternal Night.

Bash growled. Fuck that bloody tree and that damned inscription, and fuck the nymera in white. She'd called him her *son*, then had the gall to vanish and leave him reeling. Not that he believed a word she said. Bash's mother had died right after he'd been born, and the portraits in the grand hall depicted her as having kind eyes and bright blonde hair more luminous than gold.

His father told him it was his mother who named him. Sebastian. The late king never called him that, and Bash always wondered why. It was well known that his father loved his mother. The people spoke of her beauty, of her generosity, how perfect she had been, but she felt more like a fairy tale to Bash growing up, some goddess who watched over him from above.

The abomination who visited his waking nightmare wasn't his mother.

Bash shifted to his side, the unforgiving ground not helping his sore muscles. Another oddity, really, as Azantians healed rapidly, and his body should've felt better by now. Yet the farther he traveled into the woods, the heavier his limbs became and the more they ached.

Hunger had taken hold of him as well, and he'd kept his eyes out for food, though no small game flitted among the underbrush. He'd have to look for any edible plants or berries instead. Margrete would know which were safe. Bash had brought her every book on plants he could find in the

Azantian library—which was a lot, considering it had taken five men to carry them all up. His princess was ravenous that way—always seeking information and never satisfied when she closed the cover of a book. A part of him believed she studied so hard to make up for her lack of knowledge elsewhere, namely her power. He had no doubt she'd conquer that too.

Bash felt her now, deep in his bones. She might not be here, in his arms and safe, but she lived, even if he couldn't explain the reasoning behind his certainty. Morning would come soon enough, he assured himself, and then he'd have the energy to move, the energy to find her.

In the meantime, he had to remind himself of who Margrete was. Whether or not this island was indeed a place of evil, she'd faced greater foes before...and overcame them. Margrete was a fighter. Stronger than him, even.

Bash closed his eyes, repeating the sentiment over and over. Convincing himself that if anyone was in danger, it was him.

He fell asleep hours later, overcome with exhaustion. It pulled him deeper and deeper into the dark void, where his mind separated from his body, and soon, he floated.

Bash dreamed of black woods.

He knew he was dreaming, that his physical body slept unbothered beneath a fallen tree. Though the fact that even in sleep he'd envisioned the island absolutely infuriated him. Why couldn't he think of Margrete or Azantian and allow his mind a reprieve?

In this haze, Bash spotted the broad tree from earlier, the one with the bloodied inscription. It stared back at him as if it owned a pair of unblinking eyes, and he heard the hissing of unintelligible whispers. Voices that didn't belong to humans wafted through the branches, reaching his ears and sending shivers down his spine.

Bash wasn't foolish enough to touch the carving this time. He stood rooted in place, tilting his head to the sky and searching for stars. Of course, there weren't any.

"I've always wondered what made you so worthy."

Bash whipped his head in the direction of the new voice. It was deep, tainted with sin and cruel magic. A part of him recognized it.

"Hello, Azantian king."

A man leaned casually against the bleeding tree, his head cocked to the side as his bright blue eyes appraised Bash. Blond hair the color of morning sunshine crowned his head, curling around his temples and into those inhuman eyes.

Bash didn't speak. Silence was a better weapon when facing an unknown enemy. Unnerve them first. It typically worked, though he should've known his tactics wouldn't have any effect on the otherworldly male before him.

"I see your wheels turning." The stranger sighed, shoving up from the trunk. "I'm disappointed though. I'd have thought you would've recognized me straight away." His eyes fell across Bash's form, his mouth curling in a sneer.

Bash straightened in response.

"Then again, you're not as cunning as I'd believed. Another disappointment. I would've preferred a more...interesting opponent."

The blond stepped closer, his impressive height towering over Bash by at least a foot.

"Though you stand firm," the man continued, undeterred by Bash's silence. "You're not running like a frightened little mouse at the sight of me. Most humans flee straightaway, so I suppose that adds points in your favor."

Bash schooled his features into boredom. He knew who this man was, and still he asked, "And you are?"

His tone was apathetic, like he hardly cared for the god's answer. He felt immense pleasure when a muscle in Darius's jaw flickered.

He recovered quickly.

"I am the one who is going to take your life. *Eventually*," Darius added with a snarl. "Though I'll have to be patient until the time comes when I can steal your soul. Everything must unfold as planned, and you, dear king, are going to be my favorite pawn."

"I'm no one's pawn," Bash said, stepping closer. The blond snickered, though his eyes fell to Bash's feet, seemingly surprised by the advance.

"You don't even know what you are, though by the time you realize it, it'll be far too late. And how I will relish that moment."

Bash noted that the man wore all black except for a golden ring on his right hand. He squinted, though he couldn't make out the design on the ring's face. Then again, he didn't need to look. He knew he'd find two entwined circles.

Darius's insignia. The same mark that had been branded on Ortum's skin when they'd found his dead body. The same mark that had once been painted in blood on Azantian's throne.

His disgust must have shown on his face, because Darius clapped his hands in delight.

"There you go! I was waiting for that careful mask to fall."

"Darius."

The name echoed between them.

"Sebastian," the God of the Sea replied, making a mockery of his given name. "The great King of Azantian. The mortal who won the heart of the sea itself, it seems."

Now the hair on the back of Bash's neck rose.

"What do you want?" He kept his voice firm. It was a tone used when he rested on his throne, seated before his subjects.

"I want so many things," Darius replied, shrugging. Only five feet separated them now. "Though I might've grown greedy over these last few weeks. But since I'd waited a thousand years for my revenge against my dearest brother, I figured I could wait just a little bit longer to have the throne *and* the one who calls to me from across the sea." He sighed dramatically. "And how she calls! I swear, she's practically screaming my name, though she may not know *why*. Being the benevolent god I am, I plan to remedy that soon, and then she'll know my truth. *Her* truth."

Of course. Darius wanted Margrete. He'd made his intentions clear the night of the captain's attack when he'd looked at her with longing just before sending Bash barreling below the waves. That was the emotion Bash had tried to forget—the *desire* in Darius's eyes.

"That'll never happen," he snapped, moving in a semi-circle around his foe. "She's not calling to you, and you won't get anywhere near her to explain your so-called truth." Lies were the only language Darius spoke. "And her power is her own, Darius, and not yours to take. Malum made sure of that."

Darius snickered once more, beginning to mirror his movements, his cruel smile never falling. "I don't need to take it from her, not when she'll willingly *share*."

Now it was Bash's turn to laugh. Margrete was his guiding light. She'd rather die than allow a corrupt god to use her. To trap her like her father had for most of her life.

"I'm amused you find that statement humorous, king." A vein in Darius's forehead throbbed, his nose crinkling with disgust. He took a giant step into Bash's space. He held his ground with effort, despising how he had to tilt his head up to meet the god's face. "I wonder if you'll be laughing when you lay dying in a pool of your own blood, a dagger in the hands of the woman you love the most."

"Delusional," Bash ground out. "Margrete would never hurt me."

"Maybe not the Margrete you know," Darius replied, cocking his head and tsking. His confidence made Bash's fists clench. "But soon, very soon actually, your beloved will undergo the same trials my brother and I endured. Unfortunately, the trials affect everyone on the island, though I don't care if the others succeed or if they all die in the process." He grinned, his canines poking into his bottom lip.

Bash curled his hands even tighter, craving the blood of the god who taunted him. Darius appeared to sense his swelling rage. His eyes flitted to Bash's clenched hands with a grin.

"We'll have to agree to disagree on the outcome," Bash said, uncurling his fingers, struggling to regain his calm. Darius's mask slipped just the slightest. His left eye twitched. "You don't know how strong Margrete is, and I can't wait for her to destroy you."

If anyone could do it, it was Margrete.

She might not know how to use her new powers, but under pressure, she thought quickly on her feet. Bash felt confident in her ability to protect, especially if someone she loved was at risk.

"I suppose we'll find out soon," Darius said, nostrils flaring. He hadn't moved from where he hovered over Bash, who kept himself in place by a fraying thread of control. "In the meantime, enjoy the trials. The second one is my personal favorite." He scanned Bash with disdain. "Though it already appears as if you're succumbing to madness."

Bash sucked in a breath through his teeth. He couldn't touch the god, not in this dream world. Trying to attack would only show his weakness.

Bash didn't answer, but he did smile, doing his best to unnerve the God of the Sea. A fucking *god*. He never would've thought he'd ever go against a divine entity and *taunt* him.

Love made him reckless. It also made him stronger than any heartless immortal.

"Oh, I cannot wait to watch as she turns you to ash," Darius said, dipping his head in farewell, his sea-colored eyes growing muddled. He walked backward, toward the trees, and out of range of Bash's fury. "Farewell for now, king."

Bash watched stoically as the God of the Sea melded into the shadows, the night eating him alive.

CHAPTER TWENTY

MARGRETE

MARGRETE HELD BAY ALL NIGHT. THE WARRIOR MIGHT NOT HAVE realized it, but tears wet his cheeks as he slept. As she wiped them away, she wondered what he'd endured when the hallucinogenic fog had fallen across his mind.

He hadn't asked her for the details of her own nightmare, and she wouldn't push him for answers he wasn't ready to give. Gods knew she still reeled from the sensation of being confined in that box, sinking into the waves and slowly drowning.

It all felt so real.

When the hesitant sun rose the following dawn, Margrete's determination to find Bash only grew. Still, their first priority was to find fresh water today. Two days without it had made them weak, and Margrete licked her chapped lips at the mere thought of quenching her thirst. It had gotten to the point where it hurt to swallow. If the trials were real, as she suspected, they wouldn't stand a chance if they could hardly move.

"Morning," Bay croaked, rising to his elbows. He stared down at her as she lay upon his folded-up jacket. He'd insisted last night that she lay on it, practically shoving it beneath her head when she started to refuse. Her friend was stubborn—a trait she loved.

Margrete gave Bay a solemn smile. "We need water," she said, stating the obvious. Bay only nodded, likely avoiding the struggle to speak. Dark circles bruised the skin below his eyes, and his lips twisted in a grimace. She could tell it took effort for him to hold himself up.

"We'll head north," Bay finally grated out, tilting his chin in that direction. "There has to be a stream somewhere nearby. We walked all day yesterday."

They began the trek right after they burned Jace's body. Azantian custom dictated the dead be sent out to sea on a raft of solanthium blooms, and an archer would shoot a flaming arrow, igniting the body and the craft of flowers.

They'd settled on using only the flames. Carrying his body back to the coast while dehydrated would kill them all.

Mila hadn't met Margrete's eyes since yesterday. Margrete spotted the redhead across their camp curled next to Grant, who gently rubbed her back. His eyes held the weight of a parent watching their child endure heartbreak.

Margrete hastily glanced away.

"She doesn't blame you." Bay rose to his feet. "Grief can turn even the softest heart to steel. Give her time."

Margrete understood the situation well enough. She gave Bay an understanding nod and stood, wiping the dirt from her clothes. Her shirt had several tears in it, and she scented the dried blood marring her skin where the branches had nicked.

"Ready?" she asked Bay, ignoring his words. There was nothing else to say on the matter, and wallowing in pity would do nothing. She would gain the young woman's trust another way.

Bay dipped his chin before gently waking the rest of the crew. Eight of them remained.

When everyone stood in a semi-circle around them, Bay delivered instructions to head north. Margrete could tell their faith had wavered overnight, and even Jonah's usual optimism had dulled, the boy's lips curled down in a heavy frown.

Atlas, who typically voiced her opinion, kept quiet. If someone as fearsome as Atlas had been stunned into silence after yesterday, then the warrior's vision must have been vicious. It was the first time Margrete saw her as human—well, almost human, considering her heritage.

"I chose you for our journey because you lot are the best of the best," Bay intoned, his voice rising. She imagined it hurt. "You're also Azantians, and we don't fall easily. We are the raging of the wind and the salt in the sea. The strength of the waves." The crew never lowered their gazes. They held onto his every word like a lifeline. "If I didn't believe in your abilities, in your capability to overcome the greatest of obstacles, you wouldn't be standing here now. Today we find water. Replenish ourselves." Bay's voice cracked slightly, but he continued. "And then we find our lost king. Get off this cursed island and slay the beasts that escaped our grasp. We're warriors, and warriors do not bow before anyone but the God of Death."

The God of Death: the faceless entity every soul met at the end of their life. He didn't have a name, not like the rest of the immortals, but Margrete suspected that had more to do with human superstition than anything else.

Even while he'd invoked the God of Death's title, the crew dutifully bobbed their heads in agreement. The weight that had been on Margrete's shoulders lessened, and even the air itself felt lighter, as if Bay's speech had chased away the thick mist that cloaked this place. He was the kind of person who inspired hope.

When Bay took the lead and brought them deeper into the woods, Margrete assumed her position from the day before, trailing after the final crew member. She scanned the trees as they trudged through the dense underbrush, noting how the leaves had slowly begun to change. From a brittle black, they morphed into a muted red the farther they went. She didn't wish to place any significance on the transition, but it was hard not to.

Three torturous hours later, Margrete's heightened hearing picked up the most beautiful of sounds.

Rushing water.

Bay must've heard it at the same time, because he took off in an uneven sprint. Even his Azantian body suffered, but the sound of their salvation sent him stumbling ahead, the crew at his back.

Margrete rushed after, brushing aside spindly branches and reddened leaves. She ducked beneath a low-hanging limb, and when she rose, her mouth parted in shock. Before them lay the most magnificent sight she'd ever seen.

Three separate streams flowed from different directions to join together in one single pool of the clearest blue. In the very center rested a small island of rock, the dark gray surface polished and slicked with water.

"Thank the gods," Jonah murmured ahead of her. "I'd thought we'd all die from thirst. Not how I planned on going, that's for sure." The lad scrambled for the edge of the pool. He dunked his entire head under before whipping it back and shaking the drops from his hair. An enthusiastic grin brightened his face. Margrete couldn't hide her smile.

As one, they rushed to the edge and followed the young sailor's lead. Margrete cupped her hands and drank, forcing herself to take it slowly. She splashed her face with the cool water, sighing in relief when it dripped down her chin and to her neck and chest.

They'd survive another day.

Mila and Grant stood farther down the bank, conversing in hushed tones as they, too, drank and washed their arms and faces free of dirt. Margrete caught Mila's heated stare. The redhead broke contact with a scowl, turning back to her father.

She could be as mad as she liked. Margrete was simply thankful they'd reached this oasis when they did. Another hour, and she wouldn't have been sure she'd have the strength to continue.

Margrete had just finished washing her face when she saw it. Metal catching light.

Her heart plummeted in her chest.

There, on the polished stone island, in the center of the converging streams, the sun broke free from the clouds to shine upon a single coin. She brought her hands to her side, her breath hitching.

The second coin. *The second trial.*

Bay dropped into a crouch at her side, following her stare.

He cursed. "We don't have to touch it," he said. "We don't go anywhere near that thing."

Margrete shuddered. It took everything she had to break free from the small island and turn to her friend, who still glared at the ominous coin with a furrowed brow. Seconds later, the clouds swept back into place and the metal dulled, Surria's token blending back into the stone.

"I agree," she said, though her stomach coiled into knots. "We don't touch it."

Bay stood and offered her a hand, helping her rise. "We should fill the few canteens we have with water and head back to the beach. See if there's any trace of Bash there. Either way"—he clutched her hand and entwined their fingers—"we have to leave. I've never felt something this powerful, this dark—"

A great splash sounded.

Bay and Margrete whipped around just in time to see a massive tentacle rise from the water and drop to the surface with a resounding flop. Water drenched the crew as they gaped onshore, those not in shock backing away from the pool.

Margrete's chest filled with heat, and power snaked around her insides like a living thing. The blistering magic stretched down her arms and torso, moving to reach her feet, and soon she felt it everywhere, all at once, in one nauseating rush.

The force of it nearly had her doubling over. She gritted her teeth, forcing her eyes to stay open, forcing herself to watch as the monster added another tentacle to the air. When he brought them both down, the crew couldn't move fast enough to avoid the shattering blast.

The water struck them all, and Margrete turned her head to deflect most of it. The rest of her stung from the impact, even through her clothes.

"Get away! Get back!" Bay shouted, his alarm slipping past his calm façade.

They all scrambled to the woods, sprinting away from whatever the hell that thing was. Atlas had to grab hold of a young woman in apparent shock. Margrete believed her name was Dani. Her twin, Jacks, helped the blonde warrior carry his sister out of harm's way.

Margrete waited as the crew rushed past her, counting them as they passed.

Seven.

Including herself, she counted only seven.

Margrete gazed at the pool as the beast rose high into the air, three tentacled arms supporting its bulbous head. Spiked scales of deep green and blue glimmered threateningly in the soft light, the tips of each sharper than a blade. If it possessed a mouth, she couldn't make out its opening, all the scales flowing seamlessly together. It turned her way, its arms moving fluidly beneath it.

Their eyes met.

Shining orbs of yellow held and demanded her attention. They were lifeless, looking more like gems than actual eyes, but it didn't glance away, not as it raised one of its tentacles from below...lifting a petite body inches from its face.

She saw the red hair first.

Mila.

The tentacle that held her gripped her limp body tightly, and the tip of the monster's arm coiled around to stroke the sailor's wan face.

Margrete lunged. She didn't think of the consequences of her haste, didn't pause to consider that she had only Adrian's dagger at her thigh and magic she didn't know how to command. She might very well drown or be squeezed to death, but she knew one thing—she couldn't sit around and watch.

The water parted as Margrete dove headfirst, its coldness seeping into her every pore. She opened her eyes, the fire in her chest swelling into a ravishing blaze. Just as she had when Darius sent Bash underwater months ago, she opened her mouth and breathed in the dense water like air.

It went down her throat and into her lungs, filling her so completely she thought she'd burst. Margrete jerked to a stop, mid-stroke, as her body gave a forceful shudder. A spark of light blinded her before fading altogether.

Margrete gasped, and more water filled her mouth.

She was alive. For how much longer, she didn't know.

Not focusing on what packed her lungs, or the *how* of it all, she continued her swim, teeth bared, thrusting toward the creature with near-feral intent.

Below the surface, long tentacles swirled, the movement keeping its upper body afloat. Mila was still thankfully being held above the water.

Reaching for her dagger, Margrete closed the distance between herself and the creature's first limb. Without hesitation, she brought the blade to its thick, scaled skin and sliced, drawing a hint of bluish-green blood. It saturated the water and clouded her sight, but she guided her arm up and then down, piercing its hide for a second time.

A reverberating growl shook the pool, and Malum's power quivered. That couldn't be a good sign.

Margrete stabbed the beast once more before it reacted, before its wounded tentacle reached for her. She dove, narrowly avoiding its grasp by inches. It came after her again. She dodged the assault, but her power flickered, slowly weakening. She had been a fool not to practice more on Azantian. Raising the waves for an hour a day would not help her best this creature.

The blade in her hand penetrated the monster once more, and she gritted her teeth as she shoved the knife in deeper, sawing through the toughened skin. The howling continued, and the tentacle jerked back. Margrete didn't let it go. With her hand clutching her weapon, she snaked her arm around its thick trunk, holding on as the beast swung her from side to side like a rag doll, hoping to dislodge her.

Not today.

Margrete tightened her hold, and all the while her blade cut deeper into the leg. The more the beast thrashed, the further the knife went, and soon the bottom half of its limb snapped, hanging uselessly off a band of muscle.

She smiled, and the power in her chest seemed to smile as well.

There you are. Malum's essence reacted to destruction, to the adrenaline of triumph, and as she completely hacked off the limb, her magic grew.

She seized its other leg, about to dig her knife in, when the beast lunged. In a blink, the creature was beneath the surface, Mila still wrapped in its free tentacle. Her eyes were wide with fear.

Azantians could hold their breath for much longer than the average human, but if Mila had been injured, Margrete wasn't certain she'd last as long. She suspected she had about five minutes...five measly minutes to slay this creature and save Mila.

Malum's power burned with the challenge. Searing hot energy raced down to graze her every inch, and Margrete's body stiffened. Strength, the likes of which she'd never felt, had her moving, swimming around the creature before it had a chance to catch her.

The magic flowing through her oversensitive body was addicting. Under its spell, she saw herself in a new light—strong and formidable. A woman with the capability to be feared. A warrior.

Margrete swam in circles, evading the beast's reach, tiring it out. One minute remained, and Mila's eyes shuddered as her chest suddenly went still.

With a curse, Margrete kicked upward, directly into the belly of the beast. A guttural roar shook the waters as she drove the knife deep into its soft underbelly, twisting the blade before pulling away to stab it again.

Margrete wasn't sure how many times she pierced its hide, how many times she brought her arm back and thrust the knife into it, but eventually, she saw nothing but blueish green. She breathed its blood in, tasted it in her mouth. Rotten and musky. Old and bitter.

Its life essence became her entire world, and she savored it, delighting in the creature's sluggish movements. How death slowly dug its claws into the beast's heart and squeezed.

Margrete stabbed its belly one last time.

The energy that comprised the monster was absent, its buzzing life force gone.

The tentacle holding Mila captive unfurled, her body left to descend deeper into the abyss, her arms outstretched above her head. Margrete slipped her blade back into its sheath and swam toward the helpless Azantian, her red hair a beacon in the growing dark.

Come on, Margrete coaxed, her adrenaline slipping along with the hold on her power. Now that she'd slayed the beast, Malum's essence had calmed, and she couldn't seem to wield it as she had moments ago.

She reached out for Mila, her teeth clenched so hard she feared they'd crack. The possibility of losing her was unfathomable. There had been too much death, too much despair, and Margrete knew if she didn't return to the surface with the Mila in her arms, then the rest of the crew would lose what little faith they had left.

When precious seconds ticked by, Margrete gave a final kick and wrapped her fingers around Mila's wrist. She didn't look down at the woman's face, she simply held on tightly and kicked up, the weak sunlight breaking through the top of the pool.

The water in her lungs burned, and Margrete sputtered, her head spinning.

Please be okay, she pleaded with no one and nothing. *Please live.*

Before the black spots could pull her under, Margrete broke free, shattering the surface with a choked gasp. The water she'd inhaled trickled out from her lungs as she adjusted to the air, and she wheezed as it throttled her.

Mila bobbed in the water at her side, unmoving and pale. With the world tilting and dizziness shifting her sight upside-down, Margrete swam, the sailor in tow. Shouts sounded, Bay's familiar call reaching her ears.

She barely felt him as he met her halfway, helping her haul Mila back to shore. More cries filled the air, and then a heavy hand thwacked her back as she struggled to lift off her hands and knees. Margrete raised her head and caught Grant's eye, thanking him. He gave her one last hit, and she heaved the rest of the water up and out.

"Give me some room!" Bay shouted, and Margrete crawled to where her friend thrust against Mila's chest. Her lips were parted, turning a shade of blue. She could do nothing but watch as Bay pounded on Mila's chest, just as she had Jace's the day before. This island worked to kill them off one by one, and the twisted irony of taking the two lovers first felt cruel.

Atlas hovered nearby, her lips drawn into a thin line. "Bay, I don't think—"

"Quiet!" Bay cut her off without a look.

He continued to pound on Mila's petite body, willing the life back to her lungs, attempting to get her heart thumping. Margrete reached out, grasping Mila's hand. She held her cold fingers as a warm tear trailed down her cheek. It dripped onto Mila's thigh.

Margrete could've sworn she saw a flash of light as her tear seeped into Mila's drenched clothes. She sucked in a quivering breath, her grip on the girl's hand strong enough to bruise.

Live, she thought, repeating the single word over and over. Mila had so many years ahead of her yet, so many days of grief and happiness and adventure left. She was too young to die in such a cruel place.

Live, gods damn it!

Bay jolted backward at the same time Mila's eyes opened. The girl lurched to the side, water gushing from her mouth in a seemingly never-ending stream, and Margrete reached over to pat her back.

Cheers rose up as the crew howled with joy, smiling and laughing in the face of near death. She'd survived, against all odds. She fucking fought.

Margrete smiled along with them, her limbs shaking from the leftover adrenaline. Some of them called her name, others chanted it. She fell to the ground, on her hands and knees, maniacal laughter borne of relief slipping past her lips. She'd done it, used her power to save someone. The joy she felt warmed her body, chasing away the chill. It made her feel useful, *worthy* of such a gift.

She wasn't sure if her glowing tear had saved her or if she'd simply rescued Mila in the nick of time. Either way, she was alive, and Margrete hadn't failed yet another person.

"Um, Margrete." Bay's voice cut through the celebrating crew, the weight of it sending ice into her veins. Slowly, cautiously, Margrete lifted her head.

Mila began to make choking sounds again, her frame shaking so violently, Grant had to rush over and hold her steady so she didn't hurt herself.

"Get it out," he urged, his eyes wide with panic. "Come on, sweetheart. Don't give up on me yet." His grip on her shoulder tightened visibly, the color bleaching from his skin.

Mila gave one final heave.

Water flowed from her lips...along with a silver coin. It spun before falling on its side, two bold words clearly visible.

Trust Nothing.

CHAPTER TWENTY-ONE

BASH

BASH SPENT THE NEXT DAY TRAVELING DEEPER INTO THE FOREST. His black hair and nails had remained the same, and the scales winding around his throat began to inch gradually down to his torso.

He did his best to ignore it all.

Focus on the things you can change, Adrian always said. *Holding onto the impossible is like clutching rocks and diving into the sea, hoping to float.*

His oldest and truest friend had a point. Bash missed him and his pacifying presence. He hadn't wanted to leave him on Azantian, but he was glad he had. Adrian might not have survived the wreck. Bash didn't even know if the rest of the crew lived or what horrors they endured. And Margrete might be alone, facing gods knew what kind of savage monsters—

No. He wouldn't even go down that path. Margrete could defend herself, and if she was with Bay or his men, they'd all make it out alive.

That didn't mean he wasn't anxious to get to her. Bash wouldn't be able to rest until he saw Margrete in the flesh and breathing with his own eyes.

At one point on his dismal journey, Bash thought he'd heard a shriek, a human one at that. It had come from the northeast, and he quickened his pace, his thoughts going straight to Margrete. The scream sounded female, but that might've been his mind playing tricks on him.

By midday, he'd come upon a stream and drank his fill. The water on this island tasted different, off, but it was cold and quenched his thirst. He couldn't afford to overthink something as simple as the water.

Bash heard no more screams as he trekked through the thicket, though he never ceased his ruthless pace. There had to be *somebody* out there, surely. He only hoped he wouldn't find Darius waiting for him instead. The god hadn't left his thoughts since his dream the night before.

Darius desired both Margrete *and* her power. For all he knew, Darius could have taken her by surprise and had his hands on her at this very moment, and Bash would be far too late to aid her. That thought alone gutted him at the same time it infuriated him, sending shock waves of icy rage down his spine. His wrath was so potent, he felt it shudder with every step.

By nightfall, he found shelter in a cave, if it could even be called that. Its length matched his height. Bash curled up around the fire he'd built, watching the flames dance along the edges of the stone. It felt like months since he'd last seen Margrete, and yet he knew it could only have been days.

Sleep was difficult to come by without her in his arms. Before she came into his life, insomnia had plagued him for decades, and only when he slept beside her did he find any semblance of peace. Her steady breathing soothed him, and her warm skin pressed against his chest kept his mind from wandering to places it shouldn't. He'd give anything to hold her right now.

Bash sighed, his gaze drifting to his hands. They were a constant reminder of the disease he sensed spreading through his veins.

There you are, my son.

Had the nymera's words been a turn of phrase? Or had she meant it in the literal sense? Bash grumbled, his chest trembling with frustration. His nails appeared longer than they had this morning, resembling the nymera's claws. The cursed woman in white.

He picked at them with his blade.

That monster had to have been lying. This island's sole purpose seemed to work to deceive. Yet Bash had also been visited by Darius, and that had felt real as well, so he didn't know where the boundary between truth and fantasy lay.

A twig snapped somewhere in the distance.

Bash shot upright, his dagger gripped tightly in his hand.

Ears perked, he listened, though the winds made it difficult to hear much else besides the rustling of the leaves. Any form of animal could call this place home, and Bash suspected the creatures he might encounter wouldn't resemble anything he'd read about in his books.

Another thing he missed—a time when his books of myth and legends were only impossible stories that didn't affect him. He'd grown up reading about the sea's children, about Surria, the Goddess of Wind and Sky, and her two sons. It had been a pastime of his, scouring the pages describing Charion's insatiable rage. He reread accounts of lost sailors who found their way home because of the moon goddess Selene's guiding whispers. At the time, they seemed more fiction than living beings. He missed his ignorance.

Bash cringed as another twig cracked.

Something was here, and it was close.

His mouth parted, ready to demand who dared come near, but he tampered down the instinct. If Darius believed he could sneak up on him, then he was sorely mistaken.

Another snap and then—

Bash dropped his knife.

The blade fell to the ground, the sound muffled in his ringing ears. He shot to his feet, and he didn't stop moving.

"Margrete!" He rushed to her, picking her up and off her feet. Joy spread through him as he spun her around and around, his hold likely too tight. But he couldn't control it. He thought he'd lost her and now she was here, right in front of him, in his arms. Hadn't he just wished for that very thing?

"Bash!" She breathed his name, the sound better than any song or melody. "I found you." Bash drew back just enough to peer into her blue eyes, a few tears tracking down her rosy cheeks. "When we didn't find you with the others, I thought the worst." Her voice cracked, and more tears fell. He might've shed a couple himself. He'd never felt such palpable relief.

Words escaped him entirely, but he leaned down, kissing her lips and relaying his love in another way. They felt as he'd remembered, so soft, so plush, and made for kissing him. He brought his hand to the nape of her neck and gripped the strands, pulling her impossibly close, crushing her against him. He needed to feel every inch of her, touch her, have her warmth wash across his body like the morning sun.

Margrete wound an arm around his torso as she held him firm, her grip so much stronger than he remembered.

"Princess," he gasped when he finally pulled away. She panted for air, her eyes hooded. "Gods, I've missed you."

He reached out to trace the curve of her cheek, his touch featherlight, completely opposite from how he'd handled her seconds ago. She felt so precious in his hold, so brilliant and bright and utterly *his*.

Bash knew just how damned lucky he was.

"I missed you too," she murmured, resting her head against his. Their noses touched. "I searched for you while the others slept. I knew you were close, felt your presence."

He chuckled, the noise joyous. "You shouldn't have done that, but I'm glad you did," he said, still reeling. "Where is the camp? Is it far?"

Margrete shook her head. "No, not at all." Her face lit up as she smiled. Bash's heart thumped wildly. "It's about ten minutes north. I can take you there now."

Bash nodded excitedly, ready to reunite with his crew, with Bay. And with Margrete in his sights, he felt like himself again, a king who could defeat any obstacle, his partner at his side.

"Come on then," she said, grabbing both his hands. Her smile was bright and wide, and she didn't waste a second before pulling him through the trees, her steps sure and steady. He followed, smiling at her back. Bash felt drunk off her presence, intoxicated by her nearness.

He had lied to himself earlier—he wasn't sure if he'd ever see her again.

But now...now he allowed himself the hope he'd been denied.

"Hurry!" she urged, her voice coming out shrill. Bash's brows drew together, but he didn't drop her hand.

Margrete's hair floated behind her as she ran, the chocolate curls silken and shining in the hazy moonlight. He wondered how she appeared so clean after days stranded on an island. And while she looked beautiful, Bash looked—

Wait.

Bash pulled gently on her hand, but she didn't stop. Margrete dragged him ahead, her grip becoming punishing.

"Just through here," she said as they passed two curving trees. Their branches were weighed down by deep red leaves, forcing him to bend his head to slip by.

Bash tugged on her hand again once they'd cleared the prickly trees.

"Margrete, wait. Stop for a moment." Bash's heart thundered, and his entire body felt cold. "Please, just stop."

She ignored him, laughing instead. "Such a worrier. I promise, just a few more seconds..."

Bash yanked hard, forcing her to stop this time. She bumped into his chest. Twisting around, she met his heavy gaze.

The woman in front of him looked like his Margrete, sounded like her, even smelled of her lavender perfume. But...

"Notice anything different, princess?" he asked, cocking his head.

She might look and sound like his Margrete, but the woman he knew and loved wouldn't have gone bolting into the woods after seeing his new face. She'd make them sit down and talk about what happened. Margrete was exceptionally stubborn in that regard, though he secretly enjoyed her concern. This creature—Bash released her hand and stepped back—didn't ask about his scales, his nails, his newly darkened hair.

She just stared at him blankly, no spark behind her eyes. No *fire*.

"Who are you?"

Bash reached for his dagger. His hand met only air.

A flash of silver caught his eyes, and Margrete—or the *thing* masquerading as her—drew *his* blade from behind her back.

"Looking for this?" she asked, smiling.

Bash's stomach dropped.

"Want to come here and get it?" She waved it around innocently, backing away slowly. Bash took a step, his jaw clenched tight. "Come on, take it from me," she teased, her voice turning almost cruel. Sharp and hard. It reminded him of another's voice, though he couldn't place it.

"I asked who you are," he repeated, frustration simmering in his chest. "Tell me."

His demand felt weak. Even though he knew this wasn't Margrete, his daring princess, she wore her face, and he was so eager to believe it truly belonged to her.

"Don't be silly," she replied, continuing to retreat. Bash followed. "What's gotten into you? We're almost to the camp, and I can explain everything there. Adrian has been asking about you nonstop."

Bash stopped altogether.

"Adrian wasn't on the *Phaedra*."

There was no more room for doubt.

The woman who wore Margrete's face sighed dramatically as her features turned hard.

"Oops." She chuckled. "You *have* been thinking about Adrian a lot."

How did she know what he thought about?

Bash clenched his hands into fists at his side. He wished he held his dagger, a weapon, *anything* to defend himself. This was no human.

"Well, that was entirely my fault." She waved a carefree hand in the air. "A little slip of the tongue, unfortunately." The woman tsked and stepped to the side in a blur of limbs and a flash of vibrant red hair. The strands flickered back to brown seconds later, just as the woods began to shift and turn and waver all around him. Bash stumbled in place, feeling off-balance. "W-what's happening?"

"Just a few more steps, my king." More laughter followed, the kind that reminded him of nails dragging across glass. "One. More. Step."

Bash hadn't realized he'd taken a step in his disoriented state.

He fought to keep his limbs planted firmly on the ground.

"Need some help?" Margrete's voice asked, though it grew deeper, morphing into a hollow echo.

Bash shook his head and clutched at his temples. He couldn't see straight, and every time he thought he glimpsed the woman, she vanished. Bash reached out, hoping to grasp a nearby tree, hoping to steady himself—

He took a step...

His foot met open air.

The forest faded, replaced by cliffs and spiked rocks. Bash scrambled to hold on to something, *anything*, but it was already too late.

"Sweet dreams, king."

Bash plunged headfirst over the side of the cliff.

CHAPTER TWENTY-TWO

MARGRETE

*T*RUST *N*OTHING.

A crudely etched snake encircled the inscription, its forked tongue slithering out to touch the *T*. Like the last coin, this one had a number on its other face. A simple and unadorned 2.

Margrete flipped the glowing coin between her fingers, scowling. The cursed thing had found them after all, and through the most horrific of ways. How in the living hell it got stuck *inside* Mila's throat to begin with remained a mystery. One they likely wouldn't get an answer for.

While she scrutinized the coin for the thousandth time, the others sat silently around the fire they'd constructed, staring blankly ahead. Grant had fashioned a spear with his dagger shortly after Mila's rescue, and the two lean fish cooking over the flames had been thanks to him.

Atlas was the only one who wasn't glassy-eyed. She kept sneaking uncharacteristically shy glances at Dani, who was utterly oblivious to her attentions. Margrete didn't think she'd ever heard her speak. Or her twin brother, for that matter. They tended to keep to themselves.

Even though her stomach grumbled and hunger ate away at her insides, the thought of eating made her nauseous. Or maybe she was simply nauseous because she *hadn't* eaten. She couldn't think straight anymore.

"What do you think it means?" Bay asked, nudging her with his elbow. He'd been quiet since Mila spewed the ancient coin, vomiting it up along with the rest of the water in her lungs. Ignoring the trials wasn't an option it seemed. Surria's coins would always find them.

"I think we're in for a long night," Margrete said quietly, curling her fingers around the cold metal. It felt heavier than the first.

Bay leaned his head on her shoulder. She nuzzled her cheek against him, sighing.

"We'll all take turns keeping watch. Though I doubt that'll do us much good." Bay lifted his head from her cheek. She noted how pale his skin had turned, and the circles below his eyes had gotten worse.

"Was the first trial...are you all right?" She promised she wouldn't push, that she wouldn't ask for details, but she had to know how he was doing. Bay's entire posture drooped at the question.

"I saw Adrian's corpse. It was burned. Charred." Margrete swallowed hard, trying not to flinch. "The Azantian palace had been burned down. I pulled him out, but it was too late. He was dead."

"Our worst nightmares," she said, watching the fire. They kept their voices low, mindful of the others.

"Yeah, seeing the other half of my soul burn to a crisp would top the nightmare list." Bay tried to chuckle. It was horribly weak.

"Why fire?" Margrete pressed. She could understand Adrian's death, but the fire seemed odd. Or at least, it seemed specific enough to stand out.

"I'm not sure, but I can't help but feel like I'm forgetting something," he said. "It all happened in a blur, but I swear there's a piece to the puzzle that I'm missing." Bay drew away to look into her eyes. "What did you dream of?"

Margrete stiffened. "I dreamed of drowning in the box my father used to put me inside."

Gods, even thinking about it made her tremble. She'd managed to escape the nightmare's hold, but just barely. She wished she was stronger.

Bay grasped both of her hands in one of his. His weight steadied the shaking. "You broke free, Margrete. You wouldn't be here if you hadn't triumphed over his cruelty. His torture. You're stronger than you think," he said softly, seeming to read her mind. He rested his head back on her shoulder.

Margrete held him, relaying her silent thanks. If she'd had a friend like Bay back home in Prias, she might've escaped her father long ago. She'd never had someone to share her innermost secrets with before, and she realized why her father had secluded her, why he made it all but impossible for others to get close. Love gave her strength, and he'd worked tirelessly to make her believe she was weak.

Love could be a weapon all on its own.

As it so often did, her mind returned to Bash.

"I miss him," she whispered, watching as the flames sparked and popped. It felt silly to say out loud given all they'd endured, and all they were yet to face. Still, if anyone understood, it'd be Bay.

"We'll find him. Bash is more stubborn than you, which is saying a lot," he said with a cautious smile. "And besides, you would've sensed something, right? If Bash had..." He couldn't say the words, but she knew what he meant.

Margrete nodded. "I would've felt it, just as I had before when I lost him."

"So that means he's out here, likely looking for us," Bay said firmly. "I'm not one for faith, but love has a way of making me a believer. As horribly sentimental as that sounds."

"I like it when you're horribly sentimental," she whispered, bringing her hand to his hair and rubbing at his scalp. "And thank you for telling me," she murmured. About his greatest fear.

"You're welcome, Margrete. Thank you for trusting me as well."

A hush settled as Margrete massaged Bay's head, playing with the short strands. The warrior fell asleep there, right against her shoulder, and Margrete took first watch.

She stared out into the night, unable to help but feel it was staring right back at her.

MARGRETE DREAMED OF AZANTIAN.

She wandered down the shoreline, headed for the Kardias Cave. Bay had shown it to her when she'd first arrived, and it had fascinated her ever since. How could she not be? Below the waters thrashing against the rocky walls were the gates, the ones that had been constructed to imprison the sea's children.

Margrete slipped inside, sighing as darkness washed over her skin. In this dream world, she didn't miss a step, didn't fumble. She knew every rock and crevice and walked with the righteous poise of someone who'd grown up on these shores.

A buzzing had begun to sound, soft at first, like a low humming. The waves drowned most of it, but it grew louder with every step deeper into the cave. By the time she reached the opening where the sea met the yawning mouth, that buzzing was all she could hear.

Margrete's limbs were loose and her pulse steady, which was surprising given the sense of foreboding that flooded her chest right where Malum's power lived. That essence perked up, as though listening to a familiar tune, trying to decipher if it adored or loathed the melody it heard.

"How are you liking my island?"

Margrete jerked around. Emerging from the shadows was a cloaked man towering around seven feet. Pieces of blond hair poked from the sides of his hood, which covered most of his features apart from his proud chin and curving smile.

While she knew deep down none of this was real, she still stepped back and brought her hands out before her, ready to defend herself. The song of the waves continued to play, and somewhere far away, she made out the strings of a melancholy violin.

Cocking his hooded head, the man strode deeper into the cave, situating himself at its very center. Margrete realized then that she'd inadvertently moved against the far wall, her hands flush against one of many hexagonal columns.

She straightened to her full height.

"I'll take your silence as answer enough," the man chuckled. "I didn't particularly enjoy it myself."

His words confirmed everything.

"What do you want? And how are you here? In my dreams?" she asked, boldness hardening her tone. Pride surged within, and in reply her power thrummed.

"To answer your first question, I want many things. Things I hadn't believed I would ever desire again. But I suppose old age makes you realize exactly what you want. What you've been missing for so many centuries."

Margrete pushed off from the wall. Feigning confidence she didn't feel, she walked up to the God of the Sea, stopping three feet away.

"Enough mind games. Enough riddles. Answer the damned question. How are you here?" In her dreams. Trespassing in her most sacred place.

Darius.

He'd threatened her on Azantian. Told her if she didn't come with him, he'd harm Bash. Again.

Was this all his doing? The *Phaedra*'s sinking? The island? Surria's coins?

"I'm mildly wounded you haven't felt me in your dreams before, Margrete. I thought you'd have sensed me months ago."

"*Months.* You've been stalking my dreams for months?" She let out a quivering exhale. "Why?"

If he desired her power, going inside her dreams wouldn't be the way to go about it. He would have better luck searching through ancient books on myths for a clue about how to remove Malum's protective mark.

At the thought, her hand drifted to her tattoo. Instantly, a fragile calm swept across her.

Darius smiled, the curve of his mouth wicked. "I could lie to you about why I snuck into your dreams, but truthfully, my actions have been entirely selfish. A way to...understand."

"Understand *what?*" Frustration bubbled to the surface.

Slowly, Darius lifted his hands, reaching for his hood. "I wished to understand you and what you've become," he replied coolly. His fingers played with the hem of the material, as if he was debating whether or not to reveal his true face. Margrete was tempted to rip it off.

She ignored his words and narrowed her eyes. There was no way his reasons had been that simple.

"Too afraid to show me the monster lurking behind the mask?" she asked, doing what little she could to unnerve him. In truth, his very presence always managed to turn her world upside-down. And deep down, she knew he wouldn't do anything to physically harm her. He could've hurt her a thousand times over, even with Malum's protective mark, but he hadn't. The question was why.

Darius's fingers gripped the cloth. "I'm far from afraid. In fact, I've been wanting to show you."

He flipped the hood down in a blur, and the air grew heavy.

"You're one of the few who have seen me. The real me."

Gods above and below. Darius was...breathtaking. Breathtaking in a purely devastating way. He was all sharp angles and cutting cheekbones, a strong jaw, and full, rosy lips. Such a cold stare, even with eyes that rivaled the beauty of the sea. Blues and verdant greens surrounded his pupils, and slivers of gold sparked in his irises. They were the kind of eyes one could lose oneself in forever.

Or drown in.

Margrete bit the inside of her cheek, willing her gaze to break.

"I must say, your reaction hasn't disappointed." One corner of his mouth quirked up, and for the briefest of seconds, his eyes turned soft. "For a thousand years I've worn the shells of strangers, forced to survive as a mortal. But now"—he stepped closer, close enough where she could feel his breath fan across her cheeks—"I don't have to hide any longer."

"Should I feel honored?" she asked, refusing to back away. That's what he would want. For her to cower. "I don't care what you look like, Darius. I want to know why the hell we ended up here. On this island."

What would he gain from all of this?

"You have no idea what you are." He sighed. "And I wish to remedy that, once and for all. This island reveals much, and while I despise it—likely as much as you do—it is a necessary evil."

"I know what I'm *not*," she spat. "And I am tired of being a pawn in whatever twisted game you're playing."

Darius circled her. "You're no pawn. No, no, no." He shook his head, his blond curls falling into his eyes. "You're so much more precious than that. You have no idea."

"Enlighten me then," she snapped. Again, he spoke in riddles.

"I saw your eyes widen and heard your heart pick up its pace when I lowered my hood. Whether you'll admit it or not, I affect you deeply, not that you could help it. Like calls to like."

He lifted a hand, bringing a lone finger to her face. His icy touch made her flinch, but she ground her teeth and held her breath. Cautiously, he brought his finger down the curve of her cheek and to the underside of her jaw. He tilted her face to meet his.

"You're much braver than I could've ever imagined," he said with pride. "I should never have doubted that you were the one."

"The one?" Something cold and ancient slithered around her throat and squeezed. She felt like she'd been shoved off a cliff and was falling through the air, waiting for the inevitable impact.

Darius sighed and dropped his hand. It twitched at his side. "If you live long enough and complete the third trial, then all will be revealed. Though I suspect you will." He eyed her, lingering on her lips. "You aren't one to give up so easily. A trait I've always admired."

He spoke like he'd known her for years.

Margrete scowled. "I want off this island immediately, and I want to know where Bash is. Now."

She lifted her chin as Darius's stare turned lethal, the blue morphing into steel. At the sound of the king's name, he went stiff.

"The nymeras took Bash for a reason, Margrete," he said softly, like he was speaking to a small child. "They would've killed him immediately if their blood didn't flow through his veins."

Her lips parted. What Darius insinuated wasn't possible. She'd seen the portraits of his parents, dozens of them hanging throughout the palace.

"He's not a—"

"Oh, yes, he most certainly is," Darius said, his voice filled with laughter. "I can't wait until you see him again. What a delicious surprise that will be."

"So, he *is* here."

"I never said he wasn't, Margrete. I haven't once lied to you. Unlike *him*."

The light entering the Kardias Cave flickered, and the walls turned a milky shade of slate. Margrete sensed she didn't have much longer until she woke. Her vision was unraveling.

And because this was a dream and Darius could do nothing to hurt her, Margrete reached out and grabbed his cloak. She yanked him close.

"Tell me where he is, or I swear I'll spend the rest of my days hunting you down. I may be only half-Azantian, but I *do* have the power of your brother inside of me, and it's only a matter of time before I bend it to my will."

Darius's smile stretched impossibly wide. "I'm counting on that, love. I do so enjoy it when you show your teeth."

She thrust him away as he laughed. Her ethereal body tingled, and black wisps of fog rolled to the center of the cave. Darius lifted his brows before bending into a mockery of a bow.

"Until next time," he promised when he rose. "And believe me, I cannot wait for our reunion."

As Darius and the Kardias Cave vanished, another scene shifted into place—the same one she'd seen when Darius appeared on Azantian's shores.

It was of her, staring up into Darius's eyes with profound love, her arms wrapped around his torso. The god leaned down to place a gentle kiss on her brow, his eyes shutting in peaceful bliss. If she was easily fooled, she could imagine it was real.

When Margrete opened her eyes, that image stayed with her,

haunting her long after the sun rose. It didn't help that her arms prickled where the god had touched her in that scene, and no matter how hard she rubbed at her skin, willing away his phantom touch, it remained like a brand.

CHAPTER TWENTY-THREE

BASH

Bash had been dreaming of Margrete when rain splattered onto his forehead.

He shifted to the side and opened his eyes—and nearly hurled himself off the edge of a cliff.

"Fuck!" Bash scrambled away from the perilous drop, his boots sending a few errant pebbles flying over the side and into the bottomless crevasse below. He glimpsed only rock and shadows, the pit seeming to go on forever.

Shit, shit, shit, shit.

His entire body ached as he heaved in the thick air, attempting to pinpoint the last thing he remembered. Bash shut his eyes, though even that seemed to hurt. Last night he'd been hypnotized by the flames, thinking of the life he felt he'd lost when...

A breeze gusted, cooling the sweat on his brow. He sighed, pressing himself further into the stone wall, his ribs on fire. That breeze, which held notes of eucalyptus, also held another distinct scent—a scent he woke up to every day.

Lavender.

Yes. Now he remembered, though he wished he hadn't.

Realization hit him hard, and his head throbbed as fragments of memory assaulted him. He'd seen Margrete, and she'd brought him here before vanishing.

Wait, no, that also wasn't right. Bash concentrated, picking at the pieces of distorted images, sifting through the blurry bits in search of any semblance of truth. Margrete had materialized from the woods, and then they'd run to each other and embraced, and she was so excited to bring him back to camp where he'd see Bay and—

Ah, that's right.

Not Margrete.

She might've been the perfect carbon copy of her, but her lookalike lacked that indescribable spark that his Margrete possessed. He'd been too hopeful to see the truth at first and had allowed himself to be tricked.

Bash's shoulders drooped in defeat. How he wished she would have been real and not another illusion painted by this island of horror.

Fuck this place.

On unsteady limbs, he rose and faced the cliff wall. The climb wasn't long, but it would be less than ideal. Namely, he spotted a few loose footholds that might end in his imminent death.

"Lovely," he bristled, placing his hands on the rocky slab.

He caught sight of his fingertips. Still black. Still frighteningly monstrous.

Bash began his ascent, doing all he could to avoid looking at his hands. Which, not surprisingly, proved impossible.

Thank all the gods there wasn't a mirror readily available. He wasn't a vain man—well, not entirely—but he surmised his reflection wouldn't please him. Mercifully, the scales hadn't reached his face. Yet.

Bash grunted as he lifted another few feet. Typically, he wouldn't feel such exhaustion or lack of focus, but then again, something had happened to him, and he could feel his body changing, almost as if remaking itself.

That particular line of thought wasn't doing him any favors. He had to shut it all down and just *climb*.

Bash gained purchase and used his legs to push himself higher, his fingers desperately grasping the side of the cliff for dear life. A handful of loose pebbles tumbled into his eyes, and he shook his head, blinking away the residual grit they'd left behind.

He pushed ahead. There was no turning back now.

Hoisting himself to another handhold, he realized with nauseating clarity just how much the cliff wall curved precariously inward. He should never have made it to that ledge to begin with. Based on his position and the roughened shelf he'd woken up on, he should've missed it entirely last night when he fell.

Don't focus on that, he chided himself. *Focus on not killing yourself now.*

Good thing Adrian insisted he concentrate his training on upper body strength at least three times a week.

"Shit!"

His damned hand slipped. Debris crumbled from where he'd ripped away a decent chunk of rock. The offending hand dangled at his side.

Sweat lined his brow and dripped down his spine. The breeze turned cold, tickling the dampened skin, and the lavender in the air grew more potent. Or maybe that was his imagination. Gritting his teeth hard enough to hear his entire jaw click, Bash flung his right arm, aiming for a stable hold. With his hands growing clammier by the second, he knew he'd slip soon.

Bash missed his mark. Again he swung his right arm, and again he missed.

He closed his eyes, seeking darkness as he so often did when life grew too...overwhelming. He would venture below the palace to the Adiria Cavern and just curl up and let the silence eat away at his troubles. It wasn't complete darkness he found now, but it centered him.

Bash aimed. He made contact this time, his fingers biting into the stone. He'd fucking done it.

Energy rushed into his bloodstream, and his eyes snapped open. The adrenaline felt cold, sentient, like magic that could affix to a living soul.

It was too much to handle at once, but Bash didn't have a choice.

His mind focused to a painful degree, and his eyes took in the smallest details as he roved over the porous stone. He smelled salt and lavender and blood that wasn't his own in the air. In the back of his head, a small voice whispered that it came from at least three miles inland. North maybe? Sure, his Azantian senses were heightened, but this went beyond his normal capabilities.

And his muscles. They rippled with newfound strength. They didn't burn as he climbed painstakingly to the top. He might as well have been a new man. Not the crumpled-up version of himself that had woken up broken and heartsick.

Bash brought himself to the edge and flung himself onto solid ground with a determined roar. He made it, alive and whole.

Scooting forward, he took a second of reprieve to rest and calm his racing heart before rising to his feet. He scanned the woods.

He noticed the leaves first. Yesterday they'd been black, some red ones mingling with the sea of darkness, but today they were slightly more detailed.

By *slightly*, he meant a lot.

The red leaves he'd spotted were lined in what appeared to be shimmering black ink. Swirls and chaotic lines were drawn on the brittle surface, each leaf different from the last. The designs made absolutely no sense to Bash, yet he couldn't help but reach out to pluck one from a low-hanging branch.

Instantly, the shining black ink faded.

Frowning, Bash tried another one. It, too, lost its wild patterns.

"It happens when you separate them from the island."

Bash spun around.

"Gods, must you continue to do that?" He glared daggers at the creature who'd snuck up on him.

Before him, leaning against the trunk of a gnarled tree, rested the nymera who dared call him *son*. Her pale, almost blue lips twisted into a scowl at his cutting tone, and her too-wide eyes narrowed.

Bash didn't care if she took offense. Maybe that newfound energy of his could aid him in a fight, and he was no stranger to using his fists to ignore his problems.

No one could ever say he was perfect.

"I'm the one who followed you after that wretched creature took you, and it was me who made sure you didn't fall to your death." She crossed her scrawny arms, her white dress flaring at her sides, the wind picking at the hem. Pushing off from the tree, her lithe body glided through the air the way one would move in water.

Bash eyed his new enemy. A nymera could never be trusted.

Swirling at her bare feet were silver and violet clouds. They rolled in from the woods and snaked around her body. The haze seemed to shudder in delight when it touched her skin.

"Dark magic," he spat. Gods, he was sick of dark magic. On top of everything he faced, adding in dark magic was just a hair exasperating.

"Yes. And it saved your life. You're welcome, by the way. If I hadn't been there last night when you allowed yourself to fall prey to an obvious hallucination, that nymph would've stayed to make sure the job was done. Spiteful little things, nymphs." The raven-haired nymera smiled, her canines jutting into her full bottom lip. "That particular one is notoriously deceptive, but thankfully for you, she was called back to her master at sunrise, so you're safe for now."

"Nymph? Aren't those the maidens created by Brielle?"

"The Goddess of the Deep Woods and the Hunt had no hand in making those *things*. Though she's prideful enough to take credit for it, I'm sure."

"Then who?" Bash took a brazen step forward. Five feet separated them. He suspected she could lash out at any time and rob him of his soul. And yet she didn't move an inch.

"Before we continue, I thought it best you have a name by which to call me, seeing as it's impolite that I know yours and you don't know mine."

"I don't care to learn your name, demon. I want answers."

She scoffed, unbothered. "You have your father's manners, I see."

Bash's blood boiled. "He was a good and decent man," he snapped. "You'd know nothing about those traits, would you, soul stealer?"

Her nostrils flared slightly, the only sign his words had hit their mark.

"You know so very little of your own kind, and yet you judge so quickly."

"I am not a nymera."

"Denial isn't a good look on you, my son." She straightened, and the clouds around her legs moved up to touch her hips. Bash inched back when the haze skirting around her frame flitted over to lick at his exposed skin. "Nothing can change the fact that I speak the truth. Whether you believe it or not. But I imagine you've gotten a good look at your face. Your hair. Your nails." Her eyes fell to his blackened fingers. "You call me a soul stealer as if it might offend me, but I do what I have to in order to survive. Just as you must do."

"I would never feed off another in such a way." He shuddered with disgust. "I'd rather die."

Now her smile turned strained. "You *will* die if you don't feed. And feed you must."

His fists trembled as barely concealed rage quaked his frame. He felt so much anger and fire, so much tangible fury, it hurt to breathe. He didn't want to believe her, but he also couldn't deny the obvious, unless...

"And no. I didn't *turn* you into a nymera, if that's what you were about to ask," she said. He *was* about to do just that. "One cannot be changed into one. A nymera is born."

Great. He'd hoped the lore had gotten it wrong, and that somehow this creature had twisted his appearance using dark magic. She reeked of it.

"Minthe," she said, offering a hand. He eyed it skeptically. "My name is Minthe."

"Again, I simply don't care," Bash growled, marching around the nymera and away from her. He had to find Margrete and get off this island. That was his mission. If this woman—no, creature—truly was his mother, he'd deal with that later.

"I can help," she singsonged after him. Bash didn't turn around. "You do realize you're going in the wrong way, right?" His feet stopped moving.

Bash debated facing her again, but he couldn't. That familiarity he sensed whenever he took in her depthless eyes made his skin crawl.

"Take the path on the left," Minthe instructed. "When you hit a stream, follow it until dusk. You'll find your beloved once the moon rises."

On one hand, she could very well be lying and sending him in the wrong direction. On the other, he knew he wouldn't have landed on that ledge in the first place. He should have tumbled off the cliff and to his death. Which meant she had to have been telling the truth about using dark magic to aid him. While he refused to ask *how*, he realized she could've very easily hurt him moments ago. Even now, with his back turned, she could lash out and kill him. Nymeras were supposedly as quick as the lightning that seemed to follow them wherever the horde drifted.

His options were to go right and hope for the best or to listen to the soul eater claiming to be his mother.

Bash hated both options.

He didn't say a word when he veered to the left, not giving her the satisfaction. He could feel Minthe's smile sear into the back of his skull.

Until next time, son.

He shivered as her voice drifted into his ears. "I fucking hope not."

CHAPTER TWENTY-FOUR

MARGRETE

"HAVE YOU BEEN HAVING ANY WEIRD DREAMS?" MARGRETE ASKED Bay during their trek north. They'd been walking all morning and had come across nothing but trees.

"I..." Bay stumbled over a fallen branch. He quickly righted himself, though his jaw clenched. That was answer enough.

"I see," she said. "Me too."

"I keep waiting for the other shoe to drop," Bay whispered, slowing his pace. "I don't think we faced the second trial yet, even though my dream yesterday was less than ideal."

"I dreamed of being buried alive in a coffin of snakes."

Jacks sauntered over to join the conversation, his twin at his side. Margrete hadn't thought she'd been speaking all too loudly, but she'd forgotten about Azantian hearing.

"That might just beat out my dream," Bay mumbled under his breath, shivering.

Dani, Jacks's sister, just hung her head in silence. Margrete wondered what terrors she'd endured while she'd slept. The quieter of the siblings, the black-haired beauty with deep brown skin and sapphire-colored eyes rarely spoke. Her brother seemed to do the talking for them both.

From the corner of her eyes, Margrete saw Atlas's face scrunch with concern. The blonde lowered her gaze back to the ground as if she wasn't secretly listening in on their conversation.

"Are you all right, Dani?" Margrete asked loudly, mainly for Atlas's sake. Dani barely lifted her head before giving her a subtle nod.

"She's not all right," Jacks said for her, swiping a hand through his tight curls. "And I agree. The worst is yet to come."

Atlas tripped over a branch at his words, her stumble catching Dani's attention. She hastily looked away and drifted back to her brother's side.

Jacks's declaration had certainly dampened the mood, and silence descended for the next hour.

With every step, Margrete's sense of foreboding heightened to an impossible degree. The power inside of her refused to show itself, which was altogether maddening. It sank deep below the surface where she couldn't reach it, and when she closed her eyes and sought it out, she found nothing.

So much for progress. She finally thought she'd mastered it yesterday —well, not *mastered,* but gotten a better hold on it. Maybe like the sea her magic hailed from, it couldn't be tamed or called upon at will.

"Slow!" Bay raised a hand, halting his crew. His ears perked up as he listened into the hushed woods. Cautiously, he ambled ahead, pushing aside branches and marching through the dense underbrush. They all waited for his command.

Bay peeked past the leaves and instantly hissed.

That couldn't be good.

"Everyone on their guard," he said, waving them forward. He held back the limbs as Margrete passed, his eyes sharper than any blade.

Margrete came to a halt at the tree line. Before them stood a gaping chasm separated by two cliffs, a wooden bridge strung at either side. It hardly appeared stable enough to *look* at, let alone walk across. Margrete wandered to the edge and peered over. She let out a curse.

The drop had to be more than two hundred feet.

Nestled at the bottom, a narrow stream flowed. She wondered if someone could survive such a fall. She prayed she wouldn't find out.

Margrete turned to the rickety bridge and touched the fraying cords holding it in place. Thin wooden planks led the way to the other side, though there were a few gaps where boards hung from snapped pieces of rope.

"That does *not* look promising," Jonah said. "I'm officially offering to go last." He moved safely away from the edge, bumping into Dani in the process. She shot him a curious look before averting her eyes.

"There has to be another way across," Bay mused, examining the bridge. He brought a hand to his brow, scanning the surrounding wood. The damned cliffs seemed to go on forever. "I say we find another route, because I guarantee that won't hold all of us. Hell, it might not even hold one—"

The crackling of flames halted his words. As one, the crew whipped around, finding the last thing anyone would've ever expected.

Fire and smoke. It came at them from all sides, and inching closer and surrounding them were men. Men made of fire.

"Well, fuck." Jonah stumbled back, his forehead already dampening with sweat.

"My thoughts exactly." Jacks came to his side, reaching for the dagger that would be useless in a fight against flames. The surly lad seemed the type to give it a try nonetheless.

The nightmarish figures advanced.

Were they real? Or was this yet another trick?

The first and second coin clanked in Margrete's pocket as she shifted on her feet. *Trust Nothing*, it had said, and before them appeared the impossible. Something she certainly *shouldn't* trust.

"It has to be a trick of the mind," she said confidently. "The second coin warned as much."

"I can feel the heat from here," Mila snapped, appearing beside Margrete. Her bright red hair matched the flaming creatures cornering them. It was hard to tell, but they appeared to be hovering above the ground, their long legs inches from the black soil.

"They sure look real to me," Jonah murmured, taking a jerky step backward. "And I, for one, don't want to find out."

If Margrete had to venture a guess, the creatures were herding them onto the bridge, where they would surely fall to the rocky crevasse below.

One of the demons sparked white before ushering his faceless army closer. They had to be only ten feet away now. Far too close for her liking, real or not.

Mila glanced behind her. "I say we don't play with literal fire and attempt to cross."

"I second that," Jacks said, his eyes wide with understandable alarm. "You can't stab fire."

Atlas spoke up. "But the bridge won't hold. Both options lead to death."

Now was *not* the time for Atlas's brutal honesty.

Bay swiveled between the fire creatures and the unsteady bridge swaying in the wind. He was their leader, and Margrete would follow whatever decision he made. She trusted him with her life.

He held up a hand, silencing them all. With confidence she knew he didn't feel, Bay crept to the nearest demon. In a move too quick for her to comprehend, the nimble warrior slashed his Azantian blade through the largest of the creatures. When he pulled it away, Margrete saw how the metal burned red before turning back to silver.

They were real. Gods, they were *real*.

Bay swore loudly enough to rattle the trees. The fire demon took a step forward, chasing Bay back to the bridge. She noticed how he hadn't returned his blade back to its sheath, and she wondered if it was still hot.

"We cross," he said quickly, his blue eyes sharp and full of ruthless determination. Even in the face of death, he refused to bend.

Margrete couldn't argue with the proof she'd seen, and she hastily scrambled after Bay, Mila and Grant on her heels.

Fire demons. Just what they needed. If only she had the power of the sea inside of her. Oh wait. She did.

It simply wanted to hide and watch her suffer.

Margrete clutched at the rope on either side of her, placing a hesitant foot on the first plank. Bay had already ambled onto the bridge, and he tapped at the wood with his boots before resting his full weight on it.

Margrete squinted over her shoulder.

The creatures had quickened their pace.

"Hurry!" she screamed, forcing Bay to abandon his caution. He stole a peek before hastening his steps, now moving across the wood with little care. Mila bumped into her back, sparing a quick mumble of apology. Jacks took up the rear, doing his best to appear brave and collected. He didn't entirely succeed. His sister closed her eyes and walked across, her face a cool mask. Jacks murmured something into her ear, and she nodded, her jaw clenched.

They'd just reached the middle, but Margrete knew if their supernatural assailants so much as touched the bridge, the rope would fray and they'd all fall. They had maybe seconds to reach the other side...and that simply wasn't enough time.

She heard the spark catch before she glanced over her shoulder.

There was a hiss and a snap, and one of the ropes secured to the cliff broke apart. The entire bridge shuddered and heaved dangerously to the right.

"Run!" Bay shouted, racing for the other end.

There was no hesitating, no time to check every plank of rotting wood. They just frantically ran, and still another cable crackled and snapped. Now it was only held in place by one straining rope.

Margrete spared a glance just as the fire creature reached for it—

Everything happened so quickly.

She lurched into Bay, sending him soaring through the air and onto his knees. His hand poked through one of the planks, his arm hanging in midair as he worked to free himself. The crew, in their panic, shoved at one another, causing Margrete to fly against the ropes. She screamed as the upper half of her body teetered over the frayed rail. A firm hand grasped her arm and yanked her up.

Mila.

Once Margrete caught her bearings, she shot the redhead a thankful nod. Mila didn't return the gesture but shot off for Grant, whose eyes were wide as he took in the river below their feet.

Margrete watched as Bay freed himself of the rotted wood and staggered to his feet.

"They're stepping onto the bridge!" Jacks shouted, shoving at his sister, urging her to run. Dani let out a yelp, a single tear gliding down her cheek.

Bay shuddered to an abrupt halt, forcing them all to stop halfway across.

More fire demons. On the *other* side.

"Bay!" Atlas roared. She clutched Dani's shirt, her fierce grip the only thing keeping the young woman from toppling over the side. "What now?"

What now? They were utterly fucked.

Enemies approached from both ends, and there was no way they could fend off creatures that couldn't be killed. Margrete grasped the sides of the bridge and peered over. The river would be their only hope, which didn't inspire confidence.

She found Bay's stare and held it. An entire conversation passed between them.

We're outnumbered. We're screwed. Jumping is the only way out. How the hell did we end up here again?

Margrete tried to focus on her power, on Malum's essence. She struggled to home in on the river and see if she could raise it, make it so when they fell, they'd have some kind of cushion.

She failed miserably.

The spark tried to flare, but something smothered it. She felt hopelessly mortal, and for the first time, she mourned the loss of what she never truly wanted. She *missed* her power.

Another rope snapped as the creatures on the other end reached the bridge. Margrete looked at Bay.

"Trust Nothing," she said. "We know they're real, but *that*"—she tilted her head to the sliver of a river below—"might not be what it seems."

Trust. She had to have trust and faith and all that other nonsense.

"We jump," Bay shouted, surprising the crew. Before he could toss himself off the side based on her groundless suspicions, Margrete hoisted onto the rope and threw herself over first—

For a moment she soared. She flew, eyes squeezed tight, arms outstretched like wings.

Margrete struck the water quicker than she'd anticipated, quicker than should have been possible given how far away the river appeared from the bridge.

She opened her eyes. Water surged into her mouth, her nose. She sputtered. It was deeper than they thought as well. She couldn't see the bottom, but then again, she fought to stay afloat, allowing the slow current to carry her away.

Shouts sounded overhead—

Followed by splashes.

One by one, the crew, led by her reckless faith, jumped over the side of the bridge. She twisted around when Bay landed, her friend rising to the surface and shaking the water from his head.

She saw Mila, Jacks and Dani, Jonah, Atlas.

Which left only Grant.

The river carried them farther from the bridge, but she made out a lone figure standing in the very center. He didn't jump, and she heard him shouting, asking where they'd all gone.

That's when she realized he couldn't *see* them.

It had been an illusion, the river, how far away it appeared, how hopeless. She'd jumped based on a hunch, and the crew followed her almost immediately.

All except Mila's father.

"He's scared of heights!" Mila choked on water as she thrust to shore. "Fuck! I-I should've held his hand and jumped with him." The regret in her tone caused her voice to crack.

Margrete could feel the life essence of the water now, and it pushed her to the soggy banks. It appeared her powers had returned, or maybe they'd simply been suppressed on the bridge. That had been a test. Another damned trial.

That was her only explanation.

"Jump!" Mila shouted fruitlessly, rising to her feet on the banks. "Grant, jump now!"

The older man turned around as if searching for her voice, but he held the rope tighter. He wasn't letting go. Not even when the flames worked their way to him.

Slowly, the monsters encircled him. He screamed, the flames burning a bright and searing white. They singed his body so quickly, Grant barely managed to call out Mila's name for the last time.

Mila shrieked, a bone-chilling cry of anguish.

Margrete lunged for her and wrapped her arms around her waist, her grip keeping her from throwing herself back into the river. She watched with Mila as the bridge turned to ash and the flames simmered into nothing. If it wasn't for the stench of death in the air, Margrete would've almost believed there'd never been a bridge there to begin with.

As if they'd imagined it after all.

CHAPTER TWENTY-FIVE

BASH

MIDDAY CAME AND WENT, AND BASH'S UNEASE GREW. HE COULDN'T help but feel as if Margrete was in trouble. Something churned in his gut, and his hands refused to stop trembling. He'd shake them out at his sides, but the tremors didn't cease.

He surveyed the trees for the thousandth time, looking for gods knew what. Every muscle grew taut, uncomfortably tense. He expected Minthe to pop out any second, or Darius for that matter. The God of the Sea hadn't visited him again, and Bash wasn't complaining. Still, the lack of his presence meant the immortal was likely off meddling somewhere else. Possibly stalking Margrete.

Bash quickened his pace. Minthe claimed he'd reach Margrete and the crew by nightfall. That thought alone kept him going, even as his limbs protested and his muscles burned. He'd been getting weaker the farther he walked.

It seemed like that little burst of energy he'd been gifted with hadn't lasted long. Thankfully, his anger smoldered brightly enough to fuel him.

After he left Minthe, his rage had grown. Frustration bloomed and took root, and he cursed the fact he'd been separated from his crew and Margrete. He cursed how he'd been changed and twisted to resemble a monster. And along with all that frustration, a self-loathing lived and breathed. Deep down, he knew the man he'd been was gone. Possibly forever.

There would be no going back to how things were before all of this, even if he somehow got off this island in one piece.

And his hunger...

Bash had found a few bird eggs some hours back, but he had to force himself to eat. They hadn't tasted right, and they sat in his stomach like lead. It didn't help that they hadn't even made a dent in his hunger.

Perhaps that was why he'd thrown caution to the wind and nibbled on some bright red berries he discovered. Margrete would've chastised him for being so careless, in case they were poisonous, but he just wanted that excruciating hunger to abate.

So Bash continued on, even as the fire in his belly flared, demanding *more* of what he couldn't seem to find. Not food, not water. Some unnamable thing that had him clenching his teeth in irritation. His skin felt too hot, and sweat lined his brow.

When he'd come across the stream Minthe told him of, Bash followed it without thought. He was tempted to wash away the grime and soak for a bit, but he couldn't waste time, even if the icy water looked appealing.

Bash stopped in place when he heard the faraway sound of rustling and a racing heartbeat.

Whipping around, he came face to face with a wide-eyed doe. She froze, her soft brown eyes meeting his black ones, her nose flickering as if she scented his hunger. He retained the impulses of a predator, even weaponless, and the doe's frightful stare seemed to recognize the danger.

Bash didn't realize he was moving until he'd lunged. He soared through the air, faster than should've been possible given his current state, and he latched onto the doe's back. She let out a strangled sound, one of fear and pain, but he ignored it, just eager to make the empty feeling inside of him go away.

His heart thundered as the creature thrashed and fought in his hold, and Bash noted with a sickening realization that he was smiling, *enjoying* the fear the animal radiated. He could taste it in the air, sweet and ripe and bitter. Fear tasted amazing, he decided, and he tightened his hold on his prize.

Bash couldn't stop himself as he wrapped his arm around the doe's throat and snapped its neck like it was no more than a delicate twig.

The creature went still in his arms.

Bash stiffened. The rush he felt seconds ago vanished, and the hunger only grew. He told himself he just needed to eat and then he'd feel better, but he suspected that wasn't true. The chasm widened as he started a fire, only to realize he possessed no dagger, no knife in which to skin his catch. The creature masquerading as Margrete had stolen it.

So Bash did the unthinkable.

He used his teeth.

It could've been hours or days, and he wouldn't have been able to tell. All he focused on was the scent of the doe's blood, how it wet his tongue and tasted like a delicious death. Bash lost himself in that blood, gave in to the hunger that guided him. And still the blood wasn't enough. He needed *more*.

Bash ripped a chunk out of the doe's thigh and devoured the muscles and tendons whole. He swallowed, his meal sliding down his throat with ease.

More.

Bash took another bite. And another. And one more.

Not enough.

He wanted it to stop; that unquenchable need to fill his body. Bash grew desperate, and blood dribbled down his chin as he continued to devour the doe. By the time he finished, the animal looked unrecognizable. It was nothing but torn hide and splintered bones.

Blackness swirled around his sight as he licked the last bone clean, a haze dancing around the edge of his eyes, blocking out the weak sunlight. He allowed it in.

He wasn't Bash. He was nothing at all, and the nothingness felt good.

Slumping back against a tree trunk, he shut his eyes, his belly full, yet his hunger remained.

BASH WOKE HOURS LATER.

He picked himself up, brushed at his clothes, and began walking.

It might have been many miles later when he realized the wetness and stickiness he felt tacking his clothing was actually blood. He lifted his arms. A crusty red colored his hands, stretching down to kiss the black ink on his fingertips.

Bash dropped his hands at his side, his mind a mess of distorted memories. Of Margrete. Azantian. The island. Minthe. Sinking his teeth into the doe's neck...

Blackness. Lost time. Lost *self*.

Bash marched on. If he didn't stop, then he wouldn't overthink. If he kept running, he just might be able to outrun his demons.

When he came across a small lake, he waded in and submerged himself deep below its obscure depths. In the murky water, he scrubbed his skin and clothes, not coming up for air until his body was free of red.

Bash breached the surface with a gasp and scanned the trees, blinking droplets out of his eyes. He couldn't seem to recall anything other than walking and diving into this lake, and even *those* memories had a dusting of confusion coating them.

His hands twitched at his sides, and Bash looked down, frowning when he spied a single speck of blood. He wiped it away with his thumb.

Still, he couldn't seem to get that single speck of blood out of his mind as he trudged on. Even after miles of walking, Bash couldn't shake the sense of wrongness that lingered. He closed his eyes, and almost immediately, a horrific scene played out behind his lids. A creature enshrouded by dark wisps and silver lightning wavered in and out of focus. It wore his face, his smile, his eyes...

And then the monster he envisioned leaned down, his grin turning malicious as he turned to a limp body hanging lifelessly in his hold. A woman, with deep brown strands that hung down her back, and soft, full lips that had turned the slightest shade of blue.

Margrete.

Bash rubbed furiously at his temples, willing the gruesome vision away. He stumbled as he meandered aimlessly into the woods. The image of her so frozen, so still, sent his fractured heart thumping in his chest. Time was irrelevant. It ceased to be real, and like fraying threads slipping through his fingers, Bash was unable to hold on to any single thought for long.

The last thing he saw before he collapsed to the ground and shut his eyes was the monster's jaw unhinging, *his* jaw unhinging, and then him leaning down to suck out Margrete's soul.

CHAPTER TWENTY-SIX

MARGRETE

Dusk lay over the bleary world like a mottled cloak.

The second coin jangled against the first in Margrete's pocket. Shortly after the bridge, the number 2 had vanished from the face of the token, signifying they'd completed the trial. She was tempted to toss the damned thing into the river they'd emerged from.

No one had spoken since Grant had burst into flames. Margrete had reached for Mila more than once, but the young woman shucked her off and quickened her pace, in no mood to be comforted.

A part of Margrete understood that—her need to spurn everyone and delve deep inside herself where no one could reach. She'd been guilty of doing the same thing for years.

"This looks as good as any place to make camp," Atlas announced, peering around the small clearing they'd found. She swiped at the sweat on her brow and tucked flyaway strands of blonde behind her ears. Margrete wasn't sure how she managed it, but she still looked like an impossible combination of stunning and dangerous.

Bay nodded, barely glancing up. "Let's make a fire," he instructed, marching off into the woods. His quick steps suggested he didn't want company. Margrete could only guess he carried the blame for Grant's death on his shoulders. As their leader, Bay held their lives in his hands, and he'd lost another soul to this cursed island.

Margrete watched him walk away with a heavy heart. She'd speak with him later. For now, she turned her sights on another.

Mila plopped against the base of a tree, staring into the distance with glossy eyes. Not caring if she was rebuffed again, Margrete wandered over to her side and took a seat. The woman didn't acknowledge her.

People often felt like they had to speak in order to provide comfort, but that was hardly the case. Sometimes a person's physical presence could hold more weight than words.

Margrete didn't reach for Mila as she'd done before, but she leaned back against the trunk they shared and followed her line of sight. Bay had returned with wood, and as the crew built the fire, she slowly shifted so her arm grazed Mila's. Surprisingly, the redhead didn't move away. She inched *closer*.

Mila had saved her on the bridge when she had been about to fall over. Granted, she would've survived the fall, but she hadn't known that at the time.

Maybe there was hope for a friendship after all.

They sat like that, in complete and comfortable silence, until bright orange and red flames flourished. Mila flinched when the fire sparked and crackled, and her throat bobbed. Margrete noted the water lining her eyes. She was thinking about Grant, about his final, excruciating moments.

If they didn't need the heat, Margrete would have smothered the fire herself.

Across camp, Bay stood and reached into his satchel for the berries they'd found earlier, moving to each member of the crew and gifting them with a handful. As Margrete didn't recognize most of the flora on the island, she hadn't been able to tell if they were poisonous. It was Jonah who'd spotted them first on their hike, and he'd wasted no time shoving one in his mouth. When he didn't immediately die, they all joined him.

Jonah hadn't touched any other berries since. Smart lad.

The weighted hush persisted as everyone chewed, though some in their small group simply held the berries in their palms, the day's loss taking its toll. Margrete caught Atlas staring at Dani, concern marring her features.

Dani, as usual, noticed nothing. Even when her brother slung an arm around her shoulders, she barely moved. Margrete wondered how a gentle soul like Dani had gotten involved with Bay's crew.

"You don't have to sit here."

Margrete glanced up. Mila stared back, her eyes all fire.

"I don't do anything I don't want to do," she replied, knowing exactly what Mila was doing. It would take more than glares and cutting words to push her away.

Mila scoffed and shook her head as if Margrete were some pest. But she didn't tell her to go to hell, which felt like an improvement. She would continue to stand beside Mila for as long as it took. No one should go through loss alone, even if that person didn't particularly like her. Margrete aimed to change that. Bash would've just called her stubborn. One corner of her mouth quirked at the thought.

When the moon rose high in the sky and the clouds swept across the stars, everyone bedded down for the night. Margrete laid beside Mila, her arms propped beneath her head. Hours passed, and snores proceeded, but she couldn't find rest. All she could think about in the silence was Bash.

She felt him still, just as strongly as before, but something had changed. Again, she couldn't explain her reasoning, but when she shut her eyes and pictured her king, ice prickled down her spine like tiny daggers.

They had to find him. And fast. Whatever shifted had her stomach tying into knots. She would've been a wreck had she not have known he lived, but deep down, Margrete worried...

She'd seen his darkness firsthand. Back on Azantian.

Bash was lost—not just in the literal sense—and Margrete wouldn't stop until she uncovered the reason and chased away his demons. He'd do the same for her. He would go to the underworld and back if she asked it. Margrete smiled as she pictured their last peaceful morning together back on Azantian. How she wished she could wrap herself in that memory and hold on tight.

Mila had finally succumbed to exhaustion, her cheeks red and blotchy. The young woman had yet to shed a tear, even as her body fought for release. Eventually, she'd break. Sadness was never meant to be contained.

Margrete rolled onto her side, away from the fire, and away from the woman with tears in her heart. The leaves on the trees had turned red in some places, and the color reminded her of dried blood. Another omen.

A violent tremble wracked her frame as a frigid wind gusted.

She shot upright. No one stirred, all sleeping soundly except for Atlas, who had been instructed to take the first watch. Her head kept bobbing as she fought sleep, her hooded eyes trained on Jacks's twin.

Margrete gritted her teeth as her blood turned cold. Something was near. Whether an animal, a beast, or some miraculous rescue party, she couldn't tell. She got to her feet and slid between the trees. Atlas must not have noticed, because no one called out after her.

These woods were creepy during the daytime. At night, they were monstrous.

Every branch was an arm reaching out to grab her, and whenever a twig snapped, Margrete feared it would be the last sound she'd ever hear. Still, she pushed on, drawn by that unnamable awareness simmering in her chest.

Ten minutes passed before another rush of ice trickled down her spine.

She was close.

Margrete quickened her steps and handed the reins to her intuition. It might not be the most trustworthy thing, but she would gladly take *any* sign or misplaced clue at this point.

Step by step, her body grew colder, stiffer, like she'd run for miles through dense snow. Her breath came out in a puff, and she held her fingers to her lips, warming them.

What could possibly be out here?

A twig snapped, and she jerked to a halt. Somewhere, leaves whispered against each other, and something within the darkness...*moved.*

Margrete reached for her power, sensing it shudder to life. It shifted with ease now, her inner heat stronger than before. It had been awakened months ago, and now it appeared it was finally ready to step into the sun.

More rustling sounded, and then—

Margrete took off into a run the second she saw him. She ran without thought or hesitation, and she didn't stop until she collided against the muscled torso of the man she loved and wrapped her arms around his neck.

"Bash!" she tightened her grip, wanting to believe this was real, that she truly embraced her king, her pirate, her soul's other half. If it was another cruel joke, she wasn't sure she could handle it.

The body she held flinched, and in a move too quick to comprehend, Margrete was sent flying into the air.

A strangled noise left her lips as she slammed to the ground, prostrate on the damp soil. She glanced up, sucking in a breath, just as a blur of black shadow and pale skin flashed past.

Bash.

In the span of a single heartbeat, he crossed at least ten strides of ground and pressed his spine against a far tree. He bent over, hands on his thighs, and his chest heaved as if he'd just run for miles.

Margrete watched him—*studied him*—standing there beneath a shaft of silver moonlight breaking through the trees. She blinked, sure that what she was seeing couldn't be real, or perhaps it was a trick of the light. Spiked scales collared Bash's neck, and the ends of his fingertips were stained black.

Margrete watched as he ran a hand through his hair, which no longer shone a deep auburn. No copper strands glinted in the moonlight.

His hair now matched his shimmering onyx eyes, the dark strands silken and altogether foreign.

She couldn't contain her gasp.

Margrete had *felt* him before she'd seen him, that familiar tingle of knowing dancing down her spine. So overwhelmed with joy, she hadn't taken in Bash's other features.

What the hell happened?

She pushed up from the damp ground, holding both hands out before her. Bash went rigid, his eyes never once leaving hers. He watched her as a cornered animal would a hunter.

"Bash?" She inched closer, hating how he cringed. "Are you all right?" It felt like such a silly thing to ask, as he was far from 'all right,' but she hadn't expected...well, *this*.

"Bash, please talk to me," she tried again, taking another step. He didn't move, but she scented his fear. It was pungent. Malum's power twinged in her chest, clearly uneasy. "Do you recognize me?" she asked, worry eating away at her heart. What if he didn't remember her, or what if he wasn't *her* Bash or—

"Don't come any nearer."

Four words. Four words were enough to fracture her armor. They were cold and cruel and horribly cutting. And how his lips twisted with disdain as he spoke them.

It broke her heart.

"I—it's me," she whispered, unable to disguise her hurt. "It's Margrete."

Why won't you let me touch you? Why do you look at me with such hatred?

Bash flung out both his hands, warding her away. "I told you to stop!" he roared, pressing harder against the trunk. His palms returned to the bark, and his blackened fingers dug into the coarse wood.

Mixed with the animosity she sensed was unmistakable pain. Hurt. Grief. Worry.

He broke his stare. Tilting his head in the opposite direction, he avoided her eyes as if looking too deeply into them caused him inconceivable torment.

"I don't want you to see me like this." He shook his head and briefly squeezed his eyes shut. "I don't even think you're real, so I don't know why I'm wasting my breath." He gave a derisive scoff. "You're probably another hallucination or a damned nymph."

A nymph?

"I'm real, Bash!" she ground out, placing enough force behind every word that he'd believe it. "I'm really here."

And so was he. *Real*, that was. The Bash she knew—if he showed up looking like *this*—would react the same way. He'd try to push her away and protect her. Even if he had to protect her from himself.

She grew more confident, her steps more forceful. Margrete ignored how he clenched his jaw and ground his teeth. She ignored the way his stare narrowed in suspicion, the way his hands trembled.

Margrete stood inches away, blocking his path, keeping him in place. His eyes were depthless voids as he whispered her name, and for the life of her, the desolate sound of it almost made her crumble.

She nodded, careful not to make any sudden movements. All she wanted to do was throw herself around him again and kiss him senseless. She didn't care what he looked like. As long as he was safe and beside her, the rest didn't matter.

Instead of asking what happened to him and why the scales of a nymera encircled his neck, she simply asked, "Can I touch you?"

Silence stretched, and her heart became a drum beating relentlessly against her ribs. She didn't know what she would do if he spurned her now. Bash cocked his head, his sharp gaze almost feral.

"I...I don't know what happened," he finally whispered. "I feel like I'm going mad in this place. It does something to you."

"It's all right," she rushed to say. "Whatever it is, we'll figure out a way to overcome it together." Their vow to one another. Their unbreakable promise.

Bash turned his head away, and something inside of her snapped. In a flash, she grabbed his chin and forced his face back to hers. His eyes went wide.

"Don't push me away, pirate," she said, voice hardening. "You know how much that vexes me."

The seconds ticked by as he studied her face. As he inspected her eyes and mouth and wrinkling nose.

And then—

Bash...smiled.

It was a fragile thing, soft. Like he'd forgotten how to smile in the first place. Margrete melted at the sight. Whatever else had changed, his smile hadn't. The lone dimple she adored dotted his cheek, and she resisted the temptation to lean in and kiss it.

"There you are." She grinned as well, though one tear slipped from her eye. Before she could wipe it away, Bash reached out and lifted it onto the tip of his finger. He brought it to his lips, kissing away her sorrow and relief.

Margrete's willpower vanished. Not that she'd ever had much when it came to Bash. She wrapped herself around him and nuzzled into his chest, inhaling pine and salt and *home.*

"Gods, I've missed you," she said against him, a few more tears joining the first.

Cautiously, he hugged her back, his touch gentle and unsure. She sighed and forced his arms tighter around her. "Hug me already, damn it."

A chuckle drifted to her ear, and then she was swept up in his arms and spun around and around. The forest blurred, and she lifted her head, seeing only Bash and his onyx eyes and the smile that stole her air.

Bash set her down, treating her like porcelain, like he'd break her if he so much as squeezed. His hands fell to her hips, his intense stare falling to her mouth.

"If you don't kiss me al—"

Bash cut her off with his lips.

Margrete grabbed at his black hair and wound her fingers through the newly dyed strands. He groaned into her mouth when she tugged him closer, drawing him deeper against her. She wanted him as close as she could get him until the desperate feeling inside of her went away. Maybe it never would.

Bash sucked her lower lip between his teeth, and she instantly felt his canines poking into her flesh. It was a new sensation, but she welcomed the slight sting when he pulled away, and she gripped his hair tighter. Spurred on by her reaction, his hands moved up and down her back, her hips, her bottom, his fingers grazing her ribs, the underside of her breasts. He touched her everywhere, seemingly anxious to relearn her every inch.

Margrete dropped her hands and shoved them beneath his thin shirt, shivering at the icy feel of his skin. She traced the hardness of his rippling abdomen before snaking her arms around his back.

She felt his reaction to her push against her stomach, and she smiled. Reaching between them, she brushed his thick length before cupping him through his trousers. He hissed.

"It *is* you," he said, drawing back. She nearly broke at the sight of his smirk. "Only you would tease me in such a cruel way."

"And I know it's you because you love to be teased," she said, glancing down pointedly.

Bash's smile dipped slightly at the corners.

"What's wrong?" she asked, bringing both hands to his chest. Beneath her palms, he tensed, and she felt him shifting away.

"Have you *seen* me, princess?"

If he worried his changed appearance would chase her off, he was sorely mistaken.

"I've seen you, and you're still my Bash." It was as simple as that. This island worked to change them all. Whether mentally or physically. "As long as your heart hasn't changed, I don't really give a damn what color your hair is or the color of your nails." She ran a hand through the strands. "In fact, I kind of like this look."

Bash sighed...but he didn't pull back anymore. Good.

"There's a lot I have to tell you."

She nodded, growing sober. Teasing aside, she understood the reason behind his transformation couldn't be good.

"Me too," she said. Margrete wasn't quite ready to leave their bubble, not yet, so selfishly, she lifted to the tips of her toes and placed a tender kiss on his lips. While cold, they were the same ones that worshiped her every night back home. The same ones that had her seeing stars while sending fire through her blood.

Margrete kissed her pirate until all the breath left her, and reality beckoned.

They couldn't ignore it much longer.

And while she held her love in her arms—alive and whole—a small voice inside of herself whispered fate would work to change that.

CHAPTER TWENTY-SEVEN

MARGRETE

Bay's eyes shot open the moment Margrete and Bash walked back to the small clearing where they made camp. The fire he laid before highlighted his parting lips, a sigh of palpable relief escaping. He jolted upright.

"Bash? Is that really you? Holy hell."

She was stunned none of the other crew had woken from Bay's outburst, although Mila and Atlas both stirred.

Bay ran over, practically knocking Margrete to the side as he embraced his friend and king. His brother, more like.

Like Margrete, he hadn't paused at his new appearance. Some connections couldn't be severed.

Margrete swore she saw just the hint of water lining Bay's eyes, but he didn't release his tears. His smile, on the other hand, shone with such radiance it lit up the night.

When he eventually drew back, Bay drank in his king and the new *additions* to his appearance. His shock was apparent, and he made no attempt to hide it.

"I feel as if I should ask about..." He waved his hand to Bash's neck, his hair, his hands.

"I couldn't tell you," Bash responded curtly, shifting uncomfortably on his feet. Margrete felt the shame radiating off him. "I woke up like this after a dream? Well, not really a dream. It felt far too real. This fucking island...It's hard to trust anything."

She sensed he was holding back and knew more than he let on.

"I mean, it could be worse? You could've grown fangs or something," Bay teased. Margrete grimaced, not feeling the need to bring up how his canines *had* felt more pronounced.

Still, she gave Bay a thankful nod. Leave it to him to overlook the nymera scales encircling Bash's neck, as if he'd just gotten a new tattoo. Or maybe he was simply very skilled at hiding his fear. Margrete suspected the latter.

Bay grabbed at Bash's arm and gave it a squeeze. "I was trying to be positive for her sake." He cocked a thumb at Margrete. "But I genuinely thought you were dead. Buried in the deepest trench. Shark food. Head severed and missing body parts kind of dead."

"Thanks," Bash said, scoffing, though his lips gave the slightest twitch. "I'm glad Margrete still had faith, or you might've been halfway home by now."

"That's not looking too great either," Bay murmured, shaking his head and dropping his arm. "The *Phaedra?* Yeah, absolutely nothing left to work with. We'll have to start from scratch. Or, in the case of our fantastically dire circumstances, we're going to have to build a somewhat decent raft and hope another ship—one not commandeered by pirates, of course—picks us up."

"Lovely," Bash grumbled, and Margrete shuddered at the deep timbre of his voice. While he might've been utilizing his fallback sarcasm as a defense, it didn't sound like him. His voice came out as more of a growl, and the slight reverberations she picked up in the air sent shivers down her arms and down the back of her neck.

Atlas stirred from where she'd passed out against her tree. She'd failed miserably at keeping watch. "Please tell me I'm not suffering from another hallucination," she muttered beneath her breath. Her eyes went straight for the scales and inky hair. "Oh, shit. I *am* hallucinating."

Bay shot Margrete a final questioning look, but she shook her head.

"I don't believe so, Atlas," Bay said, a hopeful grin brightening his face. "It looks like our dear Margrete found our wayward king. The specifics of which I won't question at the moment, mainly because I'm too damn happy."

His voice rose with every word, and one by one, the rest of the crew woke. Most blinked as if they couldn't believe their eyes, though they were right to distrust anything on the island, especially the sight of their newly changed king.

"Are we all seeing this?"

It was Mila who spoke up. She shot to her feet and reached for her dagger, likely thinking of all the ways to stab Bash should he be another cruel trick.

"He's alive. It's really him," Bay announced to the waking group. Bash seemed to shrink in on himself, which was unlike him, his shoulders hunching over and his eyes downcast. Margrete wove her fingers through his and tightened her grip. He lifted his eyes and gave her a ginger smile.

"Are we *sure* that's truly him?" Mila wasn't easily convinced, and Margrete couldn't blame her.

"Enough!" Bay shouted, and Mila wisely shut her mouth. "As you can all see, Bash has suffered as a result of this place. Same as us. Until we discover the meaning behind any of this, I suggest you remember who stands before you now."

Their leader. Their king.

Heads bobbed, and Mila abandoned her blade.

"We have mere hours until dawn, so I advise that you all get some more rest. Who knows what we'll face when the sun rises, and we need our energy. Tomorrow we head to the coast, where we'll build a small vessel. We're Azantians, after all, so ship-making is in our blood."

If we make it as far as the coast, Margrete thought, but didn't voice her concerns.

"You heard the man," Atlas shouted, icy command heavy in her tone. "Get some rest."

Dani and Jacks settled beside one another again, the brother eyeing Bash warily as he wrapped a protective arm around his sister. Mila, who'd suffered the wrath of the island as much, if not more, than any of them, continued to stare openly at their leader, though she did step back to lean against a wide trunk. Jonah, who Margrete rather envied, simply smiled, not a trace of doubt on his face. He gave Bash a quick bow before settling down. He closed his eyes immediately, trusting that something had gone right.

Yes, Margrete definitely envied his hopeful optimism.

Bash, unusually quiet, shuffled back, taking a distant spot beneath a gathering of trees. He wrapped his arms around his knees, his gaze glassy. She wanted to know every thought plaguing him, if only to drive away his obvious pain.

An arm caught hers before she could make her way to the king.

"Margrete," Bay whispered, eyes fierce. "You need to watch him."

His warning, so very different from his earlier elation, caught her off guard.

"I will," she promised firmly, and he released her. "We just need to get the hell off this island before it destroys more of us. And if the churning of my gut is any warning, I have a feeling the days ahead will be filled with more than a strenuous hike through the woods." She swallowed around the ever-present lump in her throat.

"I can't help but agree," Bay said. "Even if I don't have the magic of the gods in my veins, I still sense our impending doom." He smiled at the absurdity of their situation. "But I'm taking the next watch, so try to get some rest. We'll talk more in the morning." Bay patted her shoulder before walking off without a backward glance.

Margrete shook off the chilling apprehension flooding her chest and drifted over to Bash. He hadn't moved from his position, appearing more statue than man.

She hated how small he looked.

Taking a seat beside him, Margrete rested her hand on his knee, careful to not make any sudden movements. He seemed skittish. She wanted to ask what he'd endured, but Bay was right—they'd talk later. Bash looked like he'd been through enough, and what he needed was rest and her arms wrapped around him.

Instead of speaking, Margrete lowered to her side and reached out to pull Bash down behind her. She took his arm and slung it over her waist. He immediately stiffened.

"Just hold me, Bash. Please."

It might've been selfish—it likely *was* selfish—but she needed him. Needed him holding her, reminding her he was there. Alive.

Perhaps it had been her desperate *please*, but Bash gripped her back. He relaxed only slightly against her, and she noticed how he put an inch of space between them. Margrete hated that single inch.

She hoped they'd close the distance before she lost him forever.

MARGRETE WOKE WELL PAST MIDNIGHT.

It could've been the island that caused her to stir, or the fact that Bash's body wasn't pressed against hers. She shoved upright, sleep still clinging to her eyes as she rubbed at them.

She glanced over her shoulder, not surprised that the spot where Bash had lay was now empty. Still, panic flared, and her heart pounded in alarm.

Not again.

Margrete jumped to her feet, careful of the unconscious bodies spread out around the weak flames. Mila rested against a far tree, away from the others, her bloodshot eyes open and on alert. She must be on her watch.

The young woman held her stare, seeming to understand Margrete's unspoken question: *Where was their king?*

Mila sighed before tilting her head to the right, to where their small clearing ended and the thick woods began. She mouthed the words, *That way.*

Margrete dipped her head in thanks, but in reality she wasn't thrilled Mila had allowed Bash to wander off by himself. Gods knew what lurked in these woods, and Margrete had *just* found him again.

At the thought of losing him, she quickened her steps and raced into the trees. Low-hanging branches and prickly underbrush scratched at her legs, her arms, her cheeks. She cursed beneath her breath as she shoved them all aside, her eyesight gradually adjusting to the night.

Five painstakingly long minutes later, she happened upon another small clearing, though this one boasted a jagged rock formation, large as a fine Azantian home, at least thirty feet in height. The stones jutted into the night at a nearly flat angle, like the earth itself had sprouted massive fingers and reached for the moon. Sitting on top of the highest point, head tilted toward the skies, was Bash.

She let out a ragged breath of relief.

"Gods, Bash! You frightened me!"

Now that she'd found him safe and sound, she wanted to wring his neck.

"Margrete?" Bash peered over the side of the boulders as she began to climb, errant strands of black hair tumbling into his face. "What are you doing awake at this hour?"

"I woke and you were gone," she said, lifting herself higher. It took less than a minute before she reached the top, and Bash offered her his hand, helping her up.

"I could've come down," he said when she'd settled on the smooth, flat surface. This high up, she could catch glimpses of the island over the trees. The woods seemed to go on forever until the thick fog swallowed them.

"You should've woken me and then I could've come with you." Margrete knew she should give him space, but she didn't particularly want to. Her paranoia was hard to shake.

"Come here," Bash said, voice gravelly. He opened his arms hesitantly, though she noted how he curled his hands into fists to hide his blackened nails.

Margrete scooted across and into his arms. It took him another minute before he allowed himself to wrap them around her. She scowled.

"Hold me like you mean it, pirate," she said, tugging at his hands until they went flat against her belly. Her back pressed against his chest, and she shifted until she could rest her head in the crook of his neck.

Better. Much better.

Bash barely seemed to breathe, and she could feel the thudding of his heart reverberate against her.

"I know you won't hurt me," she said, believing every word.

"I look this way for a reason, Margrete," Bash whispered, his breath tickling her hair. "I know you meant what you said earlier, in the woods, but I don't feel *right*."

Margrete craned her neck until she could meet his eyes. She gave him her best glare.

"I'm pretty sure none of us on this island 'feels right.' I battled a fucking sea monster, for gods' sake."

That captured his attention. "You *what*?"

"Oh yes. And Mila nearly died. It was quite extraordinary, if I do say so myself. It's a shame you missed it."

Bash snorted. "My heart would've given out," he said, laughter that sounded genuine following his words. He absentmindedly rubbed his thumb across her stomach. "Not saying I wouldn't have had faith, but you slaying a beast would be on the list of things I'd prefer not to see in person. At least, not without some ale on hand."

"That's the Bash I know. Sarcastic as ever." Margrete placed a kiss on his neck, just above his scales. Bash flinched, but she ignored it.

"Hush," he chastised lightly, one side of his mouth curling up. His single dimple made an appearance. "I see even in my dire state, you still seek to tease me."

That wouldn't change.

Margrete spun out of his arms and twisted around before he could stop her. She straddled his hips, her arms winding around his neck. Bash's lips parted in shock, but his hands automatically fell to rest on her hips.

"You *sound* like my Bash," she said, flicking his nose. His eyes narrowed at the action. "What can I do to prove to you that nothing will change how I see you?"

Bash dropped his arms to his sides. "I can't be a true Azantian..." His gaze lowered to his body, to his black nails. "Anyone can see that."

Margrete silenced him with a finger to his lips. Whenever she found herself caught up in an endless loop of self-doubt, Bash had been there, at her side, forcing her to see all the good she'd done. She knew she could be stubborn, but he never gave up on trying to make her smile, and she wouldn't give up on him either.

And right now, all she wanted was for him to forget about the horrors of this island and the scales around his neck. She wanted him to forget everything else but them.

She didn't speak as she gently pushed against his chest, forcing him onto his back. A look of pure confusion crossed his sharp features, and when he opened his mouth to question her, she shook her head slowly back and forth.

Margrete never lost eye contact as she crawled down his body and moved to his belt. His eyes widened as she unfastened it and went to work on the buttons of his trousers.

Bash grasped her wrists, uncertainty clear in his gaze.

"You don't need to do that, princess."

She scoffed. "Did it ever occur to you that I want to?" *Desperately.*

He went to open his mouth again when she reached for his length and pulled him free. Instantly, his lips parted, and nothing but a ragged exhale came out, his argument dying on his tongue.

Margrete grinned.

Bash once told her that he had grown addicted to her taste, but what he didn't know was that she'd grown addicted to his as well.

Wordlessly, she circled his sensitive tip, her smile brightening when he let out a sound closer to a growl.

His eyes fluttered closed as she moved her hand up and down, torturing him as he'd so often done to her. "Wicked—"

Bash's voice cracked when Margrete lowered her head and took him into her mouth. The familiar taste of him had her moaning, and his shaft twitched. Bash cursed, his hands flying to her hair.

"A-are you trying to kill me, woman?" he grated out, hardly able to speak.

She smiled around him. The noises he made drove her mad with need, and knowing that *she* was causing him to unravel had her core aching. Quickening her pace, Margrete swirled her tongue as she moved, wringing out his pleasure, destroying his control. Bash tightened his fingers in her curls, his hips jerking to meet her mouth while he chanted her name.

"Y-you feel so good," he murmured under his breath. "That's it, princess. Gods, yes."

When his entire body tensed, nearing release, Bash abruptly lifted her off of him. Startled, she found his eyes, which were darker than she'd ever seen them.

"There's no way in hell I'm going to come without feeling you come first."

A rush of air left her lungs as Bash hauled her up and over his chest. Carefully, he twisted her to the side, laying her down on the rocky surface of the boulder. With nimble fingers, he moved between their bodies, quickly undoing her belt and the buttons on her trousers. He slid his hand inside of them, and she hissed at the feel of his ice-cold fingers on her warm skin. The sensation sent tingles shooting in all the right places.

"Much better," he whispered, teasing her bundle of nerves. His breath skated across her face, his lips inches away. He eased one finger in before curling it, hitting a spot deep inside. She needed more. As if reading her mind, he added another, kissing her lips when she let out a gasp. He swallowed the sound, inhaling her breath, consuming her whole.

Margrete barely had the ability to reach for his length when he thrust a third finger inside. A strangled noise left her, pure bliss shooting into her core, her center throbbing and begging for *more, more, more*. She felt so deliciously full that it was almost too much to bear.

They moved as one, breathing the same air, both chasing the pleasure only the other could bring. She murmured his name, and he responded by moving faster, bringing her closer to the edge. But Margrete wasn't ready for this moment to end.

"I've never wanted you more," she rasped, and Bash trembled in her palm. "Only you make me feel this way."

Something akin to doubt flashed across his face, but she quickly chased it away when she ran her thumb over his sensitive slit. Bash groaned, his hips bucking into her palm. He didn't have to believe her yet, but he would. She'd make sure of it.

"Show me how much I affect you, king," she said. She was so damned close. "Show me—"

They both tensed, and Bash's eyes shuttered. Wave after wave of euphoria rocked her body, her release never seeming to end. Through it all, she held his stare, and the beautifully broken look on his face only prolonged her ecstasy.

His cock jerked in her hand, and a deep, rumbling groan left him as he stared at her with an intensity that set her insides aflame.

Bash brought his mouth to hers and stole her oxygen, her thoughts, her sanity. He kissed her lips and worshiped them, his tongue delving inside and swirling with hers until they both came down from their high.

Margrete wasn't sure how long they remained that way, but eventually, Bash draped her over his chest, one arm wrapped around her waist. In blissful silence they watched the stars until Margrete's lids grew heavy.

She must've fallen asleep, because the next thing she knew, she was being carried in his arms as he walked through the trees and back to camp. She caught flashes of his scales as they glinted in the weak light of the moon.

"Sleep, princess," he whispered. And without hesitation, she closed her eyes and allowed sleep to pull her under once more. She'd never felt as safe as she did with him, even here, in this wretched place crafted by a crazed goddess.

Whatever was in store for them next, she trusted in one thing. She'd destroy the world before she allowed anyone to take Bash away from her again.

CHAPTER TWENTY-EIGHT

MARGRETE

"Margrete."

She opened her eyes at the sound of her name coming from over her shoulder. She tensed for a heartbeat, but then last night came back in a rush.

Bash.

She grinned, allowing herself a moment to feel joy, and rolled over. A contented sigh left her lips as she drank in the Azantian king.

Even with black scales winding around his neck and dipping below the collar of his shirt, Bash was still the most beautiful thing she'd ever seen. He might not appreciate her calling him beautiful. He probably would prefer 'rugged' and 'dangerous' instead.

"What are you smiling at?" he asked, a grin of his own lifting his lips.

"Just happy," she whispered. The camp was silent, which told her they had some time left before dawn.

Cautiously, she reached out to cup Bash's stubbled cheek. Rather than pushing her away or flinching as he'd done the night before, he leaned into her touch, his eyes shuttering closed. She felt his body shiver beneath her palm, and hope blossomed within her. Maybe they could fix this mess after all.

"I missed you," Bash said, his voice firm yet gentle. He brought his hand to cover the one she held to his cheek. "You never left my thoughts. Not for one single moment. It felt like a thousand years had come and gone."

"It's a good thing I'm not so easily forgettable then," she replied, scooting closer until she was flush against him. Another shiver wracked his frame.

Bash opened his eyes and let out a deep chuckle. "Believe me, you are far from forgettable. My nights were filled thinking of you."

His lips were on hers before she could take in a breath. She inhaled his air instead, smiling into their kiss. Yes, things would work out, and then they'd get off this island and go back home.

"So delicious," Bash murmured between kisses. His voice had turned gravelly, deeper. "It's like we never parted." She hesitated for a second, but when he wove his fingers in her hair and pulled her against his lips, she melted.

His other hand moved to graze her hip, his fingers gentle, unsure. She moaned when his tongue traced the seam of her lips, and at the needy sound of it, Bash's movements turned desperate. His hands were no longer unsure. He gripped her as if she'd drift away should he let go. Something felt different in his kiss, and yet it was so utterly familiar at the same time.

Margrete took his bottom lip between her teeth, tasting him, trying to remember his—

She went still. He tasted of salt and fury and a foreign spice that burned her tongue. Instinctively, she drew back.

Bash cocked his head, brows creased, lips thinning. "What's wrong, darling?"

Darling. Bash never called her that, but someone else had...

Margrete shoved against his chest just as the dark eyes she loved changed color—from inky black to brilliant blue.

"Darius," she spat, clambering away and onto her feet. She scanned the camp, realizing they were alone. None of the others were sleeping peacefully, curled up beside the dying fire. It was just her and the God of the Sea.

Another fucking dream.

Slowly, taking his time, Darius rose to his full height. Margrete watched in horror as his body shifted, and she made out the distinct sound of cracking bones. His skin rippled, his features changing and adjusting. Before her eyes, he turned into her enemy.

Margrete moved away, not stopping until her back collided against rough bark.

Darius sauntered closer. He placed one hand above her head and leaned in, though he didn't touch her again.

"Beware the blood moon, darling. It comes in three days' time," he warned, smirking. "Though, I will enjoy every second of it. I've waited long enough for its return, and longer to make things right between us." His eyes shuttered as he inhaled her scent, and before she could react, he snatched a loose strand of her hair, twirling it around and around his fingers. He seemed captivated by the sight.

She jerked her head, and Darius frowned, dropping the curl.

"What do you mean, you'll make things right between us?" she asked, chest heaving. She couldn't seem to catch her breath. He was far too near. Which was why when he drew back an inch, she slipped beneath his arm.

"Answer me!" she demanded, spinning around to face him. "And why is it that I feel like I know you? And not just since that day on Azantian, but... before?" The words flew out of her mouth before she could capture them.

Whenever she was in his presence, her pulse soared—and not out of fear. And then there had been those brief glimpses she'd seen of them embracing.

None of it made any damned sense.

Darius lifted from the tree and swiped a hand through his golden locks, fixing her in place with his stare. There were so many emotions swirling in his eyes, and her magic burned in her chest, *responding* to him in a way that unsettled her.

"I want to tell you everything," he said, and the sincerity of his voice picked further at her resolve. "But some things you must learn yourself, and I hope this surprise is one you will eventually find joy in."

Margrete clenched her hands into tight fists.

"I can see I wasn't wrong about you," Darius continued, unfettered by her glowering. "And how thrilling it will be when you realize I am the last person you should be fighting." He chuckled dryly. "One cannot hate the reflection of what they are. And you, my dear, certainly won't hate me for long."

Oh, she doubted that. But in the meantime, she wanted Darius out of her mind. *Now.*

Instantly, the scene quivered like a flame, and a flash of uncertainty twisted Darius's lips into a frown. With a raised brow, he assessed her, seemingly both impressed and disbelieving.

A rush of anger flooded her, and the woods surrounding Darius tilted and blurred. The god himself swayed, flickered, and settled back into place. His jaw remained clenched as his ethereal frame fluttered in and out of existence.

"You're growing more powerful by the day—"

Margrete lunged, her fist aimed for his handsome face.

She went flying, meeting no resistance, sailing through the air. Margrete let out a yelp just before she collided with the earth.

The air rushed from her lungs as her eyes snapped open. Margrete lay on the hard earth, a cool body pressed against her back, a muscled arm slung over her waist. She flinched.

"Margrete?"

She flipped over, expecting to see Darius.

"What happened?" Bash's voice sounded alarmed as he bolted upright, his hand going to his empty sheath. When he realized he missed his weapon, he brought his hand to her cheek. His brow creased when she sucked in a sharp breath. He dropped his arm.

Was she actually awake this time?

"I—" She didn't know what to say. Should she ask him if this was real? Ask if he was the God of the Sea in disguise? Margrete trusted nothing.

She looked around the camp. The crew were all waking, some stretching, others huddled close and speaking in whispers. Her stare drifted back to Bash.

"Princess? Tell me what's wrong." His tone held an edge, but one she recognized.

Tentatively, she reached out and touched his hair, running her hand through the strands and down to his neck. A scale pricked her finger, and blood instantly bloomed. Before she could wipe it away, Bash took her wrist and paused to meet her eyes. She lost herself in his dark irises as he slowly lifted her injured finger to his lips, and his tongue brushed over the small hurt. Her stomach fluttered in response. Without breaking contact, he kissed the tip of her finger and brought it back to her side, though he didn't release her.

She swallowed down her rising nerves, though Margrete could've sworn his eyes flashed with hazy white before turning back to black.

It didn't matter though. Without any question, she recognized the man before her, and no amount of magic could disguise the sincerity in his touch.

This was her Bash.

"I—I had another dream," she finally admitted.

Bash's jaw clenched.

Anger. Her magic sensed his rage, and it tasted repulsive and bitter.

"Darius," Bash said icily, eyes narrowing. It hadn't been a question.

She nodded. The tension in her shoulders loosened when the familiar spark of determination lit up his eyes. She felt him drifting away, moving someplace she couldn't reach. Her chest heated as though to confirm her darkest fears, and she wished her damned magic could *speak* to her. It would sure make things a lot easier.

"What did he do to you?" Bash's hold on her wrist tightened. Again, his eyes sparked.

"I thought I'd woken up and you were there, and then..."

"Then?" Bash prompted, his tone lethally calm.

"Then we kissed," she admitted. "I thought it was you, and I didn't—"

Bash immediately relaxed. "Shhh," he soothed, reaching for her cheek. The suffocating feeling in her chest dissipated, and her king's jaw unclenched. "You didn't know, and you don't have to explain yourself. I know he has a talent for infiltrating dreams and wreaking havoc on one's mind."

Margrete sighed with relief.

"I'm just glad he didn't hurt you...or worse." Bash's stare burned with intensity, and she suspected what he feared. "And you're not the only one he's visited. He came to me days ago," Bash admitted in a whisper. "He taunted me. Made threats."

"What kind of threats?"

"He wants you *and* the power, Margrete," he said, sighing. His other hand lifted her chin. "He seems to think he has a right to you. I don't know if it's because of your new powers, or if he simply has some twisted fixation on you, but know that he won't win. I won't allow it."

His vow felt familiar. Like the one he'd made on the *Phaedra* months ago when they were on their way to bargain with her father.

What Bash had to realize was she didn't need him to protect her. She needed to protect *him*. Protect him from becoming more of...well, whatever he was becoming. Margrete had to tread carefully around the subject, as she recognized the pain in his eyes whenever she looked too closely at his scales, his blackened fingertips, but she *would* find a way to stop the transition before it stole away the man she loved.

Instead of saying as much, she merely touched his forehead with her own, their noses brushing.

"We'll protect each other," she insisted. She placed a tender kiss on his lips. "But he told me something else." Bash went rigid. "I think his plan will come to fruition in three days during a red moon. And we need to be ready."

Bash briefly squeezed his eyes shut as if the countdown to their demise had begun. "If Darius taught us anything, it's that gods can be killed," he whispered, not sounding as convinced as she would've liked.

For all their sakes, Margrete certainly hoped he was right.

CHAPTER TWENTY-NINE

BAY

Something was wrong with Bash.

And not just the obvious appearance of scales and black hair and fingers. No. That wasn't what had Bay glancing over his shoulder every few minutes to inspect his king.

Bay sensed...a change. Like a shift in his old friend that felt nearly tangible. It weighed heavily on him with every step they took toward the coast. He couldn't lose the notion that his friend had turned into a foe he should watch out for. The thought was absurd, he well knew, but he just couldn't shake his apprehension. *Damned warrior instincts*, he thought, grimacing.

Margrete, if she felt the same, had said nothing. Not that he expected her to. She hadn't left Bash's side since his return.

Bay couldn't blame her. If he'd lost Adrian, and by some miracle found him alive—albeit changed—he would ignore all else. Even the warning signs. Thankfully, Margrete had him to look out for her. And he would.

Bay tilted his chin to the left, leading the crew down a path with less prickly underbrush. The barbs tore at his clothing and had somehow sliced parts of his leather boots. They'd be lucky if they arrived at the beach fully dressed by the end of this.

He suspected they had a day's walk until they found the gray sands and could begin crafting some sort of vessel to get home. Or to the nearest mainland. Building a solid raft didn't concern him—Bay had grown up with a hammer and saw in his hand, and he had confidence in his Azantian blood. He simply worried about *making* it to the coast in the first place.

Gods. He worried about so much.

Adrian is supposed to be the worrier, he thought, and a timid smile tugged at his lips. He missed his boyfriend more than he missed not being endlessly chased by death on an island full of hallucinations and fire creatures.

Bay imagined if Adrian were here with them now. His lips would be twisted in a grimace, and his forehead would be creased with worry. It was his usual look—one Bay found immensely attractive. Smart men did it for him. Men who could fell an opponent with words alone. And if by some chance Adrian's words didn't do the trick, then Bay could always use his fists.

"Are you as unnerved by all of this as I am?" Atlas fell in line at Bay's side. Thoughts of Adrian vanished, and Bay fixed his face. He couldn't drift away in happier memories when their survival was in question.

"If you mean the island itself or our king's return, then yes. Yes to both." Lying to Atlas was a pointless endeavor. She was always too eager to call him on his bullshit.

"Good," she said with a curt nod. "I was worried you'd be all lovey-eyed and oblivious like Margrete."

Bay bit back his sigh. "If someone you loved came back to you after you thought them dead, I'd hope you'd take them any way you could."

Atlas turned away, eyes up front. Bay didn't miss how her jaw ticked. He'd known of her little crush on a certain sailor for a few months now. She thought she hid it so well, but she forgot Bay noticed everything.

Besides, it was becoming obvious to everyone *but* Dani.

"That's what I thought," he said. "But stay on your guard. We don't know what happened to him, and once he's settled and we've found shelter, I plan on asking." He wasn't about to rush his *king* into speaking of whatever horrors he'd faced out here alone. He may have a more casual relationship with him than most, but certain lines shouldn't be crossed.

"Fine," Atlas snapped. "But you better ask him, or I will."

There was the stubborn warrior Bay knew and loved.

"Don't worry, friend. I don't plan on losing anyone else." The sorrow in his tone hardened his voice. Atlas picked it up like he knew she would.

A firm hand landed on his shoulder, her grip deathlike. "You're my leader. My friend. The one I'd follow anywhere. Do not for one damned second carry the losses we've faced solely on your shoulders. If you continue to blame yourself, I'll be forced to punch the guilt right out of you, and you know how much I adore a good fistfight."

The corners of her mouth quirked. Bay knew all too well how she craved the battle. The rush of the fight. He shouldn't tempt her.

"Thank you for your generous offer," he said derisively. "But for now, keep those fists to yourself. We just might need them later."

LATER CAME.

The winds shifted, and with the change came that horrid smell of rot. It reminded Bay of burning hair and decayed flesh. Such a lovely scent.

"Something is coming," Margrete said.

Bay turned to the woman he'd come to see as a sister. Her eyes were sharper than any Azantian blade, and her hand drifted to the wave tattoo at her collarbone.

"I sense...I feel eyes on us," she whispered, gripping Bash's hand. His king looked down at her, his own black eyes narrowed with concern. Bay could see the muscles in his neck grow painfully taut.

"I sense it too." Everyone stopped in place at the sound of Dani's voice.

Jacks's twin sister never spoke unless absolutely necessary. Though when she did, it held weight—a reason Bay had accepted her on his crew.

That, and he understood the twins couldn't be separated. They were all each other had, and he wasn't about to isolate two orphaned siblings. As an orphan himself, Bay had grown up knowing what it was like to have nothing and no one.

"What do you sense, Dani?" Bay asked, stepping closer to the girl. She shivered in place, cautiously peeking through her thick black lashes to address him.

"Death."

Margrete let go of Bash and walked over to Dani's side. She placed a gentle hand on her shoulder.

"Do you...do you see anything?" Margrete pushed softly. "Images? Flashes of them?"

Bay didn't have a damned clue what she spoke of, but he listened with rapt attention. As did Atlas, who edged closer to Dani and Margrete. Well, closer to Dani. Her hand fell to her dagger.

Dani rubbed at her temples and shut her eyes. "I'll sound foolish," she whispered, nearly too softly for even Bay's advanced hearing to pick up.

"You won't," Margrete assured, turning the girl in place so she faced her. "Gods know nothing would sound foolish anymore. And if it makes you feel any better, I, too, saw something. Or thought I did." A crease formed in Margrete's brow. Bay could tell she didn't want to admit whatever horrors she'd glimpsed. She wasn't fond of sharing, especially when it came to her powers.

"I could've sworn I saw someone in the woods. A hooded silhouette. A flash of red." Dani glanced at the ground. "I blinked, and they were gone, but it looked so real..."

Margrete nodded, seeming to understand. She turned to Bay. "We need to find someplace safe. Somewhere that allows us a view of our enemies should they attack. We're being followed."

A shiver raced down Bay's spine. Rigidly, he looked ahead. The dense trees made it all but impossible to see clearly, but if he squinted, he could make out the beginnings of a rocky hill. If they could reach it, maybe they could climb up and get a better view of their surroundings.

"There's a hill straight ahead. We should go there. Now," he commanded. Bay had a gut feeling if someone followed them, they'd take pleasure in the chase. Everything in this place seemed to love the hunt.

Bash gave him a trusting nod, his king seemingly content to relinquish some control.

Dani inched back to Jacks's side, and her brother placed a protective arm around her shoulder. Atlas's eyes lingered on her for a heartbeat too long before she begrudgingly shifted them to the front. She brought her dagger out of its sheath and held it before her, ready to drive it into whoever pissed her off.

"We need to hurry," Bay murmured to his second. "If Dani and Margrete are right about being followed, an attack is imminent."

Atlas didn't say a word, but she didn't need to. They both understood their precarious situation.

With quickened steps, the remaining crew waded through the brush and shoved aside spindly branches. The unnerving quiet heightened every snap of a twig and every sharp inhale. Bay's blood turned to ice, but his legs continued to move, leading his people to the rocky hill where they'd hopefully stand a chance.

Soon, the trees thinned enough for Bay to make out their destination. About two hundred feet away, a crevice opened into the side of the hill. It hardly looked wide enough to squeeze through.

Bay turned his gaze higher. The hill had to be around a few hundred feet high and provided enough footholds for them to ascend easily. He couldn't make out the top, not yet, but he hoped it would be flat. He despised climbing. And heights, for that matter. Not many knew of his fears, and he intended to keep it that way.

Back on the bridge, when the fire creatures cornered them, it had taken everything he was made of to take that leap of faith with Margrete. Adrian's face had flashed across his eyes when he'd hesitated, and that was it—Bay jumped. For him.

But that didn't mean he wasn't afraid now.

"Almost there," he whispered to his crew. A few grumbled in response. Jonah tripped over a fallen branch in his rush to the front. The lad was clumsy, but he had the promise of a good mate. Bay just prayed the poor boy would make it out of here alive to test his skill on the open waters.

A howl rent the air. Well, not a howl, more like a shriek mixed with a groan. It sounded...human.

Bay's feet stilled. He held up a hand.

The metallic ring of blades being drawn cut the air behind him. He scanned the trees as he pulled out his own dagger. The howl didn't sound again.

Five heartbeats passed. Then ten. Then twenty. When more harrowing silence ensued, Bay slowly waved his men forward, indicating that they move cautiously.

He shot a quick look over his shoulder, finding Margrete standing tall, her eyes narrowed with concentration, and her hands free of Bash's. They curled into fists at her sides, and Bay thought he saw a flare of light spark from one of them.

He turned his focus back to their approaching destination. They were almost there.

Two howls pierced the quiet. Everyone stilled again, this time their labored breathing painfully audible.

Three howls followed.

"Run!" Bay shouted just as the branches behind them began to move and an agitated rustling sounded. He heard heavy footfalls, at least a dozen men or women, and from his training, he knew they were right behind them.

As one, Bay and the crew sprinted through the trees and jumped over fallen branches and logs. A clearing approached just before the hill, and he'd never run faster.

"Shit!" Jonah hissed.

Bay paused to find the young man on his hands and knees, clutching at his ankle. A snapped branch lay behind him. Motioning the rest of the crew ahead, Bay bolted to Jonah's side and hauled him up, forcing his arm around his torso. Jonah would heal, but not as quickly as he needed to. Not with demons or monsters closing in at their backs.

"I got you!" He grunted as he shifted Jonah's weight. The lad was surprisingly heavy. Just as he feared the creatures would devour them both, another figure dashed to Jonah's other side to support him.

Mila.

"Thank you," Jonah grunted, turning to Mila. His cheeks reddened when she shot him a curt nod. They grew darker when she jerked him closer to her side.

With her help, they were able to make it to the clearing shortly after the others, though they wouldn't have long to figure out how to defend themselves. They couldn't climb now. It would be foolish to give an enemy their backs.

"Got him?" Bay asked Mila. She nodded, tightening her grip on Jonah. The young man's face pinched with pain, but he did his best to hide it.

Bay faced the trees. The branches moved, and footsteps thundered.

He held his dagger out before him, holding his breath but ready to strike, to slay whatever fresh horror would emerge from the trees.

Yet Bay should have known his dagger wouldn't be enough.

A dozen figures materialized from the woods, their eyes dripping with blood.

CHAPTER THIRTY

MARGRETE

"WHAT THE FUCK?"

Bay rarely swore. This was bad.

Margrete watched in shock, utter and complete shock, as a dozen humanlike beings stepped into the clearing. Blood dripped from their eyes like viscous tears, trickling down their hollowed cheeks to their chins. Their bodies were gaunt and sickly, and their skin maintained a dull shade of grayish-green.

"What the fuck, indeed," Atlas said, lifting her dagger. "I don't know what they are, but I can't wait to try and kill them."

"If they *can* be killed," chirped Dani, earning a pained look from Atlas. She moved in front of the young sailor, blocking her from the sight of their ghoulish assailants.

That appeared to be a common question on this island—if or how something could be killed. That, or *What the fuck is actually happening?*

The invading horde advanced with leisurely steps, no longer needing to chase and corner. As a unit, they glided into the clearing and formed an uneven line—thoroughly hindering any escape attempt through the woods.

Margrete dared a look at the rocky hill behind them. They could try to scramble up, but the creatures would be on them in a heartbeat. *Whatever* they were. Dead. Alive. Human. Beast. Margrete was smart enough to glean they weren't friends, not with how they licked their chapped lips in what she could almost mistake as hunger.

"Most are wearing armor," Mila observed softly. "It looks older. A few decades at least."

Margrete hadn't really noticed seeing as her attention had been on their *tears of blood*, but they all wore the same golden armor that appeared decades out of date. And their breastplates...a winged bird taking flight had been emblazoned on the front.

Surria's symbol.

"They *can't* be alive. I mean, *look* at them," Jonah said. "But I also don't want them to be *dead*, because if they're dead..." He audibly gulped and shut his mouth. His sentiment got across well enough. If they were dead, then the crew was screwed.

You can't kill a dead person.

Margrete grabbed Bash's hand. "Get behind me," she whispered, not lowering her stare from the advancing soldiers. A particularly brazen creature with skin peeling from his shaved and tattooed skull poked his long tongue out to wet his bottom lip, his dull, clouded eyes framed by his bloodied tears.

Bash grunted at her command to step aside. He leaned over and hissed in her ear, "Like hell I'm getting behind you. I fight at your side, princess."

"As much as I appreciate that, I'm going to try something, and I'd be grateful if you gave me some room," she whispered back, her tone sharper than she intended. Bash had to realize by now that she had the power of a god. She was their best bet at the moment, whether he liked it or not.

He didn't budge. If anything, his grip on her hand turned bruising.

"We don't have time for your stubbornness," she snapped, growing frustrated. Their monstrous foes were nearly upon them.

"I'm not moving," he growled right back. "You'll have to force me to abandon you, and you should be saving your strength for them"—he tilted his head forward—"instead of pointlessly arguing with me."

Damn him.

She heaved a sigh. Stubborn, stubborn male.

To the others, Margrete ordered, "Slip into the crevice and stay there. Do not come out, no matter what you hear. If we don't make it, then run." She would try to hold these things back for as long as possible to give her friends a chance to escape through the fissure and, hopefully, underground to another exit.

Margrete could practically feel Bay's hesitation. From the corner of her eye, she saw him shifting uncomfortably on his feet, his hands clenching into fists. A moment later, he grew still, and like a mask sliding into place, he adopted the impassioned persona of their trusted leader.

"You heard her!" Bay thundered, motioning briskly for the others to head into the cave's opening. "Get inside and prepare to run. Do not stop for anything, no matter who is left behind."

"Hurry!" Margrete urged.

The cave in question—if it could be called that at all—barely allowed enough room for Atlas to inch inside, and she grunted when the sharp edges snagged her shirt. Jonah had never moved as quickly, even with his ankle not all the way healed.

Mila wasn't as easily swayed. Only when one of the supernatural soldiers hissed and raised their blade, did she follow Jonah's lead.

But Surria's soldiers mostly kept their eyes trained on *her*. Not the others. Not Bay or even Bash. They were all staring at Margrete as though she were the only one of any interest. She wasn't sure how she felt about that, but Malum's essence certainly held another opinion.

Instantly, her chest heated, and power flooded her system like a weapon freshly sharpened for battle.

As it typically did when she was in need, or whenever her adrenaline spiked to near dangerous levels, her power showed itself in force. While thankful, Margrete still wished she could control *when* it appeared, but she wasn't about to complain now.

One of the armored creatures approached, his bloodshot eyes fixated on Margrete. He smiled a broad grin that showed yellowed incisors, the points unnaturally sharp. She could've sworn a bug slithered across his front teeth.

Bash growled, the sound rivaling the most fearsome of beasts. He moved in front of her, his eyes aimed at their foes, who chuckled with delight as they walked toward them.

She couldn't let Bash distract her, couldn't let him stand in her way. The thought had her grimacing, but it was the truth.

"Bash." Margrete yanked on his hand. She had to give him another tug before he turned to meet her gaze. "I need you to trust me."

His nostrils flared, and his eye twitched. She feared he'd break a blood vessel. He wasn't fond of the idea.

"I told you, I'm not leaving you," he snapped.

"And I don't expect you to, but I'm taking charge."

Bash hesitated, fighting against his innate need to protect. He finally, *finally* inched back with the fiercest of grimaces. He held her stare and gave her a nod.

"I'd follow you anywhere. Even to the underworld itself, princess."

She squeezed his hand, hoping it relayed all she couldn't say. The words were lodged in her throat. Thankfully, Bay had gotten most of the crew inside the cave, out of the way of the fight that was about to ensue. The soldiers were fifteen feet away now, circling her and Bash like prey.

Instead of the fear that had flowed through her veins seconds before, pure undiluted adrenaline struck her like a bolt of lightning. It shot down her spine and radiated out to touch every inch of her, the intensity of its force nearly sending her to her knees.

Bash slipped an arm around her waist, holding her steady as she adjusted. Her foundation. Her rock.

Maybe she *did* need his help after all.

They exchanged one final glance.

"Let's do this, princess."

Margrete looked at Bash, whose lips curled into a grim smile. It was time to fight.

The first creature lunged, hissing as it swiped a bony hand through the air, coming at them both with inhuman speed.

She swiftly shoved at Bash's chest, sending him sailing through the air and out of harm's way. Margrete swerved their opponent's attack as muscle memory kicked in, and she quickly thanked Adrian for all of his lessons on defense. She'd been a fool to think of them as tedious.

Another one bolted forward, a woman with a jagged scar running from her right brow to the tip of her chin. Black rot poked out from the unhealed wound.

Margrete lifted her hand.

The woman flew through the air when Margrete's magic struck, her body hurtling into space like a feather swept away by a breeze. She collided against a tree trunk with a nauseating crack.

Margrete studied her palm, her mouth parting in disbelief.

"Holy hellfire, Margrete." Bash had moved back to her side, his black eyes wide with a combination of fear and awe.

There wasn't time to inspect her hand, which still vibrated with raw energy. Two warriors clad in the same ancient-looking gold armor raced forth, their swords swinging. Blood covered most of their faces like war paint, and it dripped freely onto the black soil as they advanced.

"I got one," Bash insisted, just before he dove for the first soldier. Her king moved quicker than ever before, quicker than she'd *ever* seen him move. She held her breath as he cocked his arm back, preparing to unleash hell.

When his fist collided with the metal of the soldier's armor, the entire forest seemed to quiver. Instead of the armor deflecting the punch as expected, Bash sent the soldier onto his back. Twenty feet away.

That couldn't be possible, even for his strength, but—

"On your left!" Bash yelled, forcing her back to reality. She turned seconds before the soldier swung his sword down, and her palm lifted once more.

This time blue light—the color of the sea at twilight—blasted from her palm and straight into the man's gut.

Sizzling electricity filled the air, and Margrete watched as her magic burned right through the metal like a flame to parchment, thoroughly destroying Surria's insignia. The man barely had time to let out a grunt before he fell, his chest eaten away by blue light. *Her* light. Her power.

A wave of dizziness swept over her as she faced another foe. A woman.

This one moved with lethal poise, clearly well-trained and skilled. She drove ahead with feline grace, even though she lacked her left eye. Fresh blood still fell from the empty socket.

To her right, Bash fended off two attackers at once, doing his best to give her time. His fists were weapons by themselves, and each hit he landed sent the soldiers onto their backs.

Margrete found herself smiling.

She raised her palm, a current of fire and vibrating magic tingling from her shoulder down to the tips of her fingers. With the woman squarely in her sights, Margrete unleashed herself, and the force within her shot toward her target, blasting her head straight from her shoulders.

That wave of dizziness grew more pronounced, and Margrete stumbled. The buzz of electricity in her veins burned. Her power might as well be cooking her alive from the inside out.

Not a good sign.

"Margrete!" Bash called out as he knocked over a warrior missing his left hand. He took one look at her and grimaced, concern twisting his lips. "We need to follow the others."

Gods damn him. He knew she was losing control—or that her magic was dwindling. And here she was finally getting the hang of it too. Margrete cursed as her palms sparked with blue fire, though her light painfully sputtered seconds later.

Bash was right. She had to retreat, as much as it pained her. More were coming, running through the trees, their footsteps echoing as they pounded the dry earth. Soon they'd clear the woods and surround them.

"Let's move!" she called out, making sure Bash heard her before she twisted on a heel and shot off for the cave. Bash's steps thudded loudly, and she didn't stop moving until they both slipped into the crevice and through the narrow opening.

Darkness enfolded her in its arms, and for a second she wondered if she'd fainted, but the crushing nausea she felt was all too real.

Margrete knew what she had to do, and she had *just* enough power left to do it.

"Move deeper into the cave!" she commanded Bash. He listened without pause.

Before the surge of the approaching soldiers could breach the fissure, Margrete lifted her palm one last time and aimed well above their heads. The second her magic blasted free, chaos ensued.

Rocks tumbled all around the crew as they screamed in alarm. She fell to the earth, and darkness, the true kind, washed over her, forcing all the energy from her body. She felt the cool earth between her fingers, felt hands on her back. But most notably, the frustrated growls of the soldiers had grown muffled on the other side of the fallen rocks.

She'd aimed true, and now they were stuck behind solid rock.

CHAPTER THIRTY-ONE

MARGRETE

Bash wrapped his arms around Margrete and rested his chin on the top of her head. Even in the dark, with dust and debris still falling, she felt safe.

"Are you all right, princess?" he whispered into her ear.

She wasn't. But she was alive. They all were.

"Yes," she answered weakly. "But I hope I didn't just condemn us all."

"Anyone hurt?" Bay asked, assuming command while his king tended to her. She should feel guilt for stealing him from his duty, but to be honest, she was feeling selfish, and Margrete wanted him all to herself.

A few grumbling assents sounded in reply.

The heat in Margrete's chest seared, though it differed from the consuming heat of before, during the fight. This fire was one she could reach out in her mind's eye and grasp.

She was the wind, manipulating the flame, and the swift current forcing water downstream. Margrete pictured herself so very clearly, finally understanding how this remarkably savage *thing* inside of her worked.

She shut her eyes, concentrating on the intricate strands of icy-hot magic. Shutting out all sounds and voices, she homed in on the steadying beat of her heart, the drumming of her life force. That was the key.

She had to connect with her very soul.

Seconds and minutes and hours seemed to pass as she reached out and called forth her blossoming flames. They were tangible, a power she could touch and feel and manipulate. With her eyes still closed, Margrete peered at the well of sacred magic inside of her, and the sheer intensity of it had her heart falling into her stomach in the most thrilling of ways. For the briefest of seconds, her heartbeat stopped altogether, and then—

Mila's foul curse echoed throughout the cavern.

"Holy gods," Bay hissed.

"Well, that's convenient," Jonah quipped.

"Yeah, super convenient. But we're stuck here because of her, remember?" Mila grumbled in reply.

"Still pretty amazing. I don't see *you* doing anything, Mila."

"Enough," Bay silenced the arguing pair. "Margrete?"

She heard her name. Heard the concern in his tone. His wonder. His awe. His fear.

Bay continued to fear her when it came to her powers. She hated that.

Margrete opened her eyes.

Bash knelt before her, his face aglow with a pale white light. Light that apparently came from *her*.

That cord of magic she'd seen? She actually touched it and willed it to her command. And now, she'd turned herself into a living and breathing human torch.

Bash peered up and into her eyes, her magic piercing the black pools, highlighting the stars within them. He knelt before her, in front of his people, his crew, a king on his knees. Bash didn't seem to care. It might as well have been just the two of them in that cave.

Margrete broke the moment and grasped his arm, urging him to stand. He never took his eyes off of her.

"Have I told you lately how impossibly breathtaking you are?" Bash brought both hands to cradle her cheeks and leaned his forehead against hers. He let out a soft laugh. "I always said you were my light, guiding me home. Looks like I meant it quite literally."

This time, when warmth flooded her chest, it came from a different kind of magic.

Bash drew back to place a tender kiss on the tip of her nose. "You saved us," he said, motioning toward the fallen rocks. To where she'd blocked them in.

"Hardly." She tried to turn her cheek, but Bash wouldn't let her look away. Her light fluttered before settling upon the rocky walls of the cavern.

"No. We wouldn't have been able to face...whatever those things were." His brows pinched together. "You gave us time we didn't have, and because of that, you saved everyone in here."

Bash looked pointedly at each and every crew member. "You all should be thanking her right now. Not staring at your boots or making snarky comments." He directed that last part to Mila. To her credit, she looked rightfully shamed.

Bash held out a hand to Margrete and entwined their fingers. Like a candle, her glow danced about the walls as she moved, and an incandescent shimmer played across the faces of the bewildered crew.

"We know Darius wanted us here. We know this place is filled with dark magic. And we know there are unimaginable forces out there that want us dead. Surria's insignia on those soldier's armor made that clear." Bash's voice grew stronger with every word, and the king Margrete had come to know made a reappearance. Her heart swelled at the sight. "But we also have the magic of a god on our side," he said, tilting his head toward her. "That makes us just as formidable."

Margrete caught his eyes and held them. They swirled with so many different emotions, but his fierce trust was the one that stood out to her the most. His loyalty.

Against her will, her lips quirked.

"We need to head deeper into the cave. See if there's a way out on the other side," Bash instructed. "Though I doubt solid rock will save us from the island's intent, so stay alert and stay focused."

"You heard your king. Time to move." Bay stepped forward, and Margrete's light reached out to affectionately graze him. To his immense credit, Bay only flinched before sending a cautious smile her way.

Bash walked by her side as she turned to the dank tunnel that would hopefully lead them to freedom. The Azantian king remained silent and steadfast, his thudding footsteps a reminder that he chose to follow her into the dark, forever trusting in her, without conditions.

Just as she would do the same for him...when the time inevitably came.

"Thank you," she murmured softly, gripping Bash's hand. It felt so cold it burned.

Bash scoffed. "I wouldn't say anything I didn't mean. You should know me by now, Margrete." She turned in time to see him smile. It reminded her of his smiles before the attack. Before he was changed by the sea.

Before he began to lose his way.

His gaze roamed over her ethereal form, mesmerized.

"Stop staring at me like that," she said, her cheeks heating. Her knees were weak as she pushed forward, but she suspected that had something to do with Bash's potent stare. Of all things, she noted a hint of desire in his eyes.

"I'm always going to look at you like that, princess. That little display of yours has my damned blood heating," he replied playfully, though he conceded and turned his head back to the front. "And I can stare all I want," he added with a raised brow, daring her to question him. She didn't.

As long as *she* could stare right back.

Margrete shook her head, and the tunnel flashed with her radiance. The light she emanated danced across the walls, forming patterns that were reminiscent of the sea's reflection. The lightest of blues rippled against traces of wispy navy, making the entire tunnel feel as if it were swaying.

Gods. That would take some getting used to. If anyone *could* get used to glowing. Margrete doubted that.

Instead of denying him, she gave herself a moment to snuggle in closer, pushing her body into his as they walked. His arm fell to her hip, and his fingers played on the band of her trousers. Instantly, her thoughts turned inappropriate, which seemed impossible given the circumstances, but she had missed him and his heated touch. Yet it was so much more than that—he settled her, believed in her so profoundly, that his unwavering faith forced her to believe in herself. She felt it every time he held her or looked her in the eyes with pure adoration.

No one had ever stared at her in such a way—like she was the moon illuminating the world below.

She'd never take that look for granted.

They walked for about a half-hour, silent and lost in their own heads, when a fork appeared. Two tapered passageways, equally ominous and nearly identical, branched off in opposite directions.

Of course, everyone stopped and turned to her.

At moments like these, she wished someone else could borrow her magic. What if she chose wrong and got them all killed? What if she picked the passage that led to a gruesome end rather than the escape they sought?

Yeah, she definitely didn't envy herself.

Margrete tilted her chin and reluctantly released Bash's hand. Doing her best to block out the whispers of a skeptical Mila and Jacks murmuring behind her, Margrete stepped toward the tunnel on the left. She sniffed the air.

Damp. Musky. Rotten.

Rigidly, she twisted to the right. The air wafting to her nose smelled fresher somehow, saltier. It smelled like an exit. Or maybe that was just foolish hope.

"We go right," she said, full of false confidence.

"It smells...fresher," Dani supplied, surprising her. Margrete turned to the young woman and smiled. The sailor had sensed Surria's soldiers in the forest earlier, and now she felt the same pull toward the passageway on the right. It was something Margrete would have to explore later, when they weren't all on the verge of dying.

She didn't hesitate to move, and the others dutifully trailed behind. With every step, her trust in her decision grew. Not only did the air *taste* right, but a soothing breeze drifted to cool her dampened brow. It reminded her of how the winds on Azantian would caress her body whenever the sun heated her skin.

She always likened her powers to a sixth sense. The hair would rise on the back of her neck, and tingles would race down her spine. It spoke to her in a way that didn't require words, going well beyond intuition. Almost like the humming of a song that only she knew.

Her light guided them through the dampened tunnel, and eventually, the passageway—which had to be no more than four feet wide—mercifully opened to allow a semblance of room. They continued for another unbearably hushed hour. Then one more.

Nothing changed.

The tunnel didn't reveal a fissure to the outside world. Natural light didn't brighten the stones, and the air held a musk that reminded her they were well underground.

Then, when she thought she could bear it no longer, something *did* change.

A frigid breeze, bone-chillingly cold, gusted across Margrete's face. She shuddered and then...smiled. Her heart rate picked up to match her swift steps, and she took off in a sprint borne of sheer adrenaline. Like the feeling of sunlight on your skin after months of winter and overcast skies, a little seed of hope took root.

Bash called her name, as did Bay, and yet she didn't stop.

A melody played in her head, one only she could hear, and it sounded of bells and the whistling wind, of lapping waves and fresh raindrops falling from the skies.

"Margrete!" Bash was on her heels, his boots pounding the hard stone to keep up.

She turned the corner, taking her glow with her, and stepped into ankle-deep water.

Margrete hissed at the contact. As it did whenever she touched the sea, a bolt of electricity raced up from her toes and to the crown of her head. Malum's power thrummed with her heartbeat, and she released her magic with an exhale. The water at her feet rippled and bubbled, flowing outward from her boots. The ripple turned into a gentle wave, and it took some of her light with it.

She gasped. The water—which had shone a muted blue when she'd first touched it—transformed into a brilliant sapphire whose purity would rival the most opulent of gems.

As her magic spread, reaching farther and deeper into the cavern and across the wide expanse of the pool, Margrete took in the flecks of silver embedded in the walls. They gleamed, sparkling like a thousand tiny stars. While she openly gawked, the mystical light kept spreading, kept moving on and on as if an end couldn't be reached.

"I'd call it beautiful, but that feels like an understatement," Bay murmured, suddenly standing to her right. Margrete turned, finding his eyes wide and brimming with sheer astonishment. None of them had expected...*this*. Even Mila shot her a hesitant look of what she dared to believe was approval. That said more than anything in her book, and she felt the tension between them grow less taut.

Margrete recognized the sea's essence in the air and felt its influence in the water lapping at her boots. She heard it call out to her and whisper in her ears. She sensed how it longed to be touched, and how it begged for her to step deeper into the water.

And still, that ethereal melody only she could hear continued to play. They were near the open waters, she felt it in her very marrow, and the thrill of coming close gave her new life.

She had come *home*.

"We should rest here," Atlas said, hoisting herself onto the stony banks. A ledge surrounded the pool, wide enough for them to lay their backs against the walls and spread out comfortably. Margrete didn't care as long as they were close. "We don't know when we'll be able to rest again, and by my calculations, it's past sunset," the blonde warrior added, her tone all business.

Everyone else lifted onto the ledge while Margrete stayed rooted in place. She didn't move, she hardly breathed. Her eyes must have shut at some point, because a gentle hand on her shoulder caused them to shutter open.

She didn't glow from within as she had before, and her skin had turned back to its usual tan. Margrete didn't have time to miss her light, because two thick arms banded around her midsection from behind.

Bash didn't speak. He was merely *there*, holding her as magic hummed in her blood and her heart hammered. His arms kept her steady, and his breathing joined in with the song playing in her head.

For the first time since landing on this godsforsaken island, Margrete felt a sense of peace. She wasn't naive enough to think it would last, but for now, she planned to revel in it.

CHAPTER THIRTY-TWO

MARGRETE

Everyone else was asleep—laid out on the stone banks, some snoring, others curled into themselves. But asleep, nonetheless.

Margrete untangled herself from Bash's arms. They'd settled against a damp wall, Bash's jacket resting on her shoulders. He'd insisted she use it to protect herself from the chill. As if catching a cold was the most frightening thing that could happen. Yet she didn't protest much. It retained his smell, and every so often she had brought it to her nose and inhaled his woodsy and sea scent. But now, she needed more than his jacket.

They had to talk.

Margrete soundlessly rose to her feet and gave Bash a knowing look, one he returned with a subtle nod. Without a word, she bent down and pulled off her shoes. She took off her shirt and trousers next, stripping down to her underthings. She heard Bash's boots thud against the ground seconds later. He seemed to understand what she had in mind.

The ledge they all rested on was too small for their private conversation, and their voices would carry. Thankfully, it wasn't their only option.

Deeper into the hollow, where the overhanging rocks dropped low over the pool, another cavern was concealed. There were quite a few little grottos nearly hidden to the naked eye, but her light, or whatever had caused this place to shine, illuminated the crevices and dips in the rocky walls.

The comfortably cool water felt divine as she waded up to her shoulders, the pool working to strengthen her hold on her power. The connection sustained her magic and refilled the well that had been drained after trudging through the tunnels. She required its touch, and she sighed with relief before glancing over her shoulder.

Bash must have discarded his shirt and trousers somewhere on the banks, and he stood behind her, the supernatural light of the pool dancing off his skin.

And his scales.

Margrete swallowed hard. She hoped he hadn't noticed.

"Come," was all she said, swimming out and away from the slumbering crew, her sights aimed at a secluded grotto to their right. A splash sounded, and she knew Bash hadn't hesitated to dive in.

When the jutting rocks threatened ahead, Margrete slipped beneath the surface at the last minute, gliding through the clear, luminous blue. She emerged on the other side feeling rejuvenated, as if the brief submersion had fueled her. Maybe it had. She had learned more and more about her powers every day on this infernal island, though back home on Azantian, she felt so lost. It didn't make sense.

A part of her couldn't shake that she had a connection to this place. Like she was always meant to be here.

Bash breached the surface with a loud splash. His shaggy black hair stuck to his temples as he shook the droplets from his face. With a hopeful, heart-melting grin, he cautiously glided to her, stopping inches away.

He'd been so careful around her, especially when he touched her; it certainly wasn't with the same easy confidence from before they'd wrecked.

Margrete held her breath as Bash lifted a hand, his inky fingertips seeming to darken. His lips thinned and jaw clenched, but he slowly brought his palm to her cheek. His stare never left his hands. They were proof he'd changed into something *different*.

"It's all right, Bash," Margrete assured, shivering for an entirely different reason. It didn't matter what he looked like. His nearness had a way of undoing her.

"I—" Bash dropped his arm and waded back, his brow scrunching with frustration and uncertainty. Margrete hated it. Hated the distance. Hated what this place was doing to them. "I don't trust myself when I'm with you. I feel...*wrong*."

"Why?" she asked, stepping into his space. The water touched the tops of her breasts now. "It's *me*. You should never fear being around me, and we're going to figure this all out, remember?"

She saw the lump in his throat bob as he swallowed thickly. "You don't understand, Margrete. I haven't told you about everything that happened to me out there, and I didn't want to say anything in front of Bay or the others, but—"

"Then tell me now," she insisted, softening her tone. "Remember, nothing you say will change a damned thing. So out with it." She made a show of snapping her fingers, hoping to coax a smile from him. She failed.

Bash squeezed his eyes shut. When he opened them again, he looked just above her head, not in her eyes.

"I told you Darius visited me, but someone—well, some*thing*—else did too. A nymera. She had the scales and black eyes belonging to a nymera, but she also had legs, and she claimed to know how to use dark magic." Bash glanced past her shoulder, his jaw tight. "She called me *son*."

Margrete's eyes lifted to his torso, his neck. Those black scales that belonged to the most cunning of the sea's children.

"Do you believe her?" she finally asked once she'd gathered the courage. She knew next to nothing about nymeras, but she never heard any mention of a nymera being *made* in the lore. They were only born. Which meant...

"I believe her. Against all rational thought and logic, I can't help but believe her claim." Bash ran a hand through his hair. He made a face when some of the black strands fell into his eyes. "It would explain"—he motioned to himself—"why I look like this."

"But why would it be happening now? Not when you were young?" That's the part that didn't make sense. Well, not *just* that part. Gods, there were so many things that weren't yet clear.

"I have no idea," he confessed, his frustration evident on his face. "All I know is...I feel like I killed something back there in the forest." She went still. "But I can't remember all the details. I just have images, flashes. And it scares the shit out of me."

Just like the night when he'd gone below the palace and spoken to that voice—

"Was it her?" Margrete asked at the thought of the Adiria Cavern. They were standing in front of one another, close enough to touch, yet neither closing the distance. As much as she wanted to grab him and hold him to her, this talk was past due.

"That night, when you couldn't remember how you ended up below the palace..." she continued when he merely raised a brow. "You were talking to someone, and then you told me later you'd been hearing a voice."

Bash exhaled sharply through his nose. "It was her."

Margrete nodded, treading on the subject carefully. "And now? What does she want?" She tried her very best to sound calm, indifferent even, but her voice quivered just the slightest.

"She didn't say, but I'm going to go out on a limb and say it's not good." Bash's lips lifted stiffly at that.

Screw this.

Margrete closed the gap and snaked her arms around his bare torso. He shivered when she rested her head on his chest, right above his pounding heart. That was all that mattered—that wild and forceful beating.

"Do I frighten you?" Bash asked against the crook of her neck, his voice soft, unsure.

She lifted her head. "I'm afraid *for* you, Bash, but never am I afraid *of* you."

He should know better by now.

"But what if I change more, and what if I cannot control the dark thoughts—"

Margrete placed a finger to his lips. "I happen to think that there's beauty in the dark. And your darkness doesn't scare me. It never did."

She'd fallen so deeply and irrevocably in love with him. Love, the real kind, was never easy. You worked for it, made it better, suffered through the difficult times. That's what made it precious—the unwavering commitment to another soul, however flawed it may be.

"It *should* scare you." Bash's jaw clenched, and he went to look away.

She gripped his chin.

"No. None of that," she said, tsking. "Must I always repeat myself? You don't run from me, and I don't run from you. And if you're worried about your darkness overtaking you, know this: I won't allow it. I won't allow *anything* to take you from me. Mainly because I'm far too selfish for that. Besides, I can be enough light for the both of us. I think I've proven that today," she said, gripping him tighter.

Just as he was her foundation, she could be their walls, holding them together.

She was certain they'd switch back and forth over time. But right now, she could keep them from breaking.

"I've said this before, and I'll likely say it many, *many* times in the future, and not just because I might do something that upsets you, but I don't deserve you." He shook his head in disbelief, and Margrete let out a throaty chuckle. "Only you would take a look at me and my scales and brush it off as if I'd gotten a damned haircut." His rigid smile loosened a fraction, as did the tension in his shoulders. "I can't get rid of you, can I?" This time his lone dimple popped up, and Margrete committed the sight of it to memory.

"You're absolutely insufferable," she said, flicking his nose. She wanted his smile to remain in place so badly. "But regardless of that, you're still *mine.*"

Silence fell. Their breathing combined, joined rhythm. Became one.

Something flashed across Bash's eyes, and they turned impossibly dark. She could get lost staring too deeply into them—mapping out all the silver flecks, the constellations she glimpsed when the light hit them just right. Heat pooled into her core, chasing away the chill of the waters.

"And you're my north star, forever guiding me home." He dipped his chin. "My beautiful queen."

Margrete stilled at that. She was no queen. At least, she didn't feel like one, and besides, she hadn't given *that* much thought to it.

Bash's hands moved to her bottom, and in one quick move, he scooped her into his arms. She forgot mostly everything else but how his fingers dug into her skin as he clutched her tightly. His hooded gaze seared her insides, and he appeared ready to devour her whole. Not that she had any complaints.

"Give me your dark. Your light. Your love. Give me everything. All the pieces you deem broken. All the parts of yourself you hide from the world," she whispered, leaning to place a tender kiss on his throat, right beneath his ear and just above a spiked onyx scale. "I want them for myself, because you won my heart during my darkest days, and you kept it safe when the light finally rose again. I trust you with all my days, all my nights, and all the twilight moments in-between."

Bash brought his hand to the nape of her neck and held her in place. He looked like he wanted to say something, his mouth parting, but then he closed it and shook his head. Right before pulling her to his lips.

They were plush and soft and icy, the cold tickling her in a way she very much enjoyed. She wondered how they'd feel elsewhere...

Bash groaned when she nipped at his bottom lip, his hold on her neck turning fierce. In reply, she wove her fingers through his hair and pulled on the strands, not bothering to be gentle. With him, she could just be herself—and she held nothing back.

"Fuck, I missed you," Bash murmured in between kisses. He trailed his lips up and down the column of her throat, sucking at the tender skin and making her entire body shiver. She arched into his touch, into his mouth, relishing the feel of it.

"I never thought I'd miss anyone," he said, drawing back. She let out a frustrated groan. "It's both vexing and wonderful at the same time."

"That's the perfect description for you," she said, smiling. "Though right now you're being utterly vexing."

His mouth wasn't on her body, and her underclothes were still on. None of that pleased her.

"Impatient," he chided, moving them over to the nearest wall. "I'd like to see how anxiously you missed me."

"I'm sure it would do wonders for your ego," she breathed, leaning in to kiss him. He pulled back, shaking his head tauntingly. She growled.

"You want my darkness, princess? *All* of me?"

She nodded hungrily.

"Then show me."

His voice turned gravelly, his deep words shooting right to her core. She grew intoxicated by his voice alone.

One corner of her lips lifted as she released him and settled on the tips of her toes. He stood at perfect attention, eyeing her like the stunningly handsome predator he was.

Maintaining his stare, she pulled off her undershirt—*slowly*—enjoying how tightly he clenched his jaw, how rigid he held himself. She peeled away the thin material and flung it aside. Her bottoms came next, and Bash's gaze become molten.

"Your turn, pirate."

The muscles in his abdomen ripped as he reached down and freed himself of his undershorts. Her heart rate doubled, and it tripled when he brought all of his attention to her, his eyes greedily moving across the expanse of her body. She had to fight to keep her hands from drifting below the water. From feeling his growing hardness.

The air rippled with electricity, and not just the kind borne from divinity and magic. Margrete sensed her powers awaken as her desire spiraled out of control. Her need for Bash fueled her magic, and the waters curved around them, rising up and in the air. They surrounded her and Bash in a motionless wall, shielding the outside world from what they were about to do.

Bash eyed the mounting water, a devious smile appearing. Before she could push against him the way she wanted, he was on her, reaching out to grasp her wrists. He held them above her head, gazing down at her with a stare so dark his pupils nearly eclipsed the whites of his eyes.

She sucked in a breath, and her wall rose higher in response.

Bash moved her wrists to one hand as he leaned down to whisper into her ear, his stubbled jaw rubbing her cheek. "I should be a gentleman and make you come on my fingers first, or perhaps my mouth, but I'm far, *far* too impatient for that right now."

Margrete arched against him, fighting his hold on her wrists, desperately wanting to touch him. The bastard smiled.

"Wicked man."

Bash lowered his head and took one nipple into his mouth. The coldness of his lips felt just as delicious as she'd imagined they would. He sucked on the aching peak, swirling his tongue around the rosy bud, while his free hand kneaded her other breast, his fingers working her with ease.

He lifted his lips to her collarbone, her neck, moving up and down her skin like a man who didn't know where he wished to begin first. She pressed against him, craving his mouth on her, demanding more. Her core ached when he released a deep low sound in his throat, and she shook with delirious pleasure, knowing she was causing him to unravel.

When he rose, she captured his lips and tugged his bottom one between her teeth before kissing away the hurt. He growled as her tongue danced with his, dueling for supremacy, both of them wanting nothing more than to conquer what the other gave freely.

Bash murmured her name against her lips as he lifted her up against the wall, his arms supporting her back, protecting her bare flesh from scraping against the uneven rock. Her hands fell to his broad shoulders, her nails digging into him, holding him in place. She could feel his need for her press against her entrance, a tease of what was to come. Margrete tried to shove down, wanting to be filled with him, but Bash held her firmly in place, his fingers digging into her hips.

For a brief second, hesitation crossed his features.

He doubted she'd want him in such a state.

"I want you," she breathed, knowing he needed to hear the words. "Please, Bash. Gods, I need—"

He thrust into her, filling her up completely and cutting off her plea. She moaned into his kiss, holding onto his shoulders as he drew back, only to plunge into her heat once more. He tortured her with his slow movements, his unhurried assault, driving her to the brink but not close enough to fall off of it.

Margrete gripped the hair at the nape of his neck and pulled, kissing him as if it was their last time. Her hands roamed his chest, his rippling torso, feeling how his muscles grew taut with every passionate thrust. She whispered his name against the shell of his ear, and Bash shivered as he lowered his mouth to worship her neck, her jaw, her cheeks.

Snaking her hand between them, Margrete felt where they were joined, her fingers gliding against his cock. He let out a choked groan, and her core tightened, the feeling of him sliding in and out of her bringing her closer to shattering.

"I want you for the rest of my days," he murmured, driving into her. "I want you to never leave my side." Another forceful thrust. "I want you in my bed." She moaned when he brought his fingers to the apex of her thighs and moved them skillfully against her bundle of nerves. She was so damned close. "But most of all...I want you on my throne." He plunged into her hard enough to send her moving up the wall.

Margrete cursed. She sighed his name. Prayed to the gods.

Bash chuckled darkly, and Margrete's eyes shuttered. She briefly noticed how high the waters had risen around them, enfolding them in their own bubble.

"Is that a yes, princess?"

She couldn't speak. Did he expect her to speak? Margrete thought she might be shaking her head up and down, but she wasn't sure.

"I need words, Margrete. Say the words."

"I—" She wanted to scream yes at the top of her lungs, but something held her back. Perhaps it was because they might not make it off this island alive, or in one piece, but she had the sinking sensation that things wouldn't end well.

"Margrete?" Bash's movements slowed, and his brow creased. She could practically taste the anxiety rolling off him in waves.

He wanted her to be his queen. To *marry* him. And while she wanted nothing more, Bash had undergone much during these last few days, and she didn't want him to ask when they feared for their lives.

"Ask me again when we get off of this island," she said, panting. "Ask me when we survive and we're home, on Azantian."

Bash's stare grew clouded, and a flash of hurt tightened his features, but he forced a smile and nodded before picking up his pace.

"I'll ask every day until you say yes," he promised, kissing her lips. She felt herself nearing release, and her legs locked around his waist, preparing for the fall.

"I'd expect nothing less," she said, moving her hips in time to his. Gods, she loved this man.

Bash plunged into her core like a madman. Her words were a promise of her answer, and it was good enough for him. For now, at least.

"I love you," he rasped, right as sparks flashed behind her lids and tingles shot down her spine. Margrete's lips parted in a silent scream, her lashes fluttering against her cheeks. She tensed as wave after wave of euphoria washed over her, taking her under, stealing her very air.

She held onto him as she found her pleasure, watching him as he found his with a rumbling groan. The grotto's walls seemed to tremble as he came undone, and the waters sparked a vibrant blue.

When they'd both stilled, pressed against each other and panting, Margrete took Bash's face between her palms.

She lowered her head and kissed him sweetly.

"I cannot wait for the day until I say yes."

They stayed that way—tangled in one another—until her waters fell and the pool's light simmered to a dull gleam.

Margrete would make sure the day would come when they returned to Azantian, when the sea's children were slayed and the world was safe.

She would say yes to him then, and it would be an answer free of distress and full of hope instead.

But most importantly, Margrete would say yes when she'd killed the god who wanted to take her king away from her.

Darius had to die.

And she'd be the one to do it.

CHAPTER THIRTY-THREE

BASH

"Wake up, king."

A boot prodded Bash in the ribs, and he jerked back at the same time his eyes shot open. His arms were empty, free of the woman he'd fallen asleep curled up against, and above him, towering like the vicious bastard he was, stood Darius.

The God of the Sea bent to his knees in a crouch, and his lips twisted up at the sides as he cocked his head. "Someone looks worse than before," he mused. "Or maybe I'm just sensing all the rot you cannot hide." He wrinkled his nose as if in disgust.

Bash pushed to his feet and reached for his empty sheath with a curse.

Damn. He really needed to ask Bay for a replacement, he thought, even though he realized it didn't matter. He was dreaming. *Again.*

"As you've guessed, this little visit of ours is all in your head. And what a dark place that is." Darius scoffed, crossing both arms against his broad chest. "I'm hardly able to stomach staying inside your mind for long before even *I* want to leave. And that's saying a lot."

"What is it this time?" Bash sighed, exasperated. He didn't attempt to disguise his dislike of the ruler over the seas...a fearsome god who had the power to smite him where he stood. But Darius hadn't killed him yet, which told Bash he was saving him for something else. Meaning, he needed him alive. For now.

Besides, they'd played this little game of theirs for far too long, and he grew bored. Well, bored and fucking *annoyed*.

"So impatient." Darius tsked. "I simply came by to warn you."

"And why the hell would you do that?" Bash asked, brows raised. As if he were foolish enough to believe a single word coming from his mouth.

"Today will come with some...difficulties, and I'd prefer it if you all reached the ending of our little game in one piece. At least, the main players. The rest of the crew I couldn't care less about." Darius's sea-colored eyes turned dark. "The only way out of here is through an underwater tunnel, and I fear even an Azantian might have trouble holding their breath for such a duration. Though, you're hardly a full-fledged Azantian, I suppose."

Nymera. Darius didn't have to say the word; his inflection hung between them like a thick, suffocating fog.

"Why warn me?" Bash asked, stepping into Darius's space. "If I will be fine, and so will Margrete, then why this unwelcomed social call?" Bash's tone held the perfect amount of scorn and derisiveness. It made him smile.

"I didn't want Margrete taken off guard," Darius said through his teeth. "That is all."

"Then why not speak with her directly? I know you have before. She's told me of your unwanted visits."

Something dark and unholy crossed Darius's sharp features. A muscle in his jaw feathered. When he didn't say anything crass or cutting in reply, Bash understood...

"You *can't*, can you? Reach her, that is."

Or he would have. Undoubtedly.

The god narrowed his gaze. The air—even in this dreamscape—grew chilled.

"She grows stronger," Darius finally admitted. "I doubt she even realizes how much she's grown, how much her powers have awakened since landing on these shores. Sometimes she uses them without realizing it. It's been wondrous to watch."

He *had* been following them. Observing them. It wasn't a surprise.

"So she's blocking you somehow?" Bash's smile turned wicked, and his heartbeat grew steady, a triumphant drumming in his chest. "You can't slip into her mind."

It wasn't a question.

Darius growled, his nostrils flaring. It appeared his temper was getting the best of him. Especially where Margrete was concerned.

"It won't matter in the end," he promised, seething. "Once the third trial is complete, then *you* won't matter. All will be as it should."

"You can try and manipulate her, but you won't succeed. You don't know her at all."

"I know her better than you think I do," Darius barked, nearly losing his grip entirely. His lethal calm. "She's the one I've been waiting for. The one that will set me free."

Now Bash cocked his head in confusion.

"Set you free?"

Darius chuckled, the sound grating and forced. "I gave up something on this island many, many years ago. My *dearest* mother decreed it held me back, but I feel like it's past time it was returned to me. There is so much you don't know, mortal. So much that would shatter that cocky smile on your face."

Bash's stomach coiled into knots as Darius began circling him.

"There's a reason my brother's power chose Margrete as its home all those years ago. Did you think it was pure luck?" He laughed, the sound echoing. "I didn't believe it at first, and it wasn't until a few months ago that I knew for sure." He ceased his pacing, and Bash went rigid.

"What the fuck are you talking about?" he found himself asking, seemingly for the hundredth time. Bash was sick and tired of not knowing what the hell was happening. But he couldn't rid himself of the idea that whatever Darius sacrificed had something to do with Margrete.

"As I've said, there is much you don't know."

"Then tell me," Bash countered. "If it will shatter me so thoroughly, why keep it to yourself? We both know you want nothing more than to make me miserable. So do it. Try your best, *god*."

Darius chuckled, his eyes flicking across his form, his scales, his blackened nails. "I think we both know it wouldn't take much to break you, and by the looks of it, you're not too far away from giving in to your darkness. You never did seem to possess much willpower, so I doubt you'd be able to fight off your instincts now."

Bash clenched his fists, every muscle in his body tensing. He *was* fighting his instincts, and it took every ounce of strength he had to shut off the little voice inside of his head, urging him to simply give in.

"Don't hurt yourself thinking about it, king. All will be clear soon." Darius shook his head mockingly, false pity shining in his cruel blue eyes. "Though by that time, you might be too far gone to stop yourself from hurting Margrete. It's a good thing I'll be there to pick up the pieces once she's forced to destroy you."

It was the triumphant smile on Darius's lips that had Bash losing all control. Icy fire flared in his chest, and then he was moving with only one goal in mind—to wipe that satisfied smirk off the god's face.

Darius was wrong, and Bash would prove it.

With a roar, he barreled toward the god, his fist raised and ready to strike. But when he took aim and swung, his fist met empty air. He cursed.

"Over here," Darius taunted, and Bash spun on a heel. The god had materialized behind him, his hands shoved deep into his pockets. He raised a brow as if to ask, *Is that all you've got?*

"You're going to leave Margrete alone," Bash snarled, his hackles raised. "Whatever you think she is to you, you're wrong."

"Like calls to like, and she's been calling to me since the moment I heard her prayers on those cliffs in Prias. There's a reason for everything, dear king, and the sooner you understand there's nothing you can do to stop me, the better it'll be for you."

"Why even tell me this?" Bash asked in a snarl. "What's the point?"

"Who said there was a point?" Darius lifted a shoulder. "Perhaps I simply take great pleasure in watching you break. Watching as you put all the pieces together and realize you never were going to be enough for her."

Bash's vision became drenched with red, and his heartbeat skipped several beats.

Darius's words had struck their intended target.

He lunged.

BASH WOKE WITH A GASP. HE JERKED FORWARD, HIS EYES SHOOTING open as he prepared for Darius's assault. His heart thundered as if he were still soaring through the air, seconds from wrapping his hands around Darius's throat and stealing the life from him. Something dark coiled in his stomach at what the ancient god had claimed, and that hunger from before consumed him.

He clutched at his chest, right over his racing heart.

A hand touched his shoulder. Bash jumped.

"Shit, you look dreadful."

Bash found Atlas hovering above him, her eyes narrowed into slits. "Not just the whole scale thing"—she motioned to his neck with her free hand—"but you look like you haven't slept in weeks."

"Thanks," he forced out, his voice a throaty rasp. He scanned the grotto. Margrete stood not too far away, speaking to Bay in hushed tones, her face pinched. Bay must've said something she didn't like, because she placed both hands on her hips and tilted her chin.

"What's going on over there?" he asked Atlas, pointing at the arguing pair.

"Hell if I know. Those two never share anything with the likes of me." Bash made out the barest hint of frustration in her voice.

"Either way, I'd get ready, my king. We're headed out." Atlas gave him a comforting pat on his back and strode off to where Dani and Jacks were sharing a handful of berries. He noticed how Jacks gave most of his share to his sister.

Bash's knees were weak as he rose to his feet. Adrenaline from the confrontation with Darius still flowed through his veins like poison, and his hands trembled at his sides. He made tight fists and strode to Margrete and Bay, though he had to clear his throat pointedly to gain their attention.

"Bash." Bay addressed him with a slight bow of his head. His friend hardly met his eyes. "You feeling any better?"

He was still covered in scales and had just woken from a nightmare involving the deranged god who'd trapped them on this island, but other than that, sure, he was just grand.

"Are we ready to go?" he asked, ignoring Bay's question. The answer went beyond the obvious.

"Yes, sir."

"Good. I want to get out of this tunnel as quickly as possible." He turned to Margrete, who met his gaze with bright eyes and a cautious smile. "Can I have a quick word?" he asked her, his tone unusually stiff. Bay quietly excused himself, mumbling something about wet socks, and headed toward his crew.

She probably thought he was going to ask her why she denied him last night, why she hadn't said yes to marry him. Bash knew her reasoning, but he'd be a liar if he said it hadn't stung.

Once they were alone, situated well out of earshot of the others, Bash told her everything.

"I was visited by Darius again." She took in a sharp breath at the sound of the god's name. "He spoke in more riddles and threats, and he seems more determined than ever to get to you."

Margrete rolled her eyes. "I trust nothing that man—well, *god*—says."

"And maybe we shouldn't trust his words now, but you should hear them all the same." Bash leaned in and spoke barely above a whisper. "Darius says he's been connected to you since you were back in Prias."

Margrete made a face. "Since Prias? Not after I came to Azantian?"

"Since Prias," he said. "He also told me that he's been on this island before. Before he and Malum created their beasts that ravaged the ocean. Darius said he was forced to endure harrowing trials and sacrifice something dear to him. He insinuated *you* are connected to that sacrifice somehow."

"Impossible." She scoffed. "I wasn't even alive."

"True or not, he seemed to believe you're his missing key. His damned salvation," Bash said through gritted teeth, the words like acid on his tongue.

Margrete instantly sobered. "He's a madman."

"No arguments here."

Bash wound his arms around her waist and pulled her against his chest. When she was near, he could breathe properly, and that growing hunger in his belly ceased its aching, turning into a dull twinge.

"Just be careful, princess. He wants you, and I doubt he'll rest until this whole charade is complete."

The thought of Darius anywhere near her made him want to wrap his hands around the god's neck and squeeze. Maybe then he'd wipe off that cocky, self-satisfied smirk—

"Hey." Margrete gripped him fiercely, her nose nuzzling his chest. Thoughts of murder vanished when she lifted her head, staring at him in that special way of hers that knocked the air from his lungs. "We're going to beat him at his own game," she whispered.

Bash tugged her back and wove his fingers into her hair. He couldn't lose her now that he knew what her love felt like. It would be like never seeing the sun again or feeling its warm rays on his skin.

Bash leaned forward and placed a tender kiss on her forehead, breathing her in.

"You're right. He won't win. And I can't wait to watch as you destroy him."

CHAPTER THIRTY-FOUR

BASH

BASH DIDN'T NEED A GOD TO TELL HIM THAT DANGER APPROACHED.

He sniffed the air, tasting a hint of bitterness on the tip of his tongue. The pool continued through the main tunnel, and they waded up to their knees as they trudged through it at a less than ideal pace.

Margrete led the group, looking comfortable up front, in charge. Bash smiled as pride filled him. She would make an excellent queen...*if* she ever accepted his offer. She was a natural-born leader, with or without her magic. Margrete had triumphed over her abuser and claimed the strength in herself that Bash had recognized since the moment he saw her on those cliffs in Prias.

Bash thought about the day of the attack on Azantian often, when she floated on a wave of her own making, a vengeful goddess. He'd never experienced such malicious cruelty as she had during her life, and because of that, Bash knew he could never understand her struggle. Still, it didn't take away his pride. His complete wonder of her.

Margrete abruptly slowed, and thoughts of the past vanished.

"There's..." She paused, sniffing the air, nostrils flaring. "We're getting closer."

Her brows creased in concentration as she listened to her new magic and its ethereal whispers. The entire crew had stopped to hold on to her every word. She'd garnered their respect, and even Mila watched Margrete with a semblance of trust.

Just as suddenly as she'd slowed, Margrete picked up the pace, a victorious smile blooming. "Follow me!" she called over her shoulder, her voice light and brimming with excitement.

Bash wondered what she felt and experienced when her divine power spoke to her, but now wasn't the time to ask. First they had to survive. If they were lucky enough to do that, then he'd pester her with questions later.

Chasing after her, Bash and his crew trailed behind Margrete through the luminous blue water. She didn't stop until five minutes later.

A dead end. A solid wall of impenetrable stone loomed in front of them like a taunt.

"Margrete," Bay began cautiously, his tone lowering. "I don't think—"

She held up a hand, silencing him. Bash was surprised when Bay obliged. Then again, as Atlas had pointed out, the two had formed a greater bond during their time here, an understanding. Another realization that made Bash's heart swell.

Approaching the wall with measured steps, her boots splashing, Margrete lowered to a crouch about five feet before the stone. Placing a hand in the glowing waters, she twisted her wrist, creating a small whirlpool. Around and around she moved, eyes rapt on her hand, on the vortex of magic she fashioned from the elements that called to her.

White lights sparked from her whirlpool, and those sparks flitted deeper beneath the water, moving closer to the wall blocking them in. Bash watched in stunned disbelief as they darted to the wall. Only to go *under* it.

There was a gap. Bash inwardly seethed, hating that Darius had spoken the truth. The god had warned him of the dangerous swim, but he hadn't wanted to believe him, content to regard every one of his words as a lie. Really, it had been his own selfish pride that had stayed his tongue when he woke from his dream.

Margrete stood and turned to them.

"We need to go under and swim. It should lead us right out and to the coast."

"And how far is this swim going to be?" Atlas asked what was on everyone's mind. The warrior stepped forward with a hand on her hip, looking none too pleased.

Margrete's brows scrunched in thought. "I'd say...six hundred feet, give or take."

"Sounds like a fantastic way to die," Jonah grumbled, swiping at his long black hair.

"Always so positive," Mila added with an eyeroll. Jonah's face turned a rosy shade of red.

"Enough," Bash commanded, standing tall beside Margrete. He should've warned her, but all he could do now was bolster his crew. "This is our only way out, and if Margrete thinks we can do it, then we will try. We're Azantians, and the water is our home. We do not fear its embrace." Bash eyed every single wide-eyed man and woman. They were all tired, worn, and desperate. A dangerous combination.

And yet, it was their only option. Margrete had blocked the other entrance with enough stone that it would take them a week to dig themselves out. And then there were the undead soldiers on the other side, their eyes dripping blood and their jaws unhinged, eager for a meal.

Bash would rather face the tunnel than those *things* again.

"Time to move," he ordered, giving them all his back. He was still their king, and Margrete was the woman he planned to have at his side, an equal ruler. He would've laughed a year ago had someone told him that he'd relinquish control so easily. But it was different with her. Even his newly renovated chambers were a testament to that. It had taken some getting used to, sure, but the beautiful chaos she'd brought into his bedroom had grown on him.

Lowering his voice, he leaned close to Margrete's ear, and asked, "You sure about this?"

"Unfortunately."

"Lovely."

Bash marched to where the water met stone and bent down to slip his hands beneath the surface. The gap would hardly fit him. As he crouched, his fingers feeling around the jagged stone, a whisper of a hiss sounded. A *familiar* hiss.

He went rigid. The whisper grew in volume, morphing into a chorus of grating snarls.

He shot to his feet.

"Everything all right?" Margrete asked. "Well, not all right, seeing as we're about to play a fun game with death, but you know what I mean." She bumped his shoulder with hers, a grim half-smile on her lips.

"I'm fine," he replied lightly. He was far, *far* from all right. He recognized those hisses...had heard them accompanied by Minthe's voice.

Internally, he cursed. But on the outside? Bash made sure he looked confident and calm, and everything Margrete needed to see. Besides, if the nymeras were near, they'd be after *him*, not the others. Right?

Bash leaned down and placed a tender kiss on Margrete's lips. He wished he could hold her more closely, kiss her more deeply, but time was of the essence, and he begrudgingly pulled away. "We're all going to be fine, Margrete, I promise." He kissed her temple, praying he wasn't being the optimistic fool. "Besides. I trust in you and your ability to get us out of this mess. You've saved us before, and that was a whole hell of a lot more complicated than navigating an underwater tunnel."

"That's what I fear," she murmured, swallowing hard. "I fear everyone trusting me to save them. What if—"

"Stop that," he ordered, running a finger down her cheek and to her chin. He tilted her head. "When are you going to realize that you're a force of nature?" Margrete rolled her eyes and he tsked. "Well, then I'll just have to remind you every single day how powerful you are until you believe it yourself. We got nothing but time, princess."

Bash placed another kiss on her lips before he made himself release her and step back. It was harder to do than he imagined. Especially when she looked at him like he'd placed all the damned stars up in the sky. He didn't deserve that look, but that didn't mean he couldn't cherish it for a little while longer.

"Time to move," he said over his shoulder to the others, his cutting tone brokering no room for argument.

Sucking in precious air, he slipped beneath the water and pushed through the small opening. The water burned his eyes, but thankfully, it continued to shine brightly, allowing him to see the underwater passageway he swam through.

A muffled splash came from behind him. Margrete's hair fanned around her face like a halo, and he watched as she sucked in a lungful of water. Her eyes gleamed, seeming to glow as brilliantly as the water she inhabited, and she trained them on him. He gave her a reassuring nod before turning back and kicking his legs with every ounce of strength he possessed.

It would be a long swim, one that even an Azantian—or *half*-Azantian, if Minthe was correct—would struggle to make. Then again, nymeras were made for the water and its depths. That didn't settle his thoughts in the slightest. Still, he couldn't show his fear. If he fell, so would Margrete, and it was his turn to hold them together.

More muffled splashes met his ears, and he knew the rest had joined them. Good.

Bash cupped his hands and sliced through the water with the speed and agility he'd mastered during his life at sea. This was where he felt at home, at peace, and the soft whooshing of water and the thudding of his heart gave him strength.

A minute passed before a coldness bloomed in his stomach, moving outward to graze his ribs, his torso. It slithered to touch his fingertips and move down his legs. It felt oddly soothing, even though the pool held no warmth, and he found himself relaxing as the tingling sensation of frost spread.

Margrete kicked to his side. Adrian had done well teaching her how to swim, though he never thanked his friend for that. Something he'd have to remedy once they returned.

A small current aided his endeavors, pushing him faster, growing stronger with each thrust. He turned to Margrete. Her face pinched with concentration, her lips thinned with near tangible determination. The current had to be *her* doing. He dared a peek over his shoulder, grateful that her magic supported the others.

He'd have to remind her of her brilliance when they reached the surface.

Another minute passed, then two more. On average, Azantians could hold their breath comfortably for up to six minutes.

By his calculations, they were over halfway there.

In about two minutes he'd begin to choke for air, and his lungs would begin to burn in less time than that. Bash was a proficient swimmer, but not all of the crew could be called the same. Jonah, while one of the most promising young sailors he'd come across, wasn't as skilled. According to Bay, he had struggled during training. This worried Bash. He might be half a monster, but he was still in charge of that young man's life.

As if sensing his growing unease, Margrete let out a strangled whimper. A flare of white light flashed, and the current she commanded grew more forceful, carrying the Azantians at their backs forward. A vein throbbed on her forehead as she ground her teeth. She was using too much energy on too many people at once. Margrete hardly knew how to use her magic for herself, let alone six others. Himself not included.

Bash.

He shuddered at the familiar call of his name.

You're not going to make it. Not all of you anyway.

Minthe.

She taunted him, hidden somewhere nearby. Bash could sense her like he could sense an impending storm. His mother refused to leave him be.

That little one is already struggling. Jonah, is it? He'll be the first to drown.

Bash shook his head, ignoring the words only he could hear. Margrete kept her eyes forward, too focused on controlling the current. Minthe spoke only to him.

She grows tired. So little practice over these last months.

She'll be fine, Bash thought back, angry at her insinuation. She hadn't the faintest idea of what Margrete was capable of. *Leave me.*

Minthe's laugh echoed in his mind, a noise like nails dragging across sea glass.

You have one more minute, son. One minute before you reach the exit. But they have less than thirty seconds before they take in that first mouthful of water.

Bash instinctively looked behind him, horrified when he glimpsed Jonah slowing, his eyes wide with alarm. Even Mila, who could keep calm under the most dire of circumstances, appeared frantic, her skin turning a light shade of purple.

See. They'll be gone in...twenty seconds now.

Bash reached out and prodded Margrete. When she met his gaze, he jerked his head back, forcing her to follow his stare. She took in the struggling crew, her lips parting as fear washed across her face. She began to suck the water into her mouth in uneven movements, hyperventilating.

Which meant...

She cannot save all of you. Already she helps you more, as I expected, but her control isn't as focused on the others.

Bash doubted she realized what she was doing, using most of her magic to aid him. He knew she'd be horrified if she learned her power wasn't evenly spread.

You have ten seconds, Minthe spoke, shattering any and all remaining calm. *Make a deal with me, and I'll save them.*

For once he had just wanted to imagine things working out in his favor.

What kind of deal? Bash sounded as desperate as he felt. But he didn't care. His first duty was to his people and their safety, and he was failing.

Always failing.

It's simple. Come with me, with us.

No, Bash shook his head, suddenly dizzy. Black spots floated around the edges of his sight.

Then they will die.

And it would be his fault.

He shot a final peek back, his heart clenching when he narrowed in on Bay. His old friend had slowed to a crawl, though he still fought to move. To live.

Bash knew his answer before he thought it, and it cleaved him in two.

Save them, he thought without hesitation. *Save them all or no deal.*

Minthe laughed once again. *As you wish, dearest son.*

Margrete's current ceased, and the water stilled. Bash reached out to her, a soundless scream on his lips.

Their fingers touched, and love passed between them.

Understanding. Fear.

She would be all right, he assured himself. But he couldn't let the lives of the crew weigh on her conscience. *That* would kill her.

A flash of black fluttered past his line of sight, then the whipping of a spiked tail. Gleaming teeth. Black, serrated nails. Midnight hair.

Margrete mouthed his name as a horde of nymeras surrounded the crew on all sides of the passageway. They moved quicker than the fastest bolt of lightning, their arms reaching out to snag the closest human in their grasp. One by one, the others were taken in the arms of the enemy, of the same beasts they had been set on hunting days before.

Bash looked to Margrete now, knowing Minthe would make sure he honored their deal. He mouthed three words he felt with every fiber of his being.

Maybe in another life he could've had it all.

Bone-white arms encircled him just as Margrete cried out again, her hand outstretched as if to reach him.

But it was too late. Bash closed his eyes as the horde of nymeras carried him away from her. From his friends. His crew.

As the bony arms holding him tightened, Bash's vision prickled with black, and he fell into a void of unimaginable shadows. With Margrete out of sight, that ravenous hunger in his belly roared, begging to be satiated, growing more and more voracious. The seconds passed, but time might as well have stopped. All he could focus on now was that hunger, and it tore him apart from the inside out.

The last coherent thought Bash had was of *her.*

And even that image slipped away...until eventually, he couldn't remember her at all.

CHAPTER THIRTY-FIVE

MARGRETE

MARGRETE ROARED AS THE NYMERAS STOLE BASH FOR A SECOND time.

She thrashed against the surge of water the monsters created, the chaotic frenzy of moving limbs and serrated scales. Margrete delved within and begged for her magic to last just a *little* bit longer.

It simmered and sparked...and then went out completely.

She'd lost her focus, her control, which seemed to happen whenever Bash found himself in trouble. He was her weakness.

The nymeras scooped up Jonah, Atlas, Bay, and the twins after, whisking them farther down the passageway. Either to save or devour them, Margrete didn't know.

Then there was silence.

They'd shot through the passage like a storm of black and silver and vanished just as quickly, leaving Margrete alone and frantic.

She could still breathe, but she knew she didn't have much longer. That had been the problem as well—breathing underwater *while* manipulating a current to aid seven other souls. It had taxed her, and only the energy to breathe for herself remained.

Margrete sliced through the water, once again grateful for Adrian's lessons. She lacked his grace, but the water recognized her and flowed around her body seamlessly.

She made out nothing ahead—no Azantians or nymeras—and her pulse doubled when the glow of the pool began to fade. The tunnel narrowed precariously.

Her shoulder struck the side of the passageway, a jagged rock slicing through her skin. She smelled her blood a moment later and internally cursed. Pushing on, she fought against the pull of exhaustion, swimming until she came to two tunnels.

Leading in different directions.

She didn't have time to think as they approached, and her eyes flitted between the two passages, wondering where the nymeras would've taken Bash and the crew. But she could sense nothing but her bloodied shoulder, and it clogged her nostrils, making it impossible to detect any other scent.

Margrete shifted to the right at the last minute.

It didn't take long for her to realize she'd chosen poorly.

A rush of water picked up around her, coming out of nowhere. It carried her body forward at an alarming pace, and she couldn't stop herself from bumping into the sides of the tunnel. She became a mess of cuts and scrapes, and copper continued to fill her nostrils. She took another hit to her side, grimacing when her shirt tore and a sharp stone cut deep through muscle.

Come on, focus!

She cursed herself, her situation, the entire island itself, but none of her foul words did any good. Margrete battled the unusual current, stubborn enough to not give in. When a hint of natural light reached her, a tiny seed of hope blossomed. Like a beacon in the night, it called her forth, and her arms cupped the water with renewed purpose.

That's when the current drove her headfirst into a jutting crag.

Pain unlike she'd ever known stabbed behind her eyes, radiating down from the top of her head and to her spine.

Margrete took a final breath.

She lost the battle before she could exhale.

Pure darkness swept across her mind.

THERE WERE ARMS. THE SMELL OF SMOKE, SPICE, SALT. WEAK sunlight. Cold breath on her cheek.

Margrete blinked and tilted her head. A groan escaped.

"Shhh," soothed a familiar voice. "Don't move."

As if she could. Margrete's head throbbed something fierce, and her body might as well have been torn to shreds. Maybe it was.

She felt pain and weightlessness and...those arms. That was all she knew. And trying to lift her head? She could hardly open her eyes.

When she managed to peel back her lids, which weighed as heavy as stones, the world blurred into a mess of muted colors. The only thing not belonging to the forest was golden skin.

And blond hair.

Margrete's eyes closed again.

She didn't wake for some time.

FIRE.

She smelled the smoke before she saw it.

This time, when she took in the scene before her, her vision was slightly less fuzzy, though certainly not clear.

Her head felt better, not as if someone continuously drove a dagger through her skull. A small mercy. Her body ached, but the pain felt manageable.

She lifted her head. Her blurred sight allowed her to make out the outline of a dark cave, a blossoming fire licking at the walls. She didn't recognize a thing.

"You're almost healed."

Margrete flinched, twisting to find the source of the all-too-familiar voice. The sudden movement had her grimacing in agony.

"Don't worry, I'm not here to hurt you," Darius said, stepping out from the shadows. He wore his signature cloak, though the hood remained down, leaving his face visible. Margrete squinted, wishing she wasn't so weak, wishing her vision was clear enough so she could strike if need be.

"Get back!" she said, her voice gravelly. She lifted a hand as if that might do any good. Her magic had burrowed so far beneath her skin, she doubted it would reach her even if she could summon it properly.

Darius sighed. He almost sounded offended.

"You were knocked unconscious, passed out on the banks for any predator to take."

She recalled the current, the rocks, the frantic fight of maintaining control, and then the all-encompassing darkness.

"I've healed you, but you took quite the hit to the head. If you were anyone else, it would've ended you." Darius dropped into a crouch, his arms resting on his knees. "But you're a survivor. Just like me."

"I'm nothing like you!" she snarled, pushing further against the cave's walls. She reached for her weapon. Her fingers wrapped around steel, her blade in its sheath. Darius hadn't taken it from her, which both confused and infuriated her. He believed himself impenetrable, and maybe he was against Azantian steel, but she imagined her blade would hurt nonetheless.

Darius gazed to the far side of the cave, and as her sight cleared, she made out how the flames danced across his sharp cheekbones, his strong jaw, his haunted eyes.

For a god who usually dripped with cockiness and self-righteousness, he appeared nearly mortal. The sight was unnerving.

Darius ignored her for a long time, and she tensed when he finally opened his mouth to speak, his words calculated and carefully selected.

"I want to tell you a story not many know," he said in a whisper. He turned his head back to face her, his eyes searing with unnamable emotion. "It's a tale about two brothers who fought for centuries, never able to trust the one being who should be able to understand them. A tragedy, really." Darius scoffed before swallowing thickly. "They were warriors first and brothers second. Both so very angry. Both lonely."

Margrete held his stare, unable to look away. His words carried the same kind of weight that came with infinite grief. She recognized it all too well.

Still, she didn't want to listen to this farce of a story.

"I don't care about your lies," she said, scorn lacing her voice. "I want to know where my friends are."

Annoyance flitted across his features before he smoothed it away.

"Your precious crew and your king are fine," he snapped. "But believe me, this is something you're going to want to hear."

"I doubt that."

"Just...just listen, *please*."

Margrete tensed at the sincerity in that single word. She bit back her retort and did as he asked, if only to get this whole charade over with.

Darius continued.

"After countless betrayals and nights spent alone, one of the brothers decided to change his fate. He'd grown weary of fighting a never-ending battle, and desired a partner, someone he knew wouldn't deceive him."

Darius paused, his eyes roaming up and down her form. It wasn't a sensual perusal, more curious. Margrete tightened her hold on her blade.

"I'm sure you've heard the story of Malum and his heart. How he took it from his chest and gifted it to his mortal lover. Of course, he didn't realize how that little act would destroy him in the end, but I suppose his intentions were good."

Now his very power lay in her own heart. She felt it flutter in reply.

"His brother did something similar, though he did so many years before. When Surria decided to test the brothers' worthiness, she placed them on an island so very brutal and merciless that one of the gods took drastic measures," Darius murmured, dark shadows clouding his eyes. "What the god took from himself was a piece of his very soul."

"Gods have souls?" She never had thought too long about it.

Darius nodded. "Everything has a soul, a life force, though the souls of gods aren't the same as a human's. Our essences are crafted from magic, and our blood is filled with the rarest kind of energy."

"That explained almost nothing," Margrete grumbled.

His grim smile twitched up at the sides. "Perhaps, but I don't think some things are meant to be fully understood." He breathed out through his nose, his brow furrowing. And then, as if he suddenly remembered he was in the middle of his tale, he lifted his head and squared his shoulders. All traces of uncertainty vanished.

"As I was saying..." He cleared his throat. "The god split his soul into two perfect halves, using one to create what he'd always longed for. A partner."

Darius's stare grew dark, and Margrete shifted beneath his penetrating gaze.

"The god loved his creation, the other half of himself. She was all the good parts of him, and he cherished her. Finally, he'd found someone to share his long life with, and for the briefest of times—even on this cursed island—he was happy.

"Of course, that happiness was short-lived. After he'd completed the first two trials alongside his new companion, his dearest mother decided to take what little joy he'd found."

Something snapped within Margrete.

A flash of an image fluttered across her mind, of Darius...and a woman with near-black hair. They stood surrounded by stone, side by side. Margrete couldn't ignore how the woman's features bore a striking resemblance to her own. The scene reminded her of the other pictures she'd been seeing as of late—of her and Darius in one another's arms.

Just as quickly as it had appeared, the image dissipated. She shook her head as if to rid herself of its lingering touch.

"During the third trial," Darius pressed on, "Surria forced the brothers to commit a crime so heinous it would steal what little trace of empathy they possessed." A muscle in his jaw feathered, and his nostrils flared. Margrete's grip on her dagger loosened. She hated that she wanted to know. This story...it felt familiar in a way that made the tiny hairs on her arms stand at attention.

"Malum gave up his most cherished possession; an ancient object older than the gods themselves, whose purpose remained a mystery even to Surria. Though on that day when he relinquished it, a great tremor shook the earth, and the absence of its dark magic changed Malum forever."

She felt the urge to ask more, but she suspected from his furrowed brow that not even Darius knew of the object's meaning. Margrete made a mental note to ask Bash about it later. *When* she found him.

"And the second god..." Darius sucked in a sharp breath, drawing Margrete's focus back to his story. "He gave up something far more precious than any object. The partner he'd built was taken from him, destroyed. *Killed*." Now his upper lip curled into a snarl, and the walls of the cave shook with his rage. "Surria made *him* kill her, murder the only thing that would grant him peace."

"Why did *you* kill her then? If you loved her so much?" Margrete asked.

How could someone—even a *god*—kill the other half of their soul?

"My mother spun such horrid lies, lies I believed like a fool, claiming the woman I loved was an illusion and that she existed solely in my head," Darius snapped, his voice cutting sharper than any sword. "The truth eventually came out, after...after I killed her." He could barely get the words out, the muscles in his neck tensing. "Surria merely watched as I broke apart. All she said was that sacrifice made us stronger, and then she ordered me to wipe away my tears."

Darius glanced away from her, breathing hard. He couldn't meet her eyes.

Margrete looked at him, really *looked*. She put aside her hatred for the god and ignored the warning bells ringing in her head. With the fire casting its glow upon his face, and the muscles in his neck and shoulders taut, Margrete glimpsed the edges of another image, a memory.

She closed her eyes.

Darius sat beside a fire, much like this one, though his lips weren't curled down at the sides. He smiled, a smile so radiant it rivaled the flames. His lips were moving inaudibly, and he laughed, throwing his head back at whatever he'd said. She knew he spoke with another, but she only saw the barest reflection of a woman in his eyes.

"You see it, don't you? You understand now?"

Margrete blinked, the scene swept away.

Darius had shifted to rest a foot away, still crouched but looming above her, pain and desperation in his eyes. She let out a whimper, shoving back, fearful of the truth shining in his unhinged stare.

"Tell me you remember!"

His voice broke on the last word.

"I—" Margrete couldn't breathe or think or move. She refused to close her eyes again, because if she saw another image of a different time, she'd lose herself entirely. Nothing on this island felt real, but those memories, the brief visions she'd just had...

The island had felt familiar since the moment she stepped foot on it. But that couldn't possibly mean what he said was true. She wouldn't allow it to be true.

"It's not real," she murmured, clutching at her temples. She shook her head from side to side, beginning to hyperventilate. "This isn't real. I'm having another nightmare."

"Oh, but it *is* real," Darius said, reaching out to cup her cheek. "I heard your prayers across the sea, even before Surria's curse fell. I heard you against all odds, and at the time I thought it had to do with my brother, but I knew I had to find you and discover the real reason as to *why* your pleas reached me when no one else's did."

Margrete shook her head, but he didn't drop his hand. His touch was pure ice.

"I believed you were a useful tool against my brother. A little bit of luck I could use to end him once and for all. But how wrong I was." His thumb stroked her jaw, and she shivered. Margrete wasn't sure what upset her more—that she didn't jerk away or that she was too entranced by him to *want* to move.

"I didn't realize what you might be until I saw you lift that wave and send it into your father's ship. In that moment of clarity, I glimpsed past your mortal skin and saw a piece of the soul beneath. I ran after the battle, overcome with too much...*emotion*." He sneered at the word, like having an ounce of humanity was unimaginable. "And yet I kept visiting you, sneaking into your dreams every night for months, unable to stop. It was madness, this need." His hand dropped to his side, and she took in her first breath of air since he'd touched her. "I'd believed your soul had been trapped in the underworld all this time."

His declaration hung in the air and weighed it down. The walls of the cave started to blur once more as Margrete lost air, her chest rising and falling rapidly. She was on the verge of passing out.

"Surria, twisted as always, had me believe I'd never get the other half of my soul back, and I suspect she'd prefer my ignorance even now. No one knows how very cruel the Goddess of Wind and Sky truly is, how ruthless. Then again, one might imagine where my brother and I learned it from."

"No."

A single word. It was all Margrete could manage.

She might have repeated it, repeated it half a dozen more times, but the blackness was eating away at the world again, and her lids grew heavy.

"Yes," Darius whispered, his voice sounding far away. Her eyes lost the battle and shut. "I thought I lost you, my greatest creation. My other half. But now I've found you, and I will make sure I won't ever lose you again."

More memories assaulted her. Memories of Darius. Of entwined hands and stolen kisses. Joyful smiles and long nights. Margrete saw this very island and all of its horrors, but at her side, in every wavering memory, was a man who held her throughout. He encouraged her to triumph over Surria's trials, his smile borne of the purest kind of pride.

She saw a man—no, a *god*—who looked at her with adoration and love and awe.

Margrete readily succumbed to the ravenous darkness, knowing it was the only way to escape a truth she wished she'd never learned.

She was more than a vessel for Malum's power.

Margrete had been created from the soul of a god.

Darius's missing half reborn.

CHAPTER THIRTY-SIX

MARGRETE

MARGRETE WOKE SLOWLY.

She made out the sound of rushing water in the distance, of waves lapping against the shore. She smiled, eyes still closed, hoping to stay in whatever fleeting dream she'd found. Maybe if she never opened her eyes, she'd remain here, with the music of the sea in the background and the promise of waking in her own bed, Bash nestled beside her...

Margrete wouldn't be stuck on some island created by a goddess, forced to undergo three deadly trials. She wouldn't have a god on her heels, claiming the unimaginable.

She shot upright with a start.

Darius.

Yesterday's revelations assaulted her like the worst possible headache after a night of drinking. Cautiously, she brought her hand to her temples and rubbed. Her head still ached, though it certainly wasn't as bad as it had been.

Margrete took in a steadying breath and surveyed her surroundings. She found herself in the same cave as last night, though now soft sunlight filtered in, casting ghoulish shadows on the walls. A new day had started, which meant she'd lost precious time needed to find the others. They could be headed in the opposite direction, and she would have to race to reach them. *If* she could find them at all.

A subtle weight rested across the length of her body, and Margrete glanced down. Fine linen crafted of the deepest blue swathed her, and with tentative fingers, she grasped the material and twisted it in her hands.

The cloak was unmistakable. Darius had covered her with the garment, protecting her from the slight chill, and yet the god himself was nowhere to be seen. Not that she didn't believe he wasn't watching from afar. He'd admitted he observed them all.

Margrete prepared to toss the cloak aside when she froze. Perhaps it was idle curiosity or divine instinct, but she reached into one of the deep pockets.

She cursed as her fingers wrapped around a single polished coin, a soft glow emanating from its surface.

"Fuck me."

Margrete dropped the offensive metal as if that might save her. As if she could stop the third trial from happening by simply flinging the coin aside.

Darius's words invaded her thoughts all at once in a nauseating rush.

"I thought I lost you, my greatest creation. My other half. But now I've found you, and I will make sure I won't ever lose you again."

Margrete lurched to the side and dry-heaved.

It couldn't be true. None of it even made sense, for gods' sakes. Darius was simply a liar who wanted to use her, and he'd concocted some inane story in a foolish attempt to persuade her to join him.

Even as she repeated this explanation over and over to herself, her gut twisted, her spine tingled, and her heart—which had been racing seconds before—slowed to a steady pace. Its forceful beating drummed in her ears, the measured pounding at odds with her tumultuous thoughts.

Darius claimed she was the missing half of his soul, and that was the real reason Malum's essence had sought her out in her mother's womb when her father staged a coup on Azantian. Ortum had believed he'd made a mistake when he tried to transfer the power, but maybe it hadn't been a mistake at all.

Like calls to like, Darius had said, and if Malum's power had indeed recognized her soul, it would've been drawn to it like an Azantian was to the sea.

"No," she said aloud to herself, feeling unhinged. She stood abruptly and wiped at her mouth. Darius's cloak fell from her body and into a crumpled heap on the ground. "It's not true!" She kicked at the rumpled material, unleashing her pent-up anger upon the inanimate cloak. In her mind, she pictured the god inside of it, her boot connecting with his haughty smirk.

All her life she'd wanted to be her own person, and if Darius hadn't been lying, she *never* was, and she never could be. Or maybe souls didn't work like that. Not that she knew much about them to begin with. Darius *had* said that the souls of gods differed from those of humans.

It didn't make her any less pissed.

The coin she'd hastily tossed rested beside the smoldering remains of the fire, facedown. She refused to look at it for too long. It symbolized everything she wanted to escape.

Margrete let out more foul curses as she stormed from the cave, leaving Darius's cloak and the coin behind. Outside, the air held a biting chill, the winds brutal as they rocked the same black trees she'd grown to hate. Some of the leaves were tinged with red, black swirls etched on their surface, but besides that, she found no discernable sign of where she'd wound up.

She'd make it her new life mission to never see this place again.

Marching into the woods, she chose the first path that called to her—northwest, it seemed. If this was all some game orchestrated by Darius, she figured she'd wind up wherever he wanted her to in the end.

Her temper worked to get the best of her, and in a way, she let it. Margrete wanted to wallow for a little bit. In fact, she believed she *deserved* it.

Just when Bash had returned to her, he'd been stolen yet again, and her friends and crew were taken as well. And now she was left alone and scared and angry in the woods on some island that shouldn't exist. Margrete could be optimistic...to a point.

That point had been breached days ago.

Her steps were heavy as she pushed through the dense thicket, uncaring as to whatever creatures might be lurking.

Come and get me, she thought, rolling her eyes like a sullen child. She might enjoy a fight, if only to release her burning outrage. And the monsters here didn't frighten her—she'd seen worse monsters wearing human faces.

Laughter floated to her ears, and at the sound of it, she nearly tripped over a fallen branch.

She went completely still.

The melodious noise tugged at her heartstrings. Something about it was painfully familiar, and her brow creased, an uneasy alarm eating away at her anger.

When the laughter continued, she took off in a run for the source, the power in her chest warming the nearer she got. She prayed it was a good sign, an indication to follow rather than a warning to flee. Again, she didn't care much at this point. Why be careful when her caution had brought her nothing but pain?

Margrete followed the lyrical notes until she reached the banks of a stream. Slowly, she dipped into a crouch behind a dense patch of reeds, hiding as best she could from sight. If she found anyone but her friends or Bash, she wouldn't be caught unawares. She may be pissed, but she wasn't quite suicidal.

Two figures materialized as if from thin air, a man and a woman, both ankle-deep in the stream. Margrete choked back her gasp.

They were phantoms—tricks of light that were nothing more than a quivering image—and yet the sight of them wading through the stream, joy etched upon their faces, struck a chord deep within Margrete.

She'd seen this before, or rather, it felt like she'd lived it. A rush of dizziness had her reaching out for the trunk of a tree, supporting her weight while the spectral couple neared.

Moving at a leisurely pace, Margrete glimpsed Darius...and the soul he'd created—the woman who looked remarkably like her.

No. The woman who *had* been her.

Margrete was fixed in place, unable to pry her gaze from the couple who only had eyes for each other. The black-haired woman with the brightest blue eyes Margrete had ever seen must've said something her heightened hearing couldn't pick up, because a second later Darius's deep laughter followed. He shot her a mischievous smile and bent down to send a spray of water across his companion's bewildered face.

"You bastard!" the woman screeched, though her tone held no bite. With a wicked smirk, she, too, crouched and cupped the stream's icy water, returning the sentiment and wetting the god's handsome face. His blond hair plastered to his face, and he swiped a hand through the damp strands.

"Now you've done it, Wryn," Darius threatened, before scooping her into his arms and spinning her around and around. She giggled and protested, begging him to put her down even as she squealed with delight.

And Darius...Margrete hadn't thought he was capable of smiling in such a way—unquestionably genuine and brimming with the brightest sort of joy. It rocked her very core.

Margrete blinked.

The vision vanished...or the *memory* vanished.

It hadn't felt like one of the island's typical hallucinations. Instead, the scene held the weight that memories often did, and while the phantom pair no longer played in the stream, they refused to leave her.

She stood on trembling legs. Margrete couldn't shake the intimacy of what she'd witnessed, how her heart raced as if *she* had been the one lifted in Darius's arms.

She fought the urge to retch. Again.

A playful gust of wind picked at her hair and cooled her brow, carrying with it the god's signature scent of the sea and a rich, foreign spice. Margrete scowled. She couldn't seem to escape him.

The longer she remained on this island, the more potent these visions became, and Margrete had a sinking feeling that maybe Darius hadn't lied to her at all.

MARGRETE FOLLOWED THE STREAM AIMLESSLY.

When she bent down to cup the cool water and satiate her thirst, her palms came back with more than a mere drink. They came back heavier and carrying the final piece of a curse.

The coin had found her, just like she knew it would.

Sacrifice.

That one word glimmered beneath a layer of water. A simple word that carried much meaning.

She dropped her hands with a gasp, and the glowing silver plummeted back to the stream with a resounding splash.

Margrete continued on her path, though she didn't drink from the stream again.

CHAPTER THIRTY-SEVEN

BAY

THEY'D WASHED UP ON THE BANKS OF A RIVER.

Everyone except for Bash and Margrete. Bay foolishly hoped they would wind up together.

"We should continue in the same direction as planned. They might be headed north and toward the coast now," Atlas said. She walked at Bay's side, her eyes peeled, scanning the thin limbs of every tree as if waiting for one of Surria's creepy half-alive soldiers to jump down and attack.

Bay shivered. If he never saw one of those things ever again, it would be too soon.

They'd been walking for hours now, and the little sleep Bay had gotten last night wasn't nearly enough to sustain him. He doubted the rest of the crew had found sleep either.

"I agree." Bay gave a curt nod. "Though I'm still unsettled as to why the nymeras didn't..."

"Attack? Suck our souls from our body and feed? Tear us limb from limb?" Atlas supplied without a hint of emotion.

"Yes to all of that," Bay replied, shaking his head. "From what I know of them, they aren't notorious for their self-control, and we were an easy meal. They should've killed us right then and there in that passageway."

"Or maybe our king has something to do with their...hesitation."

Bay halted and turned to Atlas, a retort on the tip of his tongue. He wanted to defend his king, as was his instinct, but Bash *had* changed, and the nymera scales surrounding his neck couldn't be ignored. Bay might've pretended not to notice or linger on them for too long, but his blood turned to ice whenever he looked at Bash's neck, his hair, those inky fingertips.

"He has the qualities of those creatures, their distinct characteristics," Atlas continued. "We'd be fools not to suspect the worst."

"And *what* are you suggesting is the worst?"

Atlas shrugged coolly. "That there's more to our king than we thought. He claimed he woke up like that, and it may be true, but I doubt that's *all* to the story. I sensed him holding back, but I'm sure he told Margrete. Which means she kept the truth from us as well."

A part of Bay couldn't blame Margrete. If the roles had been reversed, he'd have done everything in his power to protect Adrian. Still, he wished she had trusted him enough to tell him. Bay thought they'd grown closer these last few months. But if she'd lied to him, then maybe the truth was worse than he imagined.

"What's the plan?"

They both turned at the sound of Jonah's voice. He scrambled to Bay's side, shooting Atlas with a cautious look. The statuesque warrior intimidated him, as she did many.

"Same plan as before," Bay said. "We head to the coast."

"I know they're both all right," Jonah supplied, a subtle smile lifting his lips. "If they're together, they would make a formidable force against any enemy, even those creepy things with the bleeding eyes." He shivered at the memory. "Gods, they were awful to look at."

"An understatement," Dani murmured as she drifted to Atlas's right, her gaze wandering to the stream's curving banks. Bay noticed how Atlas immediately stiffened.

"We'll be fine," Atlas said, her tone uncharacteristically soft. She swallowed thickly and cleared her throat. "We should reach the coast soon. I'd even wager we'll get to it no later than nightfall."

Dani nodded, her tight curls bouncing. She hardly seemed convinced, and her silence spoke louder than any words. Atlas rushed to break the painful hush.

"Don't you worry, Dani," she said, seeming to linger on her name. "I won't let anything happen to you...or anyone else, I mean. I've trained for this, well, not *this* in particular, but for bad situations. And this is definitely a bad situation. Not that I can't get us out of it."

Bay's lips quirked. Atlas certainly wasn't very subtle, but luckily for her, Dani was oblivious to her nervous ramblings. It was so unlike his cool and collected friend to babble.

Dani lifted her head and smiled at Atlas in a way that had even Bay feeling her warmth. The young sailor had that pacifying way about her. His mind went back to the show of intuition she displayed in the woods before the soldiers attacked. He'd have to keep an eye on her moving forward.

"Thank you, Atlas," Dani finally said, peeking up through her thick lashes at the warrior. She hastily shifted her gaze back to the stream.

Atlas's ears turned bright red at the tips. Bay wondered when his friend would find the courage to speak with Dani properly. He sensed attraction on both sides, though neither of them knew how to approach each other. Funny how even opposites could stumble when it came to matters of the heart.

If they got out of here in one piece, Bay might have to have a talk with Atlas. He looked forward to the awkwardness that would ensue—and the fierce red blush that would spread across Atlas's cheeks.

But for now, they were far from safe, and he couldn't dwell on a future they might not see.

Bay broke apart from his crew and glided in front, alone. He couldn't rid himself of those final moments in the underwater passageway. As one of the beasts wrapped their arms around Bay, he'd spotted his king, just ahead, a knowing sort of look on his face. There had been no fear, no struggle, just an odd sort of acceptance.

It was a look he couldn't shake off. Bash might not be the man he knew and loved anymore. Whether Margrete could accept that or not, Bay would stay vigilant, and if Bash threatened the crew, he'd act. Even if he had to use the blade at his side. Bay had dedicated his life to Azantian and the safety of the seas, and that duty came first.

Always.

With dour thoughts weighing on his mind, Bay trudged ahead feeling as if the entire world rested on his shoulders.

Hell, maybe it did.

CHAPTER THIRTY-EIGHT

BASH

Bash found himself surrounded by the enemy.

After exiting the underwater passageway, the nymeras swam out into the open, beyond the rocky walls of the cavern. The tunnel had led out to a raging stream, and they hauled Bash downriver.

Now, after floating in and out of consciousness for the last ten or so hours, Bash was in the center of the horde, propped up against a tree trunk in the shade just beside the riverbank. It had taken him a minute to remember himself and who he was, which should've been terrifying all by itself. But he'd forgotten Margrete's *name*. He'd pictured her face upon waking, but he couldn't recall it. Only after an hour had passed had it struck him like a punch to the gut.

He felt sick. Bash promised himself he wouldn't let himself forget again.

To his right, a dozen nymeras sunbathed on boulders rising up from the stream they'd exited, their dark fins catching the little light that penetrated the clouds. The others were on land, eyeing him warily as they pretended to talk among themselves in a crude, gravelly language he didn't recognize. They all wore thin white garments, the same as Minthe.

But the biggest shock of all?

They had legs.

The books Bash read always described their lethal fins. Not once had he heard about their ability to transform and walk on land. This new revelation unsettled him, to say the least.

Oh, and being their prisoner. That, too, didn't bode well for him.

"You're weak."

Bash glanced up. Minthe hovered above, her unnaturally wide eyes narrowed. She almost appeared concerned.

"I'm fine," he lied, a grunt leaving his throat as he shifted positions. Minthe was right—he could hardly lift his head, let alone his body. The exhaustion that flooded him since the "rescue" was overwhelming.

"You need to feed," Minthe stated simply. "If you don't eat in the next day or so, you won't make it. Your body will wither and dry out into a husk, eventually turning to dust. I bet you're already losing your grip on reality as it is."

"You paint a lovely picture," he responded dryly. "But I think I'll take my chances."

Bash tried to move to the side so he didn't have to look at her, but his body protested, and with a groan, he fell back against the trunk.

"My people raided the village of Lira days before we ventured to this island to retrieve you, so we don't need to feed anytime soon. But you? You need sustenance. Now." She cocked her head and assessed him in that cold way of hers. "I wish we had kept a better hold on you during that storm so we could've brought you food, but I should have suspected you'd manage to escape. You *are* my son, after all." Minthe sounded proud, and her viciously sly lips lifted.

Bash didn't remember much of the storm that wrecked the *Phaedra*, just struggling for air and the feel of slick hands on his body. Then darkness. When he woke next, it was on the island and beneath a pile of bones.

"How do you have legs?" he asked, hating that he gave her the satisfaction of his attention. But he had to know.

One corner of her mouth lifted. "We've always had the ability to shift, but it's not something we allow the humans—or Azantians—to know." She sighed when his forehead creased. "You call the energy we harness dark magic, but really, all magic is the same. There is no good or evil. My people, *your* people, simply utilize the more potent aspects of the art."

Bash shook his head. If their magic wasn't evil, like Minthe claimed, then why did it smell and taste so foul?

"Would you care to hear the truth now?" Minthe asked after some time had passed. The air was ripe with tension. "Or are you too stubborn for your own good?"

"Screw off," Bash growled. "I'm here, as promised, but that doesn't mean I have to listen to your lies."

Minthe let out a dramatic sigh, sounding more human than Bash could've thought possible.

"I shall tell you anyway. It might help you see things a little more clearly."

Bash strongly doubted that.

"Your father was always one for his secrets. He collected them like jewels." The woman raised a clawed finger, inspecting the jagged nail. "Sadly, he wasn't protecting you the way he thought. If anything, by *not* telling you the truth, he damned you."

The air became too heavy in Bash's lungs.

Minthe pursed her lips, a flash of disappointment there and gone before Bash could fully register it. "I wonder if he ever told you the tale of how he met your mother."

How his father met *her*, she meant.

While her chin jutted out defiantly, Bash noticed how her hands clenched into dainty fists, her claws poking into her sickly white skin.

If his father kept secrets, it must've been for the best, regardless of what this monster claimed. Bash may not be a saint, but he was far from damned. At least, not yet.

Even Bash didn't believe himself.

"It was on the night of the Full Moon Feast, days after your father celebrated the recovery of a lost artifact, some magical compass or map, and he was still on edge from the journey," Minthe said, her eyes growing clouded. With anger or sadness, Bash couldn't discern.

"As he was restless and easily distracted," she continued, "he found himself in his favorite place. I believe you refer to it as the Adiria Cavern."

Bash wasn't breathing. Not at the mention of the one place that his soul sought rest.

"I see the recognition in your eyes." Minthe grinned. "It was there, just beneath the palace, that he was lured by the call of a woman trapped inside the enchanted cavern. She was strong, much stronger than others like her, and roamed the cave freely, well above the depths of her pack's prison. But as formidable as she was, she couldn't leave the rocky walls cursed by a god.

"So she sang the song that hummed in her black blood, hoping one day someone would answer her desperate plea. When the king stumbled into the Adiria Cavern, their eyes locked instantly. They felt a *pull*, the call of something greater than what either had ever known." She scoffed, the sound brittle. "Of course, as your father was always a stubborn man, he kept his distance, believing this woman to be a monster. He fled moments later, racing up the steps and slamming the door behind him.

"But that wasn't the last time he saw her," she spat. "He came back three nights later, a song only he could hear waking him from his sleep. Descending into the cavern once more, he came face to face with the woman who wouldn't leave his thoughts, as her voice had haunted him long after their first encounter."

Bash gritted his teeth, his stomach sinking as his mind worked to comprehend the hidden meaning behind her story. The nymeras had been imprisoned beneath the palace and trapped below hundreds of feet of rock. It wasn't possible his father met this *woman* in the cavern.

Nonetheless, the truth was staring him in the face. For the first time, he noticed how similar her straight nose looked, how her high cheekbones matched his own.

Minthe interrupted his thoughts. "It was another night until he spoke to her, and one more night until she replied to him. But like all good *love* stories, they didn't need words to understand each other. And so, the song would wake him every evening, and he would creep down below the palace, entranced by this mysterious stranger.

"After many weeks passed, they began to learn one another's languages, professing their shared love for the waves and the wild sea. And don't mistake me, Sebastian." Minthe raised her onyx eyes. "Your father knew all too well of what she was. He simply didn't care."

Bash cringed at the sound of his full name, a name his father never uttered.

Minthe smirked wickedly. "As you likely guessed, it didn't take much longer for them to fall in love." She let the last part linger, and Bash glared. "You're a smart man, Sebastian. I think you can figure out how this ends."

"None of it is true." The words left his parched lips before he could hold them back.

Gods, he was so *hungry*. His stomach ached and throbbed, so unbearably empty it took everything he had to focus on the nymera's words.

"Ah, but it is, and you know it. Don't insult your own intelligence." Minthe bent into a crouch, leaning back onto her heels, her bare toes digging into the soil. "They fell in love and had a secret affair right there in the cavern. Not a soul knew, all except a wise advisor who followed him the night your mother gave birth to a son. One she named Sebastian. The advisor was a clever man with brilliant coral eyes. One of the original Azantians, I believe."

Ortum.

"He saw your father and mother beneath the palace, and he helped them sneak the baby boy away from the guards, knowing that any child resulting from their coupling would be slaughtered on sight. The advisor devised a desperate plan, one that would allow your father to keep this baby as his heir. It would take quite a sacrifice to use this kind of dark magic, but the advisor gave it freely, foolishly devoted to his king and unable to watch an innocent child be slayed.

"Using the forbidden words of the ancient language of the gods, the man cast a spell over the island, placing images of a queen into their thoughts, one who had married your father a year before. The people slept in their beds, their minds conjuring this woman as their true queen. It was a spell so mighty, it cost the advisor the only thing he had to offer. His eternal soul."

Bash sucked in a sharp exhale. Ortum was dead. Murdered by a god who had stolen his face, and now this creature told him Ortum's soul would find no rest in the underworld. His hands trembled with rage at his sides.

"When morning came, every citizen in Azantian heard the news of their imagined queen's death during childbirth. But even with her demise came joy, for she had delivered a healthy baby boy." Minthe trailed off, gazing into the dark gloom of the forest just over Bash's head. She didn't look him in the eyes, not as a single black tear glanced over her hollowed cheek.

"No one was the wiser, so they mourned this pretty illusion while celebrating the king's son. While the advisor forbid him, your father would come to your mother long after the birth, bringing the baby to nurse and visit. But as the years went by, he called on her less and less. And one day he ceased coming altogether, keeping the boy from his *true* mother." Minthe's eyes grew bitter, a living coil of rage churning in the black pools.

"The king ordered his advisor to seal the cavern, to trap her deeper below so she would never see her child again. The dutiful advisor carried out the king's command, and the *monster* who fell in love with a man, who had given him a son, was imprisoned beneath unyielding stone. For decades she heard the echoes of her son's cries, and she mourned the child she would never get to raise."

Bash's heart beat furiously. He looked at the nymera before him, taking in every detail. Pieces of her reflected him, and now that he beheld the likeness, and she had relayed her grim tale, Bash couldn't look away.

He...he felt sorry for her. He felt sorry for a monster.

"So you see, I wish I could've met you sooner, but fate hasn't been kind to me. But not to worry, I plan on making up for our lost time."

"Not interested," Bash said. Even if her story was true, he didn't wish to understand her—he wanted to be as far from her kind as possible. He might feel sympathy, but it didn't change anything.

A flash of hurt crossed her face, and her eyes creased at the sides.

"Hate me all you want, but you need to feed."

"I told you this already, but I have no interest in *feeding*," Bash spat out the words like venom on his tongue. "I'm only here now because I made a deal with you, though I don't see my crew anywhere. How do I know they live?"

Minthe cocked her head and peered directly into his eyes, her stare deadly and sharp.

"Nymeras may be dangerous to your friends, to humans, but we aren't liars. Once a deal is made, we honor it. That has always been the way of our people."

Bash scoffed. "Such a moral code you have."

"As if humans are so much better," she snapped. "They don't even attempt to disguise their deceptions. Greedy little things, mortals. Your people, your *true* people, only take what they need and move on. We never hunt in excess. Except when a nymera feeds for the first time, then the hunger they feel is unquenchable. It takes years to fade, but eventually, it lessens, and soon you'll be able to control it."

Hunger. She spoke of an unquenchable hunger—the kind Bash suffered from now.

He gritted his teeth, wishing he could fucking stand up and walk away. Why had this fatigue suddenly hit him and all at once? He had a grip on it around Margrete...

"I'd still like proof," he managed to say. "And I'm not leaving with you until I tell Margrete why I left."

He'd hate himself for an eternity if he didn't tell her why he'd abandoned her when she needed him the most.

"I will allow that," Minthe said after many careful moments of considering his request. Her eyes, while dark and depthless, were cunning, and Bash could practically see the thoughts swirling in them. "But if I let you see her and say your final farewell, you must do something for me."

Bash knew exactly where she was going with this.

"Feed on a soul, replenish yourself, and then I will show you your love, safe and sound and alive. I'm not entirely heartless, son."

Minthe pursed her lips, the only tell she might be anxiously awaiting his response.

Any and all sympathy he'd felt for her disappeared. He couldn't possibly see how he was related to this demon, this monster. A true mother wouldn't pressure their child into eating a human soul. Then again, for all Bash knew, that could be a nymera's way of showing love.

"The hunger, when it hits, hits *hard*," Minthe continued when his mouth refused to work. "I suspect you only barely held onto your control because of *her*."

And now that he'd left her side...

Apparently, Margrete being his light wasn't just a metaphor.

"So, my boy, what will it be? Death without knowing Margrete is safe? Or consume a soul and live, and profess your love one last time?"

Bash's moral compass blurred. He wanted to be selfish, to give in to Minthe and see Margrete, to say his goodbyes. And if the nymeras possessed a human snack already, then they would be dead soon anyway, whether killed by him or one of Minthe's monsters.

So maybe it wouldn't be too bad if he...

"No," he barked out before he could change his mind. "I won't do it." Margrete wouldn't have wanted him to steal a soul just to say goodbye. She would've wanted him to do the right thing, even if it cost him so damn much.

Minthe rose in one fluid motion. "Fine," she snarled. "The hard way it is."

Bash tried to lift himself up, but icy-hot pain radiated across his chest and down his limbs, rendering him exasperatingly immobile.

His hunger only increased. The futile attempt had cost him.

Minthe gave him her back and wandered over to her people. They surrounded her at once and exchanged a few hushed words. She gave one creature with short, spiked hair a nod, and he turned and headed into the trees.

He returned minutes later, dragging a human boy no older than seventeen.

Bash squinted, making out his features, trying to recall why he looked so familiar. Then it struck him—the lad was one of his sailors, one of the men who had ventured out to sea on the *Phaedra*.

Rage filled his blood and battled against the cold slithering in his veins.

"Release him!" he roared, once again trying to shove up. He failed miserably and landed on his side with an agonizing thud. Crawling onto his elbows, Bash shot Minthe his most venomous stare, though she merely shrugged a thin, bony shoulder in reply.

"Bring him here," she commanded, snapping her fingers at the dutiful male who'd fetched his Azantian sailor. Bash hated that he couldn't remember his name.

As they hauled the lad forward, the insatiable hunger in Bash's belly flourished, growing into a beast all its own. So much worse than before, this hunger only intensified the closer the sailor got, and Bash instinctively sniffed the air, inhaling the most intoxicating scent he'd ever known.

The smell reminded him of fresh rain and the morning sunrise, of crisp sea winds and the deep woods of Azantian. It smelled fucking divine.

Bash's chest rose and fell unevenly, and he couldn't help himself as he greedily sucked in the air surrounding the boy. His stomach churned, eager, wanting to be filled with whatever perverse deliciousness wafted to his nostrils.

"See, you're already responding, giving into your true nature," Minthe praised, walking alongside the prisoner and the male nymera yanking him forward. "Allow it to wash over you and free yourself. Permit the beast rein." She waved a hand to the male who clearly was her inferior, and he hauled the sailor to Bash's side and shoved him gracelessly to his knees.

While thin and exceedingly pale—likely due to dehydration and being held prisoner by monsters—the boy managed to keep his shoulders lifted defiantly back, his vibrant Azantian eyes narrowed and deter-mined. He might know the end of his life loomed, but he'd meet it with dignity.

"I won't feed from him," Bash repeated, though his voice had turned into a growl. "I'm not like you!" He shook his head, trying to move away from the offering, from the human soul he couldn't help but desire.

Yes. Bash wanted it. And he wanted it *badly*.

"Give in, Sebastian," Minthe cooed, leaning to whisper into his ear. "All your pain will go away. There will be no more hunger, no more doubt, just relief."

Bash might've shaken his head again, or attempted to speak, but the world around him caved in and narrowed until only the throbbing soul captured in the boy's chest shone clear.

The color was of the purest and most brilliant shade of gold, and its light flourished and swelled with every passing second. It blinded him, rendered him dazed, breathless.

There was nothing but its all-consuming glow.

There was no crew to find. No woman he loved more than his own life. No island full of people who relied on him. Bash had no responsi-bility other than satiating the hunger inside of him, and the struggle to fight his instincts began to diminish.

An image flashed across his mind of a deer sprinting through the woods—and him, ripping it to shreds with his bare teeth. That had been real. He knew that now.

Bash had killed days ago trying to fill this gluttonous void before, and while the soul of an animal was nothing compared to that of this mortal, he *had* to have it.

"That's it..."

Minthe rubbed his back, his shoulders, her touch gentle and coaxing—comforting him just like the mother he'd always imagined. Bash closed his eyes, overcome with unimaginable thirst, and he unhinged his jaw, taking in a deep breath and inhaling—

Gods above and below.

He might as well have been struck by lightning. The hunger inside of him screamed with delight, that throbbing emptiness seeming to reach out and seize the sweetest of all fares.

Bash couldn't remember anything tasting so delicious, so filling and *right*. He could feel the soul slip down his throat and slither into his belly. It warmed his chest, gifted his heart a new beat, changed his very nature until he eventually felt the beginnings of that relief Minthe had promised.

He didn't stop inhaling until a loud thud sounded, and the empty husk of the sailor collapsed to the soil.

The boy's body sizzled, withering away as his wan flesh turned to soot and dust. A rotten breeze picked at his remains, whisking the ashes away, leaving no trace of the Azantian who'd once lived and breathed and hoped.

Bash smiled. The hunger had finally stopped, and in its place a new sensation blossomed.

"Welcome, Sebastian," Minthe said, announcing him to the onlooking nymeras. "You have become what you were always meant to be."

Those who followed Minthe bowed their heads, a rumbling, humming sound leaving their lips. One by one, they bent to their knees, their black scales glowing in the soft daylight.

Bash took his first true breath, his head swiveling around the circle of monsters.

"My people!" Minthe lifted both arms into the air, her pointed nails reaching for the sky. "My son has finally come home to me. Your heir—"

The ground shook, and a bright, divine light exploded all around them.

Screams pierced the air and agonized shrieks made their way to his ears. Blasts flared, and the nymeras fell to the ground. But Bash hardly cared—he was too drunk off the soul he'd taken, too high from the adrenaline of the kill.

Bash was entirely unaffected when more blasts of fire rattled the ground and he fell onto his back, the overcast sky bleak. For a heartbeat, he envisioned a woman with long brown hair and kind blue eyes. He knew her, but what was her name?

A figure hovered directly over Bash, stealing away thoughts of the mystery woman. He made out no discernable features, but there was a voice. A voice he distantly recognized, and it shook his very bones.

"Time for the grand finale, king."

CHAPTER THIRTY-NINE

MARGRETE

MARGRETE TREKKED THROUGH THE WOODS FOR THE REST OF THE day, the stream guiding her northwest. She'd tried not to think about the third coin, but it was damn near impossible. Every time she looked down into the cool waters, she could've sworn she glimpsed a flash of silver.

Sometimes, when she felt particularly out of sorts, she imagined she caught sight of a feminine form in the distance and a blur of red hair. She'd blink, and the woman would vanish. Margrete impulsively pushed on in the phantom's direction like a fool, hoping it would lead her to her friends or at least something that might end her stay in this wretched place. She no longer gave a shit if the woman was a bad omen. She'd take any omen at this point, good or bad.

By twilight, Margrete heard the telltale sound of lapping waves, and when the sun dipped into the horizon, the land began to change.

She hadn't seen a flash of red hair in hours.

The woods came to an end, and the earth sloped upward, shards of brittle black grass clinging to the land. Above, the moon, which had been a wan white during the entirety of her stay on the island, was now tinged with a red that matched the leaves. Its ominous glow stained her skin and washed the world in a sickly burgundy.

With every step up the hill, her power built, throbbing inside of her like a war drum. Its pounding became a song of grit and purpose, surging into her veins and fueling her limbs, and before long, she'd reached the land's peak. The sound of the waves grew thunderous, but a blanket of warmth swathed her heart at the nearness of the sea.

Yet before she allowed herself time to celebrate one small accomplishment, she was faced with another obstacle.

There, one hundred feet away, stood two looming gates fashioned from dense slate-gray rock. Attached to the open gates was a curved wall crafted from the same stone, unusual shapes and images drawn crudely onto the sides. The circular structure had been constructed on roughened cliffs overlooking the pitch-black waters, but its sheer size obscured most of the view of the swells.

Margrete knew no good awaited her beyond those gates, but her power burned so fiercely in her chest that it forced her to continue.

She grimaced. Whatever lay ahead would either be the ending of this long nightmare or the beginning of a new one.

She'd drifted close enough by then to realize that the blurred designs she'd seen were actually stormy seas, inky waves stretching high enough to touch the tips of the walls. They were fearsome and unholy, and the divine essence inside of her both craved and despised their nearness.

Margrete envisioned Bash, as she so often did when her resolve faltered and her faith in herself dwindled. She imagined he walked beside her, whispering soothing words into her ear.

She thought of Bay, Atlas, Jonah, Mila, the twins. She said a quiet prayer for Jace and Grant and for all the other sailors buried beneath the wreckage of the *Phaedra*.

Their images softened her searing magic, just enough so she could suck in a steady breath.

There was only ahead. Margrete couldn't go back—no more than she could pretend she was still a simple mortal. She'd been chosen, whether by fate or chance, and if Darius's soul indeed comprised her, she had been a part of this game long before her first breath.

The time had come to finish it.

Margrete lifted her chin and passed through the open gates. They led to the grandest arena she'd ever seen. Rows and rows of empty seats were stacked high in the air, all encircling a pit filled with charcoal-colored sand. Each grain glimmered in the light of seven flaming torches, all stationed in a perfect circle around the sleek ring.

Margrete clenched her fists, awareness dancing down her spine. She felt eyes upon her, and she shifted her focus to a long, thin opening that had been carved on the opposite side facing the coast. She squinted in the dark at a feminine form taking shape. When the torchlight captured the deep red of the figure's hair, Margrete didn't even bother to hold in her gasp.

The woman stepped forward, sauntering into the ring with a knowing smirk. She wore a silk dress of crimson—her signature color, after all.

"What the fuck are you doing here?" Margrete grabbed her dagger and held it out before her. Sure, she could've placed all of her faith in her powers to protect her, but look where that trust had gotten her.

"Did you miss me?" Shade asked, her singsong voice grating. "I know I've missed you." Her emerald eyes flitted about the empty ring, her nose wrinkling. "Though I could've gone without returning to this place. It always did remind me of the lowest court of the underworld."

Margrete had heard tales of the so-called *courts* of the underworld, but no one knew the details aside from the dead, and they weren't keen on talking. Still, she didn't speak on that particular sentiment. She had much bigger concerns.

"I always knew you weren't what you seemed," she said, sliding to her right, away from Azantian's deceitful court treasurer. Shade mirrored the movement, and the pair circled one another, both predators battling for supremacy. The redhead didn't possess any weapon Margrete could see, but that certainly didn't mean she was defenseless.

Shade waved a mocking hand. "And here I always thought you were just some simple woman with little thought between her ears." She chuckled bitterly. "Though I must say, I'm glad I no longer have to play house on that island anymore. I grew bored with all the"—she cocked her head as if searching for the right words—"mindless comradery. Though Birdie was a particular favorite of mine. I might just have to return for her after all this is done."

Margrete glowered. "You wouldn't dare."

She hadn't approved of her sister spending time with Shade before, and now she realized just how validated her fears had been.

"She has promise," Shade continued, smirking as she goaded her. "Such a bright young thing. I suspect she'd make for an apt pupil."

"What are you?" Margrete asked, ignoring Shade's obvious attempts to ruffle her.

"I'm many things," Shade said, lifting a lean shoulder. The ink of her tattooed collarbone glimmered in the light of the blood moon. "But Azantian, I am not."

Her vibrant hair shifted to the side—*finally*—and Margrete made out the odd burn mark she'd spotted a glimpse of months ago. It almost looked like a warped bloom.

"A spy then?" she asked, averting her attention from the gnarled flower.

She couldn't be human. Margrete sensed her otherworldliness now that Shade's mask had slipped. Or maybe her own magic had grown more powerful and she could finally see the truth behind Shade's eyes.

Shade narrowed her gaze. "I suppose small minds might call me a spy. I simply think of myself as a well-placed asset, a weapon that could be used if needed. It helps that I am immortal. A limited lifespan can be such a hindrance in the grand scheme of things."

An immortal? She knew Shade couldn't be a god. Her magic didn't reach out to her like Darius's did. Although, she could very well be a lower-level deity for all she knew.

Shade and Margrete continued their circling, neither breaking eye contact. Margrete's hand tightened on her dagger's hilt, and her arm remained firmly raised, her body itching to lunge.

"And your family back on the island?" Margrete asked, hoping to keep her talking...and distracted. She subtly peered around the empty arena, searching for others, wondering when Darius would make himself known.

"Them?" Shade scoffed. "I suppose I should feel sorry for my dear *family*. Well, they weren't really my family to begin with, but they didn't know that. Their real daughter died shortly after birth, but with a little dark magic"—she snapped her fingers—"I was transformed into their sweet newborn. Another perk of immortality and friends in high places."

Darius had his hand in all of this years ago, even while cursed to live as a mortal by Surria. He must've enlisted Shade to keep tabs on his brother's island. And yet the burn mark gracing her skin wasn't Darius's insignia...

"You were sent to the orphanage after your home burned down. You killed them." It wasn't a question. Margrete remembered Bay relaying her background, however brief.

Her eyes snagged on a flicker of movement to her right, nothing more than a shadow. She brought her stare back to the front. Someone was coming.

Shade's lips twisted in a mockery of a grimace. "Accidents happen, dearest Margrete."

"Who do you work for then?" Margrete asked, though she knew the answer. She continued to assess the arena, hastily looking for more shadows.

The last thing she needed was to get caught off guard.

"Oh, come now, don't play dumb." Shade tsked. "We both know who I work for."

"But your mark isn't his," Margrete said, jerking her chin at her neck. "I don't recognize it."

Shade scoffed. "Who created me has nothing to do with who I place my allegiance with." She stopped abruptly. Margrete tracked her cunning gaze as Shade turned to that narrow slit facing the waves.

Another figure entered the arena, ominous black shadows dancing around his shoulders. Even the light of the torches seemed to recoil from him.

"Ah, and here he comes!" Shade squealed, stepping back to rest against the outer walls of the ring. She casually crossed her arms and observed Margrete and the incoming figure as if preparing for the beginning of a show.

Margrete took in the ghostly form, whose seven-foot frame she instantly recognized. Darius had grown tired of watching, it seemed. He strode forward, his steps insufferably confident, like he already thought he'd won this twisted game they played.

Margrete followed the first instinct that struck her.

Bringing her arm back, she sent her dagger slicing through the air with a hissing whoosh.

Darius caught it by the blade's end with one gloved hand, a mere inch from his throat. The serrated edge cut through his thick leather gloves, and Margrete's lips parted as a single drop of blue blood fell to the sands.

He bled. *Good.*

"Now that wasn't very nice." Darius smiled, his blue eyes dancing as he dragged them up and down her form. "Though I'd be remiss if I didn't commend you on your impressive aim, darling."

He flung her blade to the side as if it were a mere toy. It thudded to the ground, far away from Margrete. She would've gladly used it to slice open his throat and watch him bleed. It might not have killed him, but it would've brought her much joy. Already the split in his leather glove had woven itself back together. She surmised his wound had healed seconds after he released the blade.

"And Shade, good work as always. Except next time, do try *not* to lure my pawns off a cliff and to their deaths. At least not *before* I've had a chance to play with them."

Margrete had the nauseating suspicion of who that certain someone was...especially when Shade's lips formed the perfect pout. She couldn't wait to kill her.

"But I was growing so bored stuck here, and I've always imagined how his blood would taste." Shade licked her lips seductively.

Darius brought the full weight of his stare to Margrete. The memory she'd seen earlier by the river came back to her—the man standing feet away couldn't be the same one laughing and frolicking in the stream, spinning his companion around and around.

"Have your memories been coming back?" Darius asked, as if reading her mind. A flicker of warped hope brightened his severe features. "They should be. The longer you stay on this island, the easier they will be to access."

"I don't want them," she snarled, wishing she had another blade to hurl his way.

Darius's jaw clenched, and his nostrils flared. "Once they return, you'll be happy they did," he said icily. She suspected he worked to keep his voice calm. "The woman I knew would desire nothing more than to remember."

Margrete took a brazen step forward, and electricity shot down her frame.

"I doubt she'd be thrilled that you killed her."

Darius's barely concealed calm snapped.

He was before her in a flash, mere inches away, his breath tickling her cheeks. His blond hair hung in his eyes, his proud jaw tensed. Margrete could all but taste his rage on her tongue.

"I would take it all back in a heartbeat," Darius spoke through gritted teeth. "Not a day has gone by where my regret doesn't eat away at me. Where it doesn't destroy me."

He lifted a hand as if to cup her jaw, but she flinched, and he dropped his arm, his eyes narrowing.

"It'll take time, but you'll remember," he said, seeming to try and assure himself more than her. "I know you feel the connection between us, the *pull*, and I am a patient man, especially when it comes to the woman I love."

Margrete laughed. She couldn't help it. Perhaps the days of unrest were finally catching up with her or she was truly losing her mind, but she laughed in the face of a very, *very* angry god.

When she eventually calmed herself, she peered up at him and shook her head.

"You wouldn't know the first thing about love, Darius. Not only did you *make* the woman you claim to love, but you killed her. All so you could become the god your dearest mother wished you to be."

"I told you Surria spun her lies," Darius argued, his voice harder than the stone surrounding them. "She knew I wouldn't have been able to rule the seas without sacrificing my heart, and she would have no doubt stripped me of my powers, allowing Malum to be left to his own wicked devices." He scoffed at the mention of his deceased brother. "Everyone always assumed he was the *good* one, but Malum might have been the worst of us all. Certainly, the most deceptive."

"I wonder," Margrete began. "Did your lover plead with you during her final moments? Did you hesitate before wiping her from this earth? Or did you *want* to believe Surria's lies, if only to claim your full power?"

She'd struck a nerve. Another one, it seemed.

This time, instead of reaching for her cheek, Darius lifted his hands as if to grab her throat. He paused just before he touched her skin, his fingers hovering menacingly. They twitched with rage.

"Wryn wanted me to rule the seas as much as I did." He dropped his arms to his sides and took a step back, his eyes turning dark. "She all but told me to do whatever needed to be done, and she would've forgiven me for believing Surria's deceptions. But her soul has come back to me. *You* have come back to me."

From the corner of her eye, Margrete noted Shade inspecting her fingernails, seemingly bored.

"And Shade? You put her on Azantian even while cursed. Be truthful. Have you always known what I was?" Margrete found it hard to believe that Darius had only just realized who she was to him.

Darius observed his stunning minion with disinterest, which made Margrete wonder what Darius waited for. He clearly planned for something to happen in this place, but he'd yet to act. She carefully marked her two exits: the gates and the narrow opening both Darius and Shade had entered from.

"Shade is a nymph. While she might have been born with Calista's magic, she didn't belong in the Court of Dreams and Eternal Love, and I happened to find her on one of my many travels as a human, right after my mother cursed me and my brother. She's been such a help orchestrating all of this." He motioned to the island. "I may be a god, but I cannot be everywhere at once."

Margrete sensed how Darius's impatience grew, and every now and again his eyes flickered to the gates as though expecting someone to walk through.

"What are you waiting for?" Margrete asked, lifting her hands mockingly. "Isn't this what you wanted? Me? Alone and at your mercy?"

Darius nearly growled as he closed the gap, his nostrils flaring and his brow scrunched.

"I never wanted you at my mercy. I wanted you to fucking remember!"

Pain. Margrete felt pain roll off his body in deadly waves.

"We were so happy, *I* was so happy, and then it was all taken from me like a sick joke. I've never forgiven my mother for her cruelty, and my brother sat back and laughed as I cut down the only thing that ever mattered to me. He *laughed*."

Margrete's heart twinged. She couldn't help it. Her empathy was turning into a weakness.

"I've been so angry for so many centuries, and just when fate seemed to favor me, the soul that mirrored my own had fallen in love with another. A man who wasn't worthy of her brilliance, her power." Darius glanced at his boots, his voice turning into a whisper. "And when she gazed upon me with such hatred, such venomous disgust, it nearly broke me all over again. *You* nearly broke me."

Darius was panting by the time he finished, his eyes wide and filled with heart-clenching agony. His stare seared into her, pleading, begging for her to say something, anything.

For a moment, Margrete lost herself in those eyes. Within those hypnotic pools, she envisioned herself wearing another's skin. She saw Darius towering above her, much like he was now, but instead of the raging fury emanating from his frame, she felt an all-consuming passion, a love so fierce it nearly drove her to her knees.

Back and forth, the vision played, from the present to a time over a thousand years past.

Margrete must've swayed, because two hands found her waist and held tight, keeping her in place.

Darius's touch sent another rush of images tumbling into her mind. All were of the god and the woman owning half his soul, and all depicted a blossoming love that Margrete couldn't deny as being one of pure enchantment.

She couldn't deny it because she *felt* it in her marrow. She couldn't deny it because she'd *lived* it.

Yes, the connection between her and the phantom memory of Wryn strengthened and grew, and for a split-second Margrete forgot who she was entirely.

But then black eyes blazed across her mind, the silver flecks reminding her of stars. She blinked away the past, focusing on Bash until the present settled and the Darius of now towered above.

Margrete lifted her chin, capturing the god's eyes, searching their depths for a lie she knew she wouldn't find. And all the while, he stared back, flecks of gold brightening the otherworldly pools, a seed of hope lending his gaze an unfamiliar sincerity.

"I hate to break up this touching moment, but it looks like our dear guests have arrived."

Shade's voice shattered the connection, and Margrete stumbled back, her vision tilting, the arena a blur of unforgiving gray.

Darius didn't take his attention off her until heavy footsteps pounded the packed sands. He flinched with what she could mistake as regret.

That regret soon faded.

When Margrete turned to the incoming figures, all the sympathy she felt for the god dissipated like steam.

Chains rattled as hooded men and women were led into the arena. Seven feminine forms hauled the prisoners forward, wisps of red hair poking out from beneath the hoods of their flowing cloaks. Margrete couldn't make out any other discernible features aside from their red-painted lips. Each warden held onto a thick silver chain, tugging at them occasionally when their captives resisted or attempted to yank themselves free.

None succeeded.

Margrete guessed who she'd find beneath those hoods, and the thought of her crew, of her friends, chained and being led to their likely deaths, had her power sparking wildly.

None of them spoke or shouted, leading Margrete to believe they were gagged beneath their hoods. Or magicked.

"Finally," Shade said, huffing. "It took you long enough to get here." She shoved up from the wall and slowly marched to the first prisoner, whose hands were shackled in front of him. All the air left Margrete's lungs as Shade reached for the hem of his hood.

"I'm sorry it has to be this way, darling," Darius whispered just as the fabric fell from Shade's fingers.

Staring back at her was a monster.

One she loved with all her heart.

Bash hissed a moment before he lunged, his teeth bared and aimed for her throat.

CHAPTER FORTY

THE BEAST

HE NEEDED ANOTHER TASTE, JUST *ONE* MORE SOUL, AND THE ONE before him smelled fucking delicious. Pure and powerful, with just the barest hint of innocent lavender.

There were muffled voices and shadowy figures he glimpsed through the thin hood. They might have been his enemies, the masked people who chained and blinded him, but he didn't care about anything other than sinking his teeth into the creature whose light shone through the linen.

More, more, more.

Wisps of crimson clouded his vision, blocking out everything but that luminescent glow. If only he weren't shackled. He'd be on her in an instant.

So fucking hungry.

Make it stop.

Someone grabbed at his hood and yanked—

No other thought entered his head as he took in the female. Her eyes widened with fear, and the scent of it fueled him. Tingles raced down his arms, his hunger roaring at the sight of her, though her beauty was nothing compared to what lay within.

More, more, more.

He was nothing but an animal, giving into instinct, giving into the beast he'd finally unleashed.

Before his warden could yank on his chain, he pounced...

All he wanted was just one. More. Taste.

No. All he wanted was *her*.

CHAPTER FORTY-ONE

MARGRETE

MARGRETE COULDN'T MOVE.

One second Bash was lunging toward her, his jaw unhinged and sharp canines poking out, and the next a flare of cobalt and pearl light collided with his chest.

The blast sent Bash hurtling backward, directly into the nymph who grasped his chain.

Margrete twisted around in time to watch as Darius lowered his arm, steam fizzling from his still-glowing palm. Not a trace of exertion marred his features. She would even dare to say he appeared bored.

Muffled shouts of alarm echoed from the hooded captives, their heads swiveling back and forth, no one quite sure where to look. In truth, Margrete wasn't sure where she should look either. Her instinct screamed for her to race to Bash, but the way he'd gazed upon her...he would've killed her.

Her heart plummeted into her stomach, and her throat burned with rising acid. *Bash would've killed me.*

"Get him up," Darius said, sighing dramatically. With a flick of his wrist, one of the other cloaked women rushed to grab hold of Bash, the force of Darius's power visibly weakening him. The King of Azantian stumbled to his feet, his guard supporting most of his weight while he swayed, a dazed look softening his sharp features.

"How fun," Shade remarked, sauntering closer to the action with a mischievous grin. She clapped her hands excitedly, like their turmoil was a play performed for her sole amusement.

Darius briefly glanced her way, and whatever he relayed in his stare sobered her enough to keep silent. Shade rolled her eyes but returned to her previous position, leaning leisurely against the ring's wall.

Fearful whimpers came from some of the prisoners, a few fighting the manacles around their hands. Their captors pulled viciously on their chains and yelled obscenities, commanding them to remain silent or be killed. Fear had them stilling.

Bash, however, wasn't as easily persuaded.

Her heart thundered as he lifted his head, his depthless eyes lacking their usual spark. She saw *nothing* in them. Absolutely nothing.

"Bash?" she murmured, her knees wobbling as she took a single step forward. Her power thrummed, seeming to hiss in reproach. When Darius held up a hand, warning her to halt, her feet complied almost instantly.

She hated that her body listened, but she recognized the danger right in front of her.

The Azantian king growled, snapping his teeth at her like some depraved animal, starving and yearning for the kill. She noticed his scales had traveled further down his chest. His nails, which had been stained in ink before, were razor-sharp and thick, weapons all by themselves.

What could've possibly happened in the short amount of time they'd been separated?

His warden yanked on his chain, and Bash whipped around, nipping at her. The cloaked woman raised her hand as if to strike him, when Darius spoke.

"Shade, I thought I told you not to let your underlings hit our guests. Control your nymphs. You know how much manners mean to me."

The nymph holding Bash's chain lowered her other arm with a grimace.

"Now that we're all here, shall we begin?" Darius asked, eyes drifting to the blood-tinged moon. The red crept out around its luminous white, tainting the world with a sinister glow. The god smiled at it, his eyes twinkling.

To Shade, he commanded, "Remove their hoods."

With a nod to her nymphs, seven hoods were lifted and tossed aside, the torchlight revealing six familiar faces and one she didn't recognize.

Dani and Jacks shot one another a knowing look, the latter sporting a deep cut across his right cheek and upper lip. Atlas, for her part, held her shoulders back and glowered, even while dirt and mud streaked her face.

Jonah, for the first time since she'd known him, frowned deeply enough to form a crease through his brow, and Bay...her friend showed nothing on his face at all. He barely breathed as his eyes flickered across the arena, likely searching for a possible escape. It nearly killed her when he refused to meet her eye, almost like he blamed her for their predicament.

Maybe he did.

Darius waved his hand before them, and all at once their mouths parted, many gulping in fresh air as their invisible gags were removed.

Not seconds after, Mila hissed at Darius, her upper lip curled back, though when she met Margrete's eyes, her stare turned frigid. "This is all your fault," she shouted, struggling against her chains. "If you'd never come to our island, none of this would be happening!"

Bay flinched at that but didn't defend her, and a small part of Margrete died. Jonah merely lowered his head.

Margrete's insides churned, her pulse soaring and her control slipping. Wave after wave of guilt drowned her sparking magic, though it continued to flare, fighting to take root.

Her gaze fell to the last and final prisoner.

A nymera.

Wearing a thin white dress, the black-haired nymera watched only Bash, her midnight-colored eyes stormy and brimming with fury. She turned to Darius, her voice a cruel, deep thing.

"We had an agreement," she said through clenched teeth. "You were supposed to leave me and my son alone. The rest were yours to take."

Darius lifted one shoulder in a mocking shrug. "I remember I specifically told you *I* wouldn't kill your son," he said, his inflection not lost on Margrete. Her magic swelled, shoving aside the overflowing shame.

The God of the Sea tilted his head to Margrete. "It is she who will take his life, effectively completing the third trial and becoming a true goddess."

So that was what this all was about? Her becoming immortal like him?

Sparks of blue light ignited from her palms. Their heat seared her skin, but it never blistered, and the longer Darius's words hung in the air, the greater her fire became.

"I will do no such thing."

Margrete turned her back on her beloved king and his crew. She held her ground while facing off against the smirking god, who appeared confident she'd relent. That confidence worried her.

Darius clasped his hands behind his back and closed the distance between them. He stopped a foot away, and she had to crane her neck to maintain eye contact. Still, she never faltered, never looked away. These were her people, her *family*, and she'd protect them until the end of days.

"Let them go, Darius, or—"

"Or *what*?" he asked, his tone free of derision. "You can't hurt me. I'm as much a part of you as your beating heart." Darius spoke the words as if they were fact. And perhaps they were true. But even if she'd been created from pieces of his soul, she was her own person.

She wasn't *him*.

"I almost feel sorry for you," she mused, her palms crackling with electricity. She tracked Darius's eyes as they briefly shifted to her hands. A muscle in his jaw feathered.

"I am no one to *pity*," he whispered, dangerously soft.

"No, that's right, you want to be feared." Margrete cocked her head, and one side of her mouth curved shrewdly. "You only know how to deceive and lie and fight. Still, you have my pity because you know nothing better. Only how to break the things you are in danger of loving."

Darius's nostrils flared. "I've *had* to fight, Margrete. Not all of us were born with the option to choose a different path, though I've done more than most. More than any of the other deities. They spend their days drowning in the debauchery of the underworld, content to indulge in fantasy and opulence, but I've been here, in the mortal realm, trying to rule. Trying to do right by my title."

"And how exactly do you plan on doing right by your title? How many of your so-called brothers and sisters do you plan on killing to get what you want?"

The god inched closer, close enough that his icy breath fanned across her brow. She shuddered, tremors racing down her arms and to her flaming palms. Her fire burned brighter, its glow dancing across Darius's looming form.

"You have no idea of what you speak," he said coolly. "If you truly knew the gods, you'd believe me to be the best of them, and while you seem to think I am callous and cruel, my heart beats in time with yours." He lifted a hand, his lean fingers grasping a loose strand of hair and gently tucking it behind her ear. She hissed. "And my soul, while only one half of a whole"—he stared down at her pointedly—"hasn't succumbed to my darker ambitions."

She didn't want to imagine what he believed were his darker ambitions. In her mind, Darius was dangerous enough.

A snarl ripped her focus away from the god.

Bash whipped his head in her direction, his solid frame pulling on the chains imprisoning him. The nymph holding his manacles grunted with the effort to keep him secured.

The nymera—the one she assumed to be Bash's mother—snarled and bared her teeth, an otherworldly glow surrounding her shoulders. It reminded Margrete of the moon's light when reflected upon dark waters.

Margrete turned back to Darius, but the god had vanished.

She spun in place, finding him situated upon one of the long benches lining the arena. He leaned back and propped up his feet, a king observing his spectators.

"Shade, the dagger, if you will."

The nymph smiled wide, all her pearly teeth on display. With a flick of her wrist, clouds of red and ash spun and wove together by the force of a supernatural wind. A glinting of steel shone through the chaos of her magicked storm, and a silver dagger with an onyx hilt slowly took shape.

In the span of a breath, the blade lifted, turned, and then flew. The weapon whistled toward Margrete, just like hers had sailed toward Darius earlier.

"No!" she screamed, bringing her glowing palms before her, her lids instinctively shutting.

Seconds passed, and the cold metal didn't pierce her flesh.

Slowly, she opened her eyes and lowered her arms. The tip of the dagger hovered inches away, floating in midair. She stood stock-still. Five heartbeats passed before her senses rushed back, and adrenaline sent her stumbling away from the weapon.

Shade's smile was cruel, and Margrete knew she would've loved nothing more than to have sent the dagger through her skull. She didn't know much about nymphs, but she already despised them.

"Take the dagger, darling. Complete the trial, or none of your friends will leave this island in one piece."

Margrete looked to Bay. His lips parted as if he wished to speak, but nothing came out but a huff of air. Atlas mouthed the word *no*. And Jonah...he gave her a sad smile, a knowing one. He nodded.

Margrete knew she didn't have much time before Darius made good on his threats. She spun around and lifted her palm, a thunderous cry of battle leaving her lips.

Her light blasted from her open hand, silver flares and cobalt blue embers illuminating the arena. The nymphs screamed. Her friends shouted.

Darius smiled.

Her magic aimed true, straighter than any arrow, directed at the unmoving God of the Sea.

Only to collide with an invisible barrier of crackling power.

Her magic shimmered to dust, Darius's wall of protection eating away at her living embodiment of rage.

"Very well done," he praised. "That was quite a show of force!"

Shade snickered somewhere in the background.

"While I am pleased to see your progress, and impeccable aim, we really should get on with it." He snuck another peek at the moon. "We don't have all night, after all."

"I won't do it—"

A flash of white and blue lightning shot from Darius's palm, nearly blinding her as it struck directly behind her.

Margrete turned around.

Jonah.

His eyes were wide, his mouth open in a frozen scream.

He took a step, fumbling, reaching out for her—

His head slid right off his shoulders and fell to the ground.

CHAPTER FORTY-TWO

MARGRETE

MILA'S FACE CRUMPLED, AND THE TWINS STARED IN SHOCK. BAY fell to his knees, and even the nymera reacted, cocking her head in concern, her thin brows raised.

And Margrete? She swiveled around and aimed.

Her fire erupted from her palm, shooting across the arena. Darius shifted to the right at the last moment, a stunned look twisting his face. He hadn't expected her to react that quickly...or with such accuracy.

He bolted to his feet, his own palms sparking to life, his magic electric in the night air. Margrete felt it deep in her marrow, his innate strength, his dominant power, and her entire body convulsed. She might as well have been caught in the middle of a storm, lightning piercing the ground all around her feet, reverberations working up and down her frame.

Margrete didn't hesitate to target the god once more. The image of Jonah's head sliding off his shoulders was ingrained in her mind forever, and all she wanted to do was inflict as much pain as possible.

Her light missed Darius by a foot.

Jonah was the best of them all. Sweet, optimistic, thoughtful. He was too young to die, his whole life ahead of him yet.

Margrete swallowed the bile rising in her throat and aimed again.

Darius understood her intent. He dodged her attack easily, and sweat banded across her brow as she roared, lifting her blistering palm higher.

"Stop. Running." She seethed, gritting her teeth, twisting each time Darius evaded her. He never responded with magic of his own, though he observed her with caution.

Good. He should be careful now. He'd crossed a line and murdered a member of her crew. Darius should fucking run.

"You're going to wear yourself out before you complete the trial," he finally said, his voice audible even though he stood a great distance away. Its deep timbre shook her bones and rattled her chest. "If you don't take that dagger and spill the king's blood on these very sands, I will be forced to kill another. You must complete this trial, or you'll never ascend to the full height of your powers and rule by my side."

"You're only doing this because you're selfish and lonely and want someone to drown with you! You don't care about me or what I may become. It's always been about you!"

Margrete reared back and released another quick blast. Her right hand sizzled, steaming for many long moments after. He was right— exhaustion weighed her down. She wouldn't have much time left before her magic failed her entirely.

"Last warning," Darius threatened, flickering to the edge of the arena in a blink of an eye. "Don't make me hurt any more of your friends. Believe me, I take no pleasure in it."

Like she believed that.

Margrete raised her arm but hesitated. In that fraction of a second, Darius's magic barreled into the arena, striking true.

She turned in time to see Jacks plummet to his knees, a charred hole in his chest, his muscles and ribs jutting out. He sputtered, blood dripping down his chin to the gray sands below. Jacks mouthed his sister's name before he dropped facedown. Smoke rose from his scorched body, mingling with the smell of potent magic in the air.

Margrete stopped.

Froze.

Panicked.

Bash was beginning to gain back his strength, and the nymph holding his chain screeched when he turned and set his sights on her. In a move far too quick for Shade or Darius to comprehend, Bash was up and moving, and then he opened his mouth and bit down on the nymph's neck. Bluish-black blood spurted from the wound, wetting the sands and turning them a shade darker.

Bash snapped her neck in one fluid movement, and the nymph's shrill scream died on her red lips.

Bile rose in her throat, hot and thick and suffocating. She refused to believe her eyes, refused to see the proof of what Bash had become, even as the nymph lay motionless at his feet.

Margrete fumbled backward, her entire world falling to pieces. Her magic was almost gone, and she felt its struggle, its fight to resurface.

"Bash! Stop!" she cried, feeling helpless. "*Please* stop!"

Her king ignored her and grasped the nymph's jaw, inhaling deeply. A mist of red, the same color as her hair, wafted from her lips—directly into Bash's mouth.

When the nymph was drained of her life force, of what Margrete knew to be her soul, Bash dropped her like a broken doll.

"See? He cannot control himself," Darius taunted from somewhere behind her.

Bay was trying desperately to get to her, fighting his guard and screaming curses, but his nymph wouldn't relent.

Dani slumped to the ground, her eyes wide and glassy. Cautiously, she reached for her twin and rested a hand over the blistering cavity in his chest. Atlas grunted, her eyes trained on Jacks's sister. She thrashed against her bonds, desperate to go to her.

Bash lifted his head, black hair falling into unrecognizable eyes. Slowly, he looked Margrete's way.

"I'd hurry," Darius called out. "The next one I aim for is going to be the sister."

Margrete's heart broke into a million and one unrepairable pieces. There were mere seconds to decide who lived and who died.

Bash ran toward her, his limbs a blur of ripped black clothing and jagged scales.

Time came to a standstill as her heart stopped beating, and the screams echoing in the arena became whispers of death.

Margrete turned to the dagger hovering nearby, floating on that unholy cloud Shade commanded. She looked back and forth between the dagger and her king.

There wasn't any other option.

Was this how Darius had felt all those many years ago? Did he feel as if he didn't have any other choice, driven to violence by his own *mother*?

Margrete grabbed the hilt with a cry and swung around, ready to lift the blade. She wasn't in control of her body, and her heart beat so fast she feared it would combust. Here she stood, ready to do the unforgivable and lose what little hope remained in her soul, and she felt nothing but the sensation of drowning.

Bash tackled her to the ground before she had the chance to move closer.

A rush of air left her lungs at the impact, and she dropped the dagger. Bash snarled and snapped at her face, his long nails digging into her skin, her neck, her shoulders. She must have been sobbing, because warmth washed across her cheeks and she tasted salt.

"Bash," she spoke his name as she fended off his beast. This wasn't her pirate, not her beloved king.

This monster had been made to destroy her.

"Please, come back to me," she murmured, her palms on his chest. She used a surge of precious energy to blast him back, allowing her time to jump to her feet.

She grabbed the dagger and faced him. He crouched in an attack stance, three strides away, ready to pounce.

Gripping the hilt with both hands, she waited for him to rise, his narrowed gaze lifeless and dull. He took her in like an animal would its prey, not the way he used to look upon her every morning when they woke on Azantian. She'd roll over in his arms, and he would nuzzle her hair, his bare chest pressed against her. The Bash she knew was warm and light and *home*. He was her best friend, the only one in this world who held her heart and her soul between the palms of his hands.

And she held his heart as well.

Perhaps that was the reason she hesitated when Bash rushed her a second time, why she merely lifted her hand—which tingled with magic —and thrust the force of her power toward the man she loved.

Bash's entire frame rocked violently as her energy shot into him, stopping him mere inches away. He bared his teeth as he fought to attack, to maim, to kill, his eyes not once lowering to the weapon she held in her hand.

All he could see was his prey, not the woman he'd pledged his life to.

Margrete's hands shook, but she aimed her dagger, all the while knowing there was no way she could drive the silver blade into his body, his heart, and steal the very thing he'd entrusted her to protect.

Her magic roared, wanting to propel him backward again, to *hurt* him, but Margrete resisted long enough to speak her goodbye.

"I love you," she whispered, gazing deeply into his eyes, trying desperately to find a trace of him. There was nothing but darkness.

He fought against her power, fought to get a hold on her, and the emptiness in his eyes made her strength wane. His hands broke through the weakening barrier between them, moving to her neck, but he hissed when he touched her skin, as if burned. He let out a guttural snarl.

"In this life and the next," she swore to him. "I will love you. Always."

Margrete let go of her power. Let go of everything.

She felt her grip loosening on the dagger, felt Bash finally able to wrap his hands around her throat, his jaw unhinging as he prepared to inhale her soul.

I love you.

His eyes sparked for only a second, a fraction of a heartbeat, and shone a brilliant onyx and silver. She could see the stars she loved in his stare, and her heart stilled entirely at the sight of recognition sharpening his gaze.

He opened his mouth, and the hands around her neck relaxed. Hope surged in her soul.

But Bash let out a growl, one both animalistic and unnatural. It seemed to scrape against her insides as it ran up and down her body, like a thousand needles prickling her skin, rendering her a mess of tremors and regret. And Margrete knew then that while he fought against his demons, in the end they were winning.

Margrete closed her eyes, willing time to stop, praying this was another horrid nightmare. Maybe he'd wake up, shove aside this daze and—

Something solid thrust into her back at the same time Bash screamed, a bloodcurdling, twisted sound that cut through the night and vibrated her very bones. She opened her eyes.

The bloody tip of a dagger protruded from Bash's chest.

The anguished and broken sound he released rocked the arena. It shook the ground, the very air, and Margrete felt her own heart crumble and break as he'd driven the dagger's sharp tip into her instead. Though that would've hurt less.

Margrete gasped, looking down at the sticky blood dripping from the weapon in *her* hand. She dropped the blade like a curse.

She hadn't delivered the final blow, she *couldn't*. Margrete had been prepared to allow the love of her life to kill her because she didn't have the strength to push the dagger into his chest, and yet...

A sob broke free as the night spun dangerously all around her and all the lights and faces and muted colors blurred.

"I'm so sorry, Margrete."

Bay appeared from behind her, his hands still chained and his eyes downcast. He couldn't look at her or the dagger at her feet. She stumbled back, dazed, beyond stunned by what she knew was the truth looking her in the eyes.

He'd killed him.

"It had to be done," Bay said even as Margrete shook her head furiously. He'd forced her arm forward. Forced her to plunge the blade those last few inches and into Bash's heart. He'd taken away her *choice*.

Betrayal. The word wasn't enough to describe the turmoil roiling inside of her like a storm.

The nymph who had held Bay when he entered the arena stood back now, her arms crossed and a smug smile on her lips. She must have let go of his chains at the last second, knowing full well what he planned to do.

And Darius had allowed it. He probably welcomed Bay's treachery.

Minthe growled as she fought to get to her son, but Darius's white light encircled her chains, reinforcing their hold. The God of the Sea wasn't about to let the enraged nymera loose. Minthe howled, her sharp canines bared, her head tossed back. Her wailing sounded like a heart breaking—if a nymera *had* a heart to break.

Bay, on the other hand, wasn't a threat, at least not to the god. He was too stunned to move, let alone fight Darius or his nymphs, and he just stood there, looking down at his hands, at the blood that painted them.

Darius entered the ring, blue and white light radiating off his every pore. The crew, all except Bay, had the god's magic encircling them, keeping them locked in place and silent. His pawns. His puppets to play with whenever he saw fit.

Margrete looked away from Bay with a choked sob. He didn't matter, not right now.

Her fingers wrapped around Bash's necklace, and the coolness of its stone snapped her back into reality. Margrete dropped the gem and lurched to Bash's side, where she took his hand in hers. He was colder than ice, his skin wan and sickly.

"Oh, Bash," she whispered, smoothing his ink-black hair back from his face. "I'm so sorry." She threw herself onto his chest and sobbed, uncaring if Darius watched. When she lifted back up, his lids shuttered, his stare blank and glassy.

And then, in a moment that lasted an eternity and a blink at once, Bash slowly turned his head toward hers, the mist shrouding him evaporating.

"M-mon shana leandri le v-voux," he sputtered, blood seeping from between his lips.

My heart beats with yours. The same words he'd whispered the night before their lives changed forever. It was the night they chose each other.

"Don't you dare—"

Margrete heard nothing else but that final wheezing breath leave his lungs. The entire universe could burn up in flames and she wouldn't have noticed or cared. That sound of his life leaving him changed her, remade her into the same woman who'd once felt so utterly and hopelessly alone. Broken and *unwhole*.

Bash's eyes remained wide open and frozen. Lifeless.

Margrete's ensuing scream shook the foundation of the arena. It rocked the walls, and the ground trembled with her grief.

She would bring him back. She'd use her power and call upon the sea.

"You can't save him," Darius murmured directly behind her, seeming to read her thoughts. "He didn't die in the waters, and the rules of this island wouldn't allow such a thing."

His voice was soft, and if she thought he had a heart, she'd say it sounded remorseful. But she didn't fucking care about him or his feelings.

Margrete rose to her feet, covered in Bash's blood.

"I will destroy you," she said barely above a whisper. "But I won't kill you. No, I'll make you watch as I take your throne and everything you love. You'll *beg* me to kill you by the time I'm done with you."

Darius staggered, taken aback by the venom lacing her tone, by the sheer intensity of her murderous promise.

While she might not have driven the dagger into Bash's heart, she'd held the blade, and the act of sacrifice had been completed. Meaning...

Meaning she was now Darius's equal.

Power flooded her system, reforming her, making her into something *other*. The ground quivered as she took a step toward him. Then another.

His eyes widened, and a flash of fear clouded his bright blue eyes.

"You'll forget about him in time," he said, mirroring her movements. She continued to walk, continued to stalk his way. "You're half of *me*," he said, his brow creasing. "Think of all the things we could do together, all the good!"

Margrete shook her head slowly from side to side, her upper lip curled.

"You remembered our time here! I know you did, at least you *felt* it!

Soon all the memories will come back to you, and you won't care about him at all!" Darius was shouting now, his calm veneer long forgotten.

Electricity sparked at her fingertips, and the night air flickered. Shade and her nymphs, sensing the violent storm that approached, scattered like the cockroaches they were. They dashed to the gates, abandoning what remained of her crew.

The Azantian's chains rattled as they, too, moved back, giving her ample room. Margrete lifted her hand and flicked her wrist, and the manacles imprisoning them clattered to the soil.

Margrete never looked back at Bay. She might do something she'd regret.

Darius held up both hands, trying to placate her. It was far too late for that nonsense. His mouth moved and words poured out, but she heard nothing but the thunderous roaring of her heart and the simmering of her blood.

Margrete embraced the icy-hot rage swelling within and relished the supernatural adrenaline flooding her body. It flowed into her veins and blazed, awakening the full beast that was her power.

Inside, Margrete roared.

The walls around them began to shift and fall, to crumble and break off into pieces. They shattered to the sands and filled the air with dust. Darius hastily surveyed the collapsing arena before twisting back to her and speaking, his hand reaching into his pocket at the same time. He brought something out—a *gem*, it looked like—and brought it to his eyes, inspecting it.

Instantly, she knew what he held, as if the damned thing called out to her.

Malum's heart. The one she'd been looking for all those months after the attack. The sea god had held onto it this entire time.

Darius's brow furrowed as the gleaming heart shattered in the palm of his hands, a single spark lighting up the world before extinguishing. He brought his gaze to hers, ash filtering through his fingertips. What remained of his brother was now gone forever.

You've done it. You've finally taken it all.

His voice sounded sluggish in her mind, soft and gravelly, and she noticed how his features hardened as if speaking to her cost him. She hoped so. He tried to say more, but his voice merely wheezed and broke apart in her mind, his power not able to break through her barriers.

So consumed by fire and wrath, she didn't care about the true meaning behind his words. All she wanted was his death.

Margrete lifted her arms high into the air, white fire crackling between her palms. She took one last look at the god who stole the love of her life, who robbed her of her happiness, and she brought her hands down to the hard earth. She unleashed herself upon the island that had taken so much from her already, a wretched place now stained with Bash's cooling blood.

She thought of him, allowed her magic to wrap around his image and take hold until they became one and the same. There was her power and there was him, and her divinity yearned for the bright soul she'd shown it.

Her power felt sentient, and it grew angered, matching her rage. It burned, demanding action, demanding that the man consuming her thoughts be returned to her.

Darius mouthed her name, but it was too late. The ground cracked and split, and beneath her palms a void yawned and stretched. She opened her mouth and let loose the scream she'd kept in, the cry of anguish she'd held back, and in reply her magic blasted through the silt and soil. The void expanded and deepened.

Her right hand tingled and burned, and she looked down, taking in the sight of gray and pearl lines inking their way up her arm. They swirled and reformed, fashioning themselves into a living and breathing flame, and where the flame ended, a single black tear shimmered.

Margrete ignored her new tattoo and peered down into the abyss.

She'd shattered the island with her fury, and somehow, she'd opened up a gateway.

A narrow staircase formed out of thin air, its gilded steps reaching up from the darkness, inviting her to follow its path.

The underworld. The staircase could only lead to one place. And her anger—the anger of a goddess—had unlocked its entrance.

"I'd follow you anywhere. Even to the underworld itself, princess."

Bash's words echoed in her mind. He may have spoken them, but it was she who would make them true.

Without another glance at the destruction and chaos she'd caused, Margrete took her first step down into the pit, an unnaturally cold breeze licking at her heels. Someone shouted her name, probably Darius, or maybe even Bay, but her vision had narrowed in on the staircase that would bring her to the land of the dead.

Margrete would follow Bash to the underworld, and when she got there, she'd bring him back home.

And then she'd crush the gods themselves.

One. By. One.

Until she was all that remained.

EPILOGUE
DARIUS

MARGRETE TOOK HER FIRST STEP INTO THE UNDERWORLD.

She'd done it—opened a portal to the realm of the dead through sheer will alone. It would've impressed Darius had it not torn him apart. Even after he'd told her of *their* past, she still chose the King of Azantian. That spineless man who succumbed so easily to his baser instincts.

Darius growled, clenching his hands into fists. How very wrong he'd been to assume she'd instantly remember him. Love him.

He was a fool.

Because of him, because of the trials, Margrete had been gifted with the final spark of divine magic remaining in his brother's heart, and she'd taken it for her own. She'd taken it and wanted to *kill* him with it.

The betrayal stung.

"Margrete!" he shouted, beginning to bolt after her descending form. She paid him no mind, didn't even lift her head at his strangled cry. Darius found he didn't care if his weakness was on full display...he didn't care about much at all, which was entirely unnerving.

Just as he had the night he killed Wryn thousands of years before, a great emptiness devoured him. It was the kind of emptiness that was tangible, a poison that spread into his blood with every pound of his immortal heart.

He promised himself he wouldn't ever allow himself to feel that way again, but as he watched Margrete walk away—for what felt like the second time—that void only grew.

A flicker of movement from his left caught his eye.

While Darius had been distracted, Minthe had hauled her son's dead body through the sands of the arena. As a nymera, she moved quickly, but it was the innate need to protect her child that drove her to the shadows.

The king might have stopped breathing, but Minthe retained something he hadn't expected. Hope.

If Margrete somehow found Bash's soul, he'd have a vessel in which to return to, and Minthe knew this as well. When Darius killed Wryn, his mother had set her body aflame seconds after her last breath, rendering it impossible for him to bring her back in this lifetime. A soul could never die, but it needed a body in order to walk the earth.

Minthe may not like Margrete, but perhaps she saw her as her only chance at getting her son back.

Darius gritted his teeth, making to follow after the nymera and her dead son, but a commotion forced his attention back to Margrete. Her *friends*—if she could even call them that—began taking the steps two at a time, racing after her and into the underworld.

Fools.

The redhead led the way, followed by a tall blonde warrior who held the hand of a petite female with a tear-stained face.

Bay remained frozen before the first step, his eyes flickering to his hands every now and again, his mouth agape in shock. Darius was surprised he'd actually done it—killed his king, his oldest friend.

He allowed Minthe to slither away into the darkness, knowing he'd deal with her later. It wouldn't be hard to locate her, and he had confidence Margrete would fail. No one had ever been successful in returning a soul to its mortal body, and he doubted that would change.

For now, Darius possessed a great weapon and a possible pawn.

Margrete may not seem to care about Bay, not after his betrayal, but having the man in his arsenal would prove useful when she came to her senses and the red haze of anger dissipated. The underworld was a cruel place full of deceitful gods and duplicitous trades that often ended poorly for the desperate party.

She hadn't the slightest idea of the nightmare she walked into, and it wouldn't be finding Bash's soul that would prove difficult. Darius's fellow gods and goddesses were the reasons he stayed as far away from the underworld as possible. It was a breeding ground for trouble, and not the fun kind.

Not wasting his breath on calling out for her again, Darius marched to Bay's side and peered into the crevice Margrete had created from her uncontrollable grief. This close to the chasm, he was forced to admit to himself how impressive the act had been. Especially for a newly fashioned goddess.

A staircase led to a gateway that would bring her to the outer lands of the realm of the dead. From there, she'd encounter things far worse than the monsters he and his brother had fashioned a thousand years ago. Far worse than the nymeras or the Collossious.

Something twinged in Darius's chest.

He wanted to damn Margrete to her irrational choices and allow the divinities to destroy her. Darius wanted her to hurt as she'd hurt him, even if unwittingly. He wanted her to feel the agony currently searing in his veins and taste the bitterness on her tongue.

But he couldn't.

He...he *cared* for her. And maybe it wasn't the same kind of love the king felt, but it was as real as a god could ever experience, and it twisted him up and forced his next move.

Turning to Bay, Darius adopted his most callous of smiles. Both he and the trembling mortal were about to play the game of their lifetimes, and now wasn't the time for weakness or irrational what-ifs.

Before he could fix his mistakes and right his wrongs, Darius had to ensure Margrete survived. And whether she wanted to admit it, she *would* need him soon. A predicament that would work out well in his favor. Darius had never been the hero, but maybe he could, just *once*, play the role.

"I think you're going to be coming with me," Darius said with a strained grin, finally gaining Bay's attention. His blue eyes widened, and his entire body shook.

Poor, poor mortal. He appeared to just be coming out of his murderous stupor.

"Unless you want to be the cause of *both* of their deaths, *kingslayer*" —Darius lingered on the word, and Bay cringed—"the time has come to visit the realm of the mighty gods, goddesses, and the unholy undead."

Darius released his magic, allowing it to wind around Bay's frame and push him forward and down the stairs. The man fumbled, almost tripping down the steps, but Darius held him tightly in his grasp.

They were about to enter the lion's den, and even Darius's heart fluttered when they reached the imposing silver door at the foot of the long stairwell.

A thousand tiny symbols were etched onto the polished surface, from cresting waves to wild trees and blooms. Frozen armies were locked in battle, every kind of weapon present and ready to be used. Here and there he spotted an image of a pair of lovers or a mother and child. Joy, love, wrath, greed, war...

The gateway showed it all.

Darius tightened his leash on his reluctant ward and then pushed on the door and took his first step into the wicked dark.

He'd ensure Margrete didn't succeed—and then, Darius would make her his true queen. And if his assumptions were correct, her memories would be flooding back, consuming her, and driving away thoughts of the insipid king.

Darius smiled.

He'd be her savior, and she'd fall into his arms like she had done all those years ago.

In the meantime, he'd let her play...and fail. The underworld would destroy her, and he'd be there to pick up the pieces.

Darius yanked on his charge, and the door to the mortal realm shut with a resounding thud behind them. There was no turning back now.

Thank you for reading! Did you enjoy? Please add your review because nothing helps an author more and encourages readers to take a chance on a book than a review.

And don't miss CROWN OF SALT AND BONE, book three of the The Azantian Trilogy, available now. Turn the page for a sneak peek!

You can also sign up for the City Owl Press newsletter to receive notice of all book releases!

SNEAK PEEK OF CROWN OF SALT AND BONE

Margrete was fire and light and malice, and nothing and no one would stop her from turning the world of the gods on its head.

Drenched in the cooling blood of her beloved king, she blasted open the portal to the Underworld, shattering the ground of Darius's wretched island and storming through a tunnel belonging to the divine.

Each wrathful step jolted her bones, a harsh stinging radiating down her spine. She inhaled the copper in the air, Bash's life essence clinging to her stiffened shirt, the potent scent fanning the flames of her rage, turning her into a living, breathing storm of heartbreak. Margrete barely sensed the humanity within, as if it shrank in on itself once Bash's soul departed her world. Though she supposed she couldn't even call herself human anymore. After completing the final trial on Surria's cursed island, a great shift had occurred, and now, nothing felt *right*.

She didn't feel right.

As if to confirm, her newly branded arm prickled. The gray swirls whirled across her forearm, the single black teardrop pulsating.

After she'd battled her father, her wave had appeared on her collarbone. Now, it seemed as if this new tattoo materialized after her fight for the immortality she didn't want. Or maybe it was borne from something else entirely...

She didn't ruminate upon the thought for long.

I'm going to kill them all, she thought as a silver door loomed ahead, intricate depictions of human life and other such absurdities etched into its thick metal. Light glimmered around its edges, luminescent in the dusky corridor. It had to be the door to the Underworld.

She shoved it open and barreled through. Nothing mattered.

Bash was dead. Darius had won. She was now a goddess.

Margrete repeated this about a thousand times to herself as she marched through a narrow passageway lined with opaque ivory sconces, blue flames seeming to reach out and lick at her skin.

She'd fought against evil and lost, but the war was nowhere near over.

The thing about loss was that sometimes it didn't hit you right away, not in its true form at least. Anger was a much easier ally, and it currently beat inside her head like a drum, drowning out her inner cries. Her unseen agony.

She could accept rage with open arms, because the alternative? Stopping her advance for just one moment would allow the burning tears to fall. The sheer weight of her loss would force her to her knees where she'd curl into a tight ball and wish the world away. She'd be useless, and while giving in was tempting—oh-so fucking tempting—she feared she wouldn't have the strength to rise again.

So, she didn't give in, and she didn't allow her tears to fall, and Margrete stormed ahead as if an army was hot on her trail.

The damp walkway went on forever, and with every thud of her boots upon the stones, her resolve strengthened, despair driving her.

"Margrete! Wait!"

The voice at her back reminded her of an annoying bell. As long as it didn't belong to Bay, she didn't much care who its owner was. Margrete didn't trust herself *not* to kill him for his part in Bash's death. He was the one who'd delivered the blade into her hands, and even if he'd ultimately saved her, she still felt anger. However unwarranted.

With the entrance to the realm of the dead growing closer, Margrete's magic opened its maw and exhaled, shuddering with anticipation. She relished how it whispered in her ears, a low melody that harmonized with her own breathing. It was almost like sharing a body with two souls, her power its own being, trapped in warm flesh.

Her name sounded again, and a hand fell on her shoulder. Such a frail, weak, *mortal* hand. Margrete never realized how breakable bones could be, but she knew without a doubt she could shatter the fingers on her shoulder without so much as a thought.

She spun around, annoyed by the interruption.

Mila. She reared back, her bright green eyes wide with uncharacteristic fear. She held up two placating hands.

"What?" Margrete snapped. She'd just lost the love of her life to some twisted game orchestrated by Darius, and dealing with Mila wasn't a priority.

"Calm down, Margrete," Mila begged, her lower lip trembling. Margrete cocked her head at that; Mila rarely showed any ounce of emotion at all. The Azantian rubbed at her stained shirt, which was ripped across the midsection, her right sleeve nearly shredded entirely. She'd put up a decent fight against Shade and her nymphs, not that Margrete doubted Mila's capability once her temper was incited.

But she was hesitant now.

Terrified.

"We shouldn't just rush into this." Mila gestured to the long, empty corridor of flickering blue light, gnawing at the inside of her cheek.

"Rush into it?" Margrete repeated, stepping closer. Heat danced in her belly and her breath grew hot. "Bash was just *killed.* I'm getting him back. The gods and their games can go screw themselves."

She made to turn around when the young woman brazenly grabbed her arm. Slowly, Margrete studied the dirtied fingers around her biceps before bringing her attention to Mila. Bold. Very bold of the sailor.

"First of all, we don't know where this tunnel leads, and second of all, your eyes are fucking *glowing.* Not to mention the air around you feels charged with...magic." Mila took a wise step back, allowing Margrete room to breathe, to seethe. "You're not thinking clearly, and when you're not thinking clearly, you're dangerous. More so now."

After she'd been given a gift she'd never wanted. No. It was a curse.

"As if you ever cared about me before," Margrete said, frost coating every word. Mila never liked her—she made that perfectly clear the day Margrete couldn't save Jace on the island. "From what I remember, you were begging me to command these powers before, and when I failed, you shunned me as if I'd allowed your friend to die on purpose."

Mila clenched her jaw, the freckles on her nose wrinkling as her nostrils flared. "I may not have liked you at first, Margrete, but that's only because..." Her focus shifted. "Well, to be quite honest, seeing you lose your shit was rather refreshing. It makes you seem like an actual person."

"Instead of?"

"Instead of some gratingly perfect specimen everyone loves and obsesses over all the damn time. I've heard your name spoken more times than I want to remember since you landed on Azantian. You may think me cynical for it, but I've found that when something looks too good to be true, it's because it usually is."

Mila didn't like her because she seemed too...perfect?

That was laughable.

Before Margrete could reply, more footsteps pounded, and Dani and Atlas sprinted into the light of the nearest sconce.

The former's head remained lowered, heavy with grief, as tears streaked Dani's face.

Shit. Now Margrete felt like an ass on top of it all. The churning fire that had fueled her moments before began to simmer.

Dani had lost her brother, Jacks. She let that thought sink in, grimacing when an image of Jonah washed across her mind. The young sailor had been so eager to join them, and he'd perished at Darius's hand in the most gruesome of ways.

She sucked in a deep breath, trying to clear the haze that worked to steal her empathy. Her humanity. It would've been so much easier to allow it control. At least then she wouldn't feel as though she were teetering on the edge of a cliff.

"Why did you follow me?" Margrete asked cautiously, addressing Atlas. She shoved Jonah and Jacks from her thoughts. While a dull and profound ache throbbed in her chest, they were wasting precious time.

The warrior lifted her chin. On a bad day, she was obnoxiously proud, but now, a cloud seemed to hover over her head, weighing down her shoulders and turning her eyes a dull shade of blue.

"I followed you because that's what my king would've wanted." Atlas's right eye twitched, showing her nerves, but she quickly regained control of her emotions and lifted to her full, towering height. "And *when* we get him back, he'll probably owe me more than a promotion."

Mila shook her head, her red hair grazing her cheeks. "Now's not the time for jokes, Atlas, which is surprising coming from you." She observed the blonde with both disdain and awe. Mila had a gift of expressing scorching emotions on a delicate face.

Atlas didn't drop Dani's hand, but she stepped closer to Mila, her hackles rising. "I'm doing my damned best, Mila. Am I supposed to pretend to be some hardened piece of stone that doesn't break or feel anything other than contempt?"

"How dare you—"

"Enough!" Margrete roared, her voice shaking the walls. The blue flames captured in the sconces wavered erratically.

Dani inched forward, eyes locked on Margrete. Dark curls tumbled into her face, her golden-brown skin smudged with grime from their fight in the arena. But even covered in dirt, there was something different about the woman, and not merely because of what she'd lost. Her blue eyes appeared to glimmer with purpose, and Margrete had to force herself to turn away from their intensity.

"I'm not wasting another moment," Margrete said, "but if you desire to do so, please stay behind and don't get in my way."

She continued deeper into the Underworld, knowing this passage had to end at some point. She'd walk forever if that's what it took.

A few seconds later, heavy footsteps pummeled the rocky earth, her reluctant companions trailing behind. The part of her that still felt mortal, that still felt like *her*, questioned why she wasn't demanding they turn around and head back to the human realm. They might not last long down here—if they ever made it to the Underworld—and they certainly weren't composed of the divinity Margrete now embraced.

She didn't question her role among the immortals anymore. All of it overwhelmed her, yes, but instead of fighting it and telling herself she *wasn't* a goddess, Margrete welcomed the change with open arms. If it helped her find her love, then she'd embrace it.

She'd become a living nightmare if she had to.

Silence ensued as they walked into the unknown, and after many long minutes, the tunnel widened. Another door stood erected in the center of a rounded stone antechamber, though this time, it had been fashioned of an opulent gold that shone with thousands of glimmering gems. Margrete considered its odd position in the middle of the room with skepticism.

She came to a sudden halt, and Atlas gently bumped into her shoulder. Margrete flinched at the contact, and the sailor wisely put distance between them. It appeared that everyone was frightened of her.

For a good reason. She frightened herself.

"We're getting him back. *Together*," Atlas said at her side. Her eyes were trained straight ahead, at the brilliant gold door. "Bash is my king, but more than that, I know he'd fight for me too. For us all if he could. But," she added, her voice stern, "I wouldn't just follow *anyone* into the depths of the Underworld."

They locked eyes. Atlas gleamed with sincerity, not an ounce of doubt marring her face. For a fraction of a heartbeat, Margrete didn't feel as if she were adrift, floating between realms. She gave the warrior a curt nod, her throat suddenly constricting.

"Once we go through that portal, there may be no turning back," Margrete warned, raising her voice and turning to address the other two women. "Now's your chance to turn back. Your *last* chance."

Silence ensued, but no protests sounded.

Surprisingly, Dani was the first to break the weighty quiet. She dropped Atlas's hand and squared her slight shoulders. Her damp cheeks had long ago dried, but the tear tracks still gleamed in the meager light of the enclosure.

"I fear nothing anymore," she murmured, her voice cracking. "I lost my twin, the other half of my soul, and if there's a chance to get him back, or even to say goodbye, I'll not waste it. I'm coming for Jacks. For my friend, Jonah. And for the island I love."

"And I want to shed the blood of the god responsible for the death of my father," Mila added. "The same one who orchestrated a twisted game that killed the man I might've found a partner in." Grant and Jace—two men whom the hardened sailor had given her heart to. "I won't rest until my father's blade is slick with Darius's divine blood."

Mila's lips curled up, baring her teeth. Margrete noted her hand rested on the blade in question, the one Grant must've given her.

Too bad the honor of killing Darius would be hers. Margrete wanted to be the one to watch as the light died from his seafoam eyes.

"It's settled," Atlas said. She motioned to the door. "We're all doing this, Margrete, and we'll follow you into the dark. Now it's up to you to lead us there."

Margrete whirled away from her companions. Three people who couldn't be any more unalike. And yet, she couldn't deny that having them in her arsenal would be an advantage. She thought of Bay for a pained moment, realizing he'd stayed behind. His hesitance after such betrayal hurt more than she expected.

The warriors before her would suffice.

Atlas was strength and grit and fortitude. Dani's presence reminded Margrete of the humanity she felt drifting further and further away. And Mila...she was that voice—that *loud* voice—in her ear, calling her out on her bullshit.

As much as she wanted to storm into the Underworld alone with her magic blazing, Margrete wasn't sure what she'd be up against. She scrutinized the trio, taking her time to drink in their determined features, to make sure their convictions held true. Not one of them showed a hint of uncertainty, and Margrete knew they meant every word.

"Fine. But stay close to me and keep quiet," Margrete said, shifting once more for the door. She ambled closer until three feet separated her from the golden slab and the gilded handle in the shape of...

A liander bloom.

The knob opening the portal to the Underworld resembled a sedative disguised by petals—the same flower she'd once used on Bash the night they shared their first kiss. Her heart clenched at the memory, but she swallowed it down with a grimace.

Her emotions would get the best of her if she didn't control them.

Lifting her hand, she brought it to the cool metal handle. It was ice beneath her skin, and the contact sent a charged current dancing up and down her arm. Her fingers tightened on the knob, and her breath wavered as a crushing weight settled onto her shoulders.

This was the moment of no return. A moment she'd either celebrate or curse.

Margrete pulled on the handle and opened the door that led to nowhere and possibly everywhere.

This time, her ensuing curse was echoed by the others.

Don't stop now. Keep reading with your copy of CROWN OF SALT AND BONE available now.

And find more from Katherine Quinn at
www.katherinequinnauthor.com

Don't miss CROWN OF SALT AND BONE, book three of the The Azantian Trilogy, available now, and find more from Katherine Quinn at www.katherinequinnauthor.com

A lost king. A deadly bargain. And the ultimate sacrifice.

After losing the love of her life on an island of horrors, Margrete Wood opens a portal to the Underworld. She's claimed her full powers, becoming a powerful goddess, and she'll use her new magic to steal Bash's soul back from the realm of the dead.

Darius, the God of the Sea, has waited centuries for Margrete to return. She's the reincarnation of the woman he once loved, and he's hellbent on wiping away Bash's memory. But the Underworld is filled with ruthless gods and corrupt bargains, and when Margrete makes a deal with the God of Death himself to get her king back, Darius agrees to help—for a steep price.

With monsters of the deep to slay and a death god to appease, Margrete is forced to work with her enemy before time runs out and everything she loves is destroyed. For good, this time.

Please sign up for the City Owl Press newsletter for chances to win special subscriber-only contests and giveaways as well as receiving information on upcoming releases and special excerpts.

All reviews are **welcome** and **appreciated**. Please consider leaving one on your favorite social media and book buying sites.

Escape Your World. Get Lost in Ours! City Owl Press at www.cityowlpress.com.

ACKNOWLEDGMENTS

There are so many beautiful souls who have made this book a reality. Once again, I must thank my grandfather Benjamin Narodick for being my inspiration, always and forever. To my mother, Nancy Narodick, thank you for always reading my rough drafts and saying I'm your favorite author, even if I know you're totally biased.

To Ashley R. King, who literally texted me every single day when I wanted to give up and didn't think I was good enough. She's the real deal people, and if it wasn't for her, none of this would have been possible. You're my rock.

To my editor, Charissa Weaks, thank you for having faith in this trilogy to begin with! I'm so thankful that you saw potential in Margrete and Bash's story! I will always be beyond grateful.

Thank you, Shawn Wallin, for being my cheerleader and telling me exactly when Bash needed to "step it up." And thank you to Princess Uddon for supporting me throughout this process, and for making me literally laugh out loud when I needed it most. I'm so thankful Instagram connected us, and that I have someone to fangirl over book boyfriends with.

To Tina Moss, Yelena Casale, and the entire City Owl team, you've changed my life forever, and made my dreams come true.

Of course, I'd be remiss if I didn't thank my husband, Joshua, who is my best friend... even if he drives me crazy 90% of the time. I love you.

And to the readers, you are the reason I write, and I love you beyond words.

ABOUT THE AUTHOR

KATHERINE QUINN is a fantasy romance author and poet. She graduated from the University of Central Florida with a degree in psychology. She resides in Houston, Texas with her husband and three children.

Her love for writing began at age nine after she read her first fantasy series, *Song of the Lioness*, by Tamora Pierce. After that, she wanted nothing more than to be a dagger-wielding heroine. Unfortunately, it's frowned upon to give a child a dagger, so she settled on writing about daring adventures instead.

Coffee is her true love, and she believes everything can be fixed with Starbucks and dark humor.

www.katherinequinnauthor.com

instagram.com/Katherinequinnwrites

ABOUT THE PUBLISHER

City Owl Press is a cutting edge indie publishing company, bringing the world of romance and speculative fiction to discerning readers.

Escape Your World. Get Lost in Ours!

www.cityowlpress.com

facebook.com/YourCityOwlPress

twitter.com/cityowlpress

instagram.com/cityowlbooks

pinterest.com/cityowlpress

Made in the USA
Las Vegas, NV
22 December 2023

83460604R00206